THE FINGERPRINT OF GOD

a novel

by

Jerry W. Lindberg

THE FINGERPRINT OF GOD

Copyright © 2008 by Jerry Lindberg

Cover and graphic design by Nancy LaRoche and Derek Brigham
Illustration credits: NASA Land Sat 7
Photo credits: Split Rock Research Foundation

ISBN: 13: 978-0-9796759-3-5
ISBN: 10: 0-9796759-3-6

Published by Radius 7 Pressworks
www.radius7.com

PRINTED IN THE UNITED STATES OF AMERICA

This book is dedicated to all those explorers,
researchers and scientists who saw the signs
and ignored the danger.

A special thanks to Tim Mahoney and
Dr. Lennart Moller for their creation of,
"The Exodus Conspiracy," a documentary film
that ought to be in every church and synagogue on the planet.

Without their vision and direction, my story would
never have taken flight.

The speculative fiction in this story takes license with a set of hypotheses put forth by Dr. Lennart Moller of Sweden's Karolinska Institute. These hypotheses are also the subject of a bold new documentary, "The Exodus Conspiracy," produced by Mahoney Media Group of Minneapolis. Dr. Moller is a clinical researcher by training. He has spent three decades applying the scientific method to DNA research. He is also a man of faith, who has applied his scientific discipline towards a subject of his own personal passion – the Hebrew Exodus out of Egypt. He is living proof that science and faith need not be mutually exclusive. Dr. Moller's findings have been the source of intense controversy in the archeological, historical and theological community. What is seldom reported in the mainstream is that many historians, archeologists and allied professionals are only allowed to conduct archeological research in the Middle East as long as their findings affirm conventional conclusions. If they dig in the Middle East and make discoveries outside the cultural norms of the region, it would not be unreasonable to assume their invitation to dig would be revoked.

It's happened and is still happening.

Up until modern times, the Exodus story has never had credible forensic or scientific proof. The story, literally, requires a leap of faith many scientists cannot or will not make. The biblical account has been accepted as literal truth in some circles, a myth, fable or allegory in others. Dr. Moller's research explores new forensic and scientific evidences that suggest new interpretations can be drawn. His research begins from an assumption science typically disdains - that the biblical account was accurate. Only now, with the advent of satellite imagery, underwater technologies and modern maps can we begin to dissect the Exodus account deductively and scientifically. Only now can science shine a new spotlight on a previously formless wilderness and juxtapose the biblical road map against what we now know is the true shape of the region. The archeological and historical community, by and large, are skeptical of Dr. Moller's contentions - not because of the evidence, but because Dr. Moller doesn't belong to their established archeological fraternity.

Dr. Moller's findings, if they cannot be refuted, ought to signal a push for further research. If the findings can withstand the test of time and Moller has, indeed, begun to validate the Hebrew history, one has to wonder why God has chosen this time to expose His hand.

What would the validation of the Exodus imply ? One can only speculate.

1

 *PROLOGUE*

At the apex of the Khafre pyramid, at the exact moment of the summer solstice, a lab technician poked a hole in the veins on their hands and got a nice spurt of blood. Under a shroud of pre-dawn darkness the technician who tapped their veins was but a silhouette to Hans Tanner and Billy Kim. As grad students, the young men could have been consenting to some sort of college hazing, but they weren't.

It was something slightly more consequential.

A priest drained the blood into separate chalices. The chief priest then held the chalices aloft and recited a Babylonian poem, an incantation to Semiramis, the wife of Nimrod, the ancient man-proclaimed-god upon whom the Babylonian empire had been built. Neither Billy Kim nor Hans Tanner recognized the language. It didn't matter. Understanding the poem wasn't the point of having a dozen hooded holy men at the apex of the pyramid of Khafre at 4:36 on the morning of June 20, 1999.

Neither Billy Kim nor Hans Tanner knew all the rules of the dance they were now waltzing across the stage of history. They understood their payday, but they didn't know the price. What they didn't know about the pre-dawn ceremony was that if any one of the priests found the young candidates lacking in their training, preparation or commitment, both students would be killed – summarily shot in the back of the head and buried without benefit of ceremony or notification of next of kin. They would simply disappear. They were never told that part of the story – or that they were the third pair of candidates to be brought to the top of Khafre over the previous 18 summer solstices. They had been led to believe that if they were, for whatever reason, deemed unsuitable they would simply be sent back to school and told to shut up. The truth they never knew was that their murders were Plan B. Had they known murder was a possibility they might have been a little less smug. They were young enough, and just naïve enough to believe the ceremony playing out before them was a coronation when, in deadly truth, it was an election.

Their presence on Khafre was a moonlit mystery steeped in ancient baffling ceremony. The two young participants had been given only a hazy understanding of its significance. They had been told they were about to enter an historic brotherhood that would grant them financial and career amenities for the rest of their lives. If they had fears, they held them in check. After all, their own parents had arranged for this mystic, moonlit marriage. What the young men never knew was their parents had been compromised, threatened with their own lives if Tanner and Kim failed to agree to the election.

The young men watched anxiously as each priest drank from the cups and passed them along – their signal of acceptance that the young Tanner and Kim met all of the required qualifications and loyalty measurements the brotherhood would ask of them over the years to come.

The last priest drank of both chalices and then nodded his head slightly. The long search was over. Hans Tanner and Billy Kim were now something more than just grad students with a lot of potential. Tanner and Kim were now cogs in a well-oiled historical machine that would treat them with deference – owing to their mystical pre-dawn covenant.

The next 30 years would require they hold their secret and never, ever profane the mission they had agreed to with their own blood.

CHAPTER ONE
Gatherings of gushing goo

The beginning of any end is seldom seen in real time. Historians have the job of labeling a date or event as having been the beginning of something called "the end" at a later time.

What Ben Kowalski knew from his five decades of wrestling with history was that historians were more artist than scientist and they often got their art absolutely, positively dead wrong.

Ben Kowalski saw the beginning of the end in real time. He knew when an event happened how history would treat it before history had been written. A psychologist would have called his gift intuition, but it was too precise. Why he had this gift he didn't know. He didn't always consider it a gift. It was a curse as well. Even in his drinking days he could see events having greater or lesser impact than his peers could figure out. In part, his sense of precognition may have been why he drank as copiously as he had.

The way Ben saw history, the end began one October morning in a shopping mall in Wisconsin in the year 2020 when a third-party candidate for the presidency of the United States held a seemingly meaningless, certainly inconsequential, political rally. Ben had followed the story on television as a curious onlooker and, like the rest of the nation, found what happened an unbelievable sequence of events.

He was ironing a shirt, watching a game show when the newsman interrupted with the startling news. A presidential candidate had been shot.

The nominee of the Independence Party, Marshall Warren, had pegged 18 percent in the polls. He couldn't win the election just eight days away but, for certain, he could influence who did win. Warren was pro-choice, pro-gun, pro-environmentalist; a self-proclaimed 'progressive Libertarian and conservative traditionalist.' He was, in theory, all things to all people. He covered the full rainbow of social and political diversity. What he didn't believe in, he hedged in political gift wrapping. His campaign was an appeal to the segment of America willing to believe anything - which was considerable.

In the crowd that day was a young man whose name, Timothy Korb, would soon become a synonym for futility. In the popular lexicon the phrase 'korbed' or 'korbed up,' would become a phrase kids everywhere would subsequently use to describe anything lacking in design, thought or execution - or could flatly be called insane.

Timothy Korb had been kicked out of college for his deficient grades - which were the result of a habitual taste for marijuana, LSD and just about anything that could alter his mental state. In his pocket, Korb had a loaded snub-nose .38. He was tired of being ignored, tired of being insignificant. He was a loose cannon with a wandering, vacant statement to make and the means to do it.

When Korb had gotten up that morning, he wondered whether he should even go to Marshall Warren's political rally. Warren wasn't his candidate. Warren was simply a name, a venue for Korb to act out his wretchedly deficient drug-induced, delusional fantasy. Before crawling out of bed he lit a joint. He toked it all the way down before his feet even hit the floor. It was how he put the world on his playing field. The pot had recently begun to have some new effects on him. Unlike the past when it would make him mellow and giddy, it now made him anxious, paranoid and indecisive. He figured more pot would take away the paranoia. It didn't. He paced and fretted and finally concluded that he had to go somewhere, to do something, to be somewhere, to actually try to interact with humanity. To soothe his growing anxiety he decided that a hit of acid would take the edge off. Why he jammed the gun in his pocket was unknown to history.

When candidate Marshall Warren took to the podium, a stoned and borderline psychotic Timothy Korb pressed toward the rope line. A Secret Service agent would later remember that he had spotted the young man, but that he didn't appear too out of place - only that he looked unkempt and his demeanor was, well, stoned. The Secret Service agent later admitted that candidate Warren attracted an unusual number of those types because of his stated position on the decriminalization of marijuana. Pot-heads always attended Warren rallies. It was a given. When the speech was over, the candidate pressed forward into the rope line to shake hands. The delusional Timothy Korb was still 20 feet from the candidate when his hand slipped into his pant pocket for the .38. It was a gun he had stolen from his father, a former police detective. He had never fired it. He had never fired a gun, period.

"Guns," he had argued in college, "are, like, dangerous."

"Tell me why you think so, Tim," his prof had asked.

"I dunno. They just are, 'cuz like there's no real reason to use 'em."

"What if some guy was coming at you with a knife?"

"I just don't think that could happen, man, 'cuz I don't really have any is-sues with anyone."

Korb was about to contradict himself. He did have issues. And in the tradition of being totally korbed, he was in the process of trying to make a statement even he wouldn't have understood.

What was unknown to Timothy Korb was that the gun he gripped firmly in his pant pocket had a hair-trigger. He pulled the hammer back and felt it click. When he pulled it out of his pant pocket the hammer caught on his belt and the gun discharged into his genitals.

Timothy Korb was starting his day off poorly. For a brief moment of clarity he considered life without genitals. He knew it was not a positive development. His drug-addled brain ran a quick assessment: He was lying on a shopping mall concourse without his goodies - they were spread about the floor in gatherings of gushing goo. That was a done deal. There was no way to undo his undeniable lapse of thinking. To make matters worse, he was in a drug-induced psychosis. In his brain three billion synapses were misfiring simultaneously. He concluded through his pain and psychosis that he must finish what he started. After all, he was supposed to do something. Doing something was why he had come to the rally. Doing something was why he got out of bed in the first place. He pointed the pistol at the only part of Marshall Warren he could see through the maze of panicked chaos in front of him - his feet.

Timothy Korb was about to become a legend in mendacity. His shot hit Marshall Warren squarely in the ankle. His futile and wretchedly stupid one act play was almost complete. Video replays would show that it took the Secret Service agent precisely 2.63 seconds to defuse the situation by putting two bullets into the head of the Timothy Korb.

Guns, Korb had now clinically proven were, like, dangerous.

Normally an assassination attempt is neither so poorly executed, nor so poorly conceived. Shooting a third-party candidate in the ankle isn't nearly as sexy as knocking off a household name. Still, the Ballad of Timothy Korb was now a part of the national archives. Had he lived to see the story on the evening news he would have laughed and said 'man, I must have been totally whacked.' He might have even considered checking himself into rehab, given the psychotic nature of his act - had not the Secret Service agent extinguished the option.

Ben Kowalski saw the event at the shopping mall in different hues. He knew, intuitively, this was a development that would have a ripple effect. His sense of precognition told him that this was an event that would swing the tenuous pendulum of history.

What he didn't know was that he, himself, would be swept up in the back swing.

CHAPTER TWO
Chum puppy

The campaign of Marshall Warren was effectively shut down. The botched assassination forced him into a series of surgeries in order to reconstruct his shattered ankle. Between the surgeries and the pain pills, the underdog candidate was forced to shut his mouth for the balance of the campaign. The law of unintended consequences began to take effect. The longer he stayed in the hospital, silent, the higher his polling numbers rose.

His handlers began to see a trend. He could have been released from care on Thursday and return to the campaign stump, in a wheelchair, but his political gatekeepers saw another option, one that made eminently more sense. They kept him in a private hospital room higher than a kite on pain pills and smuggled liquor until after the election. Silence and the slow weight of guilt was a unique campaign strategy Warren's handlers played like a fiddle. Almost overnight, Marshall Warren was transformed from insignificant third party candidate to social martyr and political antihero. The longer he stayed silent, the more anxious and guilty the American public felt about having sent this helpless fool onto the battlefield of ideas totally unarmed.

By the time election day rolled around, the fate of national leadership was a jump ball. Warren received a 37% plurality. By the time the networks forecast his victory on election eve, he was "resting." That's what his campaign manager told the press. In truth, he has passed out, blissfully anesthetized and wholly ignorant that he had become the most powerful man in the world.

Hindsight would say the election of Marshall Warren was the lowest ebb in America's historical tide, but real time and hindsight are impossible concepts to make intersect on a graph. The American people, overcome with sympathy, exercised a massive, thought-free and emotion-addled vote. Polls would later indicate that many millions of people were simply saying 'why not? He's paid the price – besides, he's independent – he's got no one pulling his strings.'

Had the American people been able to look forward they would have wished someone were pulling the strings of their hobbled, hapless president. Marshall Warren didn't have a clue. He had no party. He had no faithful political allies. He had no bureaucratic savvy. Still, he would soon be sitting in the Big Chair.

His first order of business was to select a team to surround him. Everyone inside the Beltway knew selecting an executive team, not to mention, a cabinet - was a crapshoot for Marshall Warren. No one in the press or the public had ever seriously considered his victory, which meant no one had asked him on the campaign trail about a "team." It was Warren's own inflated sense of self-importance, along with his limitless war chest of inherited money that had kept him in the race. And, his vice president-elect, Marine Colonel Adam Norton, was of little value.

A Gulf War hero, the colonel was a storefront relic Warren had selected as a constitutional necessity in order to fill out his ballot. Norton didn't make public appearances. Norton had a storied, gloried past that had been made into a movie called "White Hot Rage" which had temporarily burned his story into the psyche of the American movie-going population. He had courageously led a squadron of 19 soldiers into a nighttime assault on an Al Qaeda stronghold. The close-quarter assault on Karbala had netted 108 kills in a four-hour door-to-door firefight. The colonel's reputation was Hollywood legend. His political inexperience, however, was a hand grenade of potential liability. The colonel had some mental lapses, ostensibly, because of a war injury sustained while earning his hero label. He had a propensity of speaking a little too bluntly sometimes, which was why Warren and his campaign staff kept him out of the spotlight. Warren's campaign team had made an early and prophetic assessment.

"Keep Norton in a box," Warren's campaign manager told the presidential candidate. "He can be an asset, but not without Demerol."

Norton's "lapses" were the result of a piece of shrapnel that had tore through his frontal lobes. His leadership on the battlefield had earned him a Purple Heart, a Medal of Valor and a presidential citation. It also earned him a steel plate in his skull, which is not an unpredictable outcome when the top of one's head is sheared off by jagged hot metal. His bald head was a misshapen melon with a eight inch scar where his hairline should have been. He spoke in fractured thoughts and sentences and the joke around DC was that the colonel couldn't walk through a metal detector without peeing his pants.

In his first press conference after the surprise presidential outcome, Colonel Norton strode boldly to the microphone and read a prepared statement without too much difficulty. It was afterwards, when he ignored his chief of staff's advice and opened the floor up to questions - that the public relations disaster began.

"Colonel Norton, in view of the injury to Mr. Warren, do you see yourself assuming the role of President Pro Tem?" asked the CNN reporterette.

The colonel looked to his press aide for help. His press aide, Jeannie, was a photogenic former theater major, whose major contribution to the new Administration was her ability to look disarmingly pretty while simultaneously saying nothing. She looked vacantly at the vice president. Her training as an actress had never required she learn any Latin. She shrugged her shoulders. The vice president was on his own.

"Pro Tem?" he asked.

"Yes," replied the reporter.

The colonel weighed the question carefully.

"I'm from Oregon," explained the colonel. "We never learned Spanish there."

"Colonel," the reporter explained, "Pro Tem is Latin."

She reloaded. "What I was asking is if you will assume some of the responsibilities of president while Mr. Warren is recuperating?"

"I have always assumed responsibility for everything I've done," the Colonel replied smartly. "When I was in Iraq we didn't have to answer those smart-ass questions. We knew our orders. We followed them. I was scheduled to go home the day after I took that shrapnel in my head. That didn't distract me. I did my job. I'll always do my job. I understand duty. That's more than I can say for the lot of you. You do realize that if it wasn't for soldiers like me you folks wouldn't have the freedom to write half the crap you do, don't you?"

The reporters, usually a collection of the curious, were reduced to silence. There was an awkwardness shrouding the room as the press corps looked blankly at each other. Words bottlenecked in their throats as they tried to swallow what they had just heard.

"Dismissed!" commanded the vice president. He turned on his heels and exited the room.

The "news conference" with the vice president-elect was played extensively in the days to follow. His appearance before the press fueled the comedy mills in Hollywood, New York, Chicago, Peoria and London for months as sketch after sketch lampooned the war hero as a non compes mentes, a Latin term the colonel would hear ad nauseum.

"It makes you wonder," one network wag summarized for a disbelieving nation. "What have we done and, constitutionally, can we un-do it?"

Marshall Warren limped into the White House on January 21, 2021. In the wee hours of the evening the divorced president made the rounds at a gaggle of presidential galas, balancing on crutches, drinking copious amounts of liquor and offending more than a few Washington women by asking if they wanted to see the real seat of power.

It was the first day of a new presidential Administration and red flags were going up. The president evidently didn't realize he was now living in a fishbowl. The next day President Warren failed to appear at a morning Rose Garden ceremony with the Prime Minister of Israel. His press secretary said the president's foot had flared up and he was under doctor's orders not to walk.

"What about a wheelchair?" asked one of the reporters.

The press secretary balked. He hadn't anticipated the question. A normal press secretary would have considered curve balls from the press corps but this press secretary was an actuarial. He had spent his career juggling numbers and probabilities, not people.

"It's not an option," he said.

"Which doctor?" asked another reporter.

"The house doctor. Doctor, um, I forget his name."

Another red flag. The press knew better. They had seen the president the night before. They had seen him stumble and weave in their telephoto lenses. They had heard the stories from the guests. They had taken pictures of him being "assisted" into the limo. The president, it could be surmised without the benefit of a doctor's testimony, was hungover.

Ben Kowalski shuddered. From his suburban Minneapolis mansion he surveyed the web and read the full range of commentary concerning the president's first day in office. A sense of dread washed over him as he read from the New York Times, a paper that would, at worst, be Warren's least hostile critic. His sense of precognition was validated: The worm was going to turn on Marshall Warren.

"Whatcha doin', Cowboy," his wife Ellen asked as she entered the den and plopped down on the chair next to his computer, lifting her feet up into his lap.

"Warren's not going to make it," he declared.

"President Warren? Why?"

Ben sighed. "All right, let's weigh the evidence: One, he's a buffoon. Two, he's a drunk. Three, he's got no political allies. Four, the press is already starting to circle like vultures. Five…"

"I love it when you talk politics."

He looked at her with resignation. "You hate it when I talk politics."

"Okay, I love it when you count."

"Let me guess? The boy's asleep and we're alone in the house."

"And, you're going away for a week-long book tour in the morning and I won't see you until Friday night. Now, do you want to read boring commentary or come to bed?"

It was a million dollar question. It was the moment when he was supposed to click the computer off, grab her hand and lead her upstairs.

He stared at the computer. "Hon, there's something going on here that's more than just political flak. Warren is an accident waiting to happen. Washington is full of sharks and Warren is a chum puppy. And, he's got no party. No one owes him anything. If he can manage to stay in office he'll be playing defense for four years."

"Is that so bad," she asked, knowing that the bedroom was a lost idea for the moment. "I mean, you've always said when Congress is gridlocked they're the least dangerous."

"Yeah, but he's got no party. Every member of his cabinet will be minor league caliber. I guarantee it. None of the party reptiles dare accept a nomination to serve. He's going to be left nominating a bunch of retirees, bureaucrats and underachievers. They're the only ones with nothing left to lose. And, he's a drunk."

"How do you know that?"

"I can't tell you with any clinical precision but let's just say it takes one to know one."

"Okay, let's say he is a drunk. He wouldn't be the first."

"No. You're right. But it's one more reason he's going to get bounced."

"Impeached? He's been in office one day. That's kind of a stretch, isn't it?"

"Let's put it this way: His biggest asset right now is there isn't a sane person in either party who wants Colonel Norton in the same Area Code as the nuclear football. The three words that will keep Warren in the White House indefinitely are 'President Adam Norton.'"

She paused to let the idea sink in. "Let's say you're right. What's the worst that can happen?"

"The worst is some sort of nuclear power play."

"...And, the best?"

"From what I'm seeing, there is no best-case scenario. He's radioactive, hon."

"So, does that mean we should crawl in a hole and wait for the end?"

Ben looked at his wife with wonder. Her simple question brought the matter into a day-to-day perspective. He reached up and ran his fingers through her hair, moving down her neck to the buttons on her blouse, snapping the top three buttons open.

"Not exactly. It means we should crawl under the covers and put nuclear obliteration on the back burner. At least until the morning..."

"You sure know how to sweet talk a girl, don't you?"

CHAPTER THREE
Coup

The centerpiece of Warren's patchwork administration was his nomination of Billy Kim, a five-term congressman from California's bay area as his secretary of state. The unreported story behind Kim's nomination was the number of UN ambassadors and third-world leaders who secretly communicated their desire to the Warren Administration that Billy Kim be given serious consideration for occupying the space at the top of the diplomatic pyramid.

Warren balked at the idea. Kim was a bleeding heart. Kim was a lot of things Marshall Warren found objectionable. But, he was told – Kim was willing. Eventually Warren's posse convinced the President that talking with Billy Kim wouldn't require a commitment.

"Mr. Kim, please come in. Sit down," said President Warren as he addressed the secretary-wannabe. He paused and lit up a cigar. The cigar was strategic. Warren knew that Kim despised tobacco and had made a career out of demonizing smokers. "It seems everyone wants you to be my secretary of state but me. How do you explain that?"

"Mr. President, I know that a lot of world leaders have expressed their trust in my judgment."

"Well stated. Indeed, they have. The ambassador from Saudi Arabia just sent me this gold horse," he said, placing his hand upon the metal sculpture. "It's about twenty pounds of pure gold, Mr. Kim. Gorgeous creation. Only a man with too much money – or too little influence - would dare offer this sort of gift on pure speculation. He wants you to work for me. What have you promised him, Mr. Kim?"

"Our friends from Saudi Arabia are great allies, Mr. President. They have common enemies with us. The ambassador evidently feels that our mutual interests demand someone who can reflect their concern, someone who can

work with the Saudis and exercise all avenues to assure our mutual and continued peace and prosperity."

"My God, Kim. You speak diplomat like some sort of San Francisco
fruitcake."

The president was trying to get a rise out of the congressman and was
watching his reactions closely. Kim remained stoic; knowing full well that the
word 'fruitcake' was a targeted word. He was from San Francisco. He knew
the president was trying to get a rise out of him. He swallowed, allowing the
president have his say.

"Mr. Kim," the president continued. "You would make a great secretary
of state – if I were a socialist. But, I'm not. I don't happen to share your belief
that profit is a four-letter word. This country is the engine of the world, Mr.
Kim. The engine requires fuel. But, what you don't seem to appreciate is that
American capital and brain power drives that engine. Yes, sometimes big business makes a profit, but that doesn't mean they're evil. Their profit pays your
freight, congressman. You are aware of that, aren't you?"

The congressman smiled. He knew he was being baited. He also knew he
was required to play a specific role in the next act of the play. Winning Warren's
confidence would require that he tread lightly, diplomatically, over his next few
answers.

"Mr. President, I'm not anti-American. I'm not even anti-capitalist. I'm
a man who looks at the American landscape and sees us underachieving at the
primary function of government – which is providing a safety net for the poor,
the unemployed, the underprivileged, the under-employed, the minorities…"

"Oh, cut the crap will you please? We're not having a debate for the League
of Women Voters, Kim. I can smell your BS even if they can't. Talk to me like
a man, will you? If you mention minorities or the poor one more time, I swear
I'm going to lose my bowels. I know you can speak like a damn diplomatic
panty waist. The question is whether you can talk to me like a man. What I
need to know is if you can ply your line of BS without getting me deep in stew.
Why should I give you serious consideration as secretary of state?"

"Because, Mr. President, I have been given assurances from some very
influential people that they will deal with me, but they won't deal with you."

"Like who?"

"Mr. President," the congressman said as he pulled a sheet of paper out of
his suit coat. He unfolded the paper.

"I have a list here of the people who would like to talk to you about the
superior level of cooperation you can expect if you choose me to be the next

secretary. At 9:45 we shall conference call with the Prime Minister of England. 10:15, the President of the European Union. At 10:45, his Holiness, the Pope." He paused and looked directly at the president. "I have all the names and numbers here. They have agreed to accept our call. Our call. Shall we begin, Mr. President? We don't want to begin your administration by disappointing such a distinguished list as this. Do we, Mr. President?"

In the press it was reported as a marriage made in heaven. The mainstream press couldn't have been more effusive in their praise of Billy Kim. He was one of theirs. The press wasted no verbs in singing the harmony of Billy Kim as the centerpiece of a cabinet whose names and faces were largely anonymous and under-qualified. In a cabinet of underachievers, Billy Kim was the resident rock star.

It took only three months for Billy Kim to stage his well-timed coup.

It was off by three minutes.

History would show the coup had Billy Kim's DNA all over it. The political timing was perfect and Marshall Warren was the perfect dupe. Billy Kim had a large bank of political capital, an impeccable sense of timing and the benefit of a nation dulled by the monotonous drone of prolonged prosperity and no appreciation for the liberties insuring that prosperity.

Billy Kim knew the coup would be won or lost in the public relations trenches. He had spent a career padding his resume with the sort of accomplishments that would arm him for the PR battle. He was portrayed only in the warmest terms by the press and was the darling of his party, a party that almost mystically turned a blind eye to Kim's high profile defection into the Warren Administration.

The big box office plus Billy Kim brought to Washington, though, wasn't political or policy related. Billy Kim brought the added spice of his consort and confidante, Claudia Colgate. Claudia was Billy Kim's sexy, daring and unflappable "life partner." They were the dynamic duo – part rock stars and part political icons. The cherry on the top of the media sundae was the fact that Billy Kim was unmistakably un-white. A Chinese-American, he had served as congressman from California's Bay Area for a decade. He had also served on the board of the Peace Corps, the Boys & Girls Club, the YWCA and a handful of other prominent non-profit groups. After the convoluted election of 2020, Billy Kim had accepted Warren's invitation to serve as Number Four in the constitutional pecking order - not out of a sense of duty and service, but because he had been sworn to seize the moment three decades earlier on the top of the pyramid of Khafre.

Billy Kim was acutely aware where history, circumstance and a blood promise had placed him – just three corpses away from the presidency.

He had a plan. It wasn't elaborate. It wasn't even clever. It was just secret enough not to register with most Americans. To pull off his deed, he needed cover. He needed his friends in media to do him a favor.

On a March afternoon in 2021 a phone call was made from a secure White House office to the editor and publisher of the New York Times. The conversation lasted only a few minutes. Officially, it never happened.

"Jim, you have to report what's going to happen and not read anything into it. Just report the details."

"Mr. Secretary, you're asking one of America's foremost papers to turn a blind eye to a very big story."

"No, Jim, I'm asking you to do the right thing for America. We talked about a new day dawning. This is that new day. Now, if you're a little soft on the idea tell me now."

"Mr. Secretary, I'm not sure we can do it. It's not part of what we're called to do – run cover for a political coup. You have to agree that something like you're suggesting has global implications."

"The problem with you, Jim, is you don't know precisely what the right thing is. I mean, how can anyone trust a man who keeps a mistress - Jodi, I think her name is – on his payroll, even though the young lady doesn't appear to do anything at your paper? That's not the kind of behavior one expects from someone entrusted to publish one of America's most prestigious papers. Is it, Jim?"

There was a pause as the publisher considered the implications of what Kim had revealed.

"You gonna play that game, Mr. Secretary? I have markers I can call in, too."

"I play to win, Jim. And, you can play with me, or you might find a letter to your board of directors revealing all of the secret, sordid details of a middle-age publisher with four kids in very expensive Ivy League schools, a mistress and a fondness for a certain prescription drug he purchases off the street."

Billy Kim knew when to throw a high, tight fastball.

"If you want to take me on, Jim, I suggest you find something more potent than public opinion. Maybe a 500-pound smart bomb? Oh, I forgot – we have all of those."

Billy Kim leaned closer into his speaker phone. "Listen to me closely, Jim. If you get cold feet, if you send your reporters into places they shouldn't be, you won't just be embarrassed, you'll be out of business. I will expect, too, that you will carry my sentiments to the rest of the boys on the team. You play nice with me I'll see to it that you, and all the boys, receive some protections - behind the scenes. Do we understand each other, Jim?"

The publisher considered his defeat for the moment and swallowed hard. "Yes, Mr. Secretary."

"Please, Jim – call me Billy."

Kim's clinical sense of knowing the pulse of the American people, along with his not-so-subtle nudge into the ribcage of America's vital influence peddlers, told him the coup could be pulled off. His army of pollsters had told him the American people were asleep at the switch, more concerned with the secret lives of celebrities and free government cheese than protecting the foundation of their liberties.

The plan unfolded this way: In broad daylight, two Saudi nationals – twin brothers in the US on over-extended student visas – quickly assembled and launched their two one-man helicopters from a parking garage in DC. What forensic experts would later determine, but would never report publicly, was that the engineering for the special choppers was a Chinese design. It was a secret neither Marshall Warren nor the American people would ever learn. The CIA Director, a Kim ally, had found a way to lose that part of the story.

So it was, on April 7, 2021, two choppers whisked away from a parking garage, skimming the rooftops of buildings just six blocks away from White House grounds. Before security could react, they launched their phosphorous rockets into the White House from 500 yards away. One hundred and sixty eight White House personnel, along with the vice president, would perish in a fiery conflagration that consumed the structure in less than three minutes. The terrorists didn't wait for the fire to blossom. They blew their choppers into oblivion, killing an additional 14 people on the ground in a fiery avalanche of metal and panic.

President Warren, unknowingly, had thrown a wrench into Kim's well-constructed coup. Instead of becoming ashes in history, the president had exited the grounds just three minutes prior on Marine One, bound for Camp David and a rendezvous with a Vegas showgirl. History would later document that it was the president's unrestrained libido that had saved his life and thwarted an immediate seizure of power by the devious Billy Kim

So, instead of pleasuring himself with a lithe and leggy dancer, the president spent the bulk of the day parked on an airport tarmac at an Air Force base monitoring the fate of the nation and wondering who else might have his noggin in their gun sights.

Kim's treachery was no secret inside the DC Beltway. Outside of the Beltway it was spun so hard and so often by Kim's friends in the mainstream press that middle America never saw a coup; they only saw a large white house burn and a few unfortunate lives lost in the process. In short, the mainstream press saw nothing. They quickly labeled the event as a "national tragedy," but concluded in the first 24 hours the act was the result of the twin Saudi brothers acting out of their own fanatical Islamic zeal.

That was the end of the story. Investigative journalism simply wasn't engaged in the pursuit of the facts. In the mainstream media the story developed no inertia. The hard questions were answered before they were asked. And, the idea that Billy Kim could have a hand in the deed was the sort of "irresponsible journalism" reported in the dark, dank caverns of talk radio, the Internet and the blogosphere. The thought that Billy Kim could possibly have a hand in the chain of events was reported to most news consumers as a premature, presumptive and racist conclusion. Even the simultaneous "accidental" drowning of the Speaker of the House in the Bering Sea was reported as just one more tragic coincidence instead of another act in a well-choreographed power play.

CHAPTER FOUR
Presidential hemorrhoid

Brad Pugh, on any given day, had 28 million radio listeners. In any given week he had 45 million listeners. At any given time he had 17 million listeners. He was a major player in matters of culture and media. He was, more than any other member of the media, the source from which lava flowed. The mainstream press pretended he was insignificant; for drawing attention to Pugh's popularity would have been akin to the Coca Cola board of directors drinking Pepsi at a press conference. In mass media circles Pugh was the enemy no one mentioned by name.

Brad Pugh reported what he knew and said nothing less than what he thought. Pugh's willingness to tell the Kim saga without first passing it through the filter of the elite media was the primary reason why he ended up eventually broadcasting his award-winning talk radio program from the bow of a secret submarine.

Brad Pugh called Billy Kim a tyrant frequently and without the disclaimer his peers seemed so fond of using. There was no "alleged" in Brad Pugh's exhortations against the man he labeled a constitutional imposter.

"Beware federal strangers bearing gifts," he warned his audience with regularity. Brad Pugh, more than anyone on the airwaves, put Kim's rise to power into a troubled focus. He framed the day's development in a historical context for those who had forgotten what history was supposed to look like. To say Brad Pugh was critical of Billy Kim would have been kind.

"Billy Kim has seized the reins of power through deception, treachery and thuggery. He has packed the House and Senate with his cronies and seeks to fuel his power at the tax trough. He has, almost single-handedly perpetrated a fraud of galactic proportion on the American people."

President Kim actually tried to tango, once, with Brad Pugh. In 2023, in the heat of his push to add more "resources" to national health care, Kim commanded his Secretary of Health and Human Services to go on the air and defend the virtues of the single-payer health care system the Kim Administration was trying to "inspire" through the houses of Congress. The secretary, Hiram Steinmetz, told the president he was equal to the task and willing to meet in an on-air phone interview with Brad.

Time would demonstrate that Mr. Steinmetz had overestimated the powers of his own persuasion.

"Mr. Secretary, first of all, thank you for coming on the program today. Let's cut to the chase: Why should the American voter agree to hand our health care over to the federal government?"

The secretary had been coached through the process. He had expected Brad to throw him fastballs. He was prepped and confident.

"I don't think, Brad, that government will be taking over health care. In our present model, a patient and their doctor will always have the ability to determine the best course of action."

It would be the last positive statement the secretary would make concerning national health care. Brad Pugh switched gears and threw him a knuckle ball.

"Mr. Secretary – for almost 50 years the Department of Health and Human Services has stockpiled DNA data on babies born in this country. Could you explain - for the benefit of every parent whose name, and whose child's name, is now part of a secret government database - how this information will be not be used by the Kim Administration to ration health care once a national health care plan is put into place?"

The secretary hadn't been briefed how to answer this particular question. Pugh was off-script. How much did Pugh know about the genetic profiling? It was supposed to be classified.

The secretary stalled. He considered lying but realized he wasn't talking to a reporter from the Times or the Tribune, he was talking to the Kim Administration's most vocal and potent critic.

"I'm not sure what you're talking about, Brad."

"Well, Mr. Secretary, it's standard procedure in this country that a drop of blood is taken from the heel of every baby born. It's been going on for 50 years. They do it, ostensibly, to check for PKU, which is medical shorthand for Phenylketonuria."

Brad paused to see if the secretary would interrupt. He didn't. The secretary was waiting to see just how much Brad knew.

"PKU, Mr. Secretary, is what they call an inherited metabolic disease. It's rare, but if detected early, can be treated effectively."

"I'm not sure where you're going with this Brad, but it's no secret that the government has been testing for PKU for, as you say, 50 years." The secretary was getting an uneasy feeling. He didn't want a bothersome thing like truth uncovered in real time.

Brad picked up his line of questioning. "Mr. Secretary, what about the other 52 genetic markers the government has been tracking in babies along with the PKU testing?"

There was a palpable pause in the secretary's response. Brad Pugh had opened a Pandora's Box. Opening this discussion in front of a national audience, without a net, was not in the game plan. Steinmetz felt the ice crack beneath his feet. "You seem to know so much, Mr. Pugh, you tell me what's happening."

"What's happening, Mr. Secretary, is that the government has been collecting names and data on over 230 million people in this country for the last 50 years. Most citizens now have a file with their genetic predispositions charted and monitored - everything from diabetes to heart disease to mental disease to hypertension – in all, 53 specific indicators to chart genetic predispositions. What are the assurances, Mr. Secretary, that this data will not be used in this new medical Utopia you and your boss have crafted, to determine who should, or shouldn't, get treatment – not if, but when the government is forced to ration treatment – like they do in all the other countries with socialized medicine."

There was a lot of conjecture in Brad's question and the secretary knew it. He was ready to pounce on Pugh as soon as he took a breath.

"You're inferring, Mr. Pugh. Everything you've said is baseless speculation. You're inferring that this sort of research data will naturally lead to rationing based on some sort of government survivability models..."

The secretary had stepped into Brad's snare.

"Then, you're not denying our government has been secretly compiling genetic data on Americans - not just for PKU, but a whole host of conditions for 50 years?"

The secretary didn't know it at that moment but he had exactly four days, six hours and 32 minutes left before the president would accept his resignation as the HHS Secretary.

His next response would be the fatal bullet.

"All right. Let's say you could be right. That's not saying the president's plan for a national health care program isn't the right thing to do."

"That's not what I said, Mr. Secretary. I said – and you affirmed – that secret data has been collected on the American people for almost 50 years, and that the Kim Administration has access to the data and would be compelled, if the situation were grave enough, to ration health care based on genetic predispositions. Given that the government wants ownership of the process of health care, I think it's dishonest for the government not to tell us all the cards they have in their hand. In my mind this willful omission makes the government's case a hoax, a fraud, a conspiracy…"

The secretary forgot where he was. He forgot that up to 20 million people might be listening. He saw white.

"Listen, smartass! You think you've got all the answers. I didn't come on your show to speculate. I came to speak on behalf of President Kim's vision for American health care. If you think your little microphone and your big mouth gives you the right to insult me, and the president, and torpedo the noble intentions of a whole government - just because of your distorted notion of liberty, you got another thing coming. Billy Kim is in charge of this administration, Mr. Pugh. You need to get used to that. You're not calling the shots and never have. You sit there day after day and spew your misinformation and mean-spirited opinions. You speculate! You take your best guess at how the world is run. Well, your best guess doesn't cut it. You forget who's running the country."

"You already said that."

"Well, it bears repeating. You forget that you're not the president. You forget that you're just a man with a microphone and a lot of…" and he lost his train of thought. Steinmetz was in full fume. He sputtered his way into his next sentence.

"You, you, you think exposing a government secret will earn you bonus points with the gun lobby and the oil lobby and all your other right-wing friends? That's fine, you can think what you want, but as for me – I'm not going to stand by while you bad mouth the United States of America."

Brad Pugh waited for the secretary's rant to end. On air he began to sob. Then weep. He broke down and began crying, bawling. "Ahh!" he wailed. "You hurt my feelings!"

The HHS Secretary had had enough insolence. He didn't know humor. Certainly, he didn't understand the subtleties of sarcasm.

"Kiss it, pal," said the soon-to-be-ex HHS Secretary, and hung up the phone.

Through 1500 miles of phone line Brad Pugh could almost see the beet red crimson hue on the face of the secretary. The mental image of the secretary slamming down the phone and cursing his name made Brad Pugh laugh hysterically in front of millions - who were laughing hysterically with him. Eventually Brad regained his equilibrium and implored his board man:

"Cue that up, Robbie. That was priceless. Alert the media. Put out a press release and tell our friends in the mainstream media that we just had a member of the Kim clan have a certifiable meltdown on live radio!"

"What do you think we should do about Mr. Pugh?" Billy Kim's chief of staff asked the president.

"Kill him!" snapped back the president. It was supposed to be humor.

"Sir, you're being ironic, right?"

Billy Kim waved his hand at his chief, knowing that if he really wanted to pull the trigger on Brad Pugh he would have to do it beneath the radar. He was working on it.

Brad Pugh put on a daily full-court press. He screeched at Kim's abuses and his tortured interpretation of the Constitution for three hours every day.

Pugh had often said "if what I'm saying is untrue, why aren't they charging me with treason or, at the least, filing a civil suit for slander?"

It was an interesting question. It didn't really require thoughtful analysis and was, intellectually not a hard question to answer. But, not many asked the question. The fact was no charges were filed, nor suits brought forward against Pugh precisely because the charges Pugh laid out with prosecutorial precision had foundations in fact.

President Kim had no desire to have those facts given the disinfectant of sunlight.

Kim's handlers told the president to try to ignore Brad Pugh. They asked their friends in the mainstream press to do likewise. None of the robots in Billy Kim's orbit of influence were anxious to have the facts of the president's rise to power disseminated onto a population that seemed fully capable of enjoying a long nap in the midst of a constitutional shakedown.

In time, the very utterance of Brad Pugh's name was banned in the White House. Were it possible, they would have outlawed the very thought of Brad Pugh. His name had become toxic.

Billy Kim tried, as best he could, to deflect Pugh's unending criticism but couldn't avoid some of the daily flak. Kim plotted a plan to silence Pugh legally, but he would have to wait for his moment.

Early in his second term as president, in 2025, Kim and his lap-dog Congress made their move against the mouthy broadcaster.

Pugh was ready. He had an exit strategy well thought out. He had always considered a worst-case scenario. Brad Pugh understood that one of the liabilities of being a presidential hemorrhoid was the possibility of an executive application of Preparation H. He always assumed the day would come when he would be required to do his best jackrabbit impression.

So it was, in the summer of 2025, that Brad Pugh, the voice of the malevolent minority, ended up hiding his golden-throated opposition in a rented Russian sub, broadcasting his daily diatribe to a growing audience of American skeptics from "beneath the waves of an ocean near you."

If Billy Kim thought Brad Pugh was a problem on land, he was doubly perturbed by the candor that bounced off a satellite; a candor which was regurgitated by almost 800 stations across the US, Canada and parts of Europe. Safely hidden beneath the waves, Pugh's invisibility emboldened him. Brad Pugh was not the only radio host trumpeting the truth but he was the loudest, the most forceful, and the most listened to voice in the land.

"Billy Kim is a murderous, lying, opportunistic traitor," Pugh would say. It was the kind of statement that left little doubt which side of the fence Brad Pugh's flag was planted. Those who listened tended to agree with Pugh and tended to be the most un-persuaded by the daily media whitewashing.

For the Kim folks, the silver lining to the Brad Pugh paradox was a demographic one: While Pugh was heard by many, he was not heard by most. Pugh may have been vocal – but he was a vocal minority. Kim's ubiquitous polling data told his demographic engineers that most Americans were too consumed with their own pleasures and anxieties to concern themselves with a bothersome thing like a Big Picture. Most Americans were leading good, fat lives - ergo, whoever was president must be doing a good job.

While his fans admired Pugh's *cojones*, in quiet tones they feared for his safety. After Pugh's brazen escape beneath the waves it was rumored he had a sizeable bounty on his head – whether Pugh be delivered vertically or horizontally. Pugh's fans didn't need law degrees to tell them that their radio mentor was walking a daily tightrope between litigation, libel, life or death.

Even from the forced confines of the secret Russian sub Brad never wavered from his faith in the eventual triumph of the First Amendment. He believed the American model would ultimately recover from the illegal constructs of Billy Kim. He had faith that the American experiment would transcend Billy Kim and that one day, hopefully soon, the country would welcome he and Winnie back home where they belonged.

CHAPTER FIVE
A 50-caliber solution

Lars and Ethel Larsen lived in the sprawling brick tudor next to Ben Kowalski on their quiet and secure cul-de-sac - before and after Ben had been reluctantly selected to serve as Marshall Warren's vice president and, eventually, president of the country.

The day Ben had returned from Washington, DC, post-impeachment in 2021, Lars and Ethel were ecstatic. Not only had Ben Kowalski, the reluctant politician, been impeached, but his wife and son had been estranged from his life. It was the Larsen trifecta. Seeing Ben Kowalski – his religion, his politics and his cultural point of view squashed like a bug put a lilt in their walk. The Larsen's sense of justice had been fulfilled. If they could have bottled their smugness on that day they could have sold it for a high premium.

Over the years, they couldn't hide who they were from Ben. They tried to mask it behind a veneer of civility but their contempt for Ben and his way of life were only a quarter inch beneath the surface.

In Ben's mind, they had always been obtuse and dour neighbors. The country, according to the unspoken gospel of Lars and Ethel Larsen, had gone to hell in a hand basket and their closest neighbor, Ben Kowalski, was a mirror of that hell and that hand basket. Ben could only guess the level of their dislike for him – they were too calculating to tip their hand.

On a May morning in 2026, though, the forces of science, faith and history were going to intersect on the lawn of Lars and Ethel Larsen. Neither Lars nor Ethel could see the forces of good and evil squaring off in the space above their well-manicured lawn. Lars and Ethel Larsen didn't know spirits came in flavors of good or evil. They were, by most definitions, agnostic – humanists. What they preached was the gospel of Lars and Ethel Larsen. They recognized their lawn and their rose bushes and their quiet upper crust existence. They

knew the sweet smell of freshly cut grass, the songs of finches at their elaborate bird feeder and the whistle of the teapot on their stove. They couldn't
have seen that their lawn would soon become Ground Zero for a battle of wills
which would, over the course of the next few months, drive an invisible wedge
between the two of them.

As Lars sat atop his John Deere riding lawnmower, he listened to what he
always listened to - National Public Radio. He adjusted his headphones and
wheeled his JD-420X around the rose bushes, lining up for his first unchallenged pass through the immaculate Kentucky Blue Grass. He loved mowing.
He engaged the blades.

Disgust overtook him when he spotted the limo heading up the drive of
his neighbor and nemesis, Ben Kowalski. What now, he wondered? Kowalski
frequently entertained men in suits. Lars could smell what they were. They
were preachers - so called Men of God, calling on the former president, motivational speaker, the once proclaimed 'most trusted man in America,' Ben
Kowalski.

He turned the mower off and walked over to the deck. Ethel had a pitcher
of ice-tea waiting.

"Another group of church rats. I'll bet you," Lars said, turning his head
toward the Kowalski mansion.

His wife, Ethel, looked up from her paper and peered over her glasses at
her neighbor's house. "I suppose. It's what he does, hon. Just take solace in the
fact that he was impeached. In the process he lost his wife and his son. He's
been defeated. You have to learn how to accept victory, Lars. Besides, what are
you going to do about him? How deep do you want to bury him?"

"Let's get a 50-cal mounted on the terrace. What we want to do is wait
until we get enough of them preachers in there to make it a worthwhile kill."

"That's the male in you talking. The real way to defeat their type is through
education. A good dose of Darwin at an early age is a vaccine against a lot of
what they preach."

"Darwin was a quack," exhorted Lars. He had lectured his wife for decades about the scientific thin ice Darwin skated on. "His science doesn't hold
up. They're still teaching it, sure, but the scientific community has long since
forgotten Darwin. After 150 years, his theories don't hold up. I don't know
what the answer is but it ain't God and it ain't Darwin."

Ethel exhaled. She had heard the rant before.

"You're talking on a doctoral level, Lars. Most kids and their parents don't
have a clue. They believe what they're told. Our job is to keep telling them.

That's how you win that war. What Kim is doing with public education is far more effective against Kowalski and his cronies than any rain of bullets."

"Yeah, but bullets are quicker."

"There's a law against that, dear, so you can just hold off on your 50-caliber solution. You have got to learn to let him go. He's insignificant, Lars."

At that moment Lars spotted Kowalski coming out his garden door to greet his guests. Larsen decided the time was right to be obtuse. He walked briskly to the wrought-iron fence separating their two properties, intercepting Kowalski halfway along the walk

"Hey, Cowboy! What's cooking? I keep seeing these suits day after day. You know something we don't?"

Ethel Larsen strained to hear, smirking from the patio. She was hoping her husband could annoy Kowalski. But, after 37 years of marriage, she knew her husband was not a model of logic - he lost his train of thought quickly. She would have preferred that she intercept Ben at the fence. She was so much better at condescension. She was a retired state senator. While she liked living next door to a high-profile person, she was unmoved by Kowalski's political and, particularly, his religious views. Ben Kowalski was a Christian puppet to her. She enjoyed it when they could annoy him. In her public and private conversations, she found Kowalski an easy target among her ideological kin. In retirement, one of her small pleasures was assassinating the character of her neighbor.

"Oh, hi, Lars," Kowalski shot back at Lars. Ben tried to remain under control around Lars and Ethel. He was hoping to somehow win their acceptance - a hope that diminished with each rude and dour encounter.

Ben considered opting to ignore his bothersome neighbor but decided candor was his preferred weapon.

"Some friends from Sweden are paying a call. We're exploring some archeological finds from Saudi Arabia. It all has to do with The Exodus and the Ten Commandments. You could join us," said Ben, knowing full well Lars would sooner be raped by bikers than share space with Ben Kowalski. "You might learn something. You could meet with some biblical scholars. You could challenge the veracity of the findings."

Ben knew he had Lars in troubled waters when the word 'veracity' rolled off his lips. He wanted to take the word back, but the deed had been done. Lars was now a deer in his headlights.

It was true. Lars, in fact, had been lost before 'veracity.' He didn't listen well. When his ears should have been open, his brain was engaged trying to invent a pithy comeback. He wanted to slam Ben's faith, his politics, everything, but Kowalski had disarmed him with pleasantry. Lars was defeated before he began. Still, he was hoping to save face in front of his wife. He knew she would be straining to hear him put Kowalski down.

He clicked on his brain. The dark recess where his wit resided wasn't returning his call. He wished Ben had acted like the enemy he was supposed to be. It would have made his life so much easier. He didn't want to match wits with Kowalski. Lars was deliberative and not a quick thinker. His reasoning skills had been dulled in 27 years as a civil engineer for the Department of Highways. Procedure he could deal with. Thought, actual thought, was a long-forgotten lover. He could deal with Kowalski as a comic book adversary, but he couldn't deal with him as a human being with a brain. He had to be careful of Kowalski's brain. Lars scowled.

"Tell 'em to keep their limo parked on your side of the property line," he barked.

Kowalski looked down the line of the wrought-iron fence, seeing the rear quarter panel of the limo peeking into Larsen's private property. In the absence of thought, Lars had found a technicality he could seize on.

"I'll get 'em to move," Ben said, disappointed that Lars was choosing to be a gladiator instead of neighbor. He paused. "Anything else?"

It was too late. Larsen had turned on his heels and climbed back aboard his tractor. He affixed his headphones firmly and turned up the volume on NPR. He wasn't going to give Kowalski the satisfaction of a response. He hated Ben and everything his ilk stood for.

Someday, Lars thought, Kowalski's self-righteous act is going to be exposed. In his imagination Lars pictured scores of TV trucks outside of Kowalski's home waiting for a statement from Ben clarifying some horrible, miserable, inexcusable, shameful mistake. In his fantasy, Lars imagined Ben being caught in an affair, or embezzlement or child molestation. Any one of them would do.

The Larsen's would be there like hyenas on his carcass.

CHAPTER SIX
Plausible deniability

There was no way the news could be denied. But, it could be softened. The media crowded into the ballroom at Euro Disney. The arrival of the President of the European Union had been scheduled early in the day and deliberately delayed. The reporters, cameramen and associated technicians cooled their heels, munching on expensive meats and chocolates, seafood cocktails, canapés and sinful, rich desserts. There were also bottomless glasses of champagne Mimosa that the waiters kept full, fresh and flowing. The press corps may have grown impatient, but they were sated. Somewhere in the gaggle of reporters, there were hard questions to be asked of the European Union president. The wine and the food were designed to take the rough edges off those questions.

EU President Hans Tanner was to take the stage at 8:00 AM, Paris time, but was late. The timing was strategic. He wanted to make certain his press conference took place well after the American papers had been put to bed for the work week. The American papers were the ones that mattered to Tanner. Breaking the kind of story Hans Tanner had to break could not be denied, but it could be "spun." The American publishing world still had renegade papers, a bothersome talk radio presence and a lot of cowboy citizens who refused to consider the European Union as a legitimate player on the world stage.

The American papers concerned Tanner the most. Talk radio he couldn't control – and the Internet was filled with a misinformation no one could contain. But major American metropolitan dailies and mainstream networks still carried considerable political clout. It was for their benefit he was holding the press conference. The European press didn't matter. In Europe, the papers spoke with a unified voice, or more precisely, a union voice. Tanner and the European unions fed from the same trough; their truths were sanitized through the same filter.

"Mr. President, the press is waiting…" said Brian Vandervoort, Hans Tanner's loyal chief of staff from the secluded comfort of their off-stage office. Vandervoort was a 35-year-old political science major from Hamburg University – a father, husband and political insider who helped engineer Hans Tanner's rise to European power. Vandervoort was a man chosen for his loyalty and shared vision for world politics, but also because he had a wife and kids that could be used, if need be, as leverage. Hans Tanner always considered his trump card. Tanner viewed Vandervoort as a loyal and trusted confidante with an undeniable puppy quality about him.

"Let the press wait, Brian. Patience. You must continue to trust me." He reached into his briefcase and handed the Belgian an envelope. "Look."

Vandervoort fingered the envelope and opened it. Inside was a bundle of one hundred thousand Euro dollars. The Belgian was confused.

"What is this?"

"There 100,000 Euros there. You can't be expected to maintain the lifestyle I would expect of my chief of staff on a public servant's salary."

"I didn't ask for this, sir."

"Brian, you don't understand the foundations of my Administration. If you are a mere public servant you shall do things in accord with public service. If, however, you are my servant, you will do things in accord with my wishes."

"I don't need this, sir. You know my heart. I would never betray you."

"Yes, Brian, I know that. However, if I need a favor which may be above and beyond – well, I want someone who already owes me something."

"You don't need to buy my allegiance, sir."

The boss was starting to get tired of the puppy.

"Oh, but Brian, I do. I've never shared all my plans with you. There will be, shall we say, 'considerations' which will have to be executed as we get closer to our ultimate goal."

Vandervoort considered his dilemma for a moment. He was being bribed. That much couldn't be denied. But, for what? His immediate reaction was defensive:

"Who do you want me to kill?" He knew his boss had authored covert political assassinations, but Brian was smart enough not to ask the details.

"Brian," sighed the EU President, almost as a father to an insolent child, "a world leader keeps his operatives at the street level. Political operations like the one you suggest are always kept three or four levels removed from the source. That way, even if one of your operatives sings, you're still several levels removed from them and can reasonably deny even knowing them. Plausible deniability, Brian. It would be suicidal for me to have my chief of staff implicated in something so damning as murder. But, that doesn't mean I won't need other types of cover."

"Such as?"

"Your value to me, Brian is that the press trusts you. You're not a liar. You don't know what it means to intentionally deceive. I want to use that as an asset, but to do that I need you not to question my motives. I want you to be my mouthpiece, but I don't want you sniffing behind the scenes. I just want you to report what I say the facts are. In return, that envelope will be the first of many."

"You still haven't answered my question, Mr. President. What sort of ignorance, precisely, will I be asked to plead?"

"I will tell you the whole story at a later time, but as a first installment I need you to go to China. I have already arranged the flight. Once there you will meet with a team of Chinese scientists. They will brief you on the mission. I will tell you this much: In a few months we will execute a plan at the dedication of the third temple of Jerusalem. It will be larger than life. It will require someone to do a lot of behind-the-scenes recruiting for the talent we will need to pull the deception off. No killing, Brian. I don't need my chief even close to a dead body."

There was a pregnant pause as the Belgian considered what he knew and what he didn't. The question was simple: Did he trust his boss to tell him the truth? Or, was truth removed from the equation? Was it simply a matter of loyalty? What he knew without being told was that Tanner's truth was pliable. Truth was whatever allowed Hans Tanner to climb a ladder onto a world stage. Vandervoort knew the larger plan – ultimately his boss wanted to unite the European Union under a socialist flag and use the UN to leverage his influence onto the American stage. The Belgian believed in the larger plan and wanted to be a central figure in helping establish Europe as the next change agent in world politics. Were he to say no now, he would be deprived of seeing the drama unfold. If he said no now, he would quite possibly be reassigned or terminated.

"All right, Mr. President. When do I leave?"

"Right after our press conference."

Tanner's handlers had made sure the reporters were fed and wined and that America would not read, or see, hard news of their press conference until Sunday. That would give the Tanner team a day and a half to spin, soften and counter-punch the bad news Tanner was about to let out of the corral. It was an old political axiom: Break bad news late on Friday, after the papers were put to bed.

It was a small tactical detail. But Tanner drilled everyone on his team to appreciate that they added up.

Tanner was said to be many things. He was black and white and every shade in between. His ascendancy to the presidency of the European Union had been more of a coronation than an election. As CEO and lead researcher for Global Pharmacia, a division of Bayer, Ltd, Tanner had pioneered a chemical cocktail called Triheliomelophine Ascorbic Prophase, or TAP. TAP was both synthetic and natural in its formulation. It stopped AIDS dead in its tracks and had the unfathomable quality of acting as a both a preventative and a cure for AIDS.

People remember where they were when they heard about JFK. They remember where they were when the World Trade Centers were attacked. They remembered, too, that Sunday in October, 2021, when Hans Tanner held a small green pill in his hand and announced the end of AIDS. It had made Tanner incredibly famous and obscenely rich overnight. His patent of TAP, technically, belonged to his employer, Bayer, Ltd, but Tanner seized an opportunity, claiming the formula would never have seen the light of day had it not been for his own secret leaking of the clinical developments to the press. He felt the world owed him for his courage, and so he chose to stage his legal battle against his employer on the front pages of the world papers where his legal misdeeds could be mitigated by just what a nice, caring, sensitive guy he was.

The board of Bayer, Ltd, knew a fight with the benevolent Tanner was a battle they might win in a court of law, but could never win in the court of public opinion. Bayer made a handsome cash settlement with their wayward researcher - trying to buy his silence. The decision of the company to settle with Tanner became imperative when secret documents were produced by Tanner which revealed certain clinical omissions Bayer had overlooked in the trial process. It seemed Bayer had not exactly followed the letter of the regulatory law in their research and Tanner knew it. In truth, he had authored the illegal research – a small, tactical omission the press never learned. Tanner and the board both knew the chronology of events, but chose to keep the details private because of their shared disdain for prison life.

Tanner used his inside knowledge of his (and Bayer's) indiscretions as secret leverage in order to make TAP available to the world's population virtually overnight, virtually free.

He was Time's "Man of the Year" for 2022. In 2023 he announced his candidacy as the first president of the 11-member European Union. He was Time's "Man of the Year," again, in 2023 when he was first elected president of the EU. Then, as if he needed to pad his resume, he was awarded the Nobel Peace Prize in 2024 as well.

He had swept onto the world's stage with a flourish. Certain renegade Americans seemed to find Tanner's political coronation troubling. Specifically, he made the American Christian crowd nervous - not only because of his politics but, more disturbingly, his undercurrent of Christian antagonism. He believed in science. He never spoke of faith other than to provide the politically-correct bromide that faith was a matter of individual conscience. His lack of clarity in the spiritual realm sold in Europe. Europe had become secular in all practicality. In reality, Europe had become more Muslim than Christian and more secular than anything. But, the Muslims were gaining. In the baby-making derby Muslims were outperforming the natives four-to-one and had been for almost 20 years. The numbers were reaching a flash point as Islam sought, increasingly, to weave its way into the fabric of European law, culture and history.

America, however, still had a large renegade Christian crowd who viewed Europe and Tanner with measured suspicion.

As he approached the stage at Euro Disney, Tanner thought about the Americans and how he didn't need to sway all of them, just most of them. After all, it was for their consumption that the press conference was being staged.

Tanner wore a striking Armani suit with his trademark rainbow lapel pin as he strode to the microphone. He was a formidable six feet six inches tall with a flowing shock of salt and pepper hair and a professorial-looking goatee. He approached the podium in stealth. He deliberately wanted to arrive unannounced. A buzz rose throughout the crowd. He stood in front of the assembly, quietly coughing until they put down their wine glasses and picked up their pens, cameras and recorders. When it was sufficiently quiet he calmly announced an error had been made.

"There's a problem with TAP and we owe it to everyone to minimize the damage." He paused to make sure that everyone understood. "Once taken, either as a preventative or as a cure, TAP cannot be safely discontinued."

The press had their cameras rolling, their pens were bobbing in a dance, trying to capture the words. Tanner paused. In his eyes tears were forming and his voice broke.

"We've had some fatalities that fall outside of the statistical range of acceptance. Maybe in our haste to get this product to a suffering world, we acted prematurely but this much we can say with certainty - if you've taken TAP, you have to keep taking it. For reasons we can't quite understand the liver becomes dependent on it. Without it, the liver shuts down."

The only sound in the room was a plate breaking in the kitchen. The reporters could see and sense the anxiety in Tanner.

Tanner stepped back from the microphone and put his hands on his hips. He took a deep cleansing breath. He looked at the ceiling. He bit his lip. Before stepping back to the microphone he wiped his eyes with his right hand. In the palm of that hand he had a small vial of ammoniated salts and in the act of wiping his eyes the ammonia prompted his tear ducts into hyperactivity. When he stepped back to the microphone he looked straight at the cameras and into the eyes of the world. His head moved left, then right as he composed himself. A tear escaped from his right eye and then one rolled down his left cheek, as if choreographed.

The fact that he had engineered an inexcusable abuse of research protocol would be forgiven. He was shedding tears! His humanity was on display for the world to see. He had made an honest mistake in trying to right a wrong. Generations of people would be physically at risk – in fact, addicted, because of Tanner's scientific arrogance but, at the moment, it did not matter.

He had cried.

He had played them like a fiddle. There would be no hard questions.

It was another small detail.

CHAPTER SEVEN
Common real estate

The crane lifted the Star of David, the 15-foot crown of the Jewish faith, 180 feet above the ground to a position directly in front of three Jewish construction workers. Security was tight. From 28 strategic positions around the reconstructed temple of Jerusalem marksmen scanned the roof tops for potential assassins.

They would be at least one marksman short.

From a position inside a shaft, inside a catacomb, underneath the Al Aqsa mosque, a 29-year-old Palestinian, trained in Saudi Arabia for just such a mission, poised his grenade launcher. He had a perfect line of sight. While the Israelis were training their attention above ground the fatal blow came from below. The grenade launched with a muffled "PHOOT." Immediately the Star of David and the three construction workers were blown off their scaffolding in small and large pieces. The bloody, dangling torso of one of the workers hung from his safety harness. The other two workers were simply gone.

The Palestinian didn't wait to be captured. He admired his handiwork from below for a moment before shouting "Allahu Akbar!"

A second explosion from beneath the Al Aqsa Mosque signaled his orchestrated end.

The world was stunned. But only for a moment. A new Star of David and three new construction workers would finish the job three days later. The official dedication ceremony was still months away, but the negotiated completion site for the third incarnation of the temple of Israel was now a reality. It had been built on steel struts on the site of the temple mount directly above the Al Aqsa Mosque. So now the Jews and the Muslims held a holy shrine on the same real estate. It was supposed to be a compromise.

It was trouble brewing.

CHAPTER EIGHT
Testosterone

The story of Brad Pugh's flight into the sea was a secret seldom talked about inside the Kim Administration. Only after the Administration's failed attempt to snare Pugh in their flimsy federal net could the full story be pieced together.

The truth no one dared speak inside the newly constructed White House was that Brad Pugh had outsmarted Billy Kim.

Brad Pugh and his wife, Winnie, had secured the services of their secret sub where anyone in the Internet age would look for a submersible studio – on E-Bay.

"Honey," his wife had said matter-of-factly while she scanned the web. "Look at this: You can rent a Russian nuclear sub for 1.8 million dollars a month. Isn't that a hoot?" she laughed.

Brad Pugh smiled at his wife, appeasing her sense of humor. What she couldn't see was that her husband had filed the information away. The next day he found the site and called the Russian commander.

"Captain, I can't tell you who I am just yet but I need to know something. If I would finance the project, could you make your submarine broadcast ready?"

The captain paused. "Mr. Brad Pugh, the K-815 can be made to suit your radio show needs."

So much for anonymity.

"You know me?"

"You anticipate trouble, no?"

"Maybe. Enough to be concerned, anyway."

"Your President Kim, he maybe find reason to make you political prisoner, I have been thinking for long time now. I am former Soviet party member.

They think you have big mouth only because you do. I think you are patriot, but I am much like you. My country and I are strangers. They were going to scrap this boat. I bought it from them as a business opportunity but also because I knew it would allow me to get away from Soviet Union. Mr. Pugh, I would be most happy to help you but we need to be very secret about it, yes?"

What Brad Pugh couldn't have known was that Captain Petrov was an avid listener. Petrov was a student of American history, an American wannabe who listened to Pugh faithfully over the net because Brad Pugh, more than any professor, politician or officer he had ever learned from, cut through the crap. Petrov was an ex-communist. He knew crap. He also appreciated what the present assault on American democracy meant for the fragile future of freedom itself.

"Sometimes, Mr. Brad Pugh, I think I am watching death of America. It would be tragic death, yes, because then it becomes jungle rules, yes?"

"I can see, Captain, that you understand our demons. The question is, can you keep me and my wife from being killed?"

"In a submarine, Mr. Brad, life and death are what everyone have in common. If you die, I die. If I live, you live. I assure you, Mr. Brad, I have no desire to, how you say – cash some chips in?"

Until the day they were whisked away by helicopter and spirited offshore to the K-815, Winnie Pugh never knew her casual E-Bay observation would one day result in an almost three-year exile for she and husband.

In Kim's second term the president played the sedition card. Kim roused his complicit congress out of bed at midnight, secretly passed an emergency piece of legislation and proclaimed Pugh was guilty of new kind of ambiguous sedition. Kim's NSA storm troopers raided Pugh's broadcast studio before the ink was dry on the legislation.

Brad Pugh was one step ahead of them. A Navy admiral had tipped Pugh off a week in advance that something was going down. The admiral text-mailed Pugh that the NSA had been placed on full alert for some sort of operation in Atlanta, where Brad's flagship station carried his show. He told Winnie to have her bags packed.

"Where we going, hon?"

"Well, there's something I have to tell you," admitted Brad. "I'm feeling that the heat may be on. We may need to get out of the country."

"Heat? What do you mean?" she asked in all sincerity.

Brad knew the moment had finally come for him to have a long-avoided chat with his wife.

Brad had always kept Winnie out of the loop on just how much of a target he was. Winnie was salt of the earth and had no concept of many things, certainly not political reprisals. She knew her husband was a high-profile personality and she knew he was a lightning rod of controversy but she avoided the details. She shopped. She had a daily laundry list of things to buy. She and Brad lived in a huge, secure, sprawling ranch house located in Marietta, Georgia, and were always entertaining. Politics, as a rule, bored her silly. She shopped, entertained, did crossword puzzles and watched chick flicks, cop shows and design shows with a gaggle of lady friends. Part of the reason Brad loved her so dearly was that she was totally removed from the ocean he swam in. But, the time had come for him to ask her to join him in his sea – literally and figuratively. Had he told her in advance what he feared could happen, he would only have caused her to worry and fret needlessly and she did enough of that without the added weight of a federal warrant. The concept of tyranny was a foreign concept to her. Winnie couldn't conceive of tyranny. She wasn't sure how to spell it, much less what it meant. Telling her she was about to become a victim of tyranny would have confused her. She had no frame of reference.

"Winnie, I need you to focus for a moment," he asked of his wife. She balked. He didn't talk to her like that! She was the ultimate multi-tasker and he knew it. She could coordinate a steak and lobster dinner for a room full of affiliate station managers, re-stock the appetizer tray and marshal an army of domestics without breaking a nail. Why would he suggest she couldn't focus?

"I'm listening, dear," she said as she loaded the Lazy Susan.

"No," Pugh interjected. "You have to look me in the eye. What I have to say is bigger than you think."

"How do you know what I'm thinking? Your golf team will be here on Saturday, Brad. I'm listening. I'm going to leave their wives out on the deck. They can fend for themselves. The boys are fine. I like your friends, but their wives are catty. They're really a pissy lot of girls you know. They drive me nuts…"

"Stop!" commanded Brad. He grabbed Winnie by the shoulders and sat her on a chair. He pulled a chair up across from her and moved close.

"We've been married 31 years, hon, and I've never asked you to sacrifice on my behalf but I am going to lay a situation out on the table for you right now that may result in us being separated."

He had her attention.

"What is it, Brad?"

"Kim may be coming after me?"

"President Kim? Why? What did you do to him?"

"I said some things about him."

"Were they true?"

"For the most part, yes."

"Well, then what you have is just a difference of opinion. Why can't you just work it out with him? You're both grown men. Invite him for lunch. I'll fix something nice."

"It's a little deeper than that, dear. He may want me dead."

"For God's sake, Brad, what did you say about him?"

"Have you ever listened to my show, dear? Ever?"

"Not in the last decade. I just find all that stuff you talk about so, I don't know, contentious."

"You're right, Winnie. Politics is contentious. Freedom brings out passion in some people. Let me ask you a question: Do you know how much money I made last year?"

"A lot."

"Thirty five million, sweetheart. In April I wrote a check to the IRS for 20.2 million. We kept about 14 million."

"Isn't that enough?"

"Yes, it's plenty. You're not seeing the point. They want more. A lot more."

"Well, what are you going to do?"

"Their plan isn't to tax, dear. That's just how they execute the deal. Their plan is bigger than just me. They want to take the money from anyone they label 'rich' and give it to anyone they label needy, which would be anyone who would vote for them if they would agree to let them confiscate other people's money."

She looked at him blankly. He realized at that moment that he was trying to explain fiscal policy to a woman who had none.

"So, why would he want to kill you, Brad?"

"I'm not certain that he does want me dead. But, he might!"

"Well, then, do we really have a problem, Brad? Could it be that this isn't just a big misunderstanding?"

Brad reloaded. His wife was a vessel of warmth, humanity, grace and charity but she was not a model of logic. She was, in Brad's estimation, everything he wasn't. Part of the reason he never spent a lot of time describing his wife to his audience was because it would take more than three hours a day. Winnie Pugh was an enigma wrapped in a paradox. In her innocence she made her husband laugh – sometimes out loud and sometimes privately. Today wasn't one of her funny days. Brad tried a different tack.

"Honey, I need you to pack some bags."

"Where are we going?"

"Well, that's what I need to talk to you about."

"How long?"

"It could be quite a while. If, that is, you decide to go with me."

"You're not planning on camping again, are you? You know how I hate all that outdoor stuff. I hope we're not going camping."

"Honey, I'm not going to ask you to understand all the forces at work here but people may be coming to kill me or throw me in prison. Do you understand that?"

"I don't."

"I'm not kidding. I wouldn't kid about something like this, dear. Now, I'm going to ask you a very difficult question. If you don't want to answer it now, that's fine - but I may be chased out of the country. I'll be in exile. I'll be a man without a country. I might be living on a submarine. For a very long time."

The question suddenly came into focus for Winnie and she began to cry.

"Oh, God, no. You're really leaving me?"

"If you want me to, yes."

"What do you mean?"

"I mean they'll be coming after me, not you. I might be forced into exile but that doesn't mean you have to disappear."

"You want me to stay here? Without you?"

"It's your choice, dear. I don't expect you to give up your life because of my big mouth."

She rose from her chair and walked to the window. Brad Pugh told himself that he would live with her decision and not second-guess. Asking someone to go into exile, even one's wife, was not a situation to be won through superior salesmanship. She needed to reach her own conclusion.

"Let me ask you something," she said, wiping her eyes. " If you leave, what will they do to me?"

Bingo. She asked the question he was hoping she would.

"What do you think?"

"Well, they could just let me go, but that's not real likely – particularly if they want you dead. For certain they'll seize our assets. I'll lose the house... and my husband."

"But you won't be hunted."

"No, honey, you're right. I could get a job, I suppose but – good God, I don't know how to do real work! And, who would I sleep with? Who would listen to me? My God, Brad, this is horrible." She began to cry but stopped herself.

"This sub," she asked. Does it have a crew?"

"Of course. Fourteen in all. Sixteen with you and I."

"Could I cook?

"I'm sure we could work something out," he said, but was more taken by something his wife had said. "What did you mean when you said 'who will I sleep with?'"

"I said that, didn't I? I guess I was just confused. I spoke before I thought. I do that, you know."

Brad was prepared to extract as much mileage out of it as a husband could. "I'm a little concerned," he said. "Could I trust you in a ship with 14 strange men? I thought I knew you, but maybe I don't."

When the time came she was ready. Brad had just signed off his show. She could see by the caller ID, the call was coming from Brad's disposable cell phone – the one he kept, just in case. He said "Operation Alligator. You know where to meet." And he hung up. It was supposed to be that easy. She was supposed to get in the Hummer – the one she and Brad had judiciously packed, and meet him at a helipad in 30 minutes.

But, there was a problem. In front of their sprawling ranch sat a forgettable looking, squeaky-clean, newer model blue sedan with generic blackwall tires and nondescript markings. Everything about the car reeked of government. It had been parked there all day. The detective in Winnie – the detective that had evolved from two decades of CSI re-runs, told her that the heat was on.

Through her binoculars she had stolen glances at them; one black man and one white man in gray suits. They, too, smelled of government issue. They didn't try to hide or disguise their presence. Several times they got out of the car and lit up cigarettes, something federal employees had been required to do since 2017 when Congress had made the use of tobacco on, or in, government property a federal crime.

Her conclusion was paralyzing: She was on her own. She had to meet Brad in 30 minutes, alone, if they were going to pull off their escape. She tried to think the problem through. The plan she came up with, she realized, would require a certain level of testosterone. It was a fuzzy plan, but it was the only one she could create, given her circumstances. She would have to live or, possibly, die with it.

Winnie calmly locked the house and walked into the garage. She fired up the Hummer, pulled out, closed the garage door and cruised out onto their palm-lined drive and headed east. The sedan followed 50 feet behind her. Her mind raced. She was no race car driver. In truth, she drove like a 60-year-old lady – which, in truth, she was. One thing she knew for sure was she didn't have the mental or physical tools to try to outrun them. Every cop she had ever watched on CSI was trained in the art of high-speed chases, and she reasoned that these cops probably went through the same sort of training as TV cops.

She stopped at a convenience store. The sedan pulled into a parking spot at the adjoining dry cleaners. She went inside and considered, momentarily, calling her husband. She couldn't do it. Calling him for help might jeopardize the mission. He would be required to come and get her and that would throw the whole timing of their escape out the window. She had to act.

She walked out of the store and fired up the Hummer. She backed out. The sedan mirrored her movement. She shifted the behemoth Hummer into drive and pulled forward for 20 feet and stopped. She backed up, cutting the wheel all the way left and found herself at a 45-degree angle to the sedan. Before they knew what hit them she put the pedal to the floor and creamed their left front quarter panel, using the Hummer's massive bulk and horsepower to push the sedan backward into the dry cleaner storefront, collapsing the sidewalk awning onto the car and punching out the glass of the store. The sedan pulled forward and into the lane, attempting to counter-punch their matronly assailant. Their move forward gave Winnie a clear line on their front end. She backed up in a smoky screech of rubber. She had to make certain the deed was complete. "You never wound the king," Brad had said time and again.

The last thing she saw before ramming the sedan were the two agents bailing, rolling out of harm's way. The Hummer performed its duty admirably. The front left tire actually went up onto the hood of the sedan and bent the axle of the car so the tires were pointing outward like a rookie skier.

Coursing with adrenaline and bravado she peeled out onto the service road and gunned the Hummer out onto the highway ramp. She was up to 85 miles an hour before she realized that she couldn't risk being stopped by some enterprising State Patrol car. She slowed down and tried to breathe normally.

When she was comfortably assured she was neither being followed, nor breaking any traffic laws she blew the ballast out of her lungs.

"YAAAHOO!" she screamed.

She finally understood testosterone.

CHAPTER NINE
EYE-pod-OH-zis

While Lars Larsen concerned himself with the lines of his cut lawn and Ethel disparaged the presence of aphids in her roses, Ben went behind closed doors with his board of directors inside the residence reporters had labeled with a conscious intent 'The Kowalski Compound.' It was implied from the word 'compound' that Kowalski and his Christian causes were conducted from a cloistered, military outpost. The inferences of a Christian operation being run from a military compound were never tempered by the very real consideration that Ben Kowalski was a rich man and a former president and had larger-than-life security concerns requiring him to live life inside a security fence.

From the outside, it did look like a compound. Even Ben conceded it was a fortress. It was a huge brick edifice with wrought iron security fences all around and ubiquitous cameras on poles recording every activity. Inside the mansion there were rows of computers, conference rooms and offices. The main floor consisted of 2200 square feet where 12 telemarketers plied their trade, calling churches to publicize what had come to be called the Holy Harvest. Kowalski didn't invent the Holy Harvest, but he had agreed to lend his considerable resources to promoting it. He had name recognition. He had visibility. He had a history. He had money. He was always in demand because of everything he had, but particularly because he had money. As a man with a large cache of disposable income he had eventually found it necessary to hire himself a flak catcher whose main function was to draft rejection letters to individuals looking for financial considerations. He couldn't do it himself.

With the distant drone of Larsen's John Deere in the background, Dr. Arne Karlstrom, from the Karolinska Institute in Stockholm, held Kowalski's attention. The meeting had been arranged by Ben's chief of staff, Leon Amanti. While Ben may have earned a bank full of money, he was not an organization man. Leon kept the ship on course. Ben was the heart and wallet of the empire. Leon was the brains.

On the LCD projection screen, Karlstrom was illustrating to Kowalski and his board of directors how history had misinterpreted Scripture. Karlstrom's hypothesis was a compelling one. Ben had been given a written brief to read, but never did. He was then given a five-minute verbal briefing by Leon before the meeting began. Leon knew Ben wouldn't find the time to read the brief. What Karlstrom was putting forth as a thesis, Ben surmised, could be a tool to win the skeptic. Ben had almost given up on the skeptics. He had no clue how to move them off their fences. They were frozen by their own pride. To reach through the shroud of the popular culture into the heart of the skeptic was a Rubic's Cube Ben had tried to unlock for almost two decades. The Swedish doctor, Leon had argued, might hold a key to that lock.

Karlstrom was a slight man in a black turtleneck. He had a 50-year-old face and the beard of a teenager. He spoke excellent English but there was a word that threw the American ear: Hypothesis. When he said it, it sounded like a train wreck. EYE-pod-OH-zis. It took several train wrecks before the Americans recognized it as an actual word.

"The Bible wasn't wrong," said Karlstrom. "Geographers were. Back in the year 1450 BC, or thereabouts, the tribe of Hebrews left Egypt after being granted a reluctant permission by Pharaoh. They were headed for Mount Sinai, the Mountain of God," said Karlstrom, using his laser pointer as a visual guide to 'swoosh' his way across the LCD-projected image of the Middle East.

He paused to take a sip of water. Leon Amanti winked at Kowalski, as if to signify his endorsement of Karlstrom. Leon had liked Karlstrom from their first phone conversation. The Swede, Amanti quickly determined, was not pretentious. He was a serious man with a funny undercurrent. Amanti wanted to reassure Ben with his eyes that the Swede demanded attention. Ben shrugged. Yes, Ben was intrigued, but not sufficiently intrigued to open his checkbook just yet.

"The Hebrews," Karlstrom continued, "were being led to Mount Sinai on God's instructions by Moses, a former high official in the Egyptian royal family. Moses, the Bible claimed, demonstrated many powers that convinced the Hebrews he was a man they ought to give consideration. Once in the wilderness on their three-day sojourn to pray in the desert, they cut and ran. One-point-five to two million Hebrew slaves were busting out. Once separated from Pharaoh, they were pursued by the Egyptian army and fled across the Red Sea.

Yam Suph is what the Hebrews called the Red Sea. The waters of Yam Suph, the Hebrew texts said, had been parted by God when Moses raised his staff. The anxious and tired Hebrews walked across Yam Suph to the other side, to the land of Midian."

Karlstrom looked at the board and asked: "Is everyone with me?"

"We're familiar with the story, Dr. Karlstrom. I assume you're giving us your context," replied one of the board members.

"Precisely. Some of the story gets incredible and the secular reader gets very annoyed and lost by some of the descriptions in the text because they demand an acceptance of divine intervention."

"The story reads like a fairy tale, doctor," said Ben.

"Yes. We all know that. But, Moses, wasn't using hyperbole. I hope to demonstrate," he said as he switched the LCD projector to a series of artists renditions of the Exodus story.

"The Egyptian army, kept in a cloud by God until the right time, followed the Hebrews through the split in Yam Suph to their doom. Safely standing on the shores of Midian with the Hebrews ashore, Moses raised his staff again and the sea crashed down on the Egyptian army. All 250,000 of Pharaoh's army, including Pharaoh, perished in the crash of a wave. One moment there was chaos, the next moment there was silence. The screams and death throes of Pharaoh's army were silenced by billions of tons of Yam Suph. God's Word had been delivered. The Jews had been delivered. They were God's chosen people. They had been led by Moses, the servant of God, to the land of Midian and the Mountain of God across Yam Suph."

Karlstrom seated himself, making eye contact with the board. "The story has survived 3450 or so years." Karlstrom took a deep breath and another sip of water. He turned to the board members and changed his tone, as if confiding in them.

"There you have the nub of biblical history condensed into about a two-minute summation and I dare say I was brilliant, don't you think?" The room laughed.

Karlstrom continued with a new sobriety at just the right interval.

"I gave this same presentation to a group of archeologists at the Chicago Museum last week." He paused. "They laughed at my presentation. It seems that in the academic world our Bible is a source of great humor."

To believe the story, everyone at the table knew, required a tremendous amount of faith. The story couldn't be proven.

Karlstrom was there to suggest it could be.

"The problem," Karlstrom continued, "isn't with history or the Bible or whether or not the story is true. I am convinced that it is true." He stopped and looked at the ceiling, almost as if he were waiting for a response.

"When I announced my conviction of this truth last week, this is the point of the presentation where the archeologists laughed." He smiled and sighed. He almost seemed regretful. "I should have known better than to introduce a matter of faith to a room full of scientists."

"We're not scientists," injected Leon Amanti. "Don't address us like we are."

Karlstrom seemed to ignore Amanti's remark. He didn't look at Amanti directly. He didn't want a cheerleader. He wanted the evidence, not someone else's interpretation, to make the case. He readjusted his focus to the projection screen.

"The problem is with the maps. Yam Suph, the Hebrew name for the body of water the Hebrews crossed, has no Greek translation. In history it had been translated as 'Red Sea,' even though there is no way to track the origin of the words. But, let's put language aside for a moment. If we read Moses' account literally, we can see the route precisely if we can read Moses' map. The issue, up until this particular moment in technological evolution, is there has been no way to interpret the landmarks he was referring to."

Karlstrom clicked the projector to show a satellite photo of Egypt, the Red Sea, the Sinai Peninsula, the Gulfs of Suez and Aqaba, Saudi Arabia and Israel.

"The Red Sea is here," he said, pointing with his laser pointer to a large area south of the Sinai Peninsula. "The Red Sea is also here," he said, pointing to the Gulf of Suez. "And, also here," he said, circling the Gulf of Aqaba.

"Now, let us look at a map of the Red Sea, circa 150 A.D." The map showed a grainy drawing of the Red Sea which included a small dimple of water where the Gulf of Suez exists today and nothing where the Gulf of Aqaba today exists. "The Red Sea is considered to exist on only the west side of the Sinai Peninsula."

He racked the projector to the next picture. "Let us fast-forward to 1910 AD. This is what the maps tell us about the world as it was known just 100 years ago." The Gulf of Suez was more prominent in the 'modern' map but it was by no means to scale. The Gulf of Aqaba resided on the map as being little more than a small bay in the Red Sea - instead of a separate 160-mile long sliver of ocean. "When the Red Sea was interpreted to be the site of the crossing, their sense of geography left something to be desired. Moses had crossed a body of water he, and subsequent Greek-speaking interpreters, called the Red Sea. No one could have located it on a map, though. There were no accurate maps. Literally, they were guessing."

Amanti had read Karlstrom's briefing and was up to speed on the hypothesis. He felt compelled to interject. "So, Dr. Karlstrom, what you're saying is that Moses recorded the route - it's just that his landmarks have been hidden by our own ignorance of the true shape of the region?"

"Precisely. The Gulf of Aqaba has been hidden from maps up until the latter part of the 20th century. Before then, in a very real sense, it literally didn't exist."

Karlstrom paused. He put his hands on his hips and took a deep breath. "The facts are these: Until the last 40 or 50 years it has been impossible to interpret Moses' road map of the wilderness. Until the last 40 or 50 years man has not had the ability to connect the dots."

He racked the projector back to the modern satellite picture of the Middle East. He pointed his laser at a white point of land about 60 miles down from the upper crest of the Gulf of Aqaba.

"This is a beach head on the western shore of the Gulf of Aqaba, in Egypt. It's about 25 square kilometers of hard sand, the result of ancient run-off from the surrounding mountains of the Sinai Peninsula. Today it's called Nuweiba. This is where we hypothesize that the Israelites made the crossing. If we follow the ancient trade route across Sinai it would lead us to a site at the northern tip of Aqaba called Ezion-Geber. Today it is known as Eilat. However, in Exodus, we are told that Moses receives specific instructions to 'turn back' away from the trade route and into 'the mouth of the gorge.' When they 'turn back' the Bible tells us they are boxed in by mountains and the sea on both sides and eventually deposited, and encamp, at Yam Suph, at Pi Hariroth. The route that satisfies these descriptions goes along what is known today as the Wadi Watir. Modern satellite imagery can give us a 3D picture of the topography of the region. If Moses was giving us an accurate description of the journey, we can conclude there is only one place in the region that satisfies all of these conditions."

The LCD presentation had taken an aerial view of Sinai, zooming into the winding, tortuous path of the Wadi Watir, through the mountains and onto the beach head at Nuweiba.

The room was quiet. After several moments many in the room repositioned themselves in their chairs. It was an interesting EYE-pod-OH-zis, but amounted to nothing more than academic conjecture. No one wanted to be the first to speak.

"I'll bite. Prove it," said Kowalski.

Karlstrom smiled. "Oh, it's provable. The problem with the story as it is known today is men have relied on men to point the way. Old maps, old legends, myths and a lot of oral tradition have been our only guide - up until now. The old assumptions were predicated on maps and interpretations men had made and, we know now, were made with a lot of bad guesses. Today we can see the true shape of the region. If we follow the road map that Moses gave us in Scripture, it will lead us right to Nuweiba, across Yam Suph and to the land of Midian, to the real Mountain of God. In Scripture, Midian was clearly identified as the home of Moses and his father-in-law, Jethro. Maps as recent as the 20th century still identify Midian as being on the eastern side of the Gulf of Aqaba. Yet, the traditional Mount Sinai is located, where, here," he said, circling a spot in the middle of the Sinai Peninsula, clearly on the western side of the Gulf of Aqaba.

"The traditional site of Mount Sinai was established by Constantine's mother, Helena, about 1700 years after the Exodus. She wasn't exactly a scientist. She was, by any historical analysis, bowing to an oral tradition of the day. Understand: In the book of Exodus, Moses told us where he had been, which direction they headed, how he got there, his time frame and some of the interesting geography on the way. The names he had for the ancient landmarks don't coincide with a lot of what we can identify today, but some of them do. With modern science we can piece the puzzle together. The mystery isn't whether the Red Sea crossing occurred. Approximately 3500 years ago Moses recorded the route in the best terms he could muster at the time, but he was trying to describe an uncharted wilderness. It would be no different than if we were dropped on the moon and asked to draw a map of it from simple visual observation. Only now, in the 21st century, do we have the means to know where to look for the evidence. Right here. At Nuweiba," he said, circling the beach head with his laser pointer.

He racked up a picture from the underwater. It looked like a wheel.

"An American diver took this picture. He was working under contract in the oil fields of Saudi Arabia and rented a boat to go fishing. That's what he told the Saudis, anyway. He had a magnatometer with him and recorded that the sea bed is loaded with debris that has elements of metal in it and, although coralized, I don't think it requires a great amount of imagination to see the potential for this piece of coral having a wheel as its origin. Could it be a wheel from Pharaoh's army? The diver said it looks like a battlefield down there.

That was his word."

"Why didn't he bring any of it back?" asked one of the board members.

Karlstrom paused and took a cleansing breath. The board was now definitely on Karlstrom's turf. The doctor was getting comfortable, gaining some assurance that these men were neither skeptics, nor worse, hardened scientists.

"Both the Saudi and Egyptian governments own whatever is at the bottom of the sea. If they catch anyone trying to retrieve artifacts they will jail them. If they retrieve anything that might point toward a Hebrew miracle they might kill them. Either way, they would certainly lose the evidence."

Karlstrom turned his attention back to the map. "The Gulf of Aqaba is about 12 miles wide. Not a drop of the gulf is in international waters. Whatever rests below the surface belongs, legally, to either the Egyptians or the Saudis. They show every indication of keeping the bottom of the gulf unexplored."

Kowalski moved uneasily in his chair. The board was looking at him to ask the obvious. It was Kowalski's money - it ought to be Kowalski's question.

"If you can 'prove' this, do you know what it means?"

"Yes. And I think you know too. If Pharaoh's army rests outside of Nuweiba and if we can document it, it means we will have forensically exposed the fingerprint of God."

There was a long pause. Everyone at the table exchanged glances. It had larger implications than any of them could digest at the moment – each of them feeling a sense of smallness when compared to the historical largeness being heaped onto their plates.

"And, not everyone will be pleased," added Karlstrom. "In particular, there is a lethal strain of Islam, the jihadists, who will see this as an attack on their faith. Most Muslim scholars will acknowledge the history of the Exodus as being directly linked to their own faith but the extremists will vehemently object to any evidence which points to the conclusion that the Hebrews were God's chosen people. To the Muslim extremist, this is the kind of news which simply cannot be allowed any oxygen." He paused to let the concept sink in. He seemed almost uncomfortable with the realization that research, data, evidence – truth - could conceivably have a political enemy.

"Oh, and one other thing," the Swede said, racking the projector to a satellite photo of the mountain range on the Saudi side of the Gulf of Aqaba. He pointed his laser pointer at a mountain, one in a range of four, about 20 miles inland from the Gulf. "This is Mount Sinai, the Mountain of God, Mount Horeb - call it what you want. You can argue about my conclusion after I'm done, but I am convinced. I have studied high-resolution satellite pictures of every inch of this range for years. This mountain, Jabel El Lawz, meets 26 specific physical biblical requirements. They are chronicled in your report."

Ben looked at Leon Amanti. Leon nodded, which meant it was in the documentation. Ben concluded at that moment he should have taken the time to actually read the report.

Arne Karlstrom began to seat himself but before he did he stood. "Yes," he said with an additional burst of excitement. "My geographer faxed me a piece of information this morning. He happened to be charting Jabel El Lawz on his drawing table and ran a T-square up against a satellite photo. The peak of Jabel El Lawz is exactly, precisely, in the same global longitude as the historic temple of Jerusalem. The line runs right from the peak of Jabel El Lawz right to the center of the temple mount. Is it possible that God is, in a sort of ironic, or even comic way, pointing us to His holy mountain?"

Ben stood. It was a lot to consider.

"What happens if the world learns this is truly the Mountain of God - Mount Sinai? What's your best guess as to how Israel will react?"

Dr. Karlstrom hadn't thought about it. It was a political question. Geopolitics were foreign to him. He could only speculate.

"I suppose, if it became widely accepted as the true Mount Sinai you would see Israel marching out into the desert to worship there."

"But, it's in Saudi Arabia..."

"It is now. History, however, rewrites boundaries everyday. Wars redefine boundaries all the time. If anyone of you can look at the Middle East today and say there won't be war, I'll eat my doctoral thesis."

Kowalski stroked his chin. Karlstrom wanted over $130,000 to conduct his secret expedition to the Gulf of Aqaba. Ben looked at the board of directors and he looked at Arne Karlstrom. Then, he put his hand over his mouth and it almost appeared that he was emotionally dumbstruck. Without making eye contact with anyone he quietly asked for a moment alone with Dr. Karlstrom.

It was an odd request, but none of the men said anything. What it came down to, in truth, was a matter between Ben and Arne anyway. It was Ben's money. None of the eight other men in the room were too surprised.

When everyone had exited the room, Ben pulled a chair up close to Dr. Karlstrom and looked him in the eye. There were tears in Ben's eyes.

Ben began almost in a whisper, as if confiding in the Swede. "You don't know this about me, my friend, but I have this sense. Sometimes I get feelings. Sometimes I see things before they happen. As a man of science, I'm sure you wouldn't understand…"

Arne felt compelled to tell him that he did understand. "Precognition? Prescience? It's not something science can quantify, but it doesn't mean it doesn't exist."

"You could say the same about faith."

Arne paused. They were sparring. He didn't want to talk about faith. He wanted to talk about science. He wanted to cut to the chase. "What do you think?"

Ben rose from his chair and motioned Arne to the window overlooking the Larsen property. His neighbor Lars was outside methodically mowing his prize-winning lawn. "See that man on the tractor?" Ben asked.

Arne was a little put off. He wasn't sure where Ben Kowalski was leading him, but Ben had the checkbook. He was willing to play along.

"What about him?"

"What you are looking at is a duplicate of about four billion other people on this planet. He's a cynical, self-centered, self-anointed unbeliever. He and his wife not only doubt the word of God, they mock it."

Ben paused to watch Lars for a moment before continuing. "You need to understand the big picture. Those two unbelievers have tremendous implications," Ben said, pointing his finger repeatedly in the direction of the Larsen's. "I've been an evangelist of sorts over the years, preaching God's message as it related to modern, secular business - positioning God's word against the template of modern problems…." He was done with his preface. It was a disclaimer of sorts, but it was necessary for what was to follow.

"One-on-one evangelizing isn't my gift. I just don't know how to make the Lord's word sing," he confessed. "But, if I could make that miserable excuse for a man - or his wife - move out of their comfort zone long enough to consider that maybe, just possibly, they are not the center of the universe and that God has a master plan for them - my life would be complete." Ben exhaled, but he wasn't done. He was in mid-tirade.

"Unfortunately, there is no combination of words in the English language to move them away from their cynical secular view. I know. I've tried. I used to treat them as a game. Now it's gotten personal. I'm walking a tightrope with them. On the one hand, I would love to reach them with The Word. On the other hand, I would like to stake them to the ground, cover them with honey and laugh hysterically while the ants ate their flesh." Ben looked at Arne to amplify his point. Arne wasn't sure if he was dead serious or being dramatic.

Ben continued: "That guy on the lawnmower and his wife are the embodiment of our mission. Do you see that? Do you?"

Arne was lost.

"I'm trying to find artifacts on the bottom of the ocean. Remember?" Arne was trying to circle the wagons back to the issue at hand.

"I'm getting there," Ben said. He was on a roll. He leaned up against the window and zeroed his focus in on Lars Larsen. For a moment there was an almost manic edge to his voice. "Somewhere along the line someone planted a seed in them. I know it! There is a light of faith in there somewhere. They won't believe me or you or anyone. They tap dance with the truth. The question is: Can they dance for a lifetime?"

Arne wasn't sure if Ben Kowalski was sane. He was beginning to wonder if time hadn't turned Ben into a religious fanatic - a walking, talking monument to something Arne didn't stand for at all. Still, Ben had the money. Arne decided the best thing to do was to sit down and listen.

If being crazy was a strategy to keep Arne quiet, it was working.

Ben turned away from the window and sat across from Arne. He re-focused. The Larsens were forgotten for a moment. "You realize what you plan on doing could be dangerous, don't you?" Ben said.

"Stepping off the curb can be dangerous. But, it's how you get across the road."

"Touche'," Ben said. "Let me ask you a larger question: Assume what you're looking for is there - physical evidence of the Red Sea crossing. It's been there for 3500 years. Why hasn't it been discovered up to this point?"

Arne had the answer quickly. He didn't have to think about it. "Two reasons. First, until the advent of digital satellite imaging, the road map Moses gave us in The Exodus relied on a formless wilderness. No one knew where to look. Secondly, anyone who asked to explore there would be refused by the Egyptian and the Saudi governments. I know. I tried."

"They know there's evidence there?"

"Yes."

"You say that confidently."

"Physical evidence of the Red Sea crossing would be a frontal assault on Islam. They have a reason to keep the truth hidden and that is precisely what they're doing."

"What I'm trying to say is that if your true mission is uncovered, your theory stays a theory. They'll kill you and your people without blinking an eye."

"Is that what you see in your premonition, Ben?"

The question caught Ben by surprise. It wasn't what he saw in his premonition but the question was certainly valid.

"No, no. What I'm seeing is beyond that. I'm seeing you succeeding in your mission. It's what we do with the evidence that scares the beejeebers out of me."

Arne's heart lifted. He knew at that moment he had the money. He had made the sale. He could quit selling. He sighed.

"You're not a linear thinker, are you, Ben?"

Ben laughed. "No. No, I'm not."

"When you asked me what would happen if Israel learns that this is the true Mountain of God? - there's prophecy surrounding that. The Old Testament prophets spoke of a future time when the Hebrews will be called back to Mount Sinai to re-establish their marriage covenant with Yahweh. You have to do a lot of cross-referencing. Probably the most compelling is the story of Hosea, the prophet. He has a prophetic vision where he is told to marry a harlot. The harlot is, metaphorically, Israel. Then, in Hosea we have an almost romantic recapturing of the "harlot" heart in the wilderness by the Father. The Father says he will allure her and she will sing there as she did in her youth. Ben, where else could that marriage covenant take place except at the Mountain of God?"

Arne stopped. He didn't want to sound like he was preaching. He wanted Ben to draw his own conclusions.

"That's how I interpret the Scripture," said Arne. "There's a whole lot more, if you want. But, you're the one with the precognition. You tell me how it happens."

Ben laughed. "You know, my friend, I did have a vision." He was about to tell the first person ever about one of his private visions. He paused, almost as if he were embarrassed to share his dream, but decided there had never been a better time to share what he had seen in his mind's eye.

"I had a very vivid dream. I saw millions marching out of Israel into the wilderness. It stuck with me for a long time. Up until this moment, I had no context for it - I didn't know what it meant."

Dr. Karlstrom sighed. There was no way to know what Ben's words meant. "If that's true, Ben, then we're onto something."

"If it's true, it means Israel will one day judge your evidence and reach your conclusion. The Jews are a small slice of humanity..."

"But, Ben, it's foretold that they will return to the mountain. They have to see the evidence. If my hypothesis is correct we will deliver that evidence."

Ben rose and walked to the window, trying to digest the words. His eyes couldn't help but catch the sight of his neighbor, Lars, on his rider mower.

"My victory comes when they get it," he said, pointing out the window to the Larsen home. "Lars and Ethel Larsen will believe the physical evidence. The day I can make them ask the questions they need to ask, I'll know two things. First, that my job is done and second, that my larger premonition is true."

"Which is?"

"You tell me, doctor. Why do you think God would allow us to peer into history like this? Finding physical evidence of The Exodus will draw all of us into two camps - humanity will have to make a choice. If divine intervention can be proven the real question isn't 'what does it mean' - for the believer that will be self-evident, but rather, the larger question becomes is 'why now?'"

The white peninsula is called Nuweiba. It is located on the eastern side of the Sinai Peninsula, which is in Egypt. Across the Gulf of Aqaba is modern Saudi Arabia (ancient Midian). Nuweiba is about 25 square kilometers of hard-packed sand. The white road leading into Nuweiba is called the Wadi Watir (a wadi is a dry riverbed). The mountains surrounding Nuweiba are of the 4000-5000-foot variety. A two-lane highway has been built in the wadi and one can easily surmise that if Pharaoh's army followed them down the wadi, the Hebrews would, indeed, be trapped between the mountains and the sea.

Photo courtesy NASA Landsat -7.

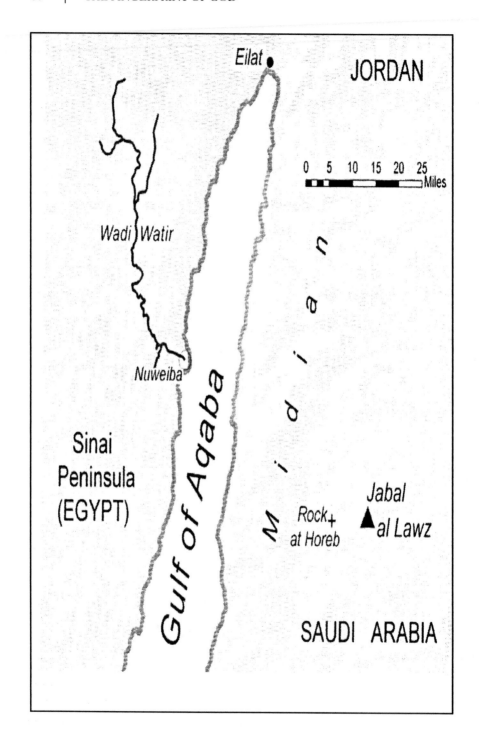

CHAPTER TEN
Dirt

Ellen Kowalski had been broke, then rich and then broke. Now she was rich again. She preferred being rich. As the estranged wife of the impeached former President of the United States, Ben Kowalski, she was leveraging who she once was for who she now was. She had written a book – a chronicle of the man she had wed. Not the man who had repented and spent two decades atoning for his wayward past, but the man who had spent his early adulthood as a drunk, a womanizer and a liar.

After all, she was trying to sell books.

As she had the final touch of make-up applied to her face in the Green Room of the Jennie Farmer Show, she stood and admired what she saw. She was satisfied except for the nagging realization that TV cameras tended to widen the body and add 10 pounds, it was said. She was at her ideal weight now after months of haranguing and denial at the hands of her publicist. Adding 10 pounds, illusory or real, put her back to where she was before the book. She hated the thought.

Three months prior she had been locked away in a motel room with a computer and her insufferable publicist, a very attractive, yet tough-as-nails brunette named Elsa. Elsa didn't like Ellen's writing style. It bordered, too often, on truth. And truth, while true, was rarely marketable. Elsa kept twisting Ellen's thoughts. Elsa wanted dirt. Ellen hated her almost more than poverty.

"Do you want to write a book or do you want to sell a book?" the publicist asked, emphasizing the word 'sell,' with a little more zeal each time.

In the end, Ellen consented to money. She had been given a handsome $750,000 advance for her memoirs as the estranged wife of the once most trusted man in America. Ellen had a lavish lifestyle and a 14-year-old son to support in an equally lavish townhome. The problem she faced, in the short

term, was that she couldn't spend a nickel of her advance until her pit-bull publicist was satisfied that they had a book. Being locked in a cage with Elsa had
been the necessary walk across the hot coals to get to the other side.

Ellen stepped into the staging area just off the set. From her position she
could see Jennie Farmer. She took one last look at herself in the mirror and
pronounced herself fit for service. She wet her lips.

The stage manager asked her if she needed anything. Ellen shook her
head. She was confident and relaxed. The Valium saw to that. She couldn't remember life before Valium. Without the benefit of her pharmaceutical friend,
she would never have had the nerve or the pomposity to do what she was now
about to do. She thought about Tonya Harding, the figure skater, and how she
had turned her promising career into a dumpster dive for cash. She wondered
if history would hang the same label on her.

"In the end, who cares?" she muttered. "I got out and I got rich."

"Pardon?" the stage manager asked. Ellen shrugged her off.

Onstage, Jennie Farmer read from her Prompter. "Our next guest was
married to the President of the United States, the once-proclaimed 'most trusted man in America.' However, in her blistering new book we discover that the
man behind the healing of a wounded America may have just been a wolf in
sheep's clothing. The book is entitled 'The False Prophet.' Behind the scenes
in the Kowalski household life may not have been any different than yours…or
mine. Well, not mine!"

Jennie, the comedienne, paused for the requisite laughter. "Please welcome the former First Lady, Ellen Kowalski."

CHAPTER ELEVEN
An adventurous bosom

Who was Claudia Colgate? The world wanted to know. Virtually every time Billy Kim appeared on camera she was over his shoulder or on his arm. She was his trademark babe. The world eventually came to know her cleavage well. It was arguably the most oft photographed flesh on the planet. Guitarists play their 'axe.' Claudia Colgate played her 'jugs.' And, she played them with clever invention, knowing that males everywhere were programmed, first, to ogle, then to breathe. In time, the world came to understand that her curves concealed a brain. In time, the world came to know that her classic Mercedes Benz body housed an equally impressive motor. She was the complete package. She had brains and a body. She also had a fitness pro and a wardrobe manager and a make-up man and a publicity team at her beck and call. She had quite a few things going for her, not the least of which was the fact she had shared Billy Kim's bed for 15 years.

Her brains and her beauty, however, meant little without a pulse. She had always considered that time could prove her an obsolete cog in Billy Kim's wheel. Her asset was also her biggest liability: She was one of the few people on the planet who knew the full measure of Billy Kim's bloody and ruthless trail.

In an underground bunker in a secret Chinese bunker she considered how to keep her brains and her beauty operating as a single, pulsing unit. Billy Kim was about to betray her. She knew it. She couldn't say for certain how she knew, but Billy's treachery was beginning to show signs of coming into season. It might have been the uncharacteristic way he had been treating her. He had opened doors, asked her what she wanted for dinner or how he had shooed away the security team in order to spend a little private time with her. That wasn't Billy. Billy Kim was, on his best day, inconsistent, inconsiderate and detached. Billy was her live-in lover, sure, but over time he had learned Claudia's allegiance could be taken for granted.

She had been having a recurring dream. In her dream her employer, lover and president, Billy Kim, was trying to kill her. She had dreamt that Billy's hands were around her throat, strangling her. She fought, but she could neither scream nor strike back. In a panic she woke - wondering where the thought had come from; what part of her subconscious mind had constructed the scenario where Billy would find it necessary she be extinguished.

The answer didn't require a medical degree – even though she had one: She knew an unhealthy amount of stuff.

She was in China, 60 feet underground in a bomb shelter she called the bunny hole. She had campaigned against the trip to China but, like most things Billy planned, he prevailed. She was feeling vulnerable. She wasn't sure she could trust him anymore.

She tried to pin Billy down before coming to China but he was elusive.

"Why do you need me to go to Yulin?" she asked. "I've been to Yulin three times. I've learned all I need to learn. I just don't understand."

"Dear, we've been through this before. You need to understand the operation from top to bottom."

"I do!" she huffed. She knew she was going to lose the battle. Billy was intractable. Even when he was wrong, he couldn't be dynamited off a position.

"Okay," she continued. "Then let me bring Rachel or one of the other girls to keep me company. Yulin is a prison sentence, Billy. I sit in the bunny hole by myself and brood. Don't make me go it alone."

"My dear, anyone who goes to Yulin will learn some of the mission. Do you want to compromise the well-being of your friends…?"

She hadn't thought about that. Billy infuriated her when he was in one of his intractable moods. History should have told her to just accept what he said as gospel and move on. The only other option was to turn her back on her acquired bank of fame and fortune and try to disappear into the night. She knew, if that were her option, Billy would employ the full resources of national intelligence to find her.

"Billy," she said turning a chair around and facing him directly. "We need to talk."

They were dreadful, horrid words. 'We need to talk' was a universally understood cold shower moment – one even the President of the United States was not immune from.

"Claudia, this is not negotiable. The details are set in stone."

"Well, don't I have a say in any of this? I don't want to go to Yulin. There's no good reason for me to go there. I'm going to be sitting in that bunny hole for days pacing the floor. Don't you care about me, Billy?"

He didn't answer. He needed her in Yulin, but he couldn't tell her precisely why. He would have liked to employ logic with Claudia but she didn't appear to be in the mood for anything that could be mistaken for thoughtful analysis.

Claudia decided to shelve her tantrum for the moment and wait for her chance to approach the problem from another angle.

"Billy, tell me this Jerusalem plan isn't half-cooked," she asked.

"Dear, we've had a team of planners on this for longer than you and I have been alive. You know that."

"But, what if it gets, you know, leaked."

"All the potential leakers have been accounted for, dear. You know that."

She did know that. She knew that there were countless Chinese bodies in secret, unmarked graves just beyond the perimeter of the Yulin complex. She also knew of at least a dozen other mysterious disappearances that would never make the nightly news.

"But, what if someone, I don't know, accidentally figures out what the plan is?"

"Accidents cannot be accounted for. If one happens, we'll deal with it."

Claudia shifted in her chair. In spite of their minor spats and differences she and Billy were a team. Part of her responsibility was to make certain all contingencies were given their due. She had an uneasiness, a dread about Jerusalem she couldn't escape in spite of Billy's unceasing optimism. The Jerusalem deception wasn't complicated, she knew, but it would require a picture-perfect execution and a fully untraceable cover-up by their army of pollsters and paid media allies.

The cynic in her had to speak. "Internal polling says that the Christians aren't going to buy it, you know. That's a lot of people."

"Internals show that the Jews won't buy it either. Nor, will a substantial amount of the Muslims. That doesn't matter. What matters is that a majority take the hook and swallow it."

"There will be skeptics."

"It wouldn't work if we didn't have skeptics, dear. When the final nail is driven through the Christian coffin, our stage is set. We've seen to it that our media friends have been compensated, in advance, for their cooperation. If we control the messenger, we control the message. You worry too much, Claudia. The plan is fool-proof."

"No plan is fool-proof. That would require there be no fools. Look around you sweetheart. Even fools have their limits."

Billy wanted to change the subject. Claudia's ceaseless pessimism wore him down. He knew he needed her but he didn't always like her. She could ask the same question in 31 different flavors if she were allowed. She wasn't his wife, but the way she nagged him sometimes, she might as well be.

"Dear," he said in a tone suggesting he were changing the subject. "I spoke with President Tanner last night. His chief of staff, Brian Vandervoort, will be there. He's getting the full debriefing. I want you to show him around. He's going to be in charge of recruiting some key allies for the big show. He has President Tanner's full confidence and I want you there to show him the operation."

"Do you want me to go to bed with him?" she asked matter-of-factly. It was not an odd question. President Kim had often used her feminine assets as a means of fusing, or defusing, situations. She knew she owed her high-pro-file fame and notoriety largely to her willingness to bed whomever Billy Kim thought needed to be compromised. It was part of the service she offered in return for her proximity to power.

"If I wanted you to bed him I would have specified that," he said. "At some point Hans may ask you to seduce him, but that's further down the line – when his marriage can be used as leverage. For the time being you can keep your lovely legs crossed and just flirt."

She smiled. Her involvement in a plan that could require some well-slung mud was a sign of Billy's continued confidence in her. It was a small assurance, but they added up. As for flirting, that was like breathing. If Presidents Kim and Tanner wanted someone primed for a later fall, it was just another part of her full-service contract.

"Is he the blond with the mustache? The tall one?"

"Yes."

"Not a problem," she purred. "He's cute. Not as bad as that Afghani Taliban colonel you set me up with. Billy, that man was a pig."

She didn't have to ask if the Taliban colonel was dead. She had seen his obituary run on CNN.

"He's not an issue anymore, is he, Claudia?"

"No, the GPS I planted in his holster saw to that, didn't it?"

"I will neither confirm nor deny that."

Claudia sighed. Normally she never asked questions about Billy's operations. First, because she wouldn't get a straight answer – particularly from

Billy - and, second, truth was not his ally. Truth was Billy's Cinderella; a secret lover he kept locked in the castle tower. He had the key, but kept it tightly to himself.

She edged closer. "Billy, I don't ask for much from you. I know you've opened a lot of doors for me and given me chances I would never have had on my own," she began. "But, I really don't want to go to China just to give a guided tour to a to a tall, blond stranger I won't be required to seduce."

He looked at Claudia with resignation. "How about I agree to think about it?"

Alone, 60 feet beneath ground in a Chinese province on the edge of the Gobi Desert, Claudia Colgate closed her eyes and created movies in her head. Billy had had his way with her. He always did. So, she tuned out the dreadful and potentially dangerous thoughts careening around inside her skull and imagined herself in a living library of personal movies. Imaginary movies were nothing new to her. In her movies, she was always the heroine. She saved the world. She had her heart broken and she broke hearts. All the action centered on her. She always commanded center stage. Fans adored her. Critics loved her. Old ladies and old men wanted their sons to marry Claudia Colgate. She bounded around her bunny hole, creating lines of script that always seemed to paint her in tragic, yet heroic hues. In her movies her cup was always overflowing.

Her imagination and memories eventually led her back to her breakthrough moment; the time when she had been catapulted into the mainstream of the American conscience. In the wake of Billy's successful orchestration of Articles of Impeachment against Ben Kowalski, she had become an American curiosity – right up to the moment she appeared on The Tonight Show with comedian Ed Montague. It was the moment she became The Next Big Thing.

America wanted to find out who the hood ornament was Billy Kim had been wearing on his arm. Claudia agreed to bring her adventurous bosom to Hollywood and spend a few minutes on TV mentally sparring with Ed Montague. It turned out to be an interview that was replayed on countless venues. Ed himself insisted that that show be replayed as a "best of" almost every time he took a vacation, which was often. The replay and transcripts of the interview peppered the Internet for years. Claudia, herself, had watched the replays countless times – thrilled at just how clever and provocative she was in her maiden performance. She never told America she had a promising young comic writing much of her material.

In her bunny hole she decided to plug into the zip and re-live the moment of her public unveiling.

"Claudia, the American people want to know more about you. You're a pediatrician?"

"I was a pediatrician. Today I sleep with the President of the United States." (Laughter).

"Which do you find pays better?"

"I never though of it in those terms. I suppose being a doctor put more money in my pocket but it kept me rather anonymous." She heaved her ample breasts forward in her beguiling, braless evening gown and sighed. "But, I had other assets most lady pediatricians couldn't bring to the dance, if you know what I mean." (Howls and catcalls).

"Now, you're not married to the president. How can I delicately phrase your relationship with President Kim?"

"Oh, I suppose you could say I'm his live-in girlfriend. Or, you could say I'm his consort or his concubine."

"How do you like to phrase it?"

"I prefer to say he's my piece." (Laughter). "Let me rephrase that because I know that Billy is going to object. Let's just say that we have an agreement. I don't think he would object to my saying that."

"Well, you just said it. You have to live with the consequences. All I can say is our president is one lucky man."

"Ed, it's not as if sex is that important to us."

Ed puts his hands up to signal 'stop.' "Wait! I think there's something in my ears. What did you just say?"

"Sex is not that important."

Ed Montague then mouthed the words 'not important?' for the camera and the audience. (Laughter).

Claudia continued. "Seriously. Billy's got world politics to worry about and I'm kind of an ambassador-at-large. We really don't see that much of each other anyway."

"Claudia, the rumor is that – how can I say this delicately – that you and the president have an 'open' relationship. Care to define that?"

"Sure. What are you doing after the show?" (Howls and catcalls).

Smiley Fisker, the leader of the band then interjected.

"Ed, the band wants Claudia to know that they're not doing anything after the show."

"I think not, Smiley," said Ed Montague. "Your probation officer is here. Tonight's 'community service' night, remember?" (Laughter).

The band members grumbled and groaned. (Laughter).

Ed shouts at his producer. "Bernie, get my wife on the phone and make certain she's not watching tonight's show…Okay, dear," he said, turning back to Claudia. "We were talking about open relationships."

"Let's just say that Billy and I have a mutual understanding. We leave all the options open. Life is just too short not to be spontaneous. At the end of the day we still have a bed to share. That's what's important."

"Bernie, make certain my wife is watching the show tonight, okay? (To his wife at home)…"Hear that honey? How can you argue with spontaneity? Eventually I'll find my way home!" (Laughter).

"You make fun of it, Ed but yesterday's model is gone. The model for relationships has been so constricting, so limiting – particularly for women - for so long. So many relationships have been ruined because of petty jealousies, when they could have been avoided if both the man and woman had a pact in place. There's an old joke that goes: 'Did you hear about the new Playboy magazine for married men? It has the same centerfold month after month after month after month…'" (Laughter).

She continued. "The fact is that most people would like to have more than one port in the storm, if you know what I mean. I think someday they'll find a gene that tells us monogamy is not natural. Trust me. I'm a doctor."

Ed seized the line with a quick retort. "Ah, doctor, the band would like to know at what point you ask them to turn their head and cough? (Laughter).

"All I'm trying to say is that a little variety adds spice to relationships that might otherwise just stagnate, don't you think?"

"I'm thinking, I'm thinking! (Comic pause). Well, I've thought it through and you've sold me. Where do I sign up?" (Laughter, howls). "Let's get serious for a moment, shall we? You studied for eight year to be a doctor."

"Yes. I quit my practice when Billy was running for congress."

"You are an amazing creature, my dear. You have a brain, you can insult musicians with the best of them, and you know biochemistry and anatomy and you've seen innards and stuff."

"I've stuck my hands in those innards."

"Okay, now you're not so sexy all of the sudden! Here's my question: How could you walk away from being a doctor and end up soiling your reputation in Washington?"

"I've got news for you, Ed. I didn't have to go to Washington to soil my reputation. Besides, what's a reputation? A lot of people think I'm a slut. That's fine. Everybody's entitled to an opinion and most of them aren't any better or worse than my own. The bottom line is I'm totally happy in my own skin…"

"I think I would be happy in your skin, too. If you know what I mean…" (Laughter).

"Seriously. I'm totally happy. I lead a full life. I have no regrets. If someone wants to rain on my parade it doesn't bother me. I won't lose any sleep over it because I'm living the life I want to live, in the place I want to be, with the man I want to be with. So, you can judge me, that's fine, but if you want to condemn me then please, please, please, reserve the right for me to cast my judgment on you. And, if you can't hold up to that kind of scrutiny then I say…to hell with you!" (Raucous applause).

"Say what's on your mind. Don't be shy now."

"I'm sorry, Ed. It's just that I get truckloads of mail everyday from people who quote Scriptures and can't even spell my name and yet they feel compelled to tell me what a vile person I am. That's it? That's the best you got? You're rotten? You're evil? You're going to hell? First off, you're assuming I believe in the idea of heaven and hell. Come on! I'll engage you in the debate, but first, get a clue! Don't just call me names and believe you won the debate. A lot of people in this country want simple answers because they can't handle independent thinking. Life isn't that simple. It requires more than just reciting Scripture or condemning others because they don't happen to live the life you want them to. (More raucous applause).

"Do you want to sit in my chair, hon? I mean, it seems as though I've become unnecessary. Maybe I'll just join the band. (Pause). Naaah, then I'd have to learn how to sleep until noon."

"And live under a bridge." (Ed breaks up, laughs uncontrollably. Howls, catcalls at the band. The laughter goes on for nearly a minute).

"You are a pistol, young lady."

"I like your band, though, Ed. Some of them are cute."

"The implication, of course, being that some of them aren't?"

"Okay. Whatever you say."

"You realize that they're all going to go home tonight and wonder if you think they're one of the cute ones."

"That's what you get from men with low self-esteem. (More catcalls).

"You are brutal."

"You know what they call a musician who just broke up with his girlfriend, don't you? – homeless!"

She clicked the zip file closed on her computer and closed her eyes, allowing herself to bask in the warmth of her own brilliance. She had made quite a splash that night. The Tonight Show had been a launching pad for her. Almost immediately, her agent was steamrolled with requests for personal appearances, endorsements and other talk show gigs. Her stint with Ed Montague elevated Claudia Colgate, almost overnight, from hood ornament to Hollywood icon. There was hardly a water cooler in the country where Claudia's name didn't come up as a matter of course.

It was three short weeks later that she appeared as a guest hostess on MTV and, shortly after, was featured on "The New, New, Hollywood Squares." Her public persona had blossomed.

She had risen into the stratosphere to a place where pediatricians weren't supposed to tread – she was a star!

CHAPTER TWELVE
Catharsis

He insisted on going into the super market alone. He hated having two Secret Service agents shadow his every move. Shopping was something he liked to do. He didn't mind the stares, the pointing, the gratuitous "Good morning, Mr. President." Actually, he liked it. He could talk to the butcher, the cracker salesman, the check-out gals. It made him feel normal.

Ben Kowalski would never have seen it under normal circumstances. He purposely avoided looking at the tabloids. He wouldn't give them the satisfaction. He knew the lessons of the tabloids first-hand. As an author and motivational speaker the 'bloids would constantly convolute his message. They sold papers by mocking, distorting and twisting his words. The press, he knew all too well, had an ax to grind. It's how they sold papers. They didn't build up, they tore down. But, out of some sort of primal reflex his eyes were drawn to an image which shocked him into a new reality. Whatever hope he had kindled for resurrecting his marriage and romance with his estranged wife, Ellen, was about to be dashed against the check-out lanes.

Ben had developed a shopping market routine over the years. It was a mind game he played in check-out lanes. He averted his eyes from the magazines in the rack. By ignoring the magazine rack he was thwarting a whole industry. Tabloids were published on the premise that Ben's own uncontrollable prurient interests would force him to eyeball their products. He was supposed to salivate at the covers of cleavage, innuendo and slime. Instead, Ben would turn to the candy rack. He would look at the ceiling. He would chat with other customers. He would not succumb to the lurid offerings in the magazine racks. It was part of the pact he had made with Jesus after he had come out of detox. Ben didn't just pledge to turn his back on booze in 2008. After all, booze was just one component of the weaknesses that had ravaged his soul.

No, Ben formulated a battle plan of the flesh. He trained himself to not allow sexual temptation to be lured by his eyeballs. It didn't always work and it required discipline, but in time he found out that it could almost be done. To pull it off required he grow a faith more consistent with what existed outside of the popular culture. So, he grew his faith, in part, by refusing to worship at the altar of pop culture. Then, he preached what he had learned. He preached over the course of the next two decades to men on five continents about the temptations paraded before them in the media. He was a constant critic of the press - the salacious and lewd spin they wove into every picture or story.

"Resist with all your heart," he would implore. "Turn the filthy images around in the magazine racks. Look the other way. Recite the Lord's Prayer. Close your eyes. Ask for strength to resist."

For these urgings he was mercilessly mocked.

Yet, as he approached the checkout lane his eye caught his own name. Above his name was the unbelievable picture of his estranged wife, Ellen, with her mouth wide open in a twisted half-laugh. It covered fully half of the front page. It was the most unflattering picture of his wife he had ever seen. The headline on the tabloid, the Daily Rattle, read "Ex-Prez wife proclaims hubby 'The False Prophet.'" The sub-head read: "Ben Kowalski a womanizer, liar and drunk, claims estranged wife." Hypnotically, he pulled the paper from the rack and opened it.

As he read the story he felt the floor disappear beneath him.

A voice tried to reach him through the haze of his disbelief.

"Mr. President, I hope I'm not interrupting, but my name is Charles Harwood. I used to play football. They called me Woodshed Harwood." He was a large black man with a small son holding his hand. Kowalski looked at him incredulously. Didn't this large man know there was a personal catharsis unfolding?

Harwood sensed that his comments and his timing may not be ideal, but he had begun a sentence to a former President of the United States. He thought he should finish that sentence. Protocol demanded it.

"In 2018 my contract was up for renewal. I was holding out. I was locked out of training camp. Contract dispute, you know. I thought I was worth a lot of money. Bengals management thought otherwise. Anyway, I was overweight and partying a little too much. A lot too much. There was this accident. I was drunk. Anyway, to make a long story short... I came to one of your seminars, sir, and I can say this now, but I didn't know it then...You saved my life."

Kowalski was reading the story. He didn't hear the man. He was in shock.

Harwood looked at the tabloid in Ben's hand with the picture of Ellen Kowalski exposing her tonsils for the world. He read the headlines. Then he looked at Kowalski and it dawned on him that, perhaps, he had caught his former president at a vulnerable moment. He put his large black hand over the text Kowalski was reading. Kowalski looked up. There weren't tears in his eyes. There was nothing. He was brain-dead.

"This the first you knew?" Harwood asked.

Kowalski looked at him in all seriousness and asked, "do you know that all of this is about someone I used to be? That nothing here applies to the here and now?"

"I know that, sir. I know who you are."

"Do they know?" he said, motioning to the store at large.

"Some do, sir. Lot of 'em read this crap 'cuz it's easier than thinking."

CHAPTER THIRTEEN
Putrid odors

She was aware of the details of the murder of the Speaker of the House. She knew how it had been made to look like an accident. She knew the political machinations of the two-single man helicopters with the phosphorous rockets that struck the White House in 2021 and incinerated Vice President Norton and 168 others. She helped orchestrate the impeachment of President Marshall Warren. She was also a key and invisible player when muscles were flexed to squash the unanticipated presidency of Ben Kowalski.

Claudia Colgate's half-awake brain dredged up secret slime she had long forgotten. In her subterranean solitude she fondly relived how she had let the press believe she and Ben Kowalski – the reluctant president standing in the gap between Billy Kim and power – were having a not-so-secret affair. The implications of the affair didn't destroy the Kowalski presidency - but it did torpedo his marriage; an achievement Claudia counted as a bull's eye moment. The lie she allowed to bloom had been a strategic piece of deception designed to drive a wedge between America's most trusted couple – creating a personal crisis inside the White House for the man they needed to dethrone. It was a perfect lie – one that could neither be confirmed nor denied which, in the minds of White House press corps jackals, meant could be presumed true. The press ran with the story of the fictitious affair because it was stench – alleged stench, yes, but putrid odors sold more papers than any faint whiff of truth. The effect the story had on the Kowalski marriage was immaterial to Claudia Colgate. And, poor, innocent Ellen Kowalski would never raise an objection concerning such a personal matter as infidelity. In Claudia's estimation, Ellen was a simple woman and a simple wife with a simple mind. Ellen had a simple Christian ethic Claudia Colgate could read from a thousand paces. No, Ellen Kowalski would never publicly discuss an allegation concerning a word

— adultery - which, at the time, she had trouble even saying.

In the end, Claudia had engineered the estrangement of Ben Kowalski and his wife and son – by saying nothing. The rumor fueled itself. All she did was not deny. Claudia Colgate smiled from her Chinese bunny hole. The memory warmed her. The truth was she didn't have to lie to the swarms of media locusts. The press filled in the blanks - because nature, and reporters with ambitions, abhor vacuums – particularly when the rumors involved high-profile people alleged to be involved in naked escapades with people other than those with whom they should be naked.

Claudia Colgate had many secrets the press would never report - not because her secrets weren't press-worthy. No, she was a wealth of rumor and dirt which most editors would normally run Page One with little, if any, verification. The editors, however, were held in check by the fact that Billy Kim was on a first-name basis with the publishers of every major news organization that mattered. The editors knew better than to go snooping around her secret life without Billy Kim's blessings. And, there were large secrets - secrets buried in graveyards on six continents. All of her previous Chinese visits had been a prelude for a larger secret; a moment which would require a well-rehearsed staging at the impending dedication of the third temple of Israel. Secrets were the reason she and Billy were in China on a so-called "trade mission."

Upon waking, she instinctively reached for Billy – not as a sign of affection or, heaven forbid, sex, but as an assurance that the most powerful man on the planet was still within her reach. He had slipped out of the bunny hole to resume whatever he was quarterbacking 60 feet above ground in their secret Chinese compound at Yulin. All she could do was wait for him to beckon. She wasn't allowed access to the elevator.

She had come to China with huge trepidation. She wanted to stay home, but knew Billy well enough to understand that her refusal would be viewed as a measure of her growing mistrust.

She was swimming with a known shark, hoping he wasn't done feasting on the other species in the tank. She had done her job for 15 years, faithfully serving as a sexual partner and diplomatic liaison – though sex had become increasingly rare and mechanical. She no longer offered herself to him and he no longer pursued her. She didn't like the sexual ambivalence, but she understood why it was happening: She didn't trust him. The prospect of Billy murdering her was a growing consideration. Her sense of quiet fatalism tended to throw cold water on any fires of passion she may have once had for the man.

The ace up her sleeve was her high public profile. She was comfortable that she couldn't just "disappear" from Billy's life without a valid alibi. Still, an untimely "accident" on her part was not out of the realm of possibility. Billy Kim was a murderer and she knew he was creative. What she didn't know was the level of his feeling for her. She was beginning to wonder if he even possessed the psychological ability to love – an ability she, herself, wrestled with on a daily basis. No, Billy viewed every relationship as a matter of utility and seemed to be almost genetically incapable of loving anyone not residing in his own skin.

For a seductive, weak moment, she lay back on her bed and fantasized. Not of sex. She lived out those fantasies. Sex was her craft. Sex was a tool to accomplish an end. She fantasized of power, her true aphrodisiac.

In the early years the press had labeled Claudia Colgate as an international whore. Like most things in her public life, it had been calculated, orchestrated. She knew the press. She played their spin almost better than Brad Pugh. She knew their hot buttons and she understood the fragile relationship between approval and condemnation were often measured in scant millimeters of cleavage. She knew - in the war between taste and ratings, taste was an ugly stepsister. She also knew the media couldn't bring themselves to mock or condemn her as long as Billy Kim shared cocktails and coercion with the boards of directors of most media conglomerates. Instead, the press invented other terms to describe the woman who shared Billy Kim's bed. Instead of "slut" or "whore" they called her "complex," "intriguing," "beguiling" and "mysterious."

While they were busy finding new adjectives for "whore," she was busy building her base of power, influence and blackmail. Officially, she held the title of Ambassador At Large. It meant she was sent wherever Billy wanted to ply sexual coercion. One episode, in Billy Kim's first presidential term, had her dispatched to Saudi Arabia on Air Force Two to seduce a Saudi prince in order to stave off an OPEC production cutback. Her midnight diplomacy in Riyadh saved the American economy untold billions. When she returned to the White House, her report to Billy Kim and his cabinet was delivered with the aplomb of a conquering general.

"Kissinger couldn't have done what I just did."

Billy Kim almost choked when his Secretary of National Health Care responded under his breath: "neither could Madeline Albright. We'd have jihad on our hands."

In an otherwise humorless White House, it was one of the few times the cabinet openly laughed together.

CHAPTER FOURTEEN
Sex and excess

From the day they had made their improbable escape into the ocean, Brad Pugh broadcast his show six days a week, 52 weeks a year. Confined to a submarine, a vacation was an oxymoron. Pugh, his wife Winnie, Captain Ilya Petrov and his skeleton crew of 13 Russian sailors operated as a slippery, sleuthful studio under the sea. Pugh would broadcast his commentary, field questions from the Internet and then slide beneath the waves into the dark underworld for 21 hours of refuge, research and recharge.

In the bow of his rented Russian submarine, the K-815, Brad Pugh and his wife, Winnie, had a submersible home; a studio in which their only contact with outside civilization was an electronic exchange, but it was in real time – something live radio tends to prefer. The three hours a day the sub came up to periscope depth gave Captain Petrov the chance to exchange recirculated, filtered, electrostatically cleansed air for the real thing. Brad and Winnie came to cherish the smell of fresh air. Captain Petrov had to bring the sub to periscope depth in order for their signal to bounce off the ionosphere to the overhead Country Music Satellite operating from a safe 240 miles above them. When the periscope broke the surface, huge fans would execute a high-power air exchange which filled the sub with the distinct smell of real air.

The confines of living in a steel coffin couldn't keep the Internet in check. Each day Captain Petrov would blow the ballasts and hide just beneath the surface while Brad Pugh vented his spleen to an audience that was beginning to grow by numbers only the media dared say were insignificant.

While Winnie wasn't helping Brad run the show, she cooked. The galley was world class, befitting the Russian Navy's only-ever "pleasure sub." Winnie was queen of the kitchen. The crew came to appreciate Winnie's homey touches in their underwater world. For them, she became Mom. She made certain they were not just fed but accommodated in a manner befitting sons. Dinner, the one meal they all shared together, was strictly a sit-down, civil affair. She took great pride in the meal arrangements and she insisted on manners. The sailors quickly learned the quickest way to tick off Mom was to do what came naturally to men living in close quarters. No belching, farting or lewd stories. She didn't want to hear any of it. She would leer at the offenders with a stare that could cut through a steel bulkhead. Her stare transcended the language barrier.

"You are men, but you are not gentlemen," she would say.

At one meal she broke down crying. The men had become a little too graphic. She left, hustling down the hallway and into her quarters. Brad simply looked at the men and said "she doesn't ask for much, boys. A little courtesy doesn't cost you anything."

From that moment on the boys would seat themselves and talk quietly while Winnie asked them how their day was going, whether they had heard from their families and all of the other mindless banter that keeps families from acting like packs of wild dogs.

She also insisted that Grace be said before every meal. The Russian sailors didn't understand or appreciate the practice at first because faith was as familiar to them as flying. Brad would read a passage from the Bible and then Winnie would lead a prayer of thanks. The Russian sailors, initially, thought it was some sort of pagan ritual. They smirked. In time, however, they caught the drift of what Winnie was doing. She and Brad slowly began to instruct the sailors on a history none of them had ever learned. Brad and Winnie were seasoned enough teachers to know they had to proceed slowly. For one thing, the Russian sailors spoke broken English. Secondly, they were biblical illiterates. Everything they were hearing was for the first time. Instead of preaching, Brad and Winnie opted to focus on the lessons contained in ancient history. What the Russians quickly learned was that the Bible was fuel for lively debate and conjecture. The sailors began to express their own wonder at how such old stories could contain such timeless lessons. The idea that ethics, morality and the rule of law sprang forth from the biblical record slowly began to impress the young sailors.

When Brad read the Easter account of the crucifixion the sailors looked at one another.

"How could a man rise from the dead," asked Lieutenant Ivanov, their sonar operator. Brad could see in the faces of the sailors that the story had the lure of a fairy tale.

"A man couldn't rise from the dead," said Brad. "This was not a man."

The men accepted the words at face value and carried their disbelief around privately for days. One by one, they found Brad and began to query him about the foundations of the faith.

At the beginning of their Bible teachings, the Russian sailors treated Scripture like a trip to the dentist. Initially, they played along with the idea of listening to verses and saying Grace because it was the quickest way to get Mom to serve the food. It wasn't long, however, before they began to look forward to the larger-than-life debates originating from the ancient readings. The sailors began to view dinner not just as a means to fuel their bodies, but as a means to test their ability to reason.

Winnie's kitchen slowly became a place where the family could discuss – robustly, the timelessness of good and evil, right and wrong, sin and righteousness. The Russians sensed no theology. They were merely exploring history and trying to understand the appeal of the biblical record.

Winnie lamented the fact that everything on the menu came from a frozen, vacuum-packed, non-perishable larder; a world in which fresh fruits and vegetables were a pipe dream. Despite her culinary obstacles she managed to concoct hearty man-meals with the help of a little creative seasoning and generous helpings of TLC. In the stainless steel world where she was queen, she managed to make the galley the closest thing any of them had to a real home.

Aside from the fact that she was an exile and living in a large, cold metal tube, she was thankful. She was thankful her husband was with her. She was thankful that the Russian sailors were civil and eager to learn. But, mostly she was thankful that her home was nuclear and virtually undetectable.

Billy Kim and his intelligence people eventually came to learn of the unique history and character of the K-815. In the wake of losing the Cold War, the Russians were cashing out on whatever assets they could. In this particular sub, Captain Petrov saw a unique business opportunity. It was one of a kind. It was no ordinary sub. It was a secret Russian invention: The Pleasure Sub. It had been commissioned to serve Russian naval officers who might be considering a career change. It had hot tubs, an executive galley, a movie theater, king-sized beds, weight rooms, a sauna and digital Internet capabilities that could intercept television signals, cable TV shows, and military transmissions on frequencies inconceivable in the commercial world.

The sub's main purpose, though, was to serve the Russian Navy as a sort of underwater bar and brothel. Officers would tell their wives they were being sent to duty at sea and would disappear into the sub for a few weeks with

20 or 30 bathing beauties. By the end of their "mission" they would be quite beholding to the Russian Navy and anxious to sign up for the next tour. The sub itself had minimal offensive capabilities – one torpedo tube and a half dozen "fish" they could use if ever caught in defensive check. But, the K-815 did have some interesting features that would make it virtually invisible. The Russians had developed a sonar cloaking device which was two steps ahead of their American peers. Instead of employing the old 'run silent/run deep' tactic in order to evade detection, they ran very deep and very loud, overwhelming any sonar tracking devices with a cacophony of noise pods designed to confuse whatever torpedo or sonar locked onto them. The masking devices had been tested, but never used – mainly because the Russian Navy had a huge vested interest in making certain a sub loaded with drunken, debased senior Russian naval officers was kept well out of harm's way.

Being invisible, after all, had always been the primary mission of the K-815. She had been engineered to hide. It's mission and modus operandi were Russian tributes to Communist Party corruption and influence; a submersible monument to the gods of sex and excess. It was a sort of underwater tree house for Russian officers; a place where they could abandon protocol and spend a few misbegotten weeks immersed in 24/7 vodka and anonymous scantily clad indulgences.

The second notable feature of the sub was a clear diamond-amalgam nose cone in the bow. Through this high-tech eye, the Russian officers could give their bathing beauty bunk-mates a squid's-eye view of the ocean bottom at depths unheard of in modern naval engineering. The sub could dive to 3200 feet before approaching their crush zone. They could then extend their telescoping lamps and light up the bottom. It was a new technology and the Russians had been holding the secret close to their vests, waiting for the right moment in international tensions to make their revolutionary engineering available to the highest bidder.

Instead of decommissioning the vessel and selling it for scrap, the Russian Navy decided to sell it to their unemployed friend, Captain Petrov for $1. Petrov speculated that there was a private market for this sort of creation. To market his service, he went to E-Bay. The ship had only been rented three times - once by a rich Bahraini oil mogul for a month of unfettered debauchery, once for three months by Green Peace to spy on American fishing trawlers, and finally by Brad Pugh. The automatic rental payment of $1.8 million per month always cleared the captain's Swiss account. When the gig was over the captain would be set for life. In the meantime, he had a client to serve. He was thankful Brad had a brain and no desire for debauchery or eco-Nazism. The widowed ex-communist party member was too old to pretend he cared about making political statements. He was just trying to make a buck. Along with Pugh and his wife and his crew of 13 trusted sailors, the captain was living a dream.

Brad and Captain Ilya Petrov, isolated at sea, came to a mutual respect. Pugh respected Petrov for his ability to carve out a meaning for his life, in spite of the huge obstacles in his path. Petrov respected Pugh for his courage in speaking the truth. As a former Communist officer, he understood how lethal the truth could be.

"Greetings, freedom lovers!" Brad's signature salutation would boom from 35 feet beneath the waves. The US Navy spent a small fortune in manpower and machinery searching the Atlantic Ocean for the K-815. Naval officers had sealed orders from their president to sink the vessel, secretly, without any telltale residue of either flotsam or jetsam. The sinking of the K-815 was supposed to occur in a vacuum, late at night with the lights off and everyone tucked in their beds, blissfully dreaming of a world where there were no such bothersome things as an opposing point of view.

Still, the Brad Pugh Show kept broadcasting. Navy brass kept telling the president "the Atlantic Ocean is a very large body of water." The "needle in a haystack" excuse was offered up to President Kim routinely.

The Navy never told the president the whole story. The K-815 was in the *Indian* Ocean. Navy brass was part of the right boat/wrong ocean ruse, but kept the secret close to their inflatable vests; well aware of the truth, but unwilling to report what they knew to a president they neither trusted, nor recognized as legitimate.

Through a secret agreement with the Country Music Association, Pugh's broadcasts were picked up and delivered to over 900 stations across Europe and North America. CMA held the orbit of their satellite in secret, fully aware of what might happen if their bird of revenue were to fall prey to an unannounced government missile. When the board of directors had launched their satellite in 1996, they held a second satellite inside the bay doors; a satellite they later launched into an orbit known only to CMA. The Country Music Association board of directors had been commissioned by several wealthy Christian businessmen to engineer the second satellite as an insurance policy guaranteeing their gospel message would never be fully extinguished.

For Pugh and his wife life at sea was a solitary life, like before fame and fortune. Brad ran his own control board - there were no union engineers or staffers or research people. There was just he and Winnie, Captain Petrov and his skeleton crew of 13 Russian sailors. Winnie served as not just executive chef, but also as executive producer, which in the case of broadcasting from a submarine, meant she watched the clock for the scheduled break times.

"Remember when we had to go out for seafood?" Winnie lamented as she counted down to his broadcast theme.

Pugh's brand of truth, as long as it originated from international waters, was a bothersome condition President Billy Kim had to tolerate. Kim had to pretend that Brad Pugh was irrelevant. In truth, Billy Kim wanted the irrelevant Brad Pugh dead. Then he could really be irrelevant. But, it was essential the Kim Administration feed the illusion that America was still a land of Free Speech, in spite of the apparent contradictions.

The truth, if one cared to look at the un-spun evidence, was that Brad Pugh had been chased into the ocean because of his big mouth. The Kim forces would kill Brad if he or his crew stuck their heads out of the water. At the very least they would have him locked in a dark place without a microphone.

The ground rules to the game of political cat-and-mouse were simple - if Pugh and his rented Russian sub came closer than 12 miles to any country owing a favor to the Kim Administration, they would be turned into a grease spot on the sea. Pugh knew he owed the US Navy a huge debt in their staged incompetence at tracking him down. He also owed a huge debt to the actual and very real incompetent bureaucrats in the Kim White House. They were clueless about the military. The Kim Administration, an association of vapid bureaucrats and Yes Men, were peerless in their military ignorance and seemingly proud of the lack of military pedigrees inside of the administration. Military people didn't populate the Kim White House.

Pugh's canned intro rolled. The dulcet tones of his recorded studio announcer greeted much of the English-speaking world.

"From beneath the waves of an unnamed ocean, broadcast in harmonious geosynchronicity with an unnamed satellite and in celebration of free speech, ladies and gentlemen - Brad Pugh." A tympani roll and a "splash" sound effect were his "ramp" into the show.

Pugh's pool of news and questions came from the Internet. He highlighted a few stories and ran copies of salient tidbits on his printer. He had 21 hours a day for show preparation. He was always loaded for bear. The isolation of forced exile could not hold the Internet at bay. The Internet was at his fingertips and was his only necessary research associate. No one could bottle the net. That genie was out of that bottle and even Billy Kim couldn't contain it.

"Greetings, freedom lovers!" His voice boomed from 35 feet beneath the waves of the Indian Ocean.

He looked out the diamond amalgam bow of the sub and could only see black. It was 10:00 PM in the Indian Ocean. In America, the nation was breaking for lunch, many of them tuning in Brad Pugh for something un-spun.

CHAPTER FIFTEEN
Pre-Qualified Infidels

In the Gulf of Aqaba there is little boat traffic. Only about a dozen cargo ships a day traverse through the 160-mile finger of water that leads from the main body of the Red Sea and ends at a port in the northern crest called Eilat. Eilat is situated at the intersection of Egypt, Israel, Saudi Arabia and Jordan. Geographically it is in Israel but three other countries skirt its city limits. It is a town with barricaded border crossings at every turn. The port itself is cordoned off into four separate quadrants, each with a military presence closely monitoring all traffic. A camera shop in the Israeli section of town makes a small fortune selling tele-photo lenses to agents - covert, military, unknown and otherwise. Everyone watches the other.

Eilat is a seaside tourist town with all the trappings. What one will not find in the local travel brochures is that most tourists are photographed through long lenses by four governments. It is impossible to be invisible in Eilat. Arne Karlstrom wasn't trying to be invisible. He was trying to appear as a tourist on a diving and fishing expedition into the gulf.

Arne Karlstrom was headed toward the belly of the beast. He had campaigned Ben Kowalski for the funds necessary to test his theory about the Hebrew crossing of the Red Sea at Nuweiba. Where his discoveries would lead was an endgame no one could predict, least of all Arne. At the moment it was just a quest for the truth. Where truth would lead them was probably to trouble.

Karlstrom, a British diver named Richard Ewald, and a Coptic Christian Egyptian named Mahrous al-Sharif rented a 28-foot inboard from an Israeli charter company. They loaded their main fuel tanks, as well as a 20-gallon saddle tank, and made their way down the Egyptian side of the gulf toward the beach head called Nuweiba. It was a 60-mile trek that took them four hours at half throttle. On both the Egyptian and the Saudi side of the gulf mountains rose from the ocean 2000, 3000, 5000 feet into the clear Middle Eastern summer sky. Where the mountains allowed for a stretch of beach, Bedouins would congregate in camps, their camels and their families huddled into a makeshift city. Karlstrom and the Brit would throw on kufis over their heads when they passed them. Mahrous was their "front," taking the helm. They nodded their heads to the Bedouins as they cruised by. What they were doing had to be cloaked in secrecy. If the Islamic world were aware of what they were seeking, they would be shot out of the water. Being Christians, they were already pre-qualified infidels. Once out into the Gulf of Aqaba, they were keenly aware that the jurisdiction of the Sweden, England or Egypt couldn't protect them from trouble.

With their scuba gear onboard, Ewald, the dive captain, estimated they could descend to 120 feet at a time and stay down for 15 minutes without having to decompress. If they had to decompress they were out of luck. At the bottom of the Gulf of Aqaba, Karlstrom was looking for 3500-year-old relics of Pharoah's army. He had picked the spot of his hypothesized crossing off the Egyptian side of the Gulf of Aqaba at Nuweiba. From the one piece of available data, Arne was able to determine that there was an underwater land bridge that stretched eight miles across the gulf from Nuweiba to Saudi Arabia. He extrapolated, from the only available underwater soundings ever made of the area, there was a hard sand bottom, about a 6-degree grade across an eight mile stretch from Nuweiba to the Saudi beach. That meant, at the maximum, the crossing, if it were the crossing, had a depth of about 1400 feet, which, if the bed were hard and relatively even, could accommodate two million Hebrews, their cattle, their children and their elderly to march across the bottom to the other side. Arne noted that the slope of the incline would, technically, comply with the Americans With Disabilities Act, were it an ancient regulation.

Sleep that night was fitful. What they were about to do was an unknown quantity with huge potential implications. The sea was calm and the sky was brilliant but all three of the crew suffered from the same malady - their bodies wanted to sleep but their brains wouldn't shut off.

"What if your hypothesis is true?" asked Ewald, looking dreamily at a perfect summer sky.

"Look in your crystal ball, Richard. What do you see?"

"The press will eat you alive. They don't want that kind of truth."

Mahrous felt compelled to add his Egyptian perspective. "Truth is dangerous. He who holds onto the truth is generally a target. Consider Jesus."

"Still," Ewald added, "whether we find anything or not - I'm skeptical. I don't believe in divine intervention. I think God may have designed the universe, but from what I can see - he left us to fend for ourselves a long, long time ago."

"You agree with Nietchze, then? God is dead?" asked the Egyptian.

"No, but He appears to be asleep at the switch, doesn't He?"

The Egyptian smiled, as if Ewald has stepped into his trap. "You mistake indifference with free will. God gave us free will so that we can seek Him. Not vice versa."

Karlstrom didn't want to preach to the Brit. It wasn't the time or place and the effort wouldn't bear any fruit. Ewald's skepticism would take care of itself as the expedition unfolded. So, too, would his own. Karlstom's concerns at that moment were larger than the Middle Eastern midnight sky. What if the hypothesis were true? The implications were staggering. If evidence could be photographed that a divine cataclysmic ancient event had occurred under these waters, what would it mean? A verifiable biblical Exodus account would provide everyone, everywhere, with a new perspective.

The following morning the sun rose hot and brilliant against the deep blue hue of the gulf and the rusty red backdrop of the Saudi and Egyptian mountains that bracketed them. The beach at Nuweiba was an eight-mile long stretch of white with only one port on the southern end. The beach head had only a few vacation resorts on it. The fact was that while Nuweiba had all the trappings of a seaside paradise, it was just too remote. The only commodities not imported on Nuweiba were sand and sun. It was sand, a few palms and more sand. Period. From their boat on the sea the sandy beach head peninsula on the Sinai coast was a study in contrasts - sea, sky, mountains and sand composed the whole panorama.

Arne pondered the incredulity of where he was. They were in a narrow strait of sea between two Muslim countries - just three vacationers on a diving and fishing expedition. That's what they had told the Israeli port authority at Eilat. That was the ruse. Arne wondered if the Saudi and Egyptian government were concerned enough to care about a singular diving/fishing trip on the gulf.

There was only one way to find out.

Karlstrom knew the Saudis and Egyptians had archeological sites they wanted to protect above sea level. He had seen the aerial photographs of Jabel El Lawz, Arne's proposed location of Mount Sinai in northwest Saudi

Arabia. The satellite photos, in close-up, raised many questions. Curiously, without official explanation, the Saudis had built a fence around Jabel El Lawz. Why? It was a 7800-foot outcropping of rock that was literally in the middle of nowhere. Why put a fence around it? Arne had his theory. He had lots of theories. His theories were why he was sliding into a wet suit into a narrow strait of water between two hostile countries. He had to give his theories some weight. As a scientist, data was his oxygen.

As he prepared for the first dive Arne wondered just how incredibly ludicrous the scene 3500 years ago must have been. He didn't want to dwell on it. That was fantasy. Once they discovered something he could allow his imagination to run. Until then, he had to keep his crew and his own imagination in check. Still, the little boy in him wondered.

Ewald slid into the water off the transom and Karlstrom handed him the video camera. Karlstrom followed seconds later with his still camera. Every moment was critical. They had enough tanks for eight dives and they only had 15 minutes on the bottom for each dive. Two hours total. No more, no less. If they did find anything worth retrieving on the bottom they would retrieve it at their own risk. The Egyptian and Saudi governments both had antiquities agencies with the power of law to confiscate whatever ancient booty they might bring to the light of day. If that happened, their mission could be revealed, or at the very least, deduced.

The Egyptians or the Saudis couldn't take their film – at least, not legally. Illegally they could do whatever they wanted. Arne was not so naïve as to think justice was a debatable issue, given their status as infidels.

The clarity of the water surprised Karlstrom. It was crystal clear, like a swimming pool. As they approached the 120-foot level the bottom was a virtual underwater beach. Some green sea moss hovered like fog above the bottom in places but it was incredibly flat. Arne placed his fin in the sand and noted that it was hard-packed, coarse and firm. Curiously, at random intervals there were what appeared to be coralized garbage dumps.

Karlstrom knew enough about coral to know that it didn't grow on sand. It had to have something to attach itself to. The mass of dead coral he and Ewald approached looked like a small, fossilized train wreck. It was incredibly old. 3500 years old? He wondered.

In the closest garbage dump Arne poked a one-meter measuring stick into the jumbled mass. The stick had been brought to provide some scale for the pictures. It couldn't budge the mass of coral. It was rock hard and an indistinguishable mass of formless non-symmetrical shapes. Arne snapped a picture.

He wasn't sure what he was shooting at the moment, but he had a camera. He knew he was supposed to use it. He snapped another. On the bottom of the pile he saw a form. It was coralized, yes, but it was a form. It was symmetrical and had definition. It was a semi-circle. The missing half of the semi-circle extended into the formless mass of coral skeletons. On the semi-circle he made out three spokes of a wheel. An Egyptian chariot wheel, if his instincts were right.

Ewald was frantically motioning Karlstrom on the other side of the coral mass. Karlstrom clicked off four pictures in rapid-fire succession of the "wheel" and made his way to the other side. He looked at what Ewald was shooting. What they saw didn't require a tremendous amount of imagination. It was a coralized human rib cage. Underneath it was what appeared to be some kind of animal, a large animal - a horse or a cow sternum and rib cage.

His hypothesis had a form.

They finished three more dives that day, each dive providing more forensic building blocks to Arne's hypothesis. On one dive Ewald took his knife and cut off a spoke of a "wheel" from one of the chariots. The idea was to take the sample up to the boat and check it for metal content with a metal detector. It tested positive. The iron-colored ring in the coral "spoke" was metal. Another hypothetical building block.

That night they found a mountain rising out of the gulf and anchored the boat as close as possible to it. They turned off their running lights. They didn't need to be discovered. They had still and video footage that the Muslim world would not welcome. They had pictures of stuff that could get them killed.

What they had found on the bottom, in Arne's mind, was indisputable. But Arne knew the scientific community. After gravity and the rotation of the planets, scientists had trouble agreeing on much else. The scientific ego and scientific elitism were powerful political forces. Arne also knew that two-dimensional photos of curious coral skeletons would demand further evidence. He was hoping to raise questions because he knew the soul of scientists. They would want more proof and Arne wanted the resources to give it to them. In his mind, Arne was hatching plots to win a grant from National Geographic or even the National Oceanographic and Atmospheric Administration.

Their most curious finding of the day had been what appeared to be the coralized form of an upside-down chariot. Karlstrom knew it was Egyptian because of the vent holes. They were the same design of vent holes that were found in the chariot displayed in the Egyptian Museum in Cairo, the chariot extracted from the undisturbed tomb of King Tutankhamen - the boy king who would have been one of Egypt's three reigning kings at about the time of the Exodus.

Karlstrom knew Tut. Karlstrom's theory was that Tut was an only son and died as a result of God's plague on first-borns, which was brought on the Egyptians by God when Pharaoh refused to allow the Hebrews to pray in the desert.

But, that was another hypothesis for another day.

Sleep came quickly for the men in the boat. It was a heavy, deep, exhausted sleep. A full day of work in the sun and sea under a Middle Eastern summer sun had sapped them of their energy. Under a stunning canopy of desert stars the three men closed their eyes just once before sleep overtook them.

The following day broke gray and windy. Before diving they took depth findings along the bottom to determine the width of the land bridge. Where they were measuring the ridge, it appeared to be about a half-mile wide.

Karlstrom and Ewald took their first dive right off the edge of the "crossing bridge" to visually confirm the width and bottom topography. At the edge of the "crossing bridge" they saw the coarse sand shelf drop off into an inky, deep darkness. According to the only soundings ever made of the sea by the Russians in the 1950's, the Gulf of Aqaba was incredibly deep and steep. Under Aqaba the Great Rift fault line extended well into the African continent. It had deep canyons and dramatic, almost bottomless, underwater mountain ranges. Here, outside of Nuweiba, the normal contour of the rest of the gulf ignored predictability and seemed to follow a singular, independent design.

The rough sea was taking its toll on Arne. While Ewald was a strapping 6'2 and 190 pounds of lean muscle and 30-something youth, Arne was a wispy 5'9", 165 pounds of 52-year-old limitations. By the third dive of the day Arne was exhausted, totally spent. Ewald called off the last dive. Being overly fatigued was a red flag. Ewald, the dive captain, decided their day was done.

Ewald's decision was made easier by the fact that on their last dive that day they had found the crown jewel of the journey. On the bottom, at the 108-foot depth, there was a perfect garbage dump of formless coral. It was potentially remarkable to three-dimensional human eyes, but unremarkable in the two dimensions which transferred the images to film. When Arne looked at it he could see differing forms of things that could be in there - some animal skeletons, spears, wheel hubs, chariot planks. His eyes may have been playing tricks on him. He was seeing the forms and snapping pictures but his mind was a blur. He knew he was exhausted but he also knew this was the chance of a lifetime. Ewald was busy circling the dumps and capturing a 360-degree view on video. Arne was looking and snapping pictures of the muddled mass of images in the garbage dumps. He was wondering if his mind was drawing conclusions the evidence could support. His own eyes had become two-dimensional.

Then he saw it.

Partially buried in silt, about 30 feet apart from the dump there was a circle in the sand. It had perfect symmetry. The coral had found nothing to attach itself to. The wheel was golden and pristine. It looked like it had 3500 years ago because coral cannot grow on polished, non-porous metal.

It was a six-spoke, perfectly intact gold-plated chariot wheel.

Its gold color could be clearly identified. He snapped pictures furiously. It had to be a general's chariot wheel or, perhaps, Pharaoh's himself. He clicked away and momentarily contemplated hauling it up. He tried moving it. Nothing. The buried half of the wheel would require a force beyond men. The pictures would have to suffice. The scientist in him wanted to dig it out of the silt and bring it to the surface but the part of his brain that wanted to stay alive told him no. Besides, they were almost out of air.

They had what they came for. It was time for the fishermen to exit.

A 28-foot boat running at 30 mph would require only two hours of wide-open throttle to make it to Eilat. Karlstrom ordered Mahrous to idle the boat back to Eilat. He wanted to get there well after a darkness which was still seven hours away.

Physically exhausted, Arne was super-charged with adrenaline. He shouted at Ewald above the roar of the engine. "Are we fools for not going back for the chariot wheel?"

"Not funny," said the Brit. "That wheel would be our death sentence. We can always come back. We marked the spot with GPS. Besides, pictures don't lie. What I want to know is what's off the ridge," shouted Ewald. "Figure the tide was rolling in or rolling out that day - the day of the crossing. There must be huge piles of artifacts in the deep. You have to assume that over the centuries most of Pharaoh's army fell off one side of the ridge, down to the deep. The stuff way on the bottom, two-three thousand feet down would be petrified, not coralized. It won't be like looking at a 'Where's Waldo' puzzle. It would be like it happened yesterday."

Ewald, Arne knew, was a Christian in name only. He had been raised Episcopalian but hadn't set foot in a church since his wedding. Arne wondered about the gears that had to be turning in the British diver's head. Ewald would be a microcosm of what most of the world would have to reconcile if the evidence they had discovered became widely known.

If.

To be heard, they shouted at each other but soon gave up. They couldn't compete with the rumble and growl of 16 cylinders. When it became apparent that the noise was not going to allow for a conversation Arne sat down and propped his head against the gunwale, a life jacket serving as a pillow. There would be time to talk later. The gentle vibration of the twin 350-cubic-inch engines soon put him to sleep.

Between his sleep and the drone of the engines he never heard the cell phone ringing in his backpack.

CHAPTER SIXTEEN
Dog in a dumpster

As she rose from her sleep in her secret Chinese bunker, her bunny hole, she was alone. Billy had arisen two hours earlier and quietly padded out of their nest. She pretended not to hear him leave. She woke up feeling vulnerable. She realized if ever she were being set up for elimination, this would be the perfect time. Why was she there? Was she being set up? She had been assigned to show Brian Vandervoort the complex and she did. She escorted Tanner's chief of staff and described the full operation, explaining the Jerusalem deception as thoroughly as she could. The Belgian was impressed with the plan - and equally impressed with the daring cleavage Claudia exhibited for, what seemed, his personal viewing pleasure. Pointing to the varied parts of the compound, she would inhale, dip her shoulder and turn her head just enough to allow the Belgian a secret, unfettered glance down the front of her blouse. She could feel the level of his arousal rise with each secret peek.

When it came to trashiness, Claudia Colgate had few peers.

Then, Billy sent her back to the bunny hole.

She took the elevator to the den and fumed. Her assignment at Yulin was, apparently, to tour and tease. She was a relief pitcher, coming in to face one batter before being pulled and sent to the showers. She wondered more and more about Billy's treacherousness. Could he be so cold and calculating that he could eliminate the one person he had trusted with his political secrets for so many years?

What Billy Kim didn't know was that Claudia Colgate had prepared for the possibility of her own elimination. At Yulin, in 2016, she had been brought in as a designing consultant for upgrades being made on the complex. She had helped draw the blueprints for the Yulin upgrades. In the design, she had left herself an 'out.' With Billy Kim, she knew there always had to be a 'just in case.'

Her initial and lasting impression of the complex had always been that it would be the perfect place to send someone for a final processing. She was no fool. She had always counted herself as a potential processee.

She arose from her bed and looked at herself in the mirror. At age 43 she began to notice gravity taking a toll. Her breasts had lost some of their perkiness. Her face had grown wider. Her rear flank was in constant need of toning. Her tummy maintained a few extra pounds. MTV had cracked jokes about her weight a few years back. She fought back. Through the miracle of cosmetic surgery, she lost 10 years and 15 pounds with the stroke of a scalpel. But, even the surgical arts couldn't hold gravity in check forever

There was little she could do to reduce her dread while sitting in her bunny hole. Underground and alone, she was reduced to ruminating and reflecting on her littered path to fame and recognition.

She had begun her publicized route to international notoriety as Billy Kim's advisor in 2008 when he first ran for congress in California's 18th district. She wrote some powerful editorial commentary on behalf of Kim's vision for socialized medicine. Then, she made herself and her ample cleavage available to the promising lawmaker. Billy took an interest in the comely physician and asked her out for a date. Her idea of a date was not exactly what he expected, but precisely what the sexually inexperienced Billy Kim craved. They stayed naked, drunk and stoned, never leaving her apartment for three days.

It was, by any measure, a memorable first date.

When it was time for Billy to get back to the campaign trail she had a simple message for him: "Whenever you want it, wherever you want it, whatever flavor you want it."

Billy didn't think twice. She took away all of his social awkwardness and began their relationship from a sexual assumption. She was attractive, intelligent and sexually adventurous. Forget courting. Forget romance. Forget the baggage of unmet expectations. She gave it all to him on a platter and gave it to him on demand. It wasn't love but it was an adequate substitute. He was like a dog stuck in a restaurant dumpster - compelled to escape, but why?

As she sat on the edge of her bed in her super-secret subterranean Chinese bedroom, she wondered if it had been worth it. She wondered why her dreams had turned so dark and foreboding. She reached in her cosmetic case and pulled out a syringe and a vial. She knew Billy's modus operandi. She didn't know if she was being set up to be killed, but she knew how to play defense. She inserted the needle into the vial and withdrew a syringe full of a potent counter to Billy's preferred method of silence, potassium trichlorite.

Purposely, she walked over to the nightstand and put the needle in the drawer, covering it with some Kleenex. She considered, briefly, whether her imagination was misguided, the truth being that Billy loved her and cherished their partnership and would never consider removing her from the picture. But, she also considered the potentially fatal price of being wrong.

Outside her underground lair lay the secret Chinese complex. It was 16 square miles on the surface, surrounded by piano wire fences and armed guards. Most of the complex was underground, within which lay the sleeping quarters, the exercise rooms, the gyms, the kitchen, the classrooms, the make-up, video and stage areas. American satellite photos had defined the complex as an area of interest as far back as the 1950's, but no one in the intelligence community had ever discovered what it was. It was the Chinese equivalent of Area 51, the American desert complex that had aroused so much suspicion and speculation over the decades. A solitary dirt road led into the complex. It was cordoned off by fences and off-limits for any travel. Twice each month COMSAT intelligence would record that a truck would go into the complex and then would leave. Above ground there was nothing happening of note. There were sleeping quarters, what appeared to be a main administration building and some guard houses. It was, in a word, unremarkable.

But of late there had been curious activity at the complex. A convoy of SUV's and camo school buses had been photographed by American intelligence sources entering the compound. It was interesting, but COMSAT could conclude nothing. Had they known that their own US President, Billy Kim, was visiting the secret Chinese complex, it might have generated some attention. Kim knew they would be taking pictures from 200 miles in the air. He took precautions, dressing in a Chinese work outfit and wearing a hat. All that American intelligence was aware of was that their president was somewhere in China on a trade mission – with his own hand-picked detail of Secret Service agents. As far as anyone knew, he was rubbing elbows with a Chinese trade delegation.

What American intelligence didn't know was everything that was contained in the brain of Claudia Colgate and Billy Kim. Only they held all the puzzle pieces. Claudia considered the depth of her knowledge and a sense of dread washed over her. Billy was devious. Claudia knew a lot about the man, but was smart enough to know she didn't know everything.

The elevator whirred to life. There was a knock at Claudia's door and Billy Kim's chief of security stood waiting. "The President would like to see you in 10 minutes."

Claudia Colgate's mind clicked. Billy wouldn't send his lead goon to relay such a trivial message. She drew a quick assumption - the security chief had been sent to confirm she was where she was supposed to be. Her survival instincts kicked in. She knew enough now to become defensive. She had an exit strategy, but needed to know, definitively, if she was being set up. Her heart palpitated and she found herself short of breath. Was this it? To make certain, she loosened up her robe and let it hang open. The security man's eyes couldn't avoid what gravity and circumstance were allowing his eyes to feast on.

"10 minutes?" Claudia said seductively, hoping her inner panic wasn't bubbling to the surface. "Do you know what most men can do in 10 minutes?"

The security man almost took the bait. His primal reflexes almost led him through temptation's door. But, he fought his instincts. He closed his eyes and took a deep breath. He turned on his heels. "The president will be waiting."

It wasn't easy for him, she knew. Under normal circumstances he would have been on her like a crow on a June bug. The security man had wanted her for a long time. She knew men and their weaknesses. She had made a career understanding the primitive male.

At that moment, she knew she was being set up. She wondered if a troupe of security men would storm her apartment, inject her with potassium trichlorite and then lock her inside. That would have been textbook Billy Kim. After that, he could stage whatever accident suited the media's curiosity. She stood for a moment, waiting for the sounds of the elevator to disappear up the shaft.

She retreated back into her apartment and picked up the syringe. Her ears were alert. If she heard the hit squad coming to her door she would jam the needle in her thigh and prepare her system for the potassium trichlorite.

Without warning, a dead-bolt lock electronically triggered into the jamb of her fireproof steel door. Claudia tugged hard at the door handle and began screaming. She was locked in.

"Billy Kim, you can't do this to me!!! You think you can get away with this? I have friends with influence, too!!!"

She was acting. While she was throwing what was supposed to be her death tantrum she had moved into the bathroom and lifted a handle on the shower head. It exposed a key pad. She depressed four numbers on the keypad. A large door opened in the wall of the shower. As she disappeared down a ladder. She began mumbling to herself.

"You forget Billy Boy. I made you what you are. I know you can't be trusted. Remember, I helped design this place. Think I didn't see this day coming?

Think I didn't build in an escape plan? I thought you were gonna drug me like the others. Even had the antidote. But, Billy boy, you surprised me."

As she disappeared down into the shower wall, she grabbed a backpack she had placed on a hook inside and had replenished with every visit to the bunny hole for almost a decade. She clicked on the flashlight as she made one more plaintive plea for whoever might be listening from the outside.

"Billy, I still love you…" she said, feigning tears. She was presuming there would be a camera or, at least, a microphone hidden somewhere outside the bathroom to record her actions. She disappeared quietly down the ladder and into a tunnel which led 25 yards to a brick wall upon which a control panel allowed her to open a door in the wall as well as override the motion detectors in a four-mile quadrant around the Yulin complex. Her design had considered all the obstacles. Her last act before heading into the brush was to jam a nine millimeter clip into her pistol. It would be a long trek through the wilderness, but she was prepared. She hit the ground running.

She had barely gone 50 yards when a powerful burst of air, heat and sound knocked her off her feet. From her secret exit door she saw a wall of flames shoot forward. The explosion was supposed to be for her. She smiled. Billy would safely presume she was dead.

Above ground, Billy Kim waited for his security man to return. The controlled explosion was no surprise to Billy or any of his team. They weren't told what the explosion was other than to say it was planned and not to pay any attention to it. When the security man had appeared from his verification of Claudia's presence in the underground quarters, he nodded at the president and touched his nose with his index finger. The deed had been done. Billy Kim smiled slightly and nodded to his explosives officer. Billy Kim was free from his nagging wife. He was beginning to feel even more upbeat about the operation. He looked down the row of school buses and turned to his chief of staff.

"I just have to check it one more time," he said as he bounded to the middle of three school buses and stepped aboard.

It was an odd mix on the bus. There were mostly Middle Easterners, but there was an eclectic group of people on the bus. They sat rigidly in their seats, none of them speaking. They were all dressed in gray sweat suits. Billy Kim spotted the man he was looking for. The man looked like Jesus. Kim walked up to his aisle and seated himself next to the man.

"Who are you?" the president asked.

"Who do people say that I am?"

"Are you the Christ?"

"So it is."

"Don't you know that I have the power to crucify you?"

"You would have no power at all if it were not given by the Father."

Billy Kim smiled as he came off the bus. He shook hands with three men in lab coats and patted them on their backs.

"What we have is good. Very good."

"And, what about me? Am I good? Very good?" The voice came from behind Billy Kim.

It was Claudia Colgate.

She was dressed in a low-cut evening gown designed to buckle the knees of mortal men. Billy looked her up and down and smiled.

"We'll be in the last car," he said to the group. "Miss Colgate and I have to become acquainted...again."

The caravan had made it almost two miles down the road before the explosions occurred, obliterating the complex. Against the Chinese sky a huge fireball erupted. An American satellite captured it on video but the humans analyzing it could draw no conclusions.

The President of the United States looked over his shoulder at the distant fire and turned to his mate. "Your twin sister is silenced now. Now it's just you and me."

"I wish I could have gotten to know her. She could have told me so much about you."

"I know. That was her problem, my dear," he said as he raised her hand to his lips and kissed it.

"I don't have that problem, do I?"

"No. Which is why you're here and she's...there," he said, motioning to the fireball in the distance.

CHAPTER SEVENTEEN
The bite after the bark

Hans Tanner had 11 countries to soothe. As the first President of the European Union he was constitutionally bound to try to mold 11 cats and dogs into one political body. When possible, he tried to ply his influence in the dark. There were agenda items that needed to be crafted behind the scenes. As chief executive of the land, Tanner was supposed to be one-third of the balance of power, with the judiciary holding a third and the House and Senate holding the other third. It was an American model. In theory.

In a close election, Hans Tanner might have felt a little fearful about political reprisals, but he had won the general election with 74% of the vote - such was his magnetic appeal for conquering AIDS. He was more king than president. He preferred being king. Kings had longer tenure. He was already considering how to defeat the 'two-term' policy lawmakers had built into their constitution.

The EU was composed of 11 former sovereign countries that were democratic bodies by definition, but socialist countries in practice. Tanner's job was to cobble together a coalition of disparate interests into a "democracy" without diminishing the size or scope of the bureaucracies. The unions who propelled him to the presidency demanded no less. Packaging Europe as a democracy was a matter of public relations, a gentle twist of the language and a liberal application of political payback.

Tanner had commanded his cabinet to Brussels for a late meeting. It was not an official meeting. The press knew nothing about it. They had been assembled not to debate the issues of the day but, rather, to get their marching orders. The cabinet members Tanner had selected were political operatives and cronies he had curried favor with over the years. They were selected not so much for their wisdom, intelligence or insight. They held comfortable government positions primarily because they didn't have to be told how to follow an order.

Tanner's chief of staff, Brian Vandervoort, led off the meeting.

"Mr. President, according to the most recent polling data, your idea for a 10-cent per liter gas tax isn't gaining traction. The voters see a ripple effect across the economy that will drive up the cost of everything. They might be willing to accept it if it were tied to something universal, say prescription drugs or health care, or pensions. But, as a stand-alone tax for the sake of raising revenue, they're taking their cues from the Americans. According to our research there is a growing cynicism that taxes are choking small business."

Brian Vondervoort was a faithful chief of staff and the one person Tanner could count on to tell him the truth when others would be willing to tell him only what they thought he wanted to hear. Vondervoort was no fool. In the very construction of his analysis he had given Tanner the ammunition the European president needed to propose his next course of action. Tanner knew he could count on Vondervoort to set his table for him. It was why he had chosen the Belgian to be his chief of staff.

Tanner paused before his department heads and considered carefully what to say.

"Belguim, Spain, Portugal and Britain have refused to get on board with our gas tax. Fine. Let us propose a travel tax. All flights beginning or ending in Europe will be assessed a fee. We can negotiate the amount. The poor won't complain. They don't, as a rule, travel much anyway. We will say it is a fee specifically designed to help offset the cost of TAP. Let us see how willing they are to flirt with liver failure. TAP, after all, has been offered as a free benefit to the citizens of the European Union. In our constitution there is no provision for TAP. It's only our benevolence that is giving it to them for free. We'll surround the travel tax initiative with a public relations campaign and public awareness campaign designed to show the average European that the benefits of TAP are not a right…but a responsibility - that every patriotic European has a responsibility to see to it all of our brothers and sisters receive this free benefit - that not one child should be denied the right to a full, healthy life. American teacher's unions have used that kind of coercion successfully for decades."

He paused to let the idea sink in.

"And if any country disagrees with the tax, then we shall have to severely limit their access to TAP." It seemed like an afterthought but everyone recognized it as the bite after the bark.

His staff was silent, each one of them considering the consequence of voicing their objection. Tanner looked around the table with a sobering stare before announcing "we're all on the same page? Good. We will expect you to measure what you say to the press carefully."

Then he shifted gears.

"In the near future I will be called to speak at the dedication of the Israeli temple. I wanted to give you all a heads-up on what not to say. Some things may appear troubling on the surface but I wanted to take this time to give you ever assurance that nothing you will see will be a surprise. The reason I mention this at all is because the press may well be seeking you out for comment. Rather than say something that might come back to bite you I will give you a simple warning: Don't speculate. Try to view everything as a citizen. Don't try to interpret the meaning and don't tell any reporter what you might think. What you think has no bearing at all on a larger picture from which we will all ultimately benefit. As a matter of fact, the temple dedication would be a good time for you to be on holiday. Ideally, it would be nice if none of you were available for comment at all."

Tanner took the moment to look each and every one of the cabinet members in the eye directly.

"And it goes without saying that what I have just told you never happened. If it turns out that one of you feels compelled to talk to the press out of school it will be dealt with for precisely what it is. And what is that, Brian?"

"Sedition, sir," responded the chief of staff.

"That is all," said the president, motioning with a deft hand, toward the door.

Without discussion, the room cleared. The cabinet members, if they had any concerns, were smart enough to stay silent. They lived in opulent circumstances and knew the quickest way to go from the top of the mountain to the valley below was to speak without thinking - or, to speak at all.

When the room had cleared, Vandervoort remained behind for his personal instructions from the boss.

Tanner said, "I'll want to speak individually to the Minister of Public Affairs, the Minister of Education and the house and senate leaders. Schedule them all separately. We'll wine them and dine them. That's your job."

Vondervoort eyed his president with admiration. The Belgian performed a cursory glance around the room to make sure they were alone, stepped back and gave Tanner a Third Reich salute, right arm extended. Tanner shook his head at his chief as if to admonish him.

"Not here. Not now."

CHAPTER EIGHTEEN
Unlock the safety

Ben Kowalski picked up the phone. It was a call he didn't want to make, but was being compelled to as a father. Slowly and deliberately he dialed. His son, Jake, sat in the chair on the other side of the big oak desk. Jake was 14 and had lived with his mother for almost five years. That was about to change. Jake had a fat lip and a swollen eye.

The phone rang three times before a sleepy female voice picked it up

"Ellen? This is Ben. Jake's over at my place. He's going to stay here for a while. He walked here at four in the morning. Three miles in the dark."

There was a long pause on the other end.

"Ben, is Jake all right?"

"He's OK, I think. He's got a fat lip and a shiner."

"Yeah, he fell."

"Yeah," Ben said with a huff. "He told me."

Ben's ears were wide open. He could hear Ellen fighting her way from sleep into consciousness and he was straining to hear if perhaps there was a male in the bed beside her. He could hear her rise, no doubt rubbing her eyes and looking at the clock.

Nothing.

"Well," she said, "maybe it's a good idea for you to have him for a couple of days. Maybe longer. This book tour has been running me ragged. My publicist is always scheduling me here and there and - "

Ben cut her off. He had had enough.

"In case last night was a total blackout Ellen, you have to remember throwing Jake into the bookshelf. You do remember that, don't you Ellen? Jake says you've been having some parties lately. Says that they get a little loud – a little out of hand."

"Ben, they're all book people. You've done books."

"I don't do those kind of books and I don't hang out with those kind of people," Ben interjected.

Ellen paused. The dig he slid in was meant to cut. She shrugged it off.

"The boy and I had a little shoving match. I guess he slipped."

"That's not the way it was told to me."

"Well, you know...kids can embellish."

"Jake is quite the inventive kid, Ellen. I guess he saw this day coming. He figured out a way to put a camera into the fireplace mantle."

There was silence from Ellen's phone.

"He brought over some interesting videos of your book parties. If I didn't know better, Ellen, I'd swear that the video shows you smoking dope and snorting cocaine with a lot of rowdy people. These kind of videos can be very damaging in custody cases."

There was a palpable silence. Ellen was seething. "You can't take Jake away from me, Ben. You have no right."

"Oh, but Ellen I do have a right. You're going to have to figure out a way to get yourself some help. I can't do it for you. You don't trust me anymore." His own voice began to falter as he considered what to say next. "And, given your book, I'm not sure I can trust you. I'm not going to try to reason with you on this because the bottom line is crystal clear. Jake is not going to stay in that house one more day and there isn't an attorney in the land that can undo what this video shows. I'm sorry."

He couldn't believe he was apologizing. He hadn't done anything wrong. He hadn't told lies. He wasn't experimenting with chemicals. Still, he was saying 'I'm sorry.'

He considered saying something rational but before he could, he softly confessed to her: "I still love you. We could make it work again, but not until you get things straightened out. I can help get you connected with some people."

If he would have had a pistol in his belt he would have pulled it out, unlocked the safety and blown out his brains at that very moment. He regretted the words he had said as they left his lips

"Whatever you say, Cowboy."

She hung up.

CHAPTER NINETEEN
Gambling

Mahrous al-Sharif was a dedicated hired hand who kept his hand at the helm and the engine humming at a constant 15 knots. He kept his eye fixed on the horizon and would have done so without objection for five hours until they reached Eilat. But, he had to pee.

He throttled the engine down to an idle, slipped it into neutral, waiting for the wake to crest behind them before descending the ladder down to the on-board chemical toilet.

Arne Karlstrom's inner compass detected the loss of motion and engine sound, signaling his brain to wake. In his half-sleep he thought he heard the phone ringing on his bedstand. It was his cell phone and it was in his backpack. He suddenly realized he was in the Gulf of Aqaba and not in his suburban Stockholm tudor. He scrambled to his feet. It had to be important because the only ones with the number were at the Kowalski compound.

"Arne Karlstrom!" he answered desperately, putting one finger in his ear to drown out the rumble of the engines.

"Arne, thank God. This is Amanti. Our mole tells us you have two Egyptian naval vessels headed your way. He intercepted their radio. They're looking specifically for your boat. Left Eilat an hour ago. Figure they're making about 20 knots. By your GPS location, they should be on you in the next hour. Don't know their business but it can't be good. You copy?"

"We copy. You sure they're Egyptian?"

"Positive. Two cruiser-crafts. Six crew members each. Armed. Our mole is reliable. Suggest you find a hole to crawl into on the Saudi side. They can't follow you inland if you're found."

"We copy." Arne said.

"Arne," Amanti asked, "you're not carrying any sort of booty, are you? If you are, toss it. Mark the spot if you have to, but toss it."

"Negative. Just pictures and I'm not going to pitch them. It's why we came here. They'll have to catch us first."

"Oh, Arne, if you go inland, into Saudi Arabia, make sure you take the GPS and phone batteries with you, otherwise we're going to lose you in the wilderness."

"Right. Thanks. Pray for us."

"Likewise. Keep us posted. We can't help if we don't know where you are. Don't leave us hanging," said Amanti as he hung up.

Arne pushed himself up on the gunwale. "Mahrous, why have we stopped?"

"I'm in the head. I had to go." He stepped from the toilet, zipping up. "What happened?"

"Trouble! Two Egyptian gun boats are after us." He held up his cell phone. It was Amanti. "We have to turn back and buy some time."

Mahrous bounded past Arne to the bridge. Arne followed and pointed up the gulf. "They'll be on us in an hour, tops. We have to kick this boat in the butt and try to find some place to hide."

Ewald stepped up to the bridge, rubbing his eyes. "What's going on? Why did we shut down?"

"The Egyptians!" said Arne, holding up his cell phone for the Brit. "Amanti has a mole in Eilat. Somebody may have figured out what we're up to."

Mahrous threw both throttles to full and spun the boat around to starboard. "We can do 30 knots, tops. I know the Egyptian gun boats. We'll outrun them."

"But, we can't run forever," said Ewald. "They'll catch up and then what?"

"We didn't pull anything up from the bottom," said Arne. "All we have is pictures, but my guess is that if they're taking the time to come after us, then they have a pretty good idea what we're looking for. That means they'll take the pictures from us and let their antiquities experts figure out what we're after."

On the Saudi side of the gulf there were some prominent beaching areas but they were all exposed, out in the wide open. There were no nooks, crannies or backwaters into which a 28-foot twin engine inboard could hide. Arne's guess was that one Egyptian boat would canvas the Saudi side and one boat would cruise down the Egyptian side. If the time-line was correct Arne knew they would eventually have to find a bay, an inlet or a running wadi in which to slip their boat. His first decision was to run away from the Egyptian boats and buy some more time. They turned back where they came from and headed in a 15-degree intercept with the Saudi shore. Then, he had Mahrous open the throttle. The problem with running at 30 knots, though, was that any hidden crevice or cranny in the Saudi shore would just be a blur if they were flying by. He was gambling. He weighed all the pros and cons in his head.

They had no artifacts but they did have film, on which were pictures the sovereign state of Egypt would confiscate and destroy. In that scenario, Karlstrom had every confidence their pictures were doomed from ever being shared with anyone. Then, too, there was the fate of his crew to consider. Infidels with evidence harmful to Islam were probably not going to be driven to the border and kindly told not to come back. Once looked at, the Egyptian antiquities agency would figure out the pictures Arne had taken were meant to provide forensic evidence of Moses and the Hebrew account of the Exodus. It was proof Arne was certain they had been sweeping under the carpet for decades - ever since the technology to put two and two together had made Arne's type of expedition a possibility.

It was the kind of evidence the Islamic world would not exactly embrace.

Another option Arne considered would be to toss the cameras and all the film overboard, simply explaining they had been fishing and diving. Not an option, Arne concluded. He had been financed handsomely to do a job. Throwing the payload overboard was only a life or death decision. Still, like life or death itself, an option.

Or they could ditch their boat and run inland into Saudi Arabia. It was hostile and virtually uninhabitable but they could survive for a time there. Arne figured into his quick equations that the Egyptians would call in their Saudi allies to flush them out. Fuel, too, was now a concern. They had left Eilat with enough fuel for 16 hours running time at full throttle. Their present fuel supply would only allow about five hours of running south before reaching the point of no return. But, return to where? Eilat? If they managed to escape the Egyptians in the gulf there would be Egyptians and Saudis and, perhaps Jordanians and, maybe a few Syrians thrown into the mix just for fun, waiting to intercept them before they could dock in Israel.

How, Arne wondered, had the Egyptians targeted him? Did they know about his quest? How had they learned? That question would have to wait to be answered.

Arne saw a multitude of options in their immediate future. All of them were bleak. Then it occurred to him. Nuweiba! The very beach from which Arne theorized the ancient Hebrews had made their crossing! Modern Nuweiba was an eight-mile beach on whose southern end was a loading port for ferries. It had a man-made bay in it and a road leading out through the same route Moses and the Hebrews had traveled 3500 years ago, or so his hypothesis went. The road led through the Sinai wilderness via the Wadi Watir, an ancient dry river bed, now a two-lane highway that snaked through the mountains. Wadi Watir was regularly traversed by trucks seeking the port at Nuweiba in order to ferry up or down the Gulf of Aqaba. The problem was that the Egyptian cruiser craft(s) would, for sure, look for them in that bay.

When the Egyptians turned into the bay, however, it might provide them with the chance to make a break. It was a game of cat and mouse.

He had Mahrous kill the engine for a minute. He needed to discuss the option with his crew.

They had a stake in it, too.

CHAPTER TWENTY
Sedition

When the sea was calm they liked to surface and breathe un-recirculated air. The diamond amalgam glass bow of the submarine would give Brad Pugh a view of moonlit ocean and sky while he broadcast from his underwater world to a land of grass, concrete and human beings he was no longer a part of. Surfacing was one of the small pleasures Captain Petrov could bring to their solitary life beneath the waves. As Pugh prepared for his broadcast he checked his clock. It was 1:00 A.M. In America it was mid-afternoon. He tried to remember life before he had become nocturnal. It didn't matter. In a submarine, night and day were relative concepts anyway.

Winnie counted down his intro and fired the disc on the broadcast console. He was on the air, in the water.

"Greetings, freedom lovers. Taxes, taxes and more taxes," he bellowed. He wasn't going to waste any time.

"While President Kim is cavorting in China with his commie cronies, his education secretary, Malcolm Dubay, was busy passing talking points to his lackeys in the house and senate. Ladies and gentlemen across America, I am Brad Pugh and I am right!!! I want you to sit down and grab your wallets. We have learned from our sources in London the details of the latest raid on your money. The Kim Administration is planning on announcing a bold new initiative in education. Why education, you ask? Aren't there more pressing needs in the country? Well, yes, but when you talk about education you must remember it's…" he paused for dramatic effect while he turned up the potentiometer on his control panel. He wanted echo. "…FOR THE CHILDREN." It echoed four times before fading into a hiss of white noise.

It was drama. It was theater. It was one of the reasons he was at once the most admired and the most hated man in America. He cut to the chase. He was drama and melodrama, often simultaneously. He wasn't afraid of his critics. He didn't have to be - they couldn't find him.

"The President of the United States will be coming back from his sales conference (did I just say that?) in China and we've learned that he has decided to raid your treasury again. This time he wants...sit down...bend over, grab your ankles and take a deep breath...One point three trillion dollars to federalize all K-12 education." He paused for effect.

"One point three seven seven trillion dollars to be exact. For those of you who might have trouble grasping the figure, that's okay because he doesn't want you to grasp it. He wants you to look into the needy faces of the children. He wants you to feel the pain of the poor inner city kids. He wants you to take it personally. Forget the fact that four years ago they shoveled 300 billion dollars in new spending at K-12 education, bought every low-income kid in the country a laptop computer and relaxed the test requirements. Forget the fact that test scores have gone down in spite of the spending. The problem, as any parent with a five-year-old will tell you, isn't money. The problem is that teachers can't discipline and they can't teach because every special interest in the country has their own version of the truth they want spun into the teaching. History is a great teacher, folks. Why do we ignore it? The National Education Association and their friends in the ACLU have rewritten history so many times it can't be recognized anymore. That's assuming you can keep enough order in the class to teach it in the first place. The lawyers have seen to it that every minority interest in the country has their own special set of rules. And, if you mention the name of G-O-D in the classroom, you'll have a small school bus filled with counselors, lawyers and administrators descend on you like a cloud of locusts."

"And, now they want more. They want a contract with McDonalds and Taco Bell and Pizza Hut in order to feed your kids in the school cafeteria with, you guessed it, subsidized breakfast, lunch and dinner. They want daycare for their young moms and maternity curriculum for moms-to-be. They want free birth-control with no questions asked. And, the crown jewel, of course, is free abortions on demand to correct the damage done when Junior forgets his free condoms at home. They want free medical insurance and day care for every pre-schooler. They want special counselors for every conceivable behavior. Then, they want to unionize everybody - the copy lady, the janitor, the teacher and the school bus driver. Here's a fact...and you don't need a BA from a liberal arts college to understand it: If you can't maintain order and insist on an honest effort, all the computers, counselors or tacos in the world won't keep a kid from falling through the cracks. What everybody knows but no one will say is, the inmates are running the asylum."

"No, you're supposed to forget the facts. The spin Billy Kim and the legions of legislators on his payroll want you to consider is that the problem with the last spending orgy wasn't because it was ill-conceived. No, rather, it was because it only went part of the way. We now learn that the vein we opened for the kids four years ago was the wrong vein. Billy Kim wants to surgically tap right into our aorta and get a nice spurt of cash flowing into his favorite union, um, did I say 'union?' I meant 'cause.' Why? Because when it comes to compassion we can't do enough for..." He hit the echo potentiometer one more time..."THE CHILDREN!!!!!"

He let it echo out into a white hiss.

"Meanwhile, on the other side of the Atlantic, EU President Tanner is hinting that he wants a travel tax to be able to provide free TAP for the citizens of Europe."

"Free education? Free drugs? Everything ought to be free. Yes, Billy Kim is right. In his world everything ought to come to us by government edict. All we have to do is get someone else to pay for it and we can have heaven on earth. It's a con as old as the Garden of Eden. Oops, sorry.... I mentioned that book, didn't I? So, sue me!!! I'll tell ya - it's days like this that I'm glad all of my money is hidden in a foreign account and beyond the greedy fingers of the IRS."

"If you think I'm an angry white seditionist, you're right!"

He took a breath. His mind was shifting gears. "There's another issue being bandied about. In today's New York Times, columnist Everett Haidy examines the Supreme Court's pending ruling on flag burning. Now, those who listen to this show regularly know that I never opposed flag-burning. I always thought that the hippies and the commies and all their affiliated malcontents ought to burn the flag if it offended them because as loathsome as I thought it was, it still fell under the heading of 'political expression.' I always argued, and I gained a lot of critics for my position, they ought to have that right because I could see into the crystal ball a day when they would be in charge and I would want to do it. The problem, of course, is that if I did it to their country they wouldn't jail me, they'd kill me. Double standard? Welcome to the Kim Administration. Welcome to the 21st century in America. Welcome to the Brave New World."

He motioned for Winnie to hit the sounder that announced the commercial break.

"We'll be right back with all your comments and questions from the Internet as well as a disturbing prediction from Reverend Warren Stone, printed today in the Rocky Mountain News, in which he describes an unsettling analysis of security surrounding the upcoming Holy Harvest and the Jewish temple dedication."

Despite the worst spin the Kim Administration could put on Brad Pugh, his numbers kept growing. The Americans tuned in and kept tuning in. His audience was growing at 10% a year. "Almost as quick as the federal government," Pugh was fond of saying.

It was shortly after Kim's botched attempt to nab Brad Pugh that Kim issued an executive order threatening the 900 radio stations who carried Pugh's program. The Kim Administration warned station owners that their licenses would be terminated by the FCC if they insisted on "aiding and abetting" a seditionist. The station owners knew they would be killing their golden goose. They took it to court. Even the Ninth Circuit Court of Appeals, the most notoriously active judicial loony bin in the land, couldn't convolute the constitution far enough to silence Brad Pugh. Though, they tried.

It was under appeal.

CHAPTER TWENTY ONE
Willful ignorance

Phosphorous missiles have one value. They burn. Tipped with multiple warheads, the missiles had slammed into the front edifice of the second floor of the White House in April of 2021. It was in the fourth month of the stumbling, bumbling administration of Marshall Warren's reign of indifference and incompetence. The timing couldn't have been more lethal. Upon impact, the missiles each shot their fiery payload in 16 different directions. Their white-hot ordnance ripped through the bowels of the building, initiating 32 fierce, localized fires. The effect was immediate. Within three minutes the building was fully engaged in flames.

The Saudi assassins had assembled their one-man helicopters overnight and had blocked off the ramp's upper level. Their helipad was cleared for takeoff.

The Saudi brothers were in Washington as part of a UN attaché. They had been stopped by DC police earlier in the week for a traffic violation, but nothing was done. Both had outstanding bench warrants for a variety of unpaid misdemeanors but no action had ever been taken because immigrants - legal or otherwise, had diplomatic immunity in the nation's capital.

Their choppers were specially designed crafts that could be assembled by two men, an electric winch and a little training. Upon takeoff, the Saudi brothers were close enough to the White House that they emerged, quite literally, from out of nowhere, delivering their payload before any alarms sounded. They didn't waste any time finishing their deed. They suspended, momentarily, outside the security gate for just a second before simultaneously exploding themselves and their single-purpose aircrafts in a blazing cascade of hot metal and panic.

When the smoke had cleared and the final body count tallied, 168 people, including Colonel Adam Norton, the Vice President of the United States, had been consumed before they could find an exit.

Incinerating the White House was as much psychological as tactical. The image of America's house belching smoke and flames was meant to signal an end to an era. At the very least, it was meant to signal an end to Marshall Warren.

In the fog of the moment, images of 9/11 were rekindled in the memories of Americans. The historical blueprint of 9/11 told Americans that they were in for a period of mourning and uncertainty as the impact of the act was put into a perspective. The stock market bottomed. Air travel was suspended.

It had been presumed, in the early moments, that the incompetent, clueless President Marshall Warren had been vaporized in the attack. He hadn't. He had been whisked away just three minutes before the attack in his Marine chopper. He had a date with a showgirl from Vegas at Camp David. He had cleared his calendar and, eager with sexual anticipation, had snuck away before the phosphorous missiles had found their mark.

Almost at the same moment the house majority leader drowned in an Alaskan boating accident. The captain of the congressman's vessel had sent a "Mayday" to the Coast Guard. They were taking on water. Fast. Three days later a navy sub located the craft in 900 feet of water. The six members onboard the fishing vessel were all presumed drowned. No bodies were ever recovered.

Under optimal circumstances, Billy Kim would have stepped into the breech and seized the reins of power. He was fourth in the line of ascension. It was a seamless, perfect plan but it didn't account for President Warren's eager libido. Warren had been scheduled to be in the East Wing in a photo session with the Boy Scouts of America. He had changed his own schedule with his chief of staff that morning, owing to the unexpected availability of his "date" reading her Daytimer wrong. She was cooling her heels in the library at Camp David two hours early!

The photo shoot would have to wait. Marshall Warren had a matter more urgent than the Boy Scouts.

After the attack, Marine One was diverted. Marshall Warren was whisked away under heavy guard to the presidential hanger and put into Air Force One within minutes. With an escort of three F-16's in tow he was flown to Nellis AFB, where they sat on the tarmac for three hours while the president and his security team tried to assess what happened. Marshall Warren handled the crisis in the best way he could. He drank. He didn't want to get off the plane. He feared for what lay outside. Someone had tried to kill him and he didn't know who they were! Alcohol fortified him for a while. Then, it put him to sleep.

Ben and Ellen Kowalski had watched the events unfold from their living room in suburban Minneapolis. Neither spoke much. The pictures told the story. Ben had figured it out from the first moment. He was waiting for the network mouthpieces to echo his assessment. What the network wags didn't say told Ben volumes. They played stupid. They refused to connect the dots.

"It's a coup, stupid!!!" he shouted at his TV. They evidently didn't hear him.

The Internet was ablaze with theories. Talk radio was alight with speculation. Thinking people everywhere knew the story. Thinking people didn't need to be told what the score was. But, then, thinking people didn't rely on the mainstream media for their news. The major dailies and networks reported the facts, but refused to look at the inertia behind the attack. Their willful ignorance at who was behind the events of the day was a signal from the media to their enemies in the thinking community. They were challenging their ideological foes to beat them in a public relations battle – the winner getting to define the parameters of the democracy.

The political right, the patriots within America, responded just the way the secret Kim pollsters said they would. They threw a fit of righteous proportion. They made themselves look like ranting fools. They followed the script perfectly. The Internet, cable TV news and talk radio blared with the cries of indignation at the apparent coup being staged by Billy Kim and his cronies in congress. The mainstream media played it straight. They reported that the torching of the White House had been the product of two demented Saudi twins who were acting out their Islamic fantasies. End of story.

The undecided Americans, the ones more in tune with Hollywood than Washington, followed their own script. They performed precisely as Kim's army of pollsters said they would. They tuned into Sports Center, MTV or went for a long walk while the government rallied their bureaucracies to make certain that everyone got their government checks on time.

When the news of Marshall Warren's narrow escape was made known, the Kim machinery set into motion a backup plan to depose the randy, incompetent president.

President Warren, in the first hours after the attack, had made one on-camera appearance to the nation to calm the national nerves. Then he crawled inside of a bottle of scotch and pondered how warm the scotch made him feel. The press waited for Marshall Warren to reappear, to look brave and presidential. They kept waiting. Warren stayed on Air Force One listening to a lot of military men tell him conflicting theories about who's hand had crept up who's skirt. In spite of their impassioned advice, Marshall Warren knew what he had to do and it had nothing to do with listening to fools on the federal payroll. He went to his private chamber and picked up the phone, asking military clearance to link him up with Ben Kowalski. He needed the advice of the most trusted man in America.

"Ben, this is Marshall Warren. President Marshall Warren?"

Ben Kowalski knew who the President of the United States was. His mind whirred with the possibilities. He and Marshall Warren were on two opposite ends of the political and cultural spectrum. Why would the besieged president be calling him now?

"I know who you are, sir. I read the papers. Well, not anymore. They're the last place anyone would find the facts these days. But, I used to read the papers. You were in there. There was a picture of you, too."

The President didn't laugh. He paused. Ben could tell he was trying to collect his thoughts. What he couldn't see on the other side of the phone was the president pouring three more fingers of scotch into his glass. "Ben, I need your help."

"Sir. I've been on the radio talking to anyone who would listen. Ever since the attack. The press seems to be ignoring the obvious."

"I know. Thank you. We need all the help we can get." The pause was lengthier this time. Ben would have interrupted, but sensed that the pause was more than just drama. "B-Ben," the President said almost chokingly. "If they don't kill me they're going to impeach me."

Ben considered the tone he was hearing from the president. He was sounding like the coward Ben had always suspected him of being.

"Mr. President, you have to put this in perspective. They've put their case before the people. They've pushed the envelope as far as they can. They're not going to murder you now. It would be too obvious, even for them. If they killed you now the papers and the networks couldn't provide the cover. Do you know what I'm saying?"

The president seemed reassured by Ben's words. A detached, purely objective political assessment was what Warren ached to hear at that moment. Still, it bothered him. People wanted him dead. Being dead was disconcerting.

"OK, Ben, what if they impeach me?"

"Then you'll be impeached. You won't be dead."

"That's not what I meant. I meant, what about the country?"

"That's a good question. I'd keep the Speaker well protected."

"Ben, no one knows this, officially, but the Speaker is missing. Fishing trip in the Bering Sea. They haven't heard from their boat in over three hours."

If there were any doubt about a Kim overthrow of the presidency it was erased in that moment.

"Well, Mr. President, it appears Mr. Kim wants your job and he's banking on Americans not to connect the dots. What do you think of his chances?"

"I'm not sure. I don't listen to a lot of the crap they say about the American people. Truth be known, I couldn't tell you what the American people think. Winning the presidency was never part of the script, you know. What I want to know is who is pulling Billy Kim's strings. He couldn't have pulled this whole thing off without some help – outside help."

"Okay, Mr. President. We're in agreement. Billy Kim is not a nice person. How are you going to stop him?"

"I thought you could help."

Ben stopped. He had no clue where the president was leading. "What do you want me to do? Slip him a Mickey? Give him a ticket?"

"If they do impeach me…"

"Mr. President, they will impeach you. I don't know on what grounds, but Billy Kim has a lot of friends in congress and more friends in the press. You're outnumbered. You are the Independence Party. You have no allies. They'll trump up a charge. It doesn't matter. If enough of them want you out, you're out. It's apparent they want to try. It's also apparent to me you don't have the political capital to survive."

The president was being talked to in a fashion he wasn't used to. He was being told the truth. Ben Kowalski wasn't a reporter or an advisor with a selfish analysis. He knew the score without a lot of high-priced analysis. Marshall Warren appreciated the candor. He had been fed a steady diet of conflicting manure from his own people. Ben was the first person validating what the besieged president was feeling inside.

"Listen to me for a second, Ben. It's important you hear what I'm saying. You're right. They are going to impeach me. The constitution says in that case the vice president will take my place, but my vice president is quite dead. And, the Speaker is lost at sea. Now, by law, I'm supposed to nominate a vice president and have him approved by congress, but Billy Kim owns congress. No one will survive the nominating process. And, he owns the press. The country is being set up for something it never bargained for."

Ben wanted to interrupt and say that the country had never bargained for a Warren presidency, but stopped. The insult would have felt good personally, but it would have served no practical purpose. His personal dislike for the president didn't matter.

"Ben," the president began with a long sigh, but stopped. Ben could hear the sound of the president swallowing. His antenna elevated. The president had seemed unusually disjointed in his thinking, given the gravity of events. Ben made a snap judgment that the president had been drinking and that if he wasn't drunk, he was getting close to being drunk.

"Ben, Ben, Ben," the president began, as if lecturing his kid brother. "I've been a critic of yours for a long time. I don't like your politics, but I don't dislike you as a man. I was reading the story on you in Newsweek. Have you read it?"

"No," Ben shot back. "I don't trust them. If you'll notice, everything they quoted me on was from my books and lectures. I told them I didn't want the story run."

"They wrote a pretty glowing picture of you. Christian, ethical – a fallen sinner who has spent a career repenting and confessing and preaching the lessons you've learned. You're a real saint, according to Newsweek."

"Consider the source."

"Still, they're willing to pronounce you as the most trusted man in America."

"Why are you calling, Mr. President? To talk about what Newsweek thinks of me? I would think you've got bigger fish to fry."

"Yeah, I do. I want to stop Billy Kim. We ran down a list of vice presidential contenders - senators, congressmen, governors - even some big-city mayors. The problem is that they're all politicians. They've all made public comments that would kill them in the nominating process. If I'm going to get a vice president confirmed he has to be bullet-proof. And, he can't have worked in, or near, anything close to the 202 Area Code. And, he has to have the name recognition and integrity the majority of the people can put their trust in."

"Me?"

"Bingo. Your sins have been part of the public record for 20 years. You've written books about your failings. You've made yourself a target for condemnation from your higher being. There's nothing they can crucify you with that you haven't crucified yourself with already."

Ben felt compelled to correct the president on the spot. "He is not my higher being. He is my God. He's yours, too. You ought to try to get to know him. He's not hiding. You could talk to him now. Want me to dial him up for you?"

At that moment Marshall Warren really didn't like Ben Kowalski. At the core of everything Ben had said or written in 20 years there was always God. Marshall Warren could deal with politicians. They were self-serving and predictable in their dual allegiances. People like Ben were one-dimensional. They were boring. And confident. And judgmental. And, Warren just didn't like men whose convictions didn't leave some wiggle room for paybacks or other gentle reconsiderations.

"Well, Mr. Kowalski? Your God is calling. You going to listen, or you gonna put your tail between your legs and let the country down?"

Ben knew the president was drunk now. Sober men don't close a sale by implying the customer is a chicken. It was a barroom poke in the chest that Kowalski ignored.

"You know they'll find a way to impeach me, too. That is, if I survive the nominating process.

"Yeah. I know that. Maybe you can get a vice president confirmed, then. We'll buy time. That's all we're left to do. See if we can run the clock out. Doing nothing is giving up. You know who gives up, Kowalski? Quitters."

There was the finger in the chest again.

Kowalski swallowed. He hated drunks. He knew them well. He knew their rationalizations. He wished the technology existed to reach through the phone and break the man's nose. He closed his eyes and let the rage pass. He tried to guess why God had placed him at the busy intersection of history and insanity.

Ben took a deep breath before speaking. "Two things, Mr. President. First, I'll do it."

"Good. Secondly?"

"When all of this is over, I'd really like to kick your ass, sir."

"Good. We're on the same page."

Ben Kowalski survived the nominating process only because every citizen who saw the clear duplicity of the conspiracy marched on the offices of their elected officials to demonstrate in person. The New York Times tried to play it down, but when the nominating vote came down in congress there were close to 600,000 people on the mall in Washington making sure their lawmakers got the vote right. If they didn't, there was over half a million people, more than half of them openly and defiantly carrying sidearms, ready to express their inalienable rights in a cowboy showdown on the capitol steps. No one in congress seemed willing to call their bluff.

Congress would have to wait to pick their moment.

Ben's vice presidency lasted 16 days. On a Thursday, Marshall Warren was asked to vacate the Oval Office by his landlords in the senate. The last Ben saw of the Marshall Warren, he was boarding Marine One and bound for Hawaii. In their last conversation, they spoke little. Marshall was drunk and combative and Ben didn't want to deal with him.

"It's all yours now, Kowalski. Try not to turn it into a church, OK?"

Kowalski wanted to cold-cock the drunken fool.

Sitting in the seat of power, Ben Kowalski had no political baggage. Assuming the presidency was a seamless act for Ben because he knew it was temporary. Besides, he wasn't a politician. He didn't take himself seriously. He had some things he wanted to do under the radar of congress, but that was a matter he kept to himself. He knew the woods were full of bears. The same political snipers who had removed Marshall Warren were still on the payroll of Billy Kim, or whoever was bankrolling the grand American coup.

In the end, Marshall Warren had been impeached for being a bad manager. Congress argued that he should have been more diligent in guaranteeing that the Saudi twins would not incinerate the White House. The impeachment team argued that it had been Marshall Warren's personal lack of attention to detail that had allowed the Saudi zealots access to White House air space. The irony, Ben knew, was that if Warren had died in the attack, they would have mourned him as a courageous American hero. In the finaly analysis, Marshall Warren was impeached for the act of being just lucky enough to have survived an act of attempted murder.

Ben didn't dwell on it. He chose to live in the moment. He was President of the United States. He was going to try to extract something good out of the experience before he was dispatched by the senate. But, Ben Kowalski was no fool. Assassination was a very clear possibility. He stayed close to home, behind the fences of the Old Executive Office Building; an aging complex that had been converted to serve, temporarily, as the White House while a new one was built. Ben was now a target and he didn't need the New York Times to tell him he had a lot of enemies – though they did, with frequency. Public appearances could be lethal. He didn't know who his friends were, other than a cadre of Secret Service agents who had met with him, prayed, and pledged their lives to keep him from misfortune. He kept them close at hand.

Ben had many one-on-one meetings with members of the press but he only had one official press conference during his brief tenure. During the press conference, he didn't talk about one policy issue. Instead, he admitted his youthful failings - his boozing, his womanizing and the rationalizations he constructed to keep himself insulated from the truth. He ignored the economy. He ignored Iraq, Iran and North Korea. He ignored the attack. He shunned discussion of cabinet appointments. They didn't matter. The undeclared war none dared report was the war between Ben Kowalski and the press. His press conference was conducted in a den of vipers, so Kowalski did the best he could not to let them spew their lethal venom. They had been sent, though it would never be admitted, to assassinate Ben Kowalski's character. Ben refused to give them the bullets. He preached. He took 20 years of speeches, sermons and observations and spoke of faith and history and character and moral, spiritual and legal obligations.

The next day, the headlines proclaimed Ben Kowalski to be a religious zealot. Not too bad, thought Ben. The only target the press could zero in on with Kowalski was his faith. It didn't bother Ben. He had learned from Scripture that his belief would make him a target. He accepted being labeled as a religious 'extremist.' He considered it a badge of honor. He wore their labels and let their snide commentary roll off his back. He always had.

"Do you think, Mr. President, that your history as a devout Christian will be an impediment as you try to deal with different religious groups," one lady ABC correspondent asked.

Ben bit his lip.

"Which religious groups are you talking about?"

"None, specifically, sir. I'm speaking generically. Are there certain religious groups for whom your personal faith might present obstacles to an open and frank discussion?"

"Yes. Druids. Hate 'em. They're dirty and filthy and pernicious. They eat their young, you know." Ben smiled at the reporter.

"Seriously, sir," she said from behind a stone cold edifice.

"What's the matter with you?" he asked of the reporter. "Do you only see the world through dark glasses? You just asked me if I'm a bigot. That's not what you said, but it's what you meant. You meant to imply that I am so blinded by my own faith that I'm incapable of making sound, rational decisions on behalf of the American people. You, young lady, have to lighten up. You need to get a sense of humor. All of you do. I've never been around a more somber group of people. While you're all here, let's just have a funeral. All we need is a corpse. Any volunteers? Maybe I could get one of the Secret Service to get me a fresh kill. How about you?" he said, pointing at a Reuters scribe. "That might make a good lead story for you, eh? Criminy, I scheduled this press conference so you folks could ask real questions and what do I get? – psychoanalysis."

"Sir, you've got to admit that your faith makes a lot of people nervous. They just don't see how someone can make decisions on their behalf if they owe something to a higher power..."

Ben cut her off. "Listen, I'm going to level with you, okay? You folks in the press don't like me because I'm a Christian but you know what? – you're not going to change that. Here's what you have to learn: Being a Christian is not a bad thing. It's a good thing. You really ought to try it. It might give you something you don't have now – perspective! You think because I'm a follower of Jesus Christ that I see right and wrong in a biblical context? Well, you're right! My faith does color my judgment. It is the key component of who I am – and guess what? – that's good! You ought to see the world with a sense of gratitude for your many blessings. Really! This notion that we're all just highly evolved pond scum is tragic. Without a sense of Creation and wonder and awe all you're left with is suffering. Is that it? Are you all suffering? You need to step out from under your own dark clouds for a while. I mean, you look at a rose and all you see are the thorns. The Christian in me says I should forgive all of you for being so myopic, but my human side says I ought to turn around, drop my drawers and moon every last one of you and I would - if there weren't so many cameras here."

Ben smiled and nodded to the lady reporter. She was sweating. "I hope I answered your question."

Another scribe, a CNN reporter felt compelled to ease the tension in the room. He took the moment to pose his own question for the president.

"Sir, I know you're being ironic."

"Irony? I thought that was sarcasm. I thought it was humor, but none of you laughed. Must have hit too close to home."

"Yes, sir," the CNN reporter said, feigning laughter. "Very funny. But, what the American people have expressed in the most recent Rasmussen poll is their concern that most of America believes Christians have surrendered to the notion of Armageddon. Do you think that's an accurate assessment?"

"Ah," Ben said. "Christian fatalism. Christians are just waiting for the end, praying and passing the collection plate while we wait for the Second Coming. Is that it?"

"Well, sir, the polls seem to indicate..."

"Yeah, well polls are orchestrated dishonesty to reflect what the pollsters want to report. God doesn't do polls. Let me tell you a little secret. We Christians – we do have a secret agenda and I'm confident it will never be reported by anyone in this room because that would require that you actually read the book! Now, since none of you seem to have anything substantive to ask, I've got some important things to take care of," he said. He gave them a cursory salute and spun on his heels.

As he was exiting the room he was heard to say "I wonder what's on TV?"

He was done with them.

He torqued them off. Because of his lack of a registered political pedigree and because he came from a theologically suspicious place, they spoke to him through waxen, frozen smiles while venom leaked out of their pens. Ben knew he would be dog meat the next day.

"Sir, they're not going to report this kindly," his press secretary said afterward.

"Got news for you, Sid. 'Kindly' isn't why they're here. They were looking for an artery they could slice. I just took away their stilettos."

During his brief tenure as president the press treated Ben's faith as an armed bomb. Ben expected nothing less. Kowalski knew they were trying to intellectually defeat his faith, but he was also convinced that that was impossible. He invited them to take their best shot. When they did, he stood and explained his faith, as best he could, in such a way as to make them think. As a result, they quickly learned not to ask him about it. He could defend his faith with reason and passion and with a clear and convincing view of history. Privately, the press liked Ben. Publicly, they had to use cautious words. He shrugged it all off. He knew what they were doing, but he still hoped he could reach past them into their audiences. The press hated Ben Kowalski, the man of faith, because he represented all that was judgmental, old-fashioned and repressive. But they liked Ben Kowalski, the human. To a man, they would have let him hold their last $100.

For Ben, the press was sport. After the impeachment of Marshall Warren, Ben knew his days as president were numbered. The Kim forces were aching for a substantive reason to impeach him and had effectively blocked the three nominations for vice president Ben had brought forth. It was check, and mate.

Ben held no illusions about a second term. He held few illusions about a second month. Consequently, he didn't have to play politics. He hadn't been elected. If ever there was a president who owed nothing to special interests, it was Ben Kowalski. He chose the stage he had been thrust upon to do what he did best. Public speaking was his arena. He enjoyed it. Cameras and microphones didn't bother him. He spoke as casually on camera as he did across the dinner table. Knowing full-well that the majority of the journalists in the room were going to invert whatever he said, he tried as best he could to create questions instead of answers. "What is our national identity? What sort of precedent are we setting for ourselves and for the future? When we deny the existence of evil, are we not denying the existence of good?" They were esoteric questions designed to make people think.

He was spitting into the wind. Thinking, in this new America, was no more the province of citizens than reporting facts was to journalists.

Ben had a gnawing sense early on that his marriage was being strained by his residency in the White House. He knew Ellen hated being in the spotlight. When Marshall Warren was impeached and Ben sworn in, Ellen missed the swearing in ceremonies. It was reported that she had a bout of flu. What the world would never know was that the First Lady was agoraphobic. She was afraid of people. Crowds sent her into panic attacks.

Ben had talked to doctors about her condition, but all they could do was prescribe drugs. Ellen didn't do drugs. She didn't want drugs. She just wanted to be left alone, which was not exactly in the job description of First Lady. So, instead of taking drugs or consulting psychiatrists she stayed with her, then, nine-year-old son, Jake, in the living quarters of the OEOB. Ben didn't pay it a lot of attention. He couldn't. Billy Kim was a fire licking at the heels of the Republic. Billy Kim was staging a not-so-covert coup. Ben's marriage was immaterial to the larger picture. He loved his wife and his son dearly, but he couldn't control what was happening to Ellen. He could only react.

The word of Ellen's insecurities soon reached the world outside of the family quarters. It wasn't long before Billy Kim devised a plan to try to drive a wedge between the reluctant president and his wife. He let a strategic lie leak out through his legions of friends in the press. The rumor being circulated was that Ben and Claudia Colgate, Billy Kim's 'consort,' had met in the library of the OEOB - often and alone.

Ellen recognized the story as a lie, but it was a convenient one for her. At that moment in time there were two things that Ellen wanted more than anything. One was privacy – she was paralyzed by the number of people surrounding her in the OEOB. The second was a way to get out of DC with Ben's checkbook. She had no real money of her own.

Ben had become rich over the years, but Ellen had been denied access to the money. It had led to some monumental arguments earlier in the marriage.

It had forced Ben to put her on a household allowance. He had to. She had tried to spend large sums of money behind his back. She had forged royalty checks. She had hidden money in secret accounts. She had siphoned money off of the family budget to go on spending binges with her lady friends. Ben didn't care so much about the money except for the fact that almost all of what he had made he had promised to others. Ben had grown up dirt poor. Anything more than $1000 in his checking account made him feel rich and always had. The millions of dollars that had flowed into their family budget through the years made him nervous. He had given most of it away to ministries. He was a sucker for any preacher with a cause. There was an endless supply of them; so many, in fact, he had eventually hired a flak catcher to tell people no. He couldn't do it himself. Ellen seethed at how he just gave money away. What she couldn't understand was why he couldn't funnel money through her first. She had to grovel, to petition for it. She didn't carry the guilt he did about spending money on personal items. She had grown up on the other side of the tracks, the uptown side. Her family had money. She had no qualms about the finer things. Ellen couldn't see why Ben couldn't render unto God what was God's and still render unto her what ought to be hers. She felt that their fame had earned them certain rights, certain amenities, certain privileges. She knew how to spend money wisely. Her rich lady friends told her so. In Ellen's world, she never measured value by what was spent but by what was saved. She viewed her success as a shopper in how badly she could defeat a retail price.

Ben never did find out how much she spent on 'stuff.' When he would press her, she would get mad and close the discussion. She would only say how much money they had saved. Eventually Ben gave up asking and decided that his wife saw the financial world in a different hue than he did. He made a conscious effort to see to it that his wife lived on an allowance.

She made a conscious effort to beat him at his own game.

The lie about Ben and Claudia Colgate was all over the papers, on the TV and on talk radio. Claudia Colgate just kept saying 'no comment' to her allies in the press. Ben wouldn't dignify the charge by issuing a formal response. The press saw Ben's lack of response as a tacit admission of guilt. It got to him. One afternoon he actually sat at his word processor and crafted a finely worded denial of his alleged sexual encounter(s) with Claudia Colgate. It was the most tortured two paragraphs he had ever written. He hated it. There was no way to arrange the words without hearing Bill Clinton saying "I never had sexual relations with that woman, not once." He knew that to read the words he had written, regardless of their arrangement, would place his portrait in the same historical art gallery as a convicted liar. He decided to stay silent.

The rumor didn't go away. It festered and bloomed like an over-ripe boil - the press squeezing it every morning.

Ellen saw the story as a means to kill what had, by then, become a manic desire to escape the fishbowl she found herself swimming in. She wanted out. She shopped for an attorney. The counsel Ellen finally contracted with came from the same Massachusetts law firm that made a career out of reconstructing the Kennedy family empire. The attorney she retained seemed relieved that neither real infidelity nor alcohol was the cause of the Kowalski marital rift. The attorney devised a plan. It would require a script.

Ellen confronted her husband about the lie the press was trying to spin. He denied it. She threw a fit, just like the attorney told her to. During the tirade, Ben turned and walked out. He knew he couldn't deny a sexual liaison with Claudia Colgate. He was guilty until proven innocent. He was being forced to prove a negative. In his past life as a chronic drunk and whoremonger, he had earned his condemnation. Now, he was being condemned for something that had never occurred. If it was irony, it was painful. Early in Ellen's act Ben surmised, correctly, that Ellen's charge of infidelity wasn't the central issue. Infidelity was a manufactured excuse. She wanted to leave the zoo. He respected that. He was willing to give her what she wanted. He had no wish to make her live in pain. He walked out in the middle of her tirade. The sight of the woman he loved going through all kinds of emotional gymnastics made him feel helpless. He couldn't argue with her and he didn't want to. It was a battle he couldn't win. He just wanted to give her whatever she wanted. He left.

She stood, jaw agape, devastated. He hadn't even put up a fight.

Ben knew her discontent had nothing to do with love and everything to do with comfort. He could give her comfort. He met with her attorney and in 45 minutes signed the papers that gave her a half million dollars in cash on the conditions that she not talk to the press and that they not divorce, but rather live as estranged husband and wife. He was still in love with her and wanted reconciliation kept as a legal possibility. Ellen agreed. As she did, she considered life with a half a mil. She wondered what was on sale. In return for the half million dollar consideration, it was agreed that Ben would get to see his son for two weekends a month – more, if she agreed. The final piece of the agreement was that she reside close to his home in Minnesota once he left Washington - which, by then, was not a question of if, but when.

After 123 days of being the President of the United States, Ben Kowalski was successfully impeached. Billy Kim's character assassins finally found a political sin with enough staying power to make a public figure fall. By the time the final impeachment vote was cast Ben was on a commercial flight home. He sat next to a professional fisherman on the flight and they talked about fishing. Period. He didn't ruminate about his fate. He had served long enough to thwart Billy Kim for a while. In the mean time, he had made some critical relationships with people inside of the government who could help him in his next endeavor. In his finely-tuned crystal ball, Ben could see the day when he and his people would need some cover and used his influence as president to secure some covert agreements.

He didn't leave Washington with shame, regrets or interviews. He just left. The whole world knew that Billy Kim had set him up to fall, but publicly it was never phrased that way.

The sword Ben fell on was a comment he had made in El Paso while promoting a book in 2013. He had been asked, after a Rotary Club dinner, to comment on the book of Revelations. His comments were made in the presence of a reporter. The reporter said that, in Ben Kowalski's opinion, 'The Great Whore' referred to in Revelations would turn out to be radical Islam.

"Watch," he had said. "The Muslim faith has been hijacked by radicals. They want the whole world Muslim or they want the whole world dead." It was supposed to be a candid comment to a friendly crowd. Billy Kim's people used it as proof positive that the Christian president was a walking, talking hypocrite - a racist, religiously intolerant, xenophobic and culturally insensitive vessel of bigotry. They were the kind of charges difficult to prove in a court of law, but quite possible in the court of public opinion over which Billy Kim presided.

In the end, they impeached Ben Kowalski because he was guilty of a charge none of them could publicly tolerate - intolerance.

In this new order, there were few greater sins.

CHAPTER TWENTY TWO
Unimpeachable

Early in Billy Kim's second term, exactly five years after Kowalski had been impeached, the "white phone" rang in Brad Pugh's soundproof studio. The white phone was Winnie. She was the only one with the number. She knew his "hard breaks" came at 28:30 and 57:30. She would wait until then to call him and remind him to pick up bread, about his dental appointment, to pick up the dry cleaning. Brad had just finished describing to millions of people how Billy Kim had clandestinely negotiated with the European Union President Hans Tanner to press their global agenda forward. After the final break in the show the white phone rang. Pugh had just vented his spleen to a network of affiliates that had grown, by then, to 900 stations. He was in no mood to be hen-pecked at that particular moment. He took a deep breath and picked up the receiver.

"Yes, dear," he said theatrically, as a brow-beaten husband.

"Dear?" It was a male voice. He knew that voice. "Awful intimate salutation from someone I've never met."

It was President Kim, the snake he had just chopped up in front of God and everybody.

"Your opinion of me, Mr. Pugh, isn't very flattering. If I were the sensitive type I might be offended."

"Mr. Kim, my opinion of you is as unimpeachable as you have made yourself with your bought-and-paid for congress. I applaud you, sir. You have single-handedly set the country up for tyranny. The question yet to be determined is who's pulling your strings? You can tell me, Mr. President. I can keep a secret."

"Mr. Pugh, you overestimate me. My goal is my own and it's not tyranny but, rather, philanthropy."

"Philanthropists, Mr. President, use their own money."

Brad Pugh had reached into his waste basket and pulled out a piece of paper. On it he wrote the words "Operation Alligator" and waved it frantically to the engineers and staff on the other side of the broadcast glass. Pugh pushed a button on his console and the president's voice came booming into the control room. The staff listened in.

"Philanthropy might be a stretch, I agree," Billy Kim continued. "Call it government benevolence, then. You, Mr. Pugh, can argue the semantics in jail. You're going to be tried for hate speech and sedition. We're not exactly sure how to define it yet, but you've been attacking me everyday now for almost five years. You forget that I'm a member of a protected class. I'm an Asian-American. Assaulting me as you do is hate speech…we think. Anyway, it will take years for the courts to put it in the right perspective. Eventually, they'll get it right. In the meantime, we have a nice federal bed waiting for you. So long, my formidable adversary."

It was supposed to be that easy. Kim was supposed to be able to simply pass a law proclaiming Brad Pugh guilty of sedition and have him picked up and locked away. Using the NSA to secure the private phone number and personally making the call was pure arrogance – a chance for Billy Kim to gloat about how easy finding a restricted number was for such an influential person as he. The president had underestimated Brad Pugh.

"Mr. President, you bore me," said Pugh. "Your power doesn't impress me. You couldn't inspire a Girl Scout troop because you have a fundamental shortcoming – you don't understand natural law. Your intentions are transparent – you seek to establish tyranny on the installment plan. You're boiling the frog slowly. You see, the difference between you and me is that I understand how insignificant I am. You don't have that problem. You've surrounded yourself with paid mouthpieces who echo whatever you say and make their careers out of guessing what you want to be told. But, beware, Mr. President - it was the senators who killed Caesar. Et tu Brute?"

And Brad Pugh hung up on the President of the United States.

"Let him suck on that for a while," he said as he entered the control booth, crowding around a television monitor.

"You just hung up on the President of the United States," said a startled engineer.

"Yeah. Sometimes you just gotta do that."

"Yeah, but he's the President," said the engineer.

He looked at the engineer and said "it's okay. He works for me."

On the monitor, a closed-circuit picture of a radio station lobby stared back at them. In that lobby Brad Pugh's pictue hung prominently on the wall. There were pictures of the radio star posing with presidents, prime ministers, actors and athletes. Behind the reception desk sat an attractive red head. She neither answered the phone - it rarely rang - nor did she perform any reception-ist functions. She read. For eight hours a day she read cheap novels, biogra-phies, self-help books, tabloids, whatever.

When the agents from the National Security Agency came bursting through the front doors and into the foyer she dropped the book she was reading. The receptionist was thrilled, very excited. The NSA team burst into the offices with their pistols and rifles poised and drawn. The doors behind the reception area led to a complex of three empty offices.

The agents attacked the offices like honeybees in season. In a few short moments they had done all the entering and posturing and shouting they could in the surprisingly small space they had invaded.

Nothing. The NSA contingent of eight finally assembled in the reception area and stood glaring at the red head.

"Where are they?" the lead NSA agent commanded.

"They never told me. They told me to sit here and take the mail. I'm a temp. They said if you guys show up I get a $1000 bonus. Thank you."

In the real studio, seven miles away, Brad Pugh looked at the monitor in resignation. He stood and shook the hands of his engineers, technicians and researchers. Their gig was over and everybody knew it. The senior producer put his hand on Brad's shoulder. "You saw it coming. Operation Alligator. You were right."

"Patriots are always prepared," Brad said, opening his jacket to reveal a nine millimeter Glock in its holster. "The price of freedom is eternal vigilance. Ben Franklin."

He flipped a cell phone out of his pocket and hit the autodial. "Opera-tion Alligator, sweetheart. You know where to meet." He hung up the phone, imagining the dread his call had created in his wife. He would have to deal with that later.

He thought about his previous statement to the crew. "Or, maybe it was Thomas Jefferson. I don't remember."

It was up to Kim's chief of intelligence to tell the president the news. Pugh had escaped. The studio they raided was a "front" and the whereabouts of the real studio was still under investigation. What the chief of intelligence, a for-mer union security man, didn't know yet, but would learn in the days to come, was that Brad Pugh had an exit strategy which would deposit he and his wife on a fully broadcast-ready rented Russian sub within six hours of the raid.

Days later, when the news had become known, the president was heard from the new White House all the way into the Virginia suburbs, screaming in disbelief. "Rented Russian Sub!!! Where the hell does somebody go to rent a Russian sub?"

It was the chief of intelligence, again, who was made to answer. "E-Bay, sir." The intelligence officer was almost sheepish when he added, "it's a secret kind of sub, sir. We don't know a lot about it."

Brad Pugh had 21 hours a day for show preparation. He was always loaded for bear. The isolation of forced exile could not hold the Internet at bay. The Internet was at his fingertips and was his only necessary research associate. No one could bottle the net. That genie was out of that bottle and even Billy Kim couldn't contain it.

"Greetings, freedom lovers!" His voice boomed from 35 feet beneath the waves of the Indian Ocean.

He looked out the diamond amalgam bow of the sub and could only see black. He tried to imagine a busy American landscape through the darkness.

It wasn't the way it was supposed to be, but it was the hand he had been dealt. Brad paid the captain $1.8 million a month to rent the sub and monthly the payment always cleared Petrov's Swiss account. When the gig was over the captain would be set for life. In the meantime, Petrov had a client to serve. He was thankful Brad had a brain and no desire for treachery. The widowed captain was too old to engage in a political power play. Along with Brad and Winnie Pugh, his Estate Sale nuclear sub and his skeleton crew of 13, he lived the life he had been born to pursue.

He couldn't have been happier.

Brad Pugh and Captain Ilya Petrov, isolated at sea, came to a quiet, unspoken mutual respect. Pugh respected Petrov for his ability to carve out a meaning for life in spite of the huge political obstacles in his path. Petrov respected Pugh for his courage in speaking the truth about political obstacles.

As a former communist officer he understood how dangerous truth could be.

CHAPTER TWENTY THREE
A super-secret society

"**B**en, they're squirreled into a small bay about a mile south of Nuweiba - just off the line of sight from the Nuweiba port." Leon Amanti was pointing out the location of Arne's boat on the illuminated map. "The GPS locator can track Arne, but we can only guess where the Egyptians are."

He went on to explain the strategy. "As soon as the Egyptian boat - or boats - disappear into the Nuweiba bay to search for them, they're going to come north - above Nuweiba. Once the Egyptians leave the bay and head further south – then Arne and the crew will go back into the bay, take their cameras and begin walking down the highway, up the Wadi Watir. We have a van on the way to pick them up."

It was a good strategy, thought Ben. It had a chance to work and no one would be the wiser.

"Any artifacts from the bottom?" Ben asked.

"None. Unless they're playing both ends against the middle. They said the pictures they have will confirm the hypothesis. Oh, and Ben, you've got a visitor waiting for you out on the porch. Your neighbor, Larsen. Says it's important."

Kowalski could always count on Larsen to have bad timing. Being in the same county was bad timing when it came to Mr. and Mrs. Lars Larsen. Still, Ben had always hoped to show the crusty Mr. Larsen that patience was its own reward. It hadn't worked to date.

Ben excused himself from the business at hand. There was nothing further he could do anyway. He wanted to see what Lars had up his sleeve so he could dispense with him. When he opened the front door to greet Lars, he was expecting a complaint.

"Kowalski, I been out here 10 minutes," Lars said from behind a pair of opaque sunglasses. "They said you'd be right down."

"Sorry. They just told me. There's a lot going on in there."

Larsen shrugged. Kowalski was fully expecting a lecture about courtesy but was surprised that Lars addressed him almost respectfully.

"I know you and I ain't what you call the best of neighbors but I have a favor to ask of you." It was as close to being human that Kowalski had ever seen his neighbor.

"Lars," he said, "whatever can I do to help you?"

Lars produced a book he had been carrying. Ben recognized the book. It was his own most recent hardcover, "America In The Crosshairs."

"My daughter, Caroline, recently married a fellow in Missouri. We didn't know he was a Christian when she married him but, he is. Evidently, he's got her thinking like one of you guys now. Anyway, they want to know if you would autograph your book for them."

It had to take a lot of pride-swallowing for him to do this thing, thought Kowalski. Ben produced a fine-tipped felt pen from his jacket and thought momentarily. He wrote: "The Lord is working real hard to reach your mom and dad. They need our help. In His name, Ben Kowalski."

Lars read the message. "Is that a shot?" he asked.

"Not at all. We Christians all belong to a super-secret society. It's secret language - marching order for your daughter."

"You know I'm a conspiracy theorist, don't you?" Ben had the feeling he had just stepped in a large pile of something warm and mushy.

"Lars, I wouldn't be surprised at that, no."

Lars continued, "If this is your attempt at humor, it's not bad. Almost funny."

Almost funny. Ben had to chuckle. "Lars, how would you like to see the cutting edge of the conspiracy? - C'mon inside. Let me introduce you to the team. Really. C'mon in."

One would have thought that Kowalski had asked him to turn his head and cough.

"No. No thanks. I've done my duty. I got the autograph." He turned to leave, stopped and asked, "Oh, I was also wondering if you could keep an eye on the place for a couple days. Me and the wife are going up to our property in Canada for about four days. Over the Fourth. We need a break. The son is over in the Middle East with Special Forces somewhere and the daughter, well…we have to put all of it in perspective. We're going to just get away for a while. Try and make some sense of things." He handed Ben a slip of paper.

"Our cell number. If anything happens at the house." He handed Ben a key as well. "Could you have your boy feed the cats. Maybe play with them a little? Ethel would really appreciate it. She'll pay him."

"No charge, Lars. I'll have Jake do it. But, you know you're going to miss all the fun."

"What d'ya mean?"

"The Holy Harvest, the temple dedication. Could be a pivotal moment in history. We've got over 100 stadiums around the world that are going to be packed with the faithful - all in one voice to celebrate the roots of the faith. There are 60 countries involved. All of them will be watching the temple dedication. A lot of things will be coming together - faith, politics, history. The whole world is going to be tuned in."

Larsen shrugged his shoulders and looked askance at him. "Never heard of it."

Ben was dumbstruck. Reflexively, he asked, "where do you get your news?"

Without missing a beat, Lars said "CNN. NPR. Why?"

It explained a lot.

Before Lars could escape, Ben grabbed his elbow. "Lars!" Ben wanted to tell him volumes. He wanted to tell him all about the Red Sea evidence. He wanted to reach into his heart and explain things - his prayers for him and his wife, his hopes about him seeing the evidence God had laid out for them.

"Lars," he said. "I've been praying for you and your wife. There are things you'll need to be aware of."

Lars looked at him with a cocked eye, turned and walked away.

"I know all I need to know," he said as if Ben were an airport Hari Krishna. "Thanks for the autograph. Thanks for watching the house. I gotta go now."

Ben stood on the porch and shook his head. "Why do I try?" he asked to no one in particular.

CHAPTER TWENTY FOUR
A volley of bullets

It couldn't have gone worse. It started fine, but quickly deteriorated. The Egyptian cruiser boat did as expected. On the Egyptian side of the Gulf of Aqaba, their cruiser-craft pulled into the harbor at Nuweiba and began to survey the bay, looking for the Swede and his rented boat. When the Egyptians disappeared from view, Arne and his crew slowly idled their boat out into the gulf, intending to quietly beach on the north side of the harbor. However, they couldn't escape geometry. There was simply no place in the harbor from which a portion of their 28-foot boat was totally hidden by the bay. It had been a calculated guess by Arne. It backfired.

When the Egyptian cruiser emerged, full-throttle, out of the bay, Mahrous didn't wait for instructions. He turned the boat south and opened the throttle, heading for the Saudi side of the gulf. Where was the other Egyptian boat? Were they heading right towards it or was it further north, "up" the Saudi coast? There was a 50/50 chance they were right. The good news was that they were about a mile, Arne guessed, ahead of the pursuit boat. The bad news was they were just buying time. They had nowhere to run. The fact that the Egyptians were in a determined pursuit told him they had some knowledge of what their payload was. The question kept coming back to him - how did they know? Silence by murder or imprisonment seemed to be the two most likely Egyptian probabilities for Arne and his crew.

"We're going to beach on the Saudi side and then run like hell," he shouted at his crew. "Get the tapes and the film together. Forget the video cameras. They're too heavy. We won't need them. We'll need food and water. Don't overload yourself!"

It occurred to Arne at that moment how a Hebrew in the Exodus must have felt when it became apparent that there simply was not going to be a return to safe harbor.

Ewald watched the horizon for the other Egyptian cruiser. Eventually it came into view. "There, from the north, two miles, at the most," he shouted.

It was the first break they had caught all day. They calculated that the Egyptian Navy wasn't quite state of the art. Their own boat was actually out-running the Egyptians. The fuel gauge told Arne that at full throttle they had enough gas to cross to the Saudi side and then run for about three hours before being forced to turn back. But, to where? Still, three hours would give them time to eyeball a landing zone and probably a few minutes to get lost in the Saudi Arabian wilderness.

After 20 minutes of wide open running they came to the Saudi side of the gulf. The Egyptian boats had intersected and were chasing them in tandem but not closing distance. Mahrous kept the boat about 200 yards from the shore looking for a wadi running down to the water. A wadi would give them a path into the wilderness. He didn't want to beach the boat where their only escape was a vertical one.

"Do you think they'll shoot?" asked Ewald.

"Yes!" shouted Mahrous from the pilot's nest. "Especially if they know why we're here. Which, it appears, they do."

Mahrous cut back the throttle. He had spotted something. "There!" he shouted.

It didn't look like much but there was a narrow wadi running back between the hills. Within 90 seconds they had beached the boat. Mahrous turned the engine off and bounded down the ladder. His last step was a bad one. He caught his heel on the rung of the ladder and came crashing down onto the gunwale, landing on his shins and catapulting over the edge of the boat and into the water.

Arne and Ewald heard the crash and saw his body fall awkwardly over-board. They were busy throwing the water jugs and duffle-bags on the shore.

"Mahrous!" Arne shouted. "Tell me you're not hurt bad. Mahrous!"

"My leg," came the moan from the other side of the boat. Mahrous swam around the corner of the boat and dragged his body up on shore.

"How bad is it?"

"It could be broken, I don't know." He was wincing and trying to gain enough strength to pull himself up. He pulled up his pant leg and on his shin was a huge purple knot.

A barrage of 20 millimeter bullets ripped through the boat. They instinc-tively threw their bodies onto the beach. Fortunate for them, they were shielded by a bank of rocks. The boat, however, was widely exposed and took the full brunt of an assault that ripped the boat into uselessness. A return to the boat for any more essentials was a closed discussion.

"...But, then again, it might just be a bruise," Mahrous said, rubbing his shin. He gathered up duffel bags with a new sense of purpose. If his leg was broken, the adrenaline provided by a volley of bullets had healed it quickly. They raced up the wadi. The last evidence of the fate of their craft was a black plume of smoke rising from the beach.

They sprinted into the Saudi wilderness until Arne commanded them to stop. They listened, trying to mute the sounds of their own heavy breathing - straining to hear if they were being followed.

Now, Arne knew precisely how the ancient Hebrews had felt.

CHAPTER TWENTY FIVE
Showtime

At 3:38 AM, local time, two buses pulled into an underground entrance at a dormitory complex just outside of Damascus, Syria. Silently, the 37 occupants of the buses exited and were led by their handlers through a series of colored ropes into the ground floor of the dormitory. In their gray sweat suits they were led like sheep into a series of elevators which shuttled them to the top two floors. They were quiet; they were orderly. They knew their room assignments and they knew that breakfast would be at 07:00 sharp. They had about three hours to sleep. Without discussion they all went to bed.

At 06:30 they were roused from their sleep. None of them grumbled or rolled over for an extra minute or two of sleep as their body clocks would've liked. They had been prepared for it. They had been schooled to know exactly what the next few weeks were going to bring.

It was showtime!

CHAPTER TWENTY SIX
Hoping for a plan

Ben Kowalski lay in bed waiting for his alarm to ring. His brain was awake and engaged and he knew that a return to sleep was useless. There were too many things going on. He ran a quick inventory of the day in front of him. There were a lot of variables, but one thing he knew for sure – he needed to submit what he felt before God. He needed to alter his perspective – to see the events unfolding in front of him in something other than a human dimension. He asked his demons if they would please leave the room while he got on his knees. Always, in his deepest moments of prayer Ben Kowalski saw the path to submission. He understood the light on his path. It was prayer, and prayer only, which opened the gates to the path.

Ben knew he was playing a part in a large production, he just didn't know why. He knew enough not to question the end result as long as it was in harmony with the light he knew was leading him home.

He had three major points of business for the day. First, he had to talk to his son about Ellen. He wished he could soften the news he had to bring the boy. Ben received the call at midnight. Ellen was in jail. Drunk, disorderly conduct and possession of narcotics were the charges. She was being held in the Overland County jail in Kansas. He had left a message with the sheriff's office that an attorney would be arranging bail in the coming day. Now, he had to tell his son why his mother was in jail.

He also had three subcontractors, ostensibly employees of his, who were lost in the wilderness of Saudi Arabia. They were illegal aliens and were being sought by Egyptian, and probably Saudi forces. Both would likely want to kill them.

Finally, he was scheduled to meet with Billy Kim's director of internal affairs. The Holy Harvest was creating security issues which the Kim Administration said presented potential "dire outcomes" for the safety of those millions of people who were planning on meeting, worldwide, to worship. Ben didn't trust anything the Kim Administration planned. Their antagonism towards the faithful was an unreported story in the press. The Kim people were all socialists and agnostics. They were officially neutral in matters of faith. In truth, they were humanists who believed in the gospel of Darwin and the virtues of moral equivalence. They were countrymen, but they were not brothers.

There were four Bible passages concerning homosexuality that the Kim Administration wanted stricken from any discourse. They wanted Ben's assurance that these passages would not be uttered. They wanted the Holy Harvest to be on the record as against bigotry and intolerance – the two greatest sins in the new order. It was, without much debate, censorship, but the word was never echoed in the mainstream. Of the 60 or so stadiums at which the Holy Harvest was going to be celebrated around the planet, Ben couldn't guarantee that some of the local preachers wouldn't utter one of those four passages. Besides, how arrogant would Ben be to tell a preacher in Sri Lanka or Botswana what to preach? But, the implication he had received through the director's office was that was exactly the assurance they wanted. Ben knew it was a politically correct charade. If he could provide a lock-solid assurance that those four "homophobic" verses would not be uttered, the Kim Administration would have another half dozen verses, equally bigoted and intolerant, in their briefcases which they would declare off limits, out of bounds, culturally insensitive and/or intolerant. Ben knew it was a battle he wasn't going to win. His attorney, Reynolds Thomas, was going to be there to interpret the US Constitution - since no one in the Kim Administration seemed to have a working knowledge of the document.

The alarm rang and Ben shut it off before the second buzz. He quickly showered, shaved and slipped into a suit and tie. Officially, he had to represent the Holy Harvest to the Kim Administration. He would have liked to wear a sweatshirt and cut-offs for them, but couldn't rationalize insulting them like that. It was an insult he did consider.

Jake slept in the room next door and like most teenagers in the summer, he preferred to sleep until circumstance forced him get up. Ben was surprised when he knocked on the door and his son was awake, alert and dressed.

"Jake, got to talk." He had to get to the point. There was no way to candy-coat the truth so he just laid it out in front of the boy.

"Your mom was arrested last night. Drunk and disorderly, possession of narcotics." He waited for it to register. The boy looked at the floor.

"Can't be too surprised, I guess," he muttered.

"Son, I've got an attorney down in Kansas who is going to bail her out. She'll be back here in a day or two." Jake stood and looked out the window.

The boy paused for a long moment. "Think we'll ever get her back?"

"I don't know. We have to be there, though."

Ben was a little surprised that the news of Ellen's troubles didn't ring deep in the boy. Were there dynamics there he was unaware of?

Jake took the news, consumed it and put it away. The news about his mother seemed to be an inconvenient diversion to what Jake had on his mind.

"Hey, Dad, mind if I follow you around today? You're up to something here, aren't you?"

Ben considered the intuitive nature of his son's question and wondered what clues the boy had picked up on.

"Let's eat and I'll fill you in. Try not to be too amazed. It's pretty fantastic. You've heard about the Holy Harvest, right?"

"Yeah. Who hasn't?"

"Well, our neighbors - the Larsen's for one."

"Dad, they're old. And, stupid."

"They're not alone, son."

The meeting with the director of internal affairs was brief, cordial and pointed. The director, a stout man, was a bureaucrat. He carried the orders without expression or emotion. His job was to be poker-faced. He had once been a president of a northeastern university. He had doubled his salary by agreeing to be Billy Kim's water boy. He was strictly by-the-numbers, but it was apparent that he was just the messenger. Logic, reason and persuasiveness were lost on him. The homosexual references in the Bible were not to be uttered. End of discussion.

Ben and his attorney, Reynolds Thomas, listened carefully to the words the director said and nodded their heads. They shook hands with him. After eight minutes the meeting was over.

Jake had been allowed to sit in on the meeting on the condition that he hold his tongue. The boy didn't see or hear anything unusual. He knew that there were anti-homosexual sentiments in the world. He heard about them from almost every teacher he had, even at the private school his parents had enrolled him in. What the director said actually made sense to Jake. He had heard it time and again at school. That his father and the attorney treated the government's requests to curb the homosexual references with coolness surprised him. The boy wanted to stand up and voice his support with the director.

When the director had safely left, Reynolds Thomas turned to the boy and asked, "What did you see here?"

The boy paused. "They want you to not discriminate against homosexuals at the Holy Harvest."

The two adults looked at each other. The assessment was correct. The reasons needed to be explored.

"Son," said Ben, "if a homosexual came to the Holy Harvest would he be welcome?"

"Yeah. Unless you know something I don't."

"He would be welcome, son. Now, let me ask you this: Is it right to kill a man?"

"No."

"How about steal his property?"

"No. What's your point?"

"I'm getting to it. How about having sex out of wedlock?"

The boy paused. His father was getting into an area he wasn't sure he wanted to explore. "Dad, I'm 14. I wouldn't know."

"What do they tell you at school?"

"They really don't. They just say you need a condom." He was embarrassed.

"The point is this: homosexuality is a sin. Sex out of wedlock is a sin. Murder is a sin. Theft is a sin. Get the picture?" The boy nodded.

"Which is the worst sin?"

The boy was stumped. He guessed. "Murder?"

"No. All of them are equal. A sin is a sin is a sin. The Bible is very clear on that. I'd quote you a verse, but you might think I was preaching to you and I know you don't want me to do that. I don't want you to come to faith just because I did. You have to draw your own conclusions."

"So, are you going to take the gay stuff out of the Holy Harvest?"

Ben looked at Jake and then looked at the attorney. The attorney looked at the ceiling.

"I don't know," said Ben. "What do you think?"

"I think you ought to."

Ben and his attorney looked at each other. They both raised their eyebrows. The boy was a microcosm of what many people thought. Neither the attorney nor the once most trusted man in America could criticize the boy – he was merely echoing what he had been taught to believe.

Leon Amanti knocked on the door.

"It's time. We're trying to raise Arne on the phone."

It was early evening in Saudi Arabia. Arne and his crew were holed up in the Saudi hills. After their escape into the Saudi Arabian wilderness Arne had called to tell them what had happened. Aside from Mahrous's leg they were physically all right. Arne figured Mahrous had a hematoma. It would be painful and probably have to be lanced. In the short term, though, they were fine as long as they could remain hidden. They had moved a few miles inland. They had about a week's worth of food, water and about two weeks worth of batteries if they kept their calls to a minimum. Arne told them to call at 7:00 PM Saudi time. They would undoubtedly be hoping Ben had a plan.

He didn't.

CHAPTER TWENTY SEVEN
Horeb

Arne Karlstrom had lied to his crew. It didn't come easy and he agonized over the deception. Yet, he saw an opportunity. From the moment it became apparent that the Egyptians were not following them into the Saudi Arabian wilderness Arne had plotted something patently selfish. What neither Ewald nor Mahrous were aware of was that Arne was in his own back yard. Arne had devoted eight years of forensic study to the piece of real estate he was now being hunted on. There was probably not a man on the planet who knew the peaks and wadis surrounding them better than Arne. He didn't need a map. Where they had beached the boat was a minor, unnamed wadi which would lead them to the biblical Wilderness of Sin. Sin, or Zin, was the Babylonian name for moon. The Wilderness of Sin was named for the Babylonian moon god from the days of Nimrod, the ancient builder of the tower of Babel. The reason it had been named the Wilderness of Sin became apparent to Arne the first time he had seen an infrared satellite photograph of the area. The Wilderness of Sin was composed of limestone and sandstone hills and was a brilliant shade of white when moonlit. Literally, it was the Wilderness of the moon – not only in luminescence, but in topography. It was, by anyone's estimate, a lot of nothing. About six miles due north of them was a split in the wadi they had been on. To the right led up into a box canyon. To the left it snaked around several mountains of the 4000-foot variety into a larger wadi. The wadis in this region were coarse sand, hard packed - just like the bottom of the Gulf of Aqaba. About four miles north of them, along the main wadi was The Rock at Horeb. A group of British explorers had taken a picture of the rock back in the 1930's. Arne had had it blown up and digitally enhanced. It stood about 10 meters high and it was situated on the top of a small, 80-foot high pile of other rocks. The rock was almost perfectly split in the middle. If his theory was correct, it was the very Rock of Horeb that Moses had split with his staff, causing water to gush out like an uncapped oil well.

About three miles south of their present location was 70 Palms. There was no name for it in the Bible. It was simply an oasis that had had 70 Palms when the Hebrews were first led by Moses to it. It was there that manna was first delivered to the grumbling Hebrews. Today, according to the photos and satellite imagery Arne had viewed over the years, there were probably 200 palms. It also had about a dozen wells in it, just as the Bible had chronicled it had 3500 years ago. Arne had confirmed by satellite photo, as well as a Saudi geography textbook, that the wells were still there. If need be, it would be their water source.

Where Arne wanted to go was to the very Mountain of God. There was one curiosity there he had to examine. He rationalized that he would never be this close again. The Saudi Arabian government would never allow him to examine the area voluntarily. He had tried. As long as he was in the neighborhood, science demanded he take a reasonable risk to assure his assumptions were put to the test.

When they had been chased from the gulf and into the wilderness they had sprinted up a wadi, up a hill and behind a wall of rocks to see if they were being followed. They waited almost an hour. Then two. No reason to move. They weren't being followed and they had no place to run. Night had descended on them and a full moon rose in the eastern sky. It was like daylight. They had three wafer-thin thermal blankets in their gear and were as comfortable as three fugitives can get on beds of rock. Everywhere they looked was sand and rock and mountain in varying shades of red, brown and gray. It was like the surface of the moon. If they had wanted to light a fire they couldn't. Acacia, the only tree indigenous to the area, was abundant, but a fire may as well be an argon searchlight in the Saudi wilderness. It got down to 58 degrees overnight but no one complained.

The communication to the Kowalski compound from Arne had been brief for two reasons. First, he wanted to save batteries and, second, there wasn't a lot to be said - they were in a mountainous wilderness in the middle of nowhere with no immediate prospects for rescue. Anything else to be said was fluff.

Amanti had plotted their coordinates from the GPS locator they had welded into Arne's belt buckle. Knowing where they were wasn't an issue for the Kowalski group. Having a plan, on the other hand, was a real issue. Kowalski and his people were the only lifeline. Kowalski had the money. They had the organization. They had the resources. They had connections.

Arne and his crew had nothing but moonscape.

The Saudis, Arne was certain, knew by now they were in the wilderness. He assumed the Egyptians would communicate their approximate location to the Saudis. Their larger problem, though, was that their payload was potentially fatal for the three of them. Saudi Arabia was the capitol of Islam. Forensic validation of The Exodus was not the kind of science that would be exalted in Mecca.

The good news, from Arne's point of view was that, even in the 21st century, the Wilderness of Sin was still a wilderness. Only a few Bedouins populated it and the army had only two soldiers within 100 square miles. The closest organized army was 80 miles away in Tibuk. Arne knew exactly where the guard shack in the wilderness was. The satellite photos had told him.

Sleeping on rock proved difficult. Actually, it was impossible. The best any of them could do was catnap. Between the catnaps, Arne's mind was drawing his new game plan. It had nothing to do with escape and everything to do with validating his theory. He closed his eyes and prayed for answers. Why was he seeking to validate his theory above and beyond the safety of himself and his crew? He couldn't rationalize it. Neither Arne Karlstrom the scientist, nor Arne Karlstrom the man, could hear the argument from the rational side of his brain. His awe of where he was and his sense of predestination burned like an ember in the pit of his stomach. When Moses saw the burning bush - by Arne's estimates, about eleven miles from their present location - he must have felt the same awe. There were voices echoing in the Wilderness of Sin. Arne heard them. Whatever he was, whatever his purpose for having lived 52 years without being called home didn't matter. There were voices out here beckoning across the ages and calling Arne Karlstrom by name. Denying the calling was simply not an option. This was Arne Karlstrom's burning bush. God had put him here for a specific purpose and God was not going to allow him to die before fulfilling his part in the larger play. Arne was putting his trust in God's providence. There was no fear of failure or fear of dying in the heart of Arne. Fear was a distant star. The only sensation in Arne's chest was a compulsion, a reverent compulsion, to kiss what he had come to know through study and revelation as the true Mountain of God.

The film they carried confirmed the biblical account of the Red Sea crossing. Now Arne's mission had expanded because of unforeseen circumstances. He weighed all of the contingencies and concluded their escape would be in God's hand. Their escape was either going to happen or not happen. It didn't matter. What mattered was that God was calling Arne to complete the mission he had been called to. And like one of the apostles who had seen the risen Christ, denying the holy evidence would be worse than death itself.

At the base of Jabel El Lawz, explorers look out at the plain that would have been the campground of the ancient Hebrews. Unlike the site at the traditional Mount Sinai, this location has sufficient space to encamp 1.5 to 2 million refugees. In the center of the frame the Saudi government has placed a fence around a pile of rocks. The fenced area is the hypothetical site of the Golden Calf Altar (see subsequent photos). The Saudi government has also placed a fence at the base of the mountain and maintains a manned guard shack to protect this "Saudi archeological site." Despite their claims that this is an archeological site, no outside research of the area has been permitted. Almost all photos and videos of this area have been pirated out of Saudi Arabia.

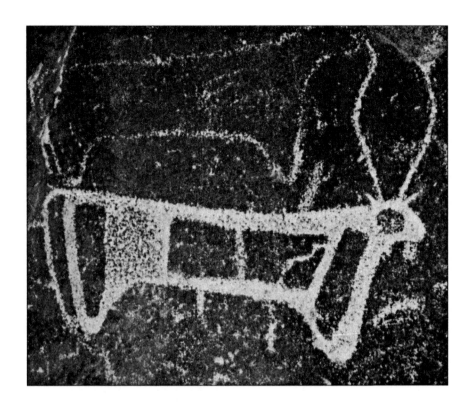

Inside the fence surrounding the Golden Calf Altar this photo was secretly taken. The drawing is consistent with the Apis bull cult, a religion unknown in Saudi history and uniquely Egyptian in origin.

Another rendering of the Apis bull shot from inside the proposed site of the Golden Calf Altar. On and around Jabel El Lawz there are some 20 specific physical "coincidences" that dovetail with the biblical account. A variety of explorers and scholars have come forward in recent years suggesting that Jabel El Lawz is the true Mount Sinai. Much of this research is documented in the book, "The Exodus Case," by Dr. Lennart Moller and the documentary film "The Exodus Conspiracy," from Mahoney Media Group. The author of this novel served as a research/production assistant on the film for five years.

The Saudis have erected a security fence around the proposed site of the Golden Calf Altar. The site features numerous calf/cow renderings which, the hypothesis goes, is the result of the Hebrews constructing the altar following Moses' lengthy disappearance up the mountain. The anxious Hebrews constructed a monument to the god they knew best – an Egyptian one. Explorers and archeologists have been routinely denied permission to conduct surveys of the area.

*All photos courtesy Split Rock Research Foundation.

CHAPTER TWENTY EIGHT
Fuming and seething

They intercepted I-94 out of St. Paul and headed north to St. Cloud. Traffic was light and the conversation was minimal. Lars and Ethel Larsen contented themselves with listening to NPR. Out of St. Paul they picked up NPR on 99.5 FM. They had a handy NPR listening guide in the glove box that told them all of the different frequencies they could pick up public radio, wherever they traveled.

Behind them, they towed Lars' fishing boat. It had grown over the years. At one time his boat was a modest 14-footer with a flat aluminum hull and an 8.5 horsepower Evinrude. The adult model he now towed was a 125-horsepower, 16-foot double hull inboard/outboard with a live-well, CD player, heavy duty trailer and custom cover. He rationalized that, in his retirement years, he owed himself a nice boat with lots of knobs and dials. The boat had sat in his four-stall garage for three summers without being fired. Before embarking for the island in Canada, he had towed it to the marina and had the mechanic check it out. The bill for the tune-up was $330. To be able to tow his boat he had purchased a Lincoln SUV with leather seats, and even more bells and whistles. Between his SUV and his boat, he was rolling over $120,000 worth of hardware up Highway 10 out of St. Cloud toward Brainerd.

On the radio they listened to a report about the cost of gas. NPR interviewed a member of congress about the free flow of crude oil into the US marketplace. The congresswoman conveniently failed to mention the US government and the Kim Administration had set the production rates of crude oil. NPR conveniently let her get away with her omission. She asserted that instead of relying on dirty old crude oil, alternative sources of energy had to be explored. To compliment her amateur thesis, the NPR reporter interviewed a professor of physics from the University of Glasgow who insisted that wind-power could be harnessed in order to reduce the planet's gluttonous consumption of oil.

While the world was waiting for the windmills, the gas Lars had pumped into his tank cost $6.03 per gallon. Filling his almost-empty tank had cost him $180.14.

Next, NPR interviewed a Muslim-American, a Sudanese business owner, about the meaning of the Fourth of July. The Muslim, a recent émigré to the US, said it was just another day to him - to him it was an interruption in his normal business. He sold coffee and cigarettes to businessmen who, because they were on a holiday, never showed up. The Sudanese man didn't like the holiday.

NPR also did a feature article about an old fellow who had served in Korea. The reporter called him one of the last American patriots. The old soldier had celebrated the Fourth of July over the years with a huge display of Americana in his front yard. Annually, he festooned his yard with a hundred flags, banners, plastic statues of American war heroes, patriotic songs and free watermelon. Over the decades, it had become an annual happening in his Cleveland neighborhood. But now, slowed by arthritis and glaucoma, the old duffer was unable to set up his yard like he had in previous years.

The report sounded like an autopsy and the reporter sounded like a coroner. The reporter concluded her feature by saying, "and so as the Fourth of July comes to this Cleveland neighborhood, 95-year old Sam Peterson and his American tribute will stand down. No more flag-waving. No more patriotic songs or banners. No more free watermelon. An era of patriotism has passed and no one, it appears, is there to unfurl the flags and proclaim the long-forgotten America Sam Peterson once knew. From Cleveland, I'm Adrienne Willings-Hawley."

The NPR "sounder" announced the end of the segment. In the two and a half hours Lars and Ethel Larsen had listened to NPR, the subject of the Holy Harvest or the Jewish temple dedication were never mentioned once.

As the SUV cruised up Highway 10 just a few miles north of St. Cloud, Lars caught the lights from the motorcycle cop in his rear-view mirror before he heard the siren.

"Damn," he said. Ethel saw him looking in the mirror. The boat obstructed her view out the back.

"What is it, Lars?"

"Cops. Speed limit's 70. I was going 82. I don't need a ticket."

"Calm down, now. Don't fly off the handle. You'll just make things worse for yourself."

"I am calm!!" he barked at his wife. He pulled the SUV to the side of the road and turned on his flashers. The motorcycle cop approached slowly. He stopped by the boat and looked under the cover before approaching Lars on the driver's side. His name tag told the Larsen's they were dealing with Minnesota State Trooper Harvey Hanscomb.

"Problem, officer?"

"I don't know, sir. Would you step outside of the vehicle please?"

Lars opened the door and stepped onto the pavement. The officer motioned him to the front of the car. Lars presented his defense. "I know I was going a few miles over the limit, but hey, there's no traffic out here today."

"Sir - can I see your license please?"

Lars dug into his wallet and pulled out the license. The trooper inserted the plastic license into his hand-held transmitter. Within seconds, the computer-link gave the officer the driver information. Officer Hanscomb pointed his hand-held transmitter at the license plate of the car and snapped a picture. The confirmation was instantaneous: The driver and the vehicle belonged to one another. The trooper scrolled up the screen for about a half a minute, studying the text. Lars looked at his wife. What could be in their file? They were textbook average people - exceedingly average, outwardly and inwardly unremarkable.

The trooper, evidently, didn't share their assessment.

"Sir, I'll need to see your vehicle registration and proof of insurance, your travel permit, gas tax stamp, boat tax clearance statement, pollution control inspection stamp and your trailer hitch permit. Oh, I also need to know if you're carrying any firearms, alcohol, tobacco, aspirin, decongestants, white gas, kerosene, live bait or any prescription drugs. I'll also need to see your seat belt and air bag deployment stickers."

Ethel got out of the car and joined Lars. She had heard enough. "Officer, I need your badge number. We are not the kind of people you shake down. I was a state senator for four terms and I can assure you that I've still got friends at the Capitol."

It was true. Ethel Larsen had served for four consecutive terms as a state senator. It didn't impress the trooper. He looked at her blankly. He knew her history. It was part of the hand-held transmission he had received. The reason he was doing the so-called "shakedown" was because she had served in the state senate. Ethel Larsen had been the committee chair of the Senate Ways and Means Committee in 2014 when the state, in the face of a budget crisis, cut the size of the Highway Patrol by about a third. Troopers who had patrolled the most heavily trafficked corridors in pairs had been forced to patrol solo over larger stretches of road. Since then, there had been six murders of state troopers. Four of them were unsolved. One of the corpses had been his partner, Harold Kastor. Trooper Harvey Hanscomb didn't pay attention to politics but he understood justice. He was about to deliver a small dose of it.

He called in his captain. It took 20 minutes for the captain to arrive in his station wagon. The captain, a short, stocky man who looked to be over 60 years of age, brought out his dog to sniff down the car and boat. The Larsen's cooled their heels, sitting in the grass, for almost an hour while the search and paperwork were completed. They passed the time by alternately fuming and seething.

When the "inspection" was done, the captain walked slowly over to the Larsen's, motioning them to stay seated. He sat down beside them, huffing a little as his stocky body sat, legs akimbo, in front of them.

The captain took off his sunglasses and looked at them both.

"I want to tell you a story Mr. and Mrs. Larsen, and I don't want to be interrupted. If I am interrupted I'm going to haul the both of you off to the county slammer in Walker. Got it?"

The anger and indignation welling up inside of the Larsen's was titanic, but they held their tongues, choosing to look off into the distance instead. Venting would come later.

The captain stuck a blade of grass in his teeth. "Mrs. Larsen, the same year your Ways and Means Committee cut our force by a third, you voted yourself a 14 percent raise and simultaneously opened the immigration and welfare floodgates of the state." He held up his hand-held data link. "It's all in here, which is another piece of law you helped pass, but that's another story. What happened was pretty predictable, really. We had a situation where we had more criminals and less officers and that's just an accident waiting to happen. That cut meant my boys were forced to patrol bigger pieces of highway. Alone. Very little back-up. On June 16, 2017 at about 2:00 AM, one of my officers made a stop about 10 miles south of here. He had no way of knowing that he was stopping a car full of very bad men. They wrestled his gun away from him, shot him in the leg with it and then dragged him into the woods where he couldn't get to his car. The coroner said he bled to death." The captain was without emotion. He was reciting the story clinically.

"Without a partner he didn't stand a chance. They were illegal immigrants. We know who they are but they're in Mexico now. The Mexican government has refused to extradite them."

The captain rose and motioned them to rise. Together they began walking up to the highway. The captain opened the door for Ethel while Lars climbed into the driver's side. Nothing was said. Lars turned the engine over and looked at the captain for some sort of signal to leave.

"Ma'am, I have learned how to forgive," said the captain. "It took me most of my life to do that, but I want you to know that I forgive you because He forgives me. I don't hold you personally responsible, but..." His voiced trailed off and he choked back a sob.

Ethel flashed a sympathetic biting of the lip. It dawned on her. She was dealing with a religious nut! Being at his mercy, though, demanded diplomacy. She tried to look humble. She would have liked to pull the gun out of his belt and shoot him in the leg, haul him off to the woods and let him bleed to death. Instead, she bit her lip.

The captain pulled a department nametag out of his pant pocket. It read "Harold Kastor, Jr." He held it up to his chest, next to his own nametag that read "Harold Kastor." He pressed the nametag into her palm. "I can't carry this any longer. You take it."

When they were safely down the road Ethel ran off a laundry list of obscenities aimed at the wide-open highway and the Minnesota State Patrol. She angrily threw the nametag out the window.

"Bastard can't hang that on me. I was just doing my job."

CHAPTER TWENTY NINE
The wrong god

His travel visa had been revoked. Ben Kowalski studied the communique from the State Department and considered the political gears that had gone into the letter. Ben and a delegation of three had wanted to be a part of an official body representing the American Assembly of Churches at the temple dedication in Jerusalem. The American government was telling him 'thanks, but no thanks.' He considered calling the local paper, the Minneapolis Star & Tribune, but thought otherwise. If they did run the story it would be buried. The bottom line was that he and his people had been snubbed. That's how the Star-Trib would report it, anyway. He knew them. They would view his side of the story as whining. Ben knew the dance.

The letter didn't surprise Ben, but it did disappoint him. What he read between the lines of the finely crafted rejection letter was that Ben's point of view was not welcome at the table. It wasn't news to Ben - it was simply another symptom of the larger disease. He didn't take it personally. He couldn't have attended, anyway. He was overwhelmed with other issues. There were a lot of alligators in his swamp and they were all chewing on him. His wife was in detox. His son was under his wing now. He had the situation in Saudi Arabia and he had the Holy Harvest beginning to show signs of crumbling around the edges.

Being snubbed by the State Department was the least of his worries.

The Holy Harvest was turning out to be a movement of both redemption and potential catastrophe. His security people were telling stories of government obstruction in most of the 60 locations across the globe where the celebration would be observed. A free and open calling to God was a noble thing, all the governments would say publicly.

Privately, what they objected to was that Ben Kowalski and his band of zealots had picked the wrong god.

Then, too, in Saudi Arabia his contract employees were being hunted in the wilderness. Arne and his crew would be captured, jailed or maybe killed. It wasn't a matter of if, but when. They were waiting for an exit strategy from Ben.

They were still waiting.

CHAPTER THIRTY
Opportunity knocking

Arne had done his best sales presentation on his own staff. Neither Ewald nor Mahrous were initially in favor of splitting up, but Arne assured them that his journey into the wilderness was calculated and inconsequential to their escape. He had decided to go it alone. For one thing, Mahrous couldn't make the journey because of the painful hematoma on his shin. Besides, wherever they were hiding in the hills didn't matter, Arne argued, because the Saudis were looking for three needles in a haystack.

They lanced Mahrous's ugly hematoma that night. Ewald sat on his chest while Arne made a six-inch cut into the flesh. As a research scientist in the field of carcinogenic pathogens Arne had made thousands of surgical cuts into biopsies and even a few cadavers. But, cadavers don't scream or flinch in pain. Arne made the cut quick. A river of blood escaped from the knot on Mahrous's shin, relieving the intense pressure of the hematoma. The problem now would be infection. Not having more than a tube of antibiotic cream in their pack, the decision was made to immobilize Mahrous and have his gaping wound exposed to the ultraviolet rays of the Saudi summer sun as much as possible. With any luck, the sand and dirt would not be blown into the wound. That was beyond what they could control.

Ewald had a pair of night vision binoculars stowed in his bag. He had absconded with them while serving as a sailor in the British Royal Navy. Given their situation, Arne decided sneaking up on the Mountain of God would best be done under cover of darkness. Ironic, he thought, that stealth would be the preferred method in approaching God's mountain.

With his night vision binoculars Arne could view the Saudi nightscape brilliantly except for one small problem - he could see 200 meters in front of him but he couldn't see 20 meters in front of him. In the night, it was like turning on a light to get your bearings, turning the light off and then running into the night stand. So, Arne would walk, stumble, look, walk, stumble and look. Even in the relatively flat wadis, the path was strewn with rocks that varied from the size of door knobs to washing machines, with many unexpected dimples in the land.

On his belt Arne had his cell phone. In his belt he had a GPS locator. He wondered if a gun would help or hurt. It was academic. He didn't have one. He had to keep moving. He had a timetable and he was determined to keep it. He had told Ewald and Mahrous that he would be gone for 28 hours.

At 2:00 AM he rounded the corner of the first mountain in the Jabel El Lawz range. The Rock at Horeb was only half a mile away. He could see it silhouetted against the Saudi sky. When he approached it, he reached in his bag for his digital camera. He climbed up the rocky slope to the 30-foot high split rock and quickly danced around it snapping flashes in the night. He wished he could shoot during the day but that was wishful thinking. He was four miles from his destination. He had to keep moving.

Halfway to the Mountain of God he slipped down into a rut and threw his back out. He lay in the dirt and dust and tried to figure out just how bad it was. His back had been giving him problems since he was 40. When he threw it out, typically, there was a shooting pain that would start in his lower back and run down both his legs. The only way he could walk would be rigidly upright and without any lateral flexion or rotation at the hips. He weighed his predicament. He wished he had a 20-year-old body again. But, at 20, he wouldn't have had any compulsion to be where he was. He would have been chasing Swedish women and drinking beer. Youth had so much resilience with so little direction. Painfully, he raised himself to his feet and took a few steps. It hurt, but he was almost to the Mountain of God. He would play with pain.

At about 5:30 AM he had found his destination. He knew from the satellite photos that he was close to what he theorized was the golden calf altar. Between him and the altar were the only two Saudi soldiers in 100 square miles. Arne could see their shack behind a fence in the moonscape, about 500 meters to his right. There were no lights on in their guardhouse. The assumption could be made that they were sleeping. Behind the fence in the guard area were a jeep and a camo four-wheeler sitting idle. Around the guardhouse was a half-mile of fence surrounding the base of Mount Sinai, the true Mountain of God. The satellite photos had always given Arne a sense of utter amazement. Why would the Saudi government pick this one little piece of real estate to protect? It made no practical sense, but here in the middle of the moon was a half-mile of fence around the base of a mountain and another fence encircling what Arne theorized was the site of the golden calf altar. Officially, the Saudis said they were archeological sites. They would offer no explanation beyond that. They were a sovereign government. Like a domineering parent, the only answer they had to officially give was, "because."

One thousand meters in front of the guardhouse there was a pile of rocks. The Saudis, for reasons they wouldn't explain, had built a fence around it. It rose about 15 feet in the air. Many of the rocks had fallen, but even after 3500 years it was apparent to Arne that this was not a random pile of rocks engineered only by gravity or groundswell. The base of the altar was too big to be man-made. At the top of the rocks, though, the centuries could not hide the fact that men had tried to engineer something of note. A small altar had been constructed on top of the bedrock to create what Arne theorized was a perfect fit for an altar to the Egyptian god of Apis, the bull god. Now, he had to prove it.

Arne walked in measured steps across the broad expanse of wadi in front of him. It was a painful trek. His back was killing him. Periodically, he would stop and fix his eyes on the guardhouse to see if any lights were on. In his pack he pulled out a pair of wire cutters and began the slow process of cutting a heavy gauge fence with wire cutters designed for a smaller application. It would be tedious work, but Arne was prepared to sweat. Then, he spotted something the Saudis couldn't have prepared for. A boulder had fallen from the altar and flexed a huge berm of earth beneath a section of the fence. Painfully, he wriggled underneath it. He was in. He looked at his watch. It was 6:38 AM and already 88 degrees. Inside the fence, under the rocks of the altar it would be stagnant and hotter. He had planned to stay under it for the day, hiding and sleeping and snapping pictures. His plan was to return to Ewald and Mahrous that evening under cover of dark. He had five liters of water in his back-pack. He uncapped one and drank a half-liter before stopping, in spite of his thirst. He would have to ration. He unhooked the phone from his belt and called Ewald.

"I'm at ground zero," he said. "Nothing remarkable. Wait for further communications."

"Copy" was the only response. Cell phone communcations were to be minimized for two specific reasons: To save wear and tear on batteries, and to thwart the possibilitiy of the Saudis triangulating their calls. Adjectives, news and hyperbole would come later.

All around Arne, under the rocks, were pictures. In the pre-dawn hours

Arne could see the carvings, the drawings. They were Egyptian in form and history. There were no Saudi equivalents to the art gallery Arne found all around himself. Their age couldn't be scientifically determined, but Arne knew without the benefit of a carbon-14 analysis how old they were – 3500 years old. The worship of Apis bulls was uniquely Egyptian. The cultures and kingdoms of Saudi Arabia had no equivalent in their histories. The Bible told of how the Hebrews, growing impatient of Moses' return from the top of the mountain, were given the okay by Moses' brother, Aaron, to make a tribute to their god. They chose the god they knew best - an Egyptian one. They constructed a monument. Arne was now hiding in that monument. He snapped digital pictures from every conceivable angle. He knew the larger meaning of the bulls carved and drawn into the rocks, but he was a part of the choir. He didn't need any convincing. Getting the pictures to the world was why he had been called to the altar.

In the distance, Arne heard the drone of engines. Jeeps, it sounded like. He knew what it meant. He didn't want to be trapped behind a fence by the Saudis. He would have to find another location.

With his binoculars he could see that there were three jeeps. Each had two soldiers in them. When they reached the guardhouse there was a flurry of activity. In a wilderness where there was supposed to be only two soldiers, suddenly there were eight. He crawled out from under the fence and headed for the nearest hill. If his back was injured, he wasn't feeling it much. The clinical side of him said it was the fear and adrenaline that made him forget the pain in his back and legs. He scurried up a hill, looking over his shoulder at the guardhouse as he did. They were all inside now. Had they seen him run up the hill they would be on his tail. They weren't.

Within 15 minutes, all eight of the Saudis were in jeeps and heading south. Arne called Ewald to give him the news.

"Got four jeeps, eight Saudi soldiers, total, heading your way. Armed. Copy?"

"Copy. Any ideas?"

"Yeah," Arne thought for a moment. "Avoid them."

The sound of the jeeps faded down the wadi and into silence. Arne looked across the landscape and stared up to the Mountain of God - not the one invented by Constantine's mother on the Sinai Peninsula, but the true mountain of faith, veneration and history. He carefully climbed down from his rocky perch and began jogging towards the base of the mountain. His back felt fine. Opportunity was knocking. Behind the guardhouse was a small stone altar. He had seen it from a high-definition satellite photograph. It was a stone anomaly, but it fit in perfectly with the description in The Exodus of the stone altar that the Hebrews had erected at the base of the mountain to make animal sacrifices to God. As Arne approached he looked for a way inside.

The idiots had left the gate open!!

He bounded up the steps of the guardhouse and went inside. There was a water cooler and a refrigerator. He quickly quenched himself and filled his water bottle. Then he grabbed a hunk of cheese, some cold cuts of lamb and beef and jammed them into his backpack. He looked quickly for a gun but found none. He ran around the back of the shack and there, 100 yards in front of him was the altar. It was about 120 feet long with two 30-degree elbows in it. There were two "walkways" through which Arne hypothesized they channeled the animals through to their sacrifice. Incredibly, there was a pit at the end of the channels which appeared to still have ancient ashes in it. He found the ashes unbelievable but then he considered that in this quadrant of Saudi Arabia the rainfall amounted to only one-tenth of an inch every decade! The altar/walkway was about three feet high and badly degraded by time but it was no freak of gravity. It was man-made. Off to his left he heard the unmistakable sound of cascading water. He couldn't see the water but he could hear it. And, in an environment where dust and dirt and heat filled one's nostrils constantly, he could smell it. He snapped pictures furiously. He had no idea how much time he had before one or more of the jeeps might return. He snapped 38 digital pictures of the altar before his danger clock told him he ought to loiter somewhere else.

Before leaving he allowed himself one personal extravagance. He climbed an incline until the face of the mountain rose almost vertically upward and he could go no further.

He kissed the mountain.

CHAPTER THIRTY ONE
A Norman Rockwell portrait

They picked up Highway 163 going north out of Walker, Minnesota. It would lead them through Ely, Orr and Cook on their way to International Falls and the border crossing. They rode along silently. Lars had turned the radio off after their encounter with the State Patrol. He could feel his wife's seething turn into something more disquieting - quiet.

After exiting from Highway 10, the road became a two-lane highway with a variety of small towns that forced them to speed up, slow down, speed up, slow down. Ethel shuddered at the mileage they were getting at $6.03 per gallon. Outside of Walker there was a hand-painted sign, a large one, posted hastily on the side of the road which said "The Lord is Coming. Holy Harvest, two miles ahead."

"What's a Holy Harvest?" Ethel asked.

"I don't know. Kowalski mentioned it. Said there was a world-wide prayer service or something like it. Supposed to be held along with the Jewish temple dedication."

They looked at each other. Neither had a clue.

It wasn't a town, it was a church where the Holy Harvest was being observed. Cars were lined up for a half mile before the church. Lars slowed his car down to a 10-mile-an-hour crawl. The road was narrow with cars on each side. There was unpredictable foot traffic of moms and dads and kids darting in and out.

"Did you hear anything about this?" Lars asked his wife.

"Nothing. I read in Newsweek about the temple dedication but I didn't think it was a big deal. Unless you're a Jew."

At the center of the throng, Lars slowed the car down and slipped into an area marked "for official vehicles only."

"What are you doing, Lars?"

"Hey, we're on vacation. We're supposed to be spontaneous. I want to find out what this is all about." He turned off the ignition and climbed out of the cab. "Coming with?"

"Thank you, no." Ethel huffed. She had a lot of issues and no time for a freak show. She put her feet up on the dash and turned on the radio.

"This is NPR," the announcer intoned.

Lars walked across the road. His eyes drank in thousands of people, most of them huddled around TV monitors. There were booths with sodas and hot dogs and it looked like a small-town summer festival. There were American flags and people everywhere. It looked like a Norman Rockwell portrait of a world Lars thought had died decades ago. It brought Lars back to his boyhood when he had been a wide-eyed youth at the Cook County Fair outside of Chicago.

There was a hand-painted sign along the pathway which caught his eye. "Prepare to meet prophecy," it said. Slightly further up the path was another sign. "Jesus is Lord." In a small clearing there were preachers dunking people in a tank. Lars recognized the baptism from his days as a Baptist youth, days he had long since abandoned. There was a rumble in the air. Heads turned.

From above, two Air National Guard helicopters buzzed the Holy Harvest. Instinctively, people covered their heads and ducked. The sound was deafening and the ground shook from the reverberation of their blades. Lars caught the sight of white clouds of something being sprayed out of the helicopters. Lars commanded his 67-year-old legs to sprint. What he got was a brisk jog. By the time he got to the car, Ethel had already positioned herself behind the wheel. Lars flopped into the passenger side as Ethel jammed on the gas.

"What the hell was that?" Lars screamed.

"That was you being spontaneous," Ethel shouted as they got out onto the highway and out of the area. She checked her rearview mirror and all she could see was clouds and panic.

They had been the luckiest ones in the camp. Their vehicle had been parked illegally and was in a position to tear down the highway first.

"Tear gas?" Ethel asked.

"Yeah, whew!" Lars said, taking a water bottle and squirting it directly into his eyes.

"Careful. You're getting the seat wet."

Lars flashed her any icy stare that could break a bone china teapot at 20 paces. She shut up.

Lars turned up the radio. The attack they had just witnessed might have some larger context. He couldn't imagine what, but he wanted news.

NPR was doing a repeat of the crusty old Cleveland patriot story. It was a four minute piece, he knew. He switched channels. None of the Twin Cities stations were in range. They were in one of those rural dead zones where FM just faded in and faded out without much clarity. Besides, they were up in corn country. All they were picking up was country music.

Ethel finally decided enough time had lapsed since her husband's angry stare. "If you're looking for news you'll have to switch to AM."

"Does this thing have AM?"

"I think so. I think you have to slide the FM button to the other side."

AM radio had never been done in their car. Lars had to study it.

CHAPTER THIRTY TWO
Am I grounded, dad?

Ben and Amanti had a plan. They couldn't tell Arne yet but, they had come up with an idea. They wanted to make certain the Saudis didn't have ears in the sky - that they weren't monitoring their phone conversations.

"Our timetable would be a lot more reliable if Arne hadn't decided to become an archeologist in the middle of a crisis," lamented Leon Amanti.

Originally, Amanti had seethed at the Swede when he saw the GPS signal moving Arne further and further inland. Then, he considered the Swede analytically. Of course Arne was seizing the moment to confirm his hypothesis. Amanti didn't want to risk calling either Arne or Ewald - their location could be compromised. He was willing to simply monitor the GPS signal and let it tell him when the three exiles would be together at their "home base" again. The GPS locator told Amanti that Arne had ventured about 15 miles from where he had been two days prior.

From their most recent phone conversation with Ewald, a day prior, they confirmed that Arne had gone off to the Mountain of God. Ewald was smart enough to code the message by saying "he went for a walk. You know where. Signing off."

Ben's plan, if it could work at all, required that the three of them be together. Now they had to wait. Ben wondered why Arne would do such a thing without telling them, but he didn't have to dwell too long on the thought – Ben knew - he would have done the same thing. A chance to set the biblical record straight would have been irresistible. Ben didn't understand the compulsion of the Swede, but he respected it.

No sooner had Ewald hung up his call from the Kowalski compound when it rang again.

"Speak. Quickly." Ewald said.

"You won't believe where I am, Richard. At Jabel El Lawz, the Mountain of God. It's incredible," he said with zeal. "I can't wait to show you the pictures. There are so many incredible things here at this mountain," he said deliberately. Ewald couldn't believe that the Swede was doing this thing, calling and perhaps compromising their position by communicating something that could easily wait.

And he hung up. Immediately, Ewald and Mahrous heard the sounds of the Saudi jeeps, which had been combing the wadis, turn and head north toward Jabel El Lawz.

The assumption Ewald made at the moment was that their calls weren't being triangulated for location, but they were being monitored. "Damn," muttered Ewald. "Stupid Swede! Why not just send up a flare!" Ewald screamed. "He's going to get all of us killed." At that moment a motor could be heard racing up to their location.

"Bloody idiot. C'mon, Mahrous. We're getting out of here."

"Ewald….Mahrous! Where are you?"

It was Arne. The Egyptian and the Brit peered from behind their lofty rock to the wadi below. Their partner was sitting, smiling on a four-wheel drive Saudi ATV.

"What's the plan? Talk to me."

"Where have you been? You just said you were at the mountain. What's happening?"

"Just throwing the wolves off the trail. I figured by now they would be listening. I needed them to leave. Am I grounded, dad?"

Ewald had made his way down the rocks and was quickly at Arne's side. He went to embrace the Swede but Arne held up his hand.

"Don't. Don't. My back. It's killing me. I threw it out." He climbed slowly off the ATV. "They left this thing behind and I thought to myself 'where would they hide the keys?' If it were me they would be on a hook, inside of the door. Some things are the same in every culture. That's where they were. So, I took this thing and I've been laying low in it ever since. Didn't want to call until the time was right. I figured if you didn't know my location, they wouldn't know."

Ewald smiled. He unhooked the phone from his belt and walked away from Arne. He autodialed and the phone rang on Arne's belt. Arne picked up the call.

"Arne here."

"Arne, they're all heading back your way. Find a hole to crawl in. Copy?"

Arne flashed a smile at his partner. "Copy."

Ewald climbed back up the hill and helped the Egyptian down to the ATV. He made a second trip up the hill and grabbed their gear. The message Ewald and Arne had sent the Saudis would keep them busy sniffing at the wrong end of the wilderness. For a while. They needed to sleep. Arne knew a nice, out of the way oasis where they could rest their heads for a while.

CHAPTER THIRTY THREE
Company song

The Secret Service agent walked up behind Ben Kowalski and whispered in his ear.

"Sir, Marshall Warren is at the door." The news caught Ben Kowalski flat-footed. "And, sir, he's quite drunk."

Ben thought about the development for a moment. Not that Marshall was drunk, no. He was usually drunk, according to the scuttlebutt. What made no sense was why he was there at all. They hadn't seen each other in, what, seven years? The only capacity Marshall Warren might call on Ben would be to seek sobriety - doubtful - or to lend something to the cause. A social visit wasn't a possibility. They didn't even like each other. Marshall had picked Ben to be the vice president only as a measure of keeping the country from the not-so-subtle seduction of Billy Kim.

Ben met him at the door and stepped out onto the porch to speak. Ben extended his hand. Marshall Warren had to switch the Styrofoam coffee cup out of his right hand and into his left. "Ben, good to see you."

Ben looked into his former boss' eyes and had to smirk. He motioned to the coffee cup. "You want me to warm up your coffee?"

"Nahhh. I'm just fine. Besides - it ain't coffee, Cowboy."

"Yes, I figured that Mr. President."

"Mr. President? - Oooh. We're pretty formal."

"Marshall, somehow I don't think you came here to visit. You know I've got a lot on my plate right now. If you've got business, I'd appreciate it if you, you know, got to it." He waited for a response.

"You're not going to invite me in?"

"Sure, Marshall. You want to come in and visit with a lot of very busy and very sober Christians you're welcome to it."

"Do I get an introduction? A little fanfare?"

Ben rolled his eyes. He motioned Marshall to stand where he was and stepped inside the door.

"May I have your attention, please?" The Kowalski compound was a beehive of activity but when the boss asked for attention, the worker bees obliged.

"Ladies and gentlemen it is my distinct honor and high privilege to present the former President of the United States, the honorable Marshall G. Warren." Ben opened the door. Marshall Warren caught his jacket pocket on the screen door handle as he stepped into the room. It threw him off stride. He tried again. And again. Finally, Ben reached over and released the pocket from the door handle. If it was funny, no one laughed.

Marshall Warren waved to the room.

"Nice to meet you all." He looked at them one by one and then looked back at Ben. "They are very sober, aren't they?"

Marshall had asked to meet with Ben alone. Ben knew better. He brought Amanti and Reynolds Thomas into the meeting. That way Ben wouldn't be saddled with telling his former boss that he was drunk, babbling, out of line and would have to go. At least, not alone. Safety in numbers.

For as loaded as Marshall appeared to be, he was incredibly lucid. It reminded Ben of himself. Ben had been a lucid drunk.

Once introductions had been made Marshall came right to the point.

"I used to have a friend in the State Department named Chuck Winston. He had been a part of NSA, CIA, foreign intel, the works. He had a half dozen aliases and could speak Russian and Chinese and a couple other languages. Global player. Anyway, when I became president he offered his services. Covertly. He knew that Billy Kim was up to some things. He just didn't know what. He knew, for example, that Billy and Hans Tanner spent two quarters in internship at the University of Cairo at the same time. Found out that they had a couple of classes together and belonged to some sort of Knights of the Brotherhood, or some such thing. I forget the name. It was some kind of pagan thing - I could never follow it all. Frankly, I still think it's all hooey, but we do know that at one point their paths intersected."

Ben looked at his watch. Marshall caught the look.

"It's very important you stay with me here because I do have a point. I promise. Anyway, Winston doesn't trust Kim and devotes all of his energy to finding out who he is. Guess what he comes up with? Nothing. Kim graduated from UC Davis with a poly-sci and, oddly, a bachelor's degree in genetic engineering. Then, his parents head back to China. They disappeared into the landscape right after Billy Kim entered college. Almost as if Billy had been given legal overseers until he became of age and then he was just cut loose to sink or swim on his own. Problem is, he's not sinking. He's got money coming from somewhere and Winston, to this day, never did find out from where, but was able to determine that he didn't have to work."

Ben felt obliged to interrupt. "Marshall, can we get the Cliff Notes version of this? We're just a bunch of church deacons trying to conduct a very large service. We've got a lot of details to attend to."

"Ben, don't sell yourself short. You guys are the only ones left willing to report what's actually going on. What is true is being smothered. Real news has been replaced with a kind of company song."

"It's called media bias, spin." interrupted Reynolds Thomas. "Are you just starting to notice it, Mr. President? It was around well before you were in office."

"I'm a drunk, but I'm not an idiot. It's deeper now. If you look at most of the major news bureaus - in the last six months there's been regime changes. Most of them have been low-keyed. Just a press release and a Page Six story. Do a Google search. I did."

They couldn't discount what Marshall was saying.

"Okay, where do we fit in?" asked Ben.

"Hear me out. So, I'm at a party in Hawaii two weeks ago and I get a call from Winston. He says he's in China. Wants me to pull some strings to get a lady fugitive out of China. Caucasian lady. Says he can't tell me the whole story. I do what I can legally, but that's not enough. We eventually had to go to the Australians to get some documents forged so he can get her out of the country. She's out in my limo, right now. She can connect all the dots."

"We're not trying to connect dots, Marshall. We've got our own fish to fry. We're not involved in any government. We're a part of a very large church movement."

"Well, if I'm reading the tea leaves correctly, you will soon be part of a very large political movement and your church is going to be right in the cross hairs - like it or not."

"Okay, Marshall," Ben conceded. "You've got our attention. Who do you have in your car and what can she tell us."

Marshall Warren motioned his Secret Service men to fetch whoever this whole meeting was about. He then pulled a half-pint of scotch out of his jacket pocket and poured an inch into his Styrofoam cup. He grabbed the pitcher from the desk and topped it off with water.

"Don't mind if I do. Anyone else? Good. I'm running low."

Marshall Warren's two Secret Service agents brought her in the side door. When she walked into the conference room one of the agents pulled a chair out for her.

The men responded in a breathless chorus: "Claudia Colgate."

She was, after all, the most notorious woman on earth. Everyone knew her. She looked a little disheveled and she was wearing clothes that were hardly befitting an international fashion template. She had on a work shirt and blue jeans that were obviously thrown on her not by a designer but, more likely, a gardener.

Reynolds Thomas, the attorney, Leon Amanti, the chief of staff, and Ben Kowalski collectively cleared their throats at the sight of the woman.

"Marsh," Ben was deliberate. "On the news yesterday, all of us saw Billy Kim get off Air Force One in Jerusalem with a woman who looked amazingly like her," he said. "You have an explanation?"

"That's where the story gets interesting."

Amanti couldn't make sense of what was going on. "Quit speaking in riddles! Is she or is she not Claudia Colgate?"

Claudia spoke deliberately. "The woman in Jerusalem is a fraud. I am Claudia Colgate."

Amanti was unsatisfied. "What are you? A twin?"

"Yes."

"So, Billy Kim dumped you?"

"No, he tried to kill me."

"And, he recruited your sister to stand in your shoes?"

"He didn't really recruit her." She weighed her words carefully and looked at them all directly.

"She was *created* to walk in my shoes."

Claudia, or whoever she was, poured herself a cup of coffee. "I don't know how willing or able you will be to believe this but that thing hanging on Billy Kim's arm yesterday in Jerusalem isn't my sister. She's my clone."

No one spoke. They were trying to judge whether this woman was yanking their collective chains.

"Cloning is unproven, dangerous and against the law," Reynolds Thomas, the attorney, was obliged to add.

Marshall Warren reacted as if he had been waiting for the set-up to his punch line.

"You know what they say: When clones are outlawed, only outlaws will have clones…I told you - we have a lot of dots to connect."

CHAPTER THIRTY FOUR
Syrup and smarm

The stage was temporary. It had been constructed for the dedication ceremonies. After that, it would be torn down. It extended out over the apron of the ancient western wall, the Wailing Wall of the Second Temple, the very temple that had been razed by the Romans in 70 AD.

Madison Avenue in New York City had a fortune invested in the event. The dedication ceremony was being heralded on every commercial media venue available on the planet. The advertising community was grateful, willing and beholding for all the money being shoveled at the event. No one seemed to be asking where the money was coming from. Cash was flowing like a winter thaw into the Muslim countries of the Middle East. Al-Jazeera, the Arab TV network, was running back-to-back infomercials between their programs promoting the event. It was unclear why the non-Muslim world would be throwing good money at a market they couldn't tap. No one seemed overly curious. If sponsors were looking for a return on investment they were going about it in a novel way. With a little digging, an enterprising journalist could find an interesting story in the machinations behind the temple hype. Enterprising journalists, though, seemed to be at a premium. The world news community seemed to accept on faith what was happening in Jerusalem as the simple yearning of a spiritually hungry world.

It wasn't faith. It was cash.

The message was simple. The Arabs were being told the event was a marriage of the common ancestry of both Jew and Arab. According to Madison Avenue, Jews and Arabs were brothers.

It needed some reinforcement.

The 30, 60 and 120-second infomercials ignored 4000 years of visceral hatred between these 'brothers.' According to Madison Avenue and Hollywood, the enmity between Arab and Jew, Jacob and Esau, could be erased in bites of 30, 60 and 120 seconds.

The faithful didn't buy it. But they were in the minority. Neither the fundamental Muslims nor the orthodox Jews recognized the new temple. Faithful Jews and Muslims argued their faith couldn't be sold.

The sponsors disagreed.

To compound the chaos, the orthodox Jews were out of joint about the construction going on, or in, the Wailing Wall. For four weeks the old Wailing Wall had been covered up with scaffolding and hidden underneath sheets of heavy black poly while Palestinian construction workers burrowed into the earth behind it. The official Palestinian lie was that the construction team was pouring foundations for a new portico being added to the Al Aqsa mosque.

Partly, this was true. They were pouring foundations beneath the poly. That was the true part. What they were pouring was the concrete to support a monstrous pneumatic tube. The workers pouring the concrete were all union Palestinians. They, too, were part of the compromise. They had all been told by their employer that if any of them talked out of class about what was happening beneath the plastic sheeting, their families would be killed. It was the kind of influence union workers, regardless of national origin, understood without being told twice.

This new temple, this compromise of a temple, was being hailed as a new chapter in relations between Palestinians, Jews, Arabs and the rest of the world. Those hailing the compromise had lot of money invested in how the world perceived what was happening.

EU President Hans Tanner and American President Billy Kim had arrived in time for a brief press conference and rehearsal two days before the beginning of the three-day temple dedication ceremonies. They met briefly, shook hands and smiled for the cameras before they were whisked away by security to their respective hotels.

The temple dedication was supposed to be a display of 'hands across the water.' It was supposed to be a celebration of life, love, joy, music, dance, happy thoughts, and whatever else could be troweled out with syrup and smarminess. The audience was by invitation only. Many political dignitaries. Image was paramount. Of the 15,000 observers allowed through the gates, half of them were just common citizens. It was important that they be of all stripes - Arabs, Jews, black, white, brown, men, women, children. The organizers wanted to be certain the temple dedication looked like a world court. What was largely unreported was that the attendees would all be required to walk through metal detectors and that every man, woman and child would be frisked. Twice.

Under the poly, under the Al Aqsa Mosque, was a chamber. In it there was a beehive of workers racing the clock. They were putting the finishing touches on a series of dressing rooms and a small rehearsal theater which were connected to the main stage by a long tunnel. At the end of the tunnel was a pneumatic tube. The tube was large enough to hold three adults.

In the underground complex a stage manager had been given a script. The stage manager had been promised a handsome payment for following the script and keeping its contents entirely secret. To make sure of his fidelity he had been assigned two plain-clothes Hamas agents who shielded him from everyone but the singers, actors and dancers. The stage manager was a subcontractor recommended by the vice president of acquisitions at CNN. He had made his mark as a production coordinator on Broadway. He was hired because he was a cool customer with actors. He understood them and he understood how to read, follow and anticipate a script. But there was a part of the script that was not held in his hands. It was the final chapter - the act where he would be shot in the back of the head upon the completion of his three-day gig, stuffed into the pneumatic tube and then encased in concrete. All he knew was that he had a chance to make some serious money for minimal work.

"People...people. Places, please!!!" he announced to the actors. "This is a dress rehearsal! We need energy!!!"

CHAPTER THIRTY FIVE
News, dammit!

Ethel Larsen was hating the trip. She had been witness to a group of Christians being tear-gassed. It didn't really bother her that they had been gassed. What bothered her most is that she had seen it with her own eyes and could never be expected to deny it. What bothered her second-most was that the incident had lit a fire in her husband. His right hand was constantly tweaking the AM dial for news about it. She wanted to scream at him, "It happened. You saw it. I saw it. Life goes on. Get over it."

Ethel also had to reconcile the fact that she had been admonished by the Minnesota State Patrol for having done her job. And then, to totally ruin her weekend, Lars had agreed to let the Kowalski group rent their house for a couple days!

Their cell phone had rung in their car about an hour after racing away from the Christian gassing. It was Ben Kowalski. The government, it was told to Lars, had cut the power to the Kowalski house. It's what Kowalski said, anyway. Probably, Ethel thought, they hadn't paid their utility bill. That would be more likely. What Kowalski asked of them was to rent their home for a day or two while they got some generators. He was willing to pay $1000 per day to rent it. He said it was a desperate situation. Lars had taken the call and seemed to be more concerned with the government having cut the power. He wanted to know the details. Kowalski explained how a utility truck with no markings had parked in their alley and a man in coveralls had disconnected the power lines to the Kowalski compound. The man on the pole was efficient. He cut the lines. They couldn't be reconnected. Lars was unbelieving at first but Kowalski, as usual, was sincere sounding.

Lars couldn't help but wonder about his own home.

"Do we have power?" Lars asked.

"Yes, I had Jake go over and check it out."

"Were they targeting you?"

"Apparently. None of the neighbors were hit. The guy was efficient. He cut off three feet from both sides so that no one could come out and just re-connect the lines. Whatever their intentions are, they were designed to knock us out of the saddle. You have any theories?"

The conspiracy theories floating in Lars' brain saw the development in a larger context, but he didn't want to speculate with his wife sitting next to him.

Lars told Kowalski about the gassing of the Christians at the roadside. They talked like they were friends! It was a disturbing development for Ethel. Kowalski, after all, was supposed to be a Larsen adversary. And, then, Lars said okay when Kowalski asked if they could rent their house for a day or two! Ethel fumed. Lars decided a fuming wife was a condition he could live with. He was familiar with it.

Lars and Ethel had been pre-registered to spend the night at Wickstrom's fishing lodge in Ely. All the way through central Minnesota, Lars had been scanning the AM frequencies on his radio for some news of what had happened at the Holy Harvest he and Ethel had escaped.

"Army helicopters don't just casually gas a peaceful church group. It's news, dammit." Lars wanted somebody to report it. Still, scan as he might, he could find no station making any reference to the incident.

"Did we imagine that?" he finally asked his wife. She said nothing. She gritted her teeth. She wished they had.

AM 980 out of Duluth didn't draw a lot of listeners. They were only approved for a 1000-watt signal and had a directional broadcast pattern that sent their signal southeast about 30 miles into Wisconsin and 30 miles northwest into the lake country of Minnesota. Lars caught their signal, but it wouldn't track for more than 30 seconds at a time.

"...In Toronto, organizers at the Holy Harvest are reporting that security is tight. Worshippers have been asked to show identification and submit to random checks at the gate."

"Those checks are illegal, Chet," said his broadcast partner. "They're asking for ID to attend a religious gathering. They can say it's for security reasons all they want, but at the end of the day, what the Canadian government is doing to these people is unconstitutional."

"I understand, too, Bob that there have been incidences of people being ushered into fields adjoining the stadium...." The signal faded. The urgency in the announcer's voices told Lars that they were reporting news. News, not conjecture, not day-old recaps, but an actual event. Lars tried to tweak the receiver to lock into AM 980. Static. Garbled, yet urgent voices. Finally, at the crest of a hill the signal locked into 980 again. They were broadcasting a hymn, 'How Great Thou Art.' Lars recognized it from his youth. He hadn't heard the melody for 50 years. It spun him backwards in time.

"It's a Christian station!" Ethel proclaimed. "Find something reliable," she barked. Lars ignored her and listened to the hymn, silently turning back the pages of his life to the time he had sung that very song in the youth choir of the Second Baptist Church of Calumet, Illinois. There were memories in this simple hymn that Lars had long since buried. He passed off what he was feeling as nostalgia, yet he couldn't manufacture the energy to search for another station. He was hypnotized. His wife wanted to bark at him to change the channel but he was softly singing the chorus: "How great Thou art. How great Thou art."

She had never seen him softly singing. It was both curious and frightening.

They arrived at Wickstrom's in relative silence. She wondered what was happening to her husband. He wondered about the significance of the events his eyes had unmistakably witnessed.

Frank Wickstrom had been a good friend over the years. He had always been gracious and helpful and kind and caring. When Lars and Ethel met him at the office he looked detached. He looked so much older than he should have. They exchanged greetings but Frank had little to say. "You've got Cabin Three. Breakfast is 6:00-8:30."

"Something wrong, Frank?" Lars asked.

Frank Wickstrom unloaded. It was as if someone pulled the cork out of his bottle. He spent the next five minutes in a tirade. Business was down. The cost of gas was killing him. His old customers weren't booking anymore.

"This is the Fourth of July weekend, Lars! Look at my lot. It's not even a third full." He went on to blast the Christians for having the Holy Harvest on a holiday weekend. He blasted the Jews for re-dedicating their temple on a holiday weekend. He said he didn't know if he could even afford to keep the doors on the place open much longer. He lamented the fact that the resort had been in the family for three generations, but now he couldn't see a future for his own kids. He talked about the new taxes the legislature had imposed on the tourist industry. Liquor and tobacco, he said, was a back-breaker. No one was buying their booze or cigarettes because of the taxes.

"They bring their own from out of state." He said half of his old business was now booking their vacations, when they could afford it, in Wisconsin where the taxes weren't so high.

It was an area Ethel didn't want to explore with him. She had voted for the higher tourist, tobacco and liquor taxes when she had been in the state senate - a fact she was sure he was unaware of but, still, she didn't want to go there. She was surprised, though. She thought the Wickstrom family didn't live 'on the edge.' In her mind, a place like Wickstrom's could absorb a few more taxes. She made a mental note that Frank Wickstrom was a whiner.

"Frank?" Ethel interrupted. "We're tired. We've got a lot of ground to cover tomorrow and maybe in the morning we can chat over breakfast."

Frank was embarrassed. He had vented to customers. Not very businesslike. He knew better. He excused himself and reminded them that he would be available if they needed him.

Last light didn't fade until almost 10:00 P.M. Ethel was under the covers and fast asleep by 9:30 - having fallen asleep with CNN on the TV. Lars couldn't turn his brain off like that. He had spent a half-hour watching CNN to see if there was any news about what they had seen. He wasn't sure how CNN could report it - Christians being gassed by the government? Christians being controlled by the government? What he had seen at the roadside church had happened. It couldn't have happened in a vacuum. A Minnesota National Guard commander didn't just decide he was going to gas a church group just for practice. The order had to come from somewhere.

CNN, as it turned out, was the only national outlet for news up in the Minnesota lake country. Lars tried to find some other source but CNN was the only game in town. CNN had led off the half-hour segment with "team coverage" of the temple dedication - something which was not news to Lars. In the 16th minute of the broadcast there was a brief 15-second mention of the Holy Harvest - how Christians across the world were celebrating their roots in concert with the temple dedication.

That was it.

Lars had read a piece in a dentist's office - years earlier - that described how CNN had 'manipulated' the cable contracts so that only CNN news came into most rural locations. They had also locked up all airports as the news of preference. He read that there was a unique set of unscrupulous circumstances that froze out the competition. He had discounted the story. He had read it in "The Economist," after all. In Lars' mind it couldn't have been true – he would have heard about it from his usual sources!

Lars slipped quietly out of the cabin and slid in behind the wheel of his Lincoln. He put the key in the ignition and turned it toward himself to 'accessory.' He tuned the digital search for 980 AM. It was dark now. The ionosphere had lowered. In the broadcast world it was the time of day when an AM signal has its strongest legs.

The message Lars was searching for came in clear as a bell.

CHAPTER THIRTY SIX
Origin

Even the assassins from Hamas were impressed by the fireworks display on the Wednesday evening prior to the opening ceremonies of the Jewish temple. Palestinians and Jews, for a slice of time, leaned on their rifles or unbuckled the dynamite around their waists long enough to momentarily forget their 4000-year-old differences. For the first time in history, fireworks were launched from bombs aboard F-15 jets. The streaking jets dropped spectacular pyrotechnics from over 10,000 feet, arcing across the sky in brilliant, explosive hues - each 'bomb' having five stages of explosions cascading and spiraling down against the ink-black sky-drop. In coordination with the ground fireworks, it was a pyrotechnics display unparalleled in history. Literally, the entire panorama of night sky was aglow with colors seemingly descending from heaven.

It was show time. It was a small prelude of what was to come the following day.

At 4:00 PM, Jerusalem time, on Thursday, Billy Kim looked into the camera. As he spoke, his head turned left to right as he addressed the crowd - which, research told them, was the most effective technique of communicating to a camera. The Humphrey Institute of Public Affairs had spent $500,000 of public money to quantify that left-to-right was three percentage points higher than the pedantic right-to-left method.

Another small detail.

On each side of the podium there were TelePrompters which gave him the text of his presentation. An administrative aide saw to it that the script did not scroll too fast or too slow for his delivery. The entire presentation was captured by a single video crew of 30. They were responsible for the pictures that would be fed by satellite to the world. Outside production crews were neither welcomed nor allowed. Ostensibly, this was to prevent the temple dedication from becoming a media circus. Event planners argued that if every news outlet that wanted to shoot pictures were allowed to do so, there would be more media than attendees. CNN won the bidding. It was going to be a CNN shoot with CNN cameras, CNN reporters, CNN producers and CNN technicians, all coordinated from a CNN production truck located just outside of the temple area.

It was late afternoon in Jerusalem and early morning in the US. Most Americans would be working and miss the president's introduction of Hans Tanner. That was fine. The important element was that the Americans get the fury of the moment capsulized on their radios throughout the workday. Then, they would race home to see the only live pictures from the temple dedication - on CNN.

Thursday was Day One. In the morning, an endless parade of dancers, singers, actors, politicians, emissaries and others to whom Billy Kim and Hans Tanner owed homage, presented their entertainment du jour. It was like the Academy Awards without a time limit. The crowd grew restless and listless. The cameras didn't show the crowd. The viewing audiences around the world were shown 'puff pieces' highlighting the historical unity and gravity of the temple dedication - how Muslims, Jews and Christians could finally proclaim a common ancestry, heritage, history and future. Simple platitudes about harmony and brotherhood dominated the airwaves like a non-stop political infomercial.

It was dull to the nth degree. "Andy Griffith" reruns would actually score higher in the ratings than the first few hours of the temple dedication. It was boring stuff, poorly paced and featured a lot of contrived entertainment - none of it compelling. Like everything else, it had been planned that way.

At 4:00 PM, Jerusalem time, Billy Kim was scheduled to introduce Hans Tanner, the EU President. The previous act had featured a Jewish chorus singing a traditional hymn. A haunting accompaniment of Jewish shofars complemented the singers. When their presentation was over, the Jews simply placed the shofars in their stands and left the stage. There were 12 of them, one for every tribe in Israel. The CNN director had asked the talent coordinator to make sure they left the shofars in their stands because they gave depth to the set and they looked like something 'authentic.'

A host of shepherd's shofars are normally pretty harmless. But, if left outside in an unpredictable wind they can sound like the doorbell to the gates of Hades. The shepherd's horns, not having brains of their own, softly or loudly bellowed as the wind blew across their mouthpieces. On the microphone the sound was barely audible for the viewing audience but live, at the temple site, the shofars sounded like a howl from beyond the clouds - a plaintive cry that echoed across the outdoor arena - bellows that seemed to originate from the gods themselves. The speed of the wind that Thursday afternoon was about the only part of the finally-tuned presentation the script hadn't anticipated.

Billy Kim had a miniature earpiece through which the director in the truck could give him cues and instructions. Directors didn't like using the IFB, the earpiece, when "talent" was on camera. Instructions and cues tended to upset the concentration and therefore, the flow of the video moment. As Billy Kim approached the podium he looked at the shofars in their stands. From his vantage point, they were loud and obtrusive. In his mind, he was wondering if the shofars wouldn't drown out what he was about to say.

CNN director Kenneth Quist clicked on the IFB to Kim and gave him a reassurance.

"Mr. President, don't pay any attention to the horns. They're barely audible over the air. Ignore them. You'll be heard just fine."

Billy Kim approached the podium. He stood against a stunning visual backdrop of a 60-foot by 90-foot satellite photo of earth taken from space.

"Today," the president began, "we stand on the verge of a new order."

They were the kind of words people expected from a politician on a world stage. What came next was unexpected.

"I draw your attention to the skies above this great monument."

From out of nowhere a black disc appeared in the sky. It zoomed into airspace above the temple and seemingly stopped on the proverbial dime. It hovered like a giant bee over a honeysuckle earth.

"Somebody, anybody...Get me that shot," screamed Kenneth Quist from inside the production truck. A shoulder-mounted camera in the front row zoomed in and then zoomed out to show the disc in the sky.

"Holy Hanna," implored the director, seeing the disc on one and then two and then six monitors in his truck. "Gentlemen, we have a story."

The disc stood still in the sky, almost like an obedient dog waiting for orders. Whatever it was, it ran virtually silent - a faint hum the only sound. From its belly the disc had a bank of green pulsing lights. Military radar would later indicate that there was nothing in the sky. Whatever it was, it eluded the electron beams of modern science. It simply didn't exist. Yet, there it was. The 15,000 in the assembled crowd saw it. The cameras saw it. The world saw it.

Allowing for the 'ooh's and ahhh's, Billy Kim continued.

"From the beginning of recorded time man has sought answers from above. Today you will see things we have been unable to tell you. Until now."

Billy Kim motioned to the disc in the sky. "Until today the true nature and purpose of the intelligence behind this has been kept a secret. Today, we can demonstrate it because today the very origin of human intelligence can be revealed for all to see."

CHAPTER THIRTY SEVEN
A three-fold strategy

Marshall Warren limped into Lars and Ethel Larsen's kitchen. He had spent the night on the couch in the family room, downstairs. Periodically, nerves in his foot would flare up. Some days were worse than others. In his Percocet days, he would have popped another pill. But, having spent a week in detox getting that monkey off his back he was unwilling to embrace it again. The depression, night sweats and crying jags Percocet addiction brought were an evil torment. Liquor was more primitive, but the hangover could usually be cured with another drink. He could live with that. He pulled a chair up next to Ben Kowalski at the kitchen table of Lars and Ethel Larsen. The Larsen home was neat, tidy, temporarily unoccupied and, most importantly, had electricity. The feds, or whoever had cut the power to the Kowalski home, had evidently had only one mission. As soon as the power disappeared, so did they.

Convincing Lars to let his crew use the Larsen home was the best sales jobs Ben had done in years. When Ben had called Lars on the cell phone he knew Ethel would be next to him. Ben heard Lars 'shushh' her several times while he explained the necessity, the urgency, of them being able to use their house for a few days. Ben then had to listen to a long list of do's and dont's Ethel dictated to Kowalski through Lars. He knew she wasn't happy. Before hanging up, Ben asked Lars if he listened to any coverage of the Holy Harvest.

"Yeah, but I can't really talk about it," responded Lars.

"Ethel would get upset, would she?"

"Yeah."

"Well, Lars, let's just say that all of this has been foretold."

There was a long, cold silence while the words registered with Lars. Lars pondered, momentarily, what to ask next and then decided not to ask anything. He didn't want to go down that road of conversation at that moment.

"Try not to mess the house, okay. We're doing something for you that we're not real comfortable with. Don't let us down, okay?" Lars hung up.

Ben recognized what Lars was doing. He was trying to save face in front of Ethel. Ethel, he knew, would be fuming. It had been Lars' intervention that allowed them to set up a temporary base of operations. Ben said a quick prayer. They had a lot to be thankful for.

Ben nursed a cup of coffee and stared out the kitchen window. He felt old. The Holy Harvest was a bust. From what he could glean from talk radio and Lars' cable TV affiliates, most of the sites of the Holy Harvest celebration had been corrupted by "out of control Christians." That's the way it was being reported. From the field reports Ben was getting through his cell phone, there was a lot of media spin going on. The Holy Harvest had been shut down - celebrants treated like sheep at a wolf convention - because governments were working in concert to make sure the Christians were sent a clear message. The message was consistent - no faith has a monopoly on the public square.

The knowledge that Arne Karlstrom had uncovered real forensic evidence of the Exodus story was of some consolation to Ben, but he seriously wondered if that knowledge would ever see the light of day before, before what? Before Billy Kim and Hans Tanner could denounce it? Before the scientific community could mock and ridicule the undeniable proof of the photos?

When Marshall Warren limped into the kitchen, Ben took a look at his sorry, hungover former boss and saw a reflection of himself years ago. He felt sorry for Marshall, but at the same time, didn't feel sorry for him. He knew that Marshall wasn't ready to quit drinking.

"You know I never really liked you, don't you?" Marshall began. It was an opening volley devoid of any pretense.

"You know, Marshall, I was never trying to win a popularity contest."

"Still, I admire what you've done," Marshall said as he pulled a half-pint of Bailey's Irish Creme out of his jacket pocket and poured it into his coffee." He pushed the bottle towards Ben. It was supposed to be comedy. Ben didn't laugh.

Marshall leaned forward. "It's a three-fold strategy."

"What is?"

"First, they take command of the school system. They guarantee that the next generation or two of kids graduate singing the company song. They've been working on that one for 50 years. Second, they kill your church - the church of Christ. That's why they were so tolerant in allowing you guys to schedule this Holy Harvest thing. They wanted all of you holier-than-thou types in controlled locations so they could crack a few skulls and then blame you for being loonies. Third, they replace your God with a god of their own."

"So, how do you know their game plan?" Kowalski asked.

"Remember I told you that Tanner and Kim belonged to the same thing - I called it the 'Knights of the Brotherhood?' Remember?"

"Yeah."

"Well, last night I made a few phone calls and got the right name. They're called the Knights Templar. They're a secret order."

"I know about 'em."

"You do? I learned about it from NSA. Who briefed you?"

"Marshall, the history of the Knights Templar is no secret. They're kind of like the ancient equivalent of Council on Foreign Relations. They got blamed for a lot of things they did and didn't do. They were kind of like a Christian Highway Patrol during the Crusades – they made certain the routes were secure for Christians, which meant they had to eliminate a lot of Muslims. It was not exactly Christianity's finest moment. History has shown that their influence was almost as much legend as fact. It was media spin."

Marshall looked at Ben with incredulity. "How do you know all this crap?" he asked.

"Oh, I don't know Marshall. There's these things called books! They're newfangled. Come from the printing press. People read 'em and learn stuff?"

Marshall ignored the sarcasm. "Well, then I don't know what kind of secret order Tanner and Kim belong to. All I know is that Chuck Winston claims they belong to some kind of unholy alliance."

"Well, that doesn't really narrow it down much, does it?"

"What do you mean?"

Kowalski stood and walked to the kitchen counter. He picked up his Bible and held it up. "It's all right here. Doesn't matter the name. Jesus warned us that many would come and claim to be the true faith but that we should be on guard against false prophets. If Tanner and Kim belong to some kind of pagan religion they can take a number."

Marshall shook his head and looked into his coffee. "Man, I wish I could do that – just divorce myself from the real world and bury myself in that book. I wish I had a crutch like that."

"That's an interesting analogy – coming from a drunk."

CHAPTER THIRTY EIGHT
Conspiracy nuts

Lars didn't want to have breakfast at Wickstrom's Resort. There was nothing Wickstrom could tell him. What he needed to know lay north of them. At 7:00 AM he shook Ethel awake and announced that they were on their way. She tried to object, but Lars was animated, insisting that he had learned some things on talk radio the night before, after she had fallen asleep, that he had to confirm. In 15 minutes they were out of their cabin and on their way to Orr, a small town just 35 miles south of the Canadian border. He said that they would have breakfast in Orr. The thought made Ethel grimace. Orr was a pitiful excuse for a town. It was a ghost town of old iron-range workers who had raised their families while they toiled in the taconite pits of northern Minnesota. Orr needed a good coat of paint or a case of dynamite. Ethel would have chosen the latter. The mines had been tapped out and the industry bankrupted, but there was a core of citizens who refused to believe that Orr wasn't staring at the prospect of a new boom. They had nothing to base their feelings on other than the dull knowledge that comes from drinking too many beers, talking to the same people for too long, and living in the same trailer house for two generations. They hung on, buying up overpriced property in the hopes that better days had to be ahead. The last time Lars and Ethel had stopped in Orr was eight years ago at a greasy-spoon café. It was coated with a smoke film and the rest room stunk.

When they pulled into town, Main Street was bustling. Everywhere there were four-wheel drive pickups, newer ones, sticking out onto a small-town street where diagonal parking was still the law of the land.

"I don't believe it," Lars muttered as he cruised slowly down their main thoroughfare.

"Ethel, honey," he began. He hadn't called her 'honey' in three years, since their 35th anniversary. "If what I think is true, you won't believe what you're about to learn." He winked at her. He hadn't winked at her in, well, longer than three years, for sure.

He pulled the pickup and trailer off onto a side street. The closest spot big enough for them to park was two blocks away. Ethel tried to object at having to park so far away from the restaurant but it wasn't registering with her husband.

"C'mon, hurry up," he said, trying to encourage his wife. "We have some people to meet."

"Doubtful, Lars. We don't know anybody in this town."

When they got to the restaurant, the 183 Café, a matronly hostess greeted them. "Smoking or non?" the hostess asked. The entire room was a blue pall of smoke from cigarettes and cigars.

"I thought smoking was outlawed indoors," commented Ethel.

The waitress smiled a faint smile at the former legislator. "Yeah, well, the geniuses in St. Paul can pass all the do-good laws they want. Doesn't mean they get obeyed. We tried enforcin' it and nearly had to close the doors. Better to be in non-compliance than bankrupt. You can voice your concern with the County Sheriff if you like," she said, pointing to the lunch counter. "He's the uniformed officer over there. The one suckin' on the Marlboro."

The waitress led them to the back of the restaurant to a booth. They ordered coffee to start. Lars looked around. In the booth next to them there was a family - a mom and a dad and three kids.

"Excuse me," Lars interrupted. Ethel looked at him strangely. Something was definitely up. Lars didn't speak to strangers. It just wasn't in his genetic code.

"Are you from around here?"

The father looked them up and down suspiciously. "Not for long. We're heading out."

"I mean, do you live here?" Lars rephrased his question.

"Yeah," the man said. "Why?"

"I heard something on the radio last night and I need to know if it's true?"

"Try me," the man said, shoving a biscuit in his mouth.

"They were saying that they've moved the borders."

"You heard this on the radio?"

"Yeah. What do you know?"

The man rose from his booth and sat next to Lars. He motioned for his teenaged son to pass him his plate of bacon and eggs. The man extended his hand.

"Charlie Dunwalt. That's the wife, Deb, and the three kids - Alex and Brian and Anna, he said. They all waved and smiled at each other warily.

"You want to know the truth?" Charlie asked. "Because what's happening is below the radar screen. Officially, no one is talking."

Ethel sat mute. To her, what was happening looked like some sort of fraternity pledge-week secret ritual. Her husband and this stranger were speaking in tongues. She looked at the mom in the adjoining booth trying to gauge if she thought her husband were as nuts as she thought Lars was. The woman sat poker-faced, her lips curled down in a kind of anguished frown.

"See these men here," Charlie said, motioning to the beehive of activity in the café. "Three months ago, half of them didn't live up here. But, we're going through a new boom. Didja see all the new pickups on the street coming in? The Ford dealership is rolling in clover. All these men have been hired by some foreign construction company to operate heavy rigs. They move dirt from one end of the county to the other. They're getting paid above union scale with triple-time after 40 hours. Know what that means? It means that they're calling all of their out-of-work family and friends to move up here to gorge themselves at the table."

"What profit is there in moving dirt from here to there?" Lars asked.

"There isn't, unless you're trying to make friends. What you heard on the radio is right. Must've been some pirate broadcast - or a Christian station. They're reconfiguring the borders. These men are putting up new crossings and fences. They're moving mountains of dirt to make elevations across the border on both sides. Elevations where armed guards can regulate the border traffic."

The politician in Ethel was getting unnerved.

"I don't get it," she said. "How could something like this not get reported? What are you saying? - That we're just going to give Canada some of our land just to make friends? It doesn't make sense."

"Ma'am, across the length and breadth of the Canadian and Mexican border there's going to be a 30-mile buffer zone. Any commerce going into or out of our country is going to be subject to a duty, a tax."

"I don't believe it. If all they wanted to do is raise revenue they would just raise taxes."

"Higher than they already are? Between the gas and the tobacco and the liquor taxes - the nimrods on the county board and the bozos in St. Paul have driven a stake right through the heart of this town."

There was that legislative gremlin again. Ethel flinched.

"Besides, the taxes won't be collected by the Canadians or the Americans. The 30-mile buffer zone will be owned, operated, managed and taxed as a sovereign government by the UN."

Ethel laughed. "You're one of those conspiracy nuts. You believe all that crap about a one-world government. None of what you say makes any sense."

"You're right ma'am. None of it makes sense. Unless you happen to be Billy Kim."

Charlie was watching Ethel when he mentioned the president's name. The reaction on her face would tell him whether he was spinning his wheels trying to explain the way of the world to her.

Ethel Larsen had campaigned for Billy Kim. She had given scores of hours and substantial amounts of money to his re-election campaign. She had 'walked the district' on his behalf. After Clinton and JFK, Billy Kim was her president. He was caring and compassionate and believed in government solutions to private pain. Charlie Dunwalt saw in her eyes that she wasn't going to swallow what he had to tell her. He got up to leave.

Lars tugged at Charlie's sleeve. He knew the man had given up talking to Ethel. "Talk to me," he implored of the stranger. "Let's go outside. I need to know."

"Lars," she said, as he got up to walk outside with the stranger. "You're an old fool."

"Order me the old fool's breakfast then. I'll be right back."

Ethel looked at her menu as long as she could without looking up. When she did elevate her gaze Charlie's wife, Deb, was staring at her. Deb grabbed her coffee cup, filled it and walked over to Ethel's booth. 'Great,' thought Ethel. 'Now his wife is going to come and beat me up. What a quaint little town.'

"Can I explain something to you?"

"Sure," Ethel said with a measured skepticism.

"My husband is kind of passionate about some things and sometimes I get upset with him because he doesn't think things through all the way."

Good, thought Ethel. She's reasonable. A fist-fight was only a remote possibility.

"But, you gotta understand. We're leaving this town. This is our last meal here. We don't belong here anymore. My husband runs a construction company and he can't hire any workers. They're all taken. We're moving to Des Moines. He's got a brother there who needs some help building houses. So, you'll have to excuse him. We've been kind of stressed and he tends to speak a little too plainly sometimes."

"I got to ask you a question." Ethel was wondering how to be delicate without offending the local woman. "Why doesn't your husband just get a job here, with them, instead of uprooting the whole family? The union will take care of you and the family."

"Oh, the union took care of us already. It's the union that took all his workers. We can't compete with the wages they offer. Besides, it's the principle. Charlie doesn't want to be a party to what's going on, you know, in the big picture."

"Oh, I understand," Ethel responded.

Ethel didn't understand at all. Deb could read it in her face. The blank expression she shot Deb was a neon sign of indifference. Ethel went back to studying the menu. The discussion was over. Ethel Larsen was transparent. Principle and paychecks didn't conflict with each other in the world of Ethel Larsen. A high-paid union job was a salve for almost all sins in the world of Ethel Larsen. Turning such a job down on principle was a sign of weakness in the worker's paradise Ethel Larsen had constructed in her own mind.

Deb nodded kindly and returned to her table. She felt sorry for this older woman. There was no verb, no adjective, no exclamation that could inspire the seed of doubt to take root in Ethel Larsen.

CHAPTER THIRTY NINE
The enemy lair

Claudia Colgate had reached an equilibrium. She knew she could no longer be the most notorious woman on the planet. In truth, she would have to become the most invisible woman on the planet. Her life now depended on it. It didn't catch her by surprise. Becoming invisible had always been a contingency. She had squirreled away a small fortune in an off-shore bank and had ready access to it. She had already arranged for her line of credit under an assumed identity. A second identity was one of the perks for having a government intelligence agency at her disposal for almost a decade. There was a small town in Mexico she wanted to get to. She had a plastic surgeon on retainer there and she was looking forward to gaining weight. Lots of weight. The mental image the world had of her was a svelte, lithe, buxom beauty with stylish long tresses. Her new persona would be chunky and plain with short-cropped "butch" hair, maybe a tattoo or two and lots of biker leather. Her new name was Rosa Carillo.

It was her exit strategy. All she needed was a car and an opportunity. In the short term, though, she was enjoying the company of the Kowalski clan. She was enjoying seeing her 10-year battle plan unfold right in the enemy lair. She could relax here. The Kowalski clan had been marginalized. They had no power - literally or figuratively. They had been taken out of the war. All of them had been reduced to mere observers. She had a sudden understanding of how screenwriters must feel on opening night. She decided she was going to enjoy it, share her insights and become 'one of the boys.' Then, she would disappear.

She walked into the kitchen at the Larsen home at precisely 6:59AM. She was timing her move. When she entered, Ben Kowalski and Marshall Warren quit talking. She had heard Marshall say something about Knights Templar. It told her they were beginning to connect some dots. When she stuck her head around the corner, it was plain from their demeanors they had been engaged in a head-butting contest. Kowalski was holding a Bible. It had been a private conversation and the implication was evident that she was not welcome. She ignored their glares. What they thought about her didn't matter. She had a timetable.

"You gentlemen will want to see what's on TV. I guarantee it," she said, jamming a chocolate covered donut in her mouth.

The conviction in her voice told them whatever she was, she was serious.

They gathered in the living room in front of the Larsen TV set just in time for President Kim to say "I draw your attention to the skies above this great monument." What happened next was, without pretense, a surprise to the CNN production crew. Cameras jumbled to catch the image of the black disc hovering above the skies of Jerusalem.

Except for Claudia, they all gawked at the screen.

"What is it?" Marshall Warren muttered.

Claudia Colgate sat, unimpressed, on the sofa. "It's a flying saucer. Don't you know a flying saucer when you see one?"

Ben turned and looked at her directly. "There are no such things as flying saucers. Don't play us for fools. We're not playing you for one. What is it?"

"Let me ask you this, Mr. Kowalski - you and I know that there are no such things as flying saucers, but what do you think Joe and Mary Sixpack will think they're seeing? Our polling groups have told us that 52% will automatically assume that it's a UFO. Why? Because research tells us they want to believe it's a UFO. Why? Because we live in a comic-book culture. People don't want truth. They prefer to believe in their own conspiracy theories. They're much less bothersome than actual facts."

The eight men and one boy all looked at the woman quizzically. She didn't appear to be making up what she was saying.

"Nothing you will see in the next three days is an accident," she added.

Amanti stepped forward. He didn't like Claudia. He didn't try to hide it, either. "Give us the Cliff Notes version, Missy. What's going on?"

"If I told you, sir, you wouldn't believe me. Watch."

It wasn't a suggestion.

As they watched from the Larsen living room to a location 7500 miles away, the underside of the black disc shot forth a bright green light - dead center onto the stage of the temple. It was so bright that people in the temple audience were repelled from the stage. Many of those in attendance screamed and threw themselves on the ground. The light ceased. Where it had been shining there was a huge plume of smoke.

A solitary man stood in a gray suit and tie.

CHAPTER FORTY
Ghost

In the production truck at the site, director Kenneth Quist was having a cow. "Somebody, anybody, center up on that shot!!! Not everyone at once! Three, hold your position on the thing, the flying saucer. What the hell is that??? Focus up, two."

The apparition - the man with the suit - stepped forward to the microphone. Hans Tanner and Billy Kim stood back and allowed the ghost an access to the podium.

It was John Fitzgerald Kennedy.

The apparition held up his hands for quiet as the crowd viewed his face on the digital Maximage closed-circuit video screen in the arena. He approached the podium to a stunned and silent crowd.

"On November 22, 1963, I was killed by an assassin's bullet."

If it wasn't really JFK the ghost had done his homework. He had the New England accent of the fallen president down to a craft. The way he swept his hair off of his face with his left-hand was reminiscent of the fallen president.

"I was saved by superior technology and compassion." He smiled. It was a genuine JFK smile. In his eyes tears formed.

"There's, ah, so much more I could tell you but that will all evolve." He turned to leave, but stopped, "It's so nice to see you. And, to be seen."

The crowd would have laughed, but they were too stunned.

The Kennedy apparition shook hands with Tanner and Kim and left by a secure exit at the back of the stage. Hans Tanner approached the podium.

"In 70 AD the Romans laid siege to this holy site. The Jewish people were dispersed to the winds of history. Today their faith and every faith will be reaffirmed because, as we can now demonstrate to you...the world is truly one community of man."

Tanner and Billy Kim left the stage. A brisk wind kicked up. The shofars in their stands howled in 12 different pitches.

The black disc silently slipped off to the east in a blur, off towards Arabia.

"Wow," said Kenneth Quist in the production truck.

"Wow," said Jake Kowalski sitting on the Larsen couch between his father and Leon Amanti.

"Yeah. Wow," they echoed in unison.

CHAPTER FORTY ONE
Ducks

The escape plan was communicated in the old Swedish dialect.

The Kowalski team located Arne's father in a nursing home in Stockholm. They told him that his son was in some 'diplomatic trouble' in Saudi Arabia and that they needed to send him a message. They didn't want to get too specific with the old fellow because he was quite feeble. They kept reassuring the old man that Arne was not in imminent danger, that it was all a bureaucratic mix-up. It was a full lie peddled as a diplomatic half-truth.

Leon Amanti had been told by the nursing home administrator that the old man was lucid but prone to dementia. Amanti had called the nursing home four times and spoke to staff and secretaries before finally reaching the home administrator. The administrator was cautious, but efficient, and very fluent in English. A career bureaucrat, thought Amanti. Eventually, Amanti found it necessary to recruit the help of a visiting priest.

At precisely 3:00 PM Saudi time, the priest dialed Arne's cell number. When Arne answered the phone he was greeted with the familiar sound of his father's voice speaking to him in the old Swedish language. Arne quickly recognized the ploy. Kowalski and his people were betting that neither the Saudis nor Egyptians would have an interpreter at their disposal versed in the old Viking language. Arne's father had been a professor of Swedish history and had taught Arne the long-forgotten tongue of his forefathers.

Arne's scientific nature could be directly connected to the feeble old voice at the other end of the line. Arne's voice softened when he heard his father speaking to him. He understood, without being told, that his father's message had to be brief. Tryggve Karlstrom read off a time and then said he was told not to talk any longer, or offer any further specifics. The ears in the sky might now be able to triangulate the call if it were on the air long enough.

When he hung up the phone Arne sat motionless for 20 seconds. His father had said 'I love you' in the Viking language and Arne wanted the words to echo in his brain while he savored the sound of his father's voice. It might be the last time they talked.

Mahrous and Ewald watched Arne's body language for something positive. What they got was Mount Rushmore. Arne looked like his soul had separated from his body.

In speaking the old language, Arne had been briefly transported back 40 years to a place in time when he and his father explored the old Viking ruins and spoke the forgotten ancient language like their Viking ancestors.

In Sweden, the old man said a quick prayer when the call was over. He wanted to know the extent of danger his son was in and asked the priest to help. The priest said he would find out what he could.

By dinner time that night Tryggve had forgotten that he had a son.

Leon Amanti had come up with the idea of having the elder Karlstrom call and communicate the plan in the old Swedish language - knowing that the Saudis or Egyptians would be monitoring the cell transmissions.

For security reasons, Arne had been given no specifics, only a time. There was one small issue. The plan required a boat.

What is a boat? thought Arne. The first requisite of a boat is that it float. It should be large enough to carry people and it should be durable enough to complete a mission, whether that mission last 50 years or 50 minutes. To that end, they agreed that they needed wood. The only wood available in 70 Palms were palm trees and none of the men were sure if a palm tree, alive or dead, would float. Cutting one up was an issue, too, because they had no ax. And, if they did fell a tree they would have to haul it roughly six miles behind the ATV to the Gulf of Aqaba.

"Tires float," said Mahrous. They looked at each other and smiled. Of course! They could take the tires off of the ATV, lash them together and float out into the sea.

In the pre-dawn hours the three aliens pushed off of Saudi soil into the Gulf of Aqaba.

The good news was that the water was warm and the sea was calm. It was summer and spending an hour or two in the Gulf of Aqaba, pushing a tire-boat out into the dark sea would not result in hypothermia. The bad news was that it quickly became apparent that there would be no return. If their rescue plane or ship did not arrive, they would probably drown or get captured. The tide was going out, carrying them south toward the Egyptian side of the gulf faster than their legs could kick. Mahrous had been placed in the center of the tire-boat along with a plastic bag containing their video tapes. Mahrous tried to sit as close to center of the craft as possible - his oozing wound wrapped in a plastic bag to keep the inevitable splashes from corrupting his "surgical site." Arne and Ewald quickly discovered that their kicking was unnecessary. They could feel the tide pulling them. They hung on for the ride, wondering where they would find themselves in the coming day - at the bottom of an ocean, in a jail, or in a hotel with clean sheets and a shower. In the pre-dawn hours, in the middle of a deserted ocean their ears were attuned to capture anything but silence. Silence, though, was all they got.

"The still discs are in a plastic bag in my zippered pant pocket," Arne said to his ship-mates.

"Why are you telling us that?" Ewald countered.

"Just in case. I'm weighing all the possibilities in my head." He made what sounded to them almost like a confession.

"God has put me, has put us, here for a reason. What we have will be shared with the world. I know it. I feel privileged to have been chosen as His instrument to point the way. It's been a pleasure to serve with you." To Mahrous and Ewald it almost sounded like defeat being grasped from the jaws of victory.

From the north, engines could be heard. All three heads turned. They listened silently. The engines idled down and then started up again. Dawn was breaking and the shroud of night would soon be lifted from them. The engines started up again and stopped again. A boat was visible.

"They're probably stopping to recalibrate the GPS signal," offered Ewald.

They weren't stopping to recalibrate a GPS signal. They were stopping to scan the horizon. What none of the exiles could know was that the ATV Arne and his crew had stripped of its tires had been located by the Saudi army about 45 minutes prior. The Saudi deduction was that the infidels had crafted a boat and cast themselves into the water. The Saudis had radioed their findings to the Egyptian craft.

Ewald waved his arms "over here!" It was a spontaneous act. It was wishful thinking. Arne pulled his hand down.

"If they're locating us by GPS you don't need to wave." Arne was wary. The boat stopped again. "I don't like this. If it was GPS location, they would hone right in on us." Nothing else need be said.

They were sitting ducks.

The Egyptian craft approached slowly, its engines idling as it sidled up next to the tire-boat. Rifles were trained on them from both bow and stern.

"Which one of you is Karlstrom?" the captain asked in perfect English.

Arne raised his hand. The boat drifted and a ladder was dropped over the side. Arne was helped aboard and one of the sailors motioned Arne to put his hands over his head. Arne complied.

"We'll take the film!" The captain pointed. "In the bags. Right there!" The officer instructed Mahrous and Ewald to hand over the payload. Reluctantly, they handed up the two plastic bags with the video, discs and still cameras inside.

Simultaneously, reflexively, all heads turned.

Off the bow of the Egyptian ship, 18,000 tons of Russian submarine surfaced with a titanic, breathtaking "whoosh."

For the Egyptian captain, whatever the Russian markings on the hull told him about geopolitics was immaterial. He had his orders.

The Egyptian craft headed off in a full-throttle escape, leaving Mahrous and Ewald behind.

Rescuing two men attached to a make-shift tire-boat by submarine cannot be done on the fly. By the time Captain Petrov's men had floated an inflatable raft out to Mahrous and Ewald, helped them up the ladder and down into the submarine, a full eight minutes elapsed.

When Captain Petrov helped Ewald descend the last two rungs of the ladder into the con, he looked him in the eye and asked a question. He was hoping to get an affirmative answer. "Dr. Karlstrom?"

"No. I'm Ewald. The Egyptians have Arne."

The Egyptian craft could proceed 30 knots at full throttle. The K-815 with its nuclear engine could max out at 42 knots underwater. Captain Petrov calculated the intercept time before the Egyptians would be in range of one of his torpedoes. He sat in his chair weighing the evidence in front of him.

He was about to commit an act of war and he was trying to calculate the consequences. He had six torpedoes on his ship. To sink the Egyptian craft was not even sport. A live torpedo would kill Arne Karlstrom, though, which was contrary to the mission Brad Pugh had originally received from his longtime friend, Ben Kowalski. He weighed the more serious implications to his ship. His invisibility would be compromised. His modus operandi, after all, had been to operate in the shadows. His crystal ball into the future was fuzzy. The political implications were hard to measure. Russia and Egypt were neither enemies nor friends. They existed in an environment of peaceful tolerance. And, where would the Arab world and the United States and Britain square off if he were to blow the Egyptian craft out of the water? And, what about Russia? He discounted his own country. They were politically insignificant. Petrov realized that he would, from this act forward, be considered a pirate.

"Load the tube," he commanded from the bridge. "Take the detonating cube out of it." He turned to Brad and Winnie Pugh. "We're going to fire an unarmed torpedo into their hull. We have to get close enough to make sure we allow for any shift in their course. We're going to put a large hole in their boat and disable them. Hopefully, they'll give Dr. Karlstrom up at that point. Anybody else have a suggestion?"

Winnie had a question. "What if we just let them go?"

"I am Egyptian," countered Mahrous. "I know how they think. They are protecting Islam." He paused. "They will most definitely kill him."

"Captain?" Lieutenant Ivanov interrupted. Captain Petrov rose and stepped to the lieutenant's console. He looked carefully at the screen, his face soured in a twisted grimace. What he saw distressed him.

"What is it?" Ewald demanded.

"The GPS locator is about three kilometers in front of us. It is neither moving forward nor backward." He paused. "It's descending. Quickly." The implications were clear. Either Arne was dead and his body had been pitched overboard or they had removed his belt and tossed it into the gulf.

The shot had been clean. The muzzle of the pistol was placed at the base of the skull and angled upward. His neck was shattered and his brain stem was mortally traumatized. A team of neurosurgeons could not have fixed the damage done.

They tied a cinder block around his ankles and threw the body overboard. Mission accomplished.

CHAPTER FORTY TWO
Higher beings and whores

The court ordered Ellen Kowalski to complete a 30-day drug and alcohol rehab. A 30-day stay on the lush and beautiful campus of the Hambelton Clinic carried a $16,200 price tag. They had world-class accommodations, world-class counselors and psychologists, a world-class reputation and would have had a four-star rating from most traveler guides. The Kansas court had allowed her to rehab at Hambelton because of its reputation. Its proximity, in Minnesota, to her son was another reason the attorney had argued it would be in his client's best interest.

Ellen hated it.

She was not one of them, one of the drunks. She was just a woman who had strayed a bit, gone on a small bender and gotten in a little trouble. To her, Hambelton was prison. There were round-the-clock counseling sessions - group and individual. She lay out her life to people she didn't know. She did it to satisfy the court. Their purpose was to break her of a behavior. What they didn't know was that her destructive behavior had already been broken. She thought about telling them she was through with the drugs and booze and pills but decided against it because they were paid handsomely not to believe her. The psychologists and counselors treated everyone courteously, professionally and clinically but they didn't trust any of them to tell them the truth. The fact that a patient was at the Hambelton Clinic was testament to the fact that they were convincing liars - not just to the world at large, but to themselves.

The hard business fact no employee of the Hambelton Clinic would ever publicly admit was that no on was released until their $16,200 was used up or forfeited.

What the professionals could never know and could never measure, was that Ellen had returned to God. In her moment of defeat, locked in a Kansas jail, she had gotten down on her knees and prayed to the very God she had tried to run away from. He had embraced her again, like the Prodigal Daughter, and assured her that He was in control, that He would direct the show from that point forward. Ellen cried, but only a little. She knew crying was self-pity and that God's plan would require her to consider her sins forgiven and not to dwell too long on them. Her job now was to seek obedience and look ahead. She talked to God a little and listened a lot. She knew there was a price to be paid for the life she had led, but she also knew there was nothing the law could do to condemn her beyond what Jesus had already paid to save her. In her Kansas jail cell, she re-discovered the faith that had buoyed her before she had been thrust into the national limelight as the First Lady. Her faith had been put to a test and she had failed. She got on her knees and asked to be forgiven.

She had come home.

Her episode in Kansas had resulted in a near rape that had a profound impact on her. Her assault and arrest was more convincing proof than an army of chem-dep counselors that her life had gotten off track. She didn't need the expensive therapy. All she needed was to get out. She didn't like the place. There were too many screwed-up people in detox and she didn't count herself as one of them.

Clinically, the club pros gave Ellen a better than even chance of not relapsing because of her strong Christian foundation. At the Hambelton Clinic they would have liked to cater strictly to a Christian clientele. They had once, but they couldn't anymore. Their clinical success rate was markedly better with faithful patients than with the secular crowd. The secular gods tended to be more pliable. A purely economic decision had been made years earlier by the Hambelton board of directors to accept federal and state money. It gave them the ability to engage in a huge expansion of their facilities. The good news was that their revenues soared. The bad news was that their relapse rate increased dramatically the minute they had to jettison God for a generic "higher being."

In her group therapy sessions Ellen tried to explain her Christian view of sobriety but it was lost in a crowded field of other "higher beings." A personal Savior with whom she had a living, albeit ignored, relationship was a strange concept to the group. They all acknowledged the wisdom, warmth and humanity of Jesus, but would stare blankly at her when she talked about Jesus the Divine, the Son of God. The others talked about their Zen experiences, their meditative safe havens, their oneness with nature, their inner peaceful places. Ellen was surprised that she was the only Christian in the group. None of them said anything against her brand of "higher being." For the purposes of non-judgmental recovery, a "higher being" was simply whatever horse could get you out of the canyon. Speaking ill against one's horse was against House Rules. It was like a congressman calling a colleague a liar. It might be true, but it just wasn't done. The same applied for "higher beings." They were all subjective and none of them were above, better, superior or more righteous than another. They were all high and they were all beings and they were all equal. What Ellen learned in group therapy was that a "higher being" had little to do with higher beings at all and a lot to do with human beings. Ellen knew that these "higher beings" were tolerated in the name of "recovery," but she knew them personally as false gods. She had paid homage to them herself in her departure from Christ. It was, to a large measure, why she was where she was. These higher beings were the gods of narcissism, of humanism, cultism and agnosticism. They had many names but they didn't have the one name that Ellen knew was capable of forgiving and fulfilling.

In the end, she could live with all the protocol and procedure required to be a client at the Hambelton Clinic, but she couldn't live with the clinical marriage of her God with the gods of the earth and the sky and the inner safe havens and the humanist creations. Her problem wasn't chemical dependency, she concluded. It was much more basic.

It was sin.

She didn't need a master's degree in clinical psychology to know that even at the world's best treatment clinic, sin couldn't be cleansed - not for $1 or for $16,200.

Ellen had touched rock bottom and knew that liquor, drugs and greed were what got her there. The counselors didn't believe her when she said she had no inclination to relapse. She was stuck. She had made a promise to the courts, and while she loathed her forced exile, she was there because of a tactical error she could neither escape nor ignore.

Her rocky road to Hambelton had begun when one of her book signings short-circuited. In Witchita, Kansas, she found herself at an after-hours party thrown by the bookstore owner. There were a lot of political activists there. There were a lot of drugs. There was a lot of booze. There were some guys who found her attractive because she was attractive and because she was high profile. And, she was alone. There was a car ride to another party in a bad part of town. There was more drugs and booze. There were some more men who spent more time leering at her than speaking to her. Under normal circumstances she would have felt threatened, but the combination of Valium, booze and cocaine in her system made her forget where she was. Besides, Elsa, her publicist and personal pit bull, was there. Elsa would protect her. It was her job.

It was 2:30 AM when the strippers arrived. They put the house into a new mind-set. All of the sudden there were attractive, undulating and loud women. Ellen found herself suddenly ignored. When the strippers started plying their trade, after hours, dancing for the men, Ellen was cajoled into a dance. She wondered where Elsa was. Elsa was supposed to stop her from this sort of thing. Ellen found out much later that her personal protector had found an attractive young stud, half her age, and was upstairs, in the attic, commingling her assets with his.

She didn't want to dance but the encouragement was robust. The men cajoled her. She didn't have to undress, they reassured her. All she had to do was dance. So, Ellen Kowalski, with a central nervous system under siege, kicked her shoes off and danced for the men. She was having fun and reasoned that one dance would satisfy them. So she thought.

Once she began dancing they changed their tone. They became insistent, animated and almost demanding that she begin to perform like the other professionals. She thought unbuttoning the top two buttons of her blouse would appease the men and quiet them down a bit. She didn't understand the forces at work at 3:00 AM at an after-hours party in a drug house in the wrong part of town. Unbuttoning the top buttons of her blouse was a down payment. All the naked and almost-naked professionals in the room couldn't compete with the attention given to Ellen Kowalski. She had her clothes on. She wasn't playing "nice" like the other girls. In this house, with these people, under these circumstances and at this hour she was violating house rules. They wanted more.

Neither the Valium, the booze, nor the cocaine could lower her inhibitions further. She wanted to quit, but the men had other ideas. They started stuffing dollar bills into the band of her skirt. She had no clue what they were doing. She had never been to a strip club. But, then it dawned on her: She was a whore!

They were giving her money in the pursuit of raw, uncut lust. It was a lust she had never before seen. In all her married years, Ben had never once had that look in his eyes. Sex had always been private, personal and shared. Ben had been a chronic womanizer before they had met. He had a library of pornography in the early years but he had abandoned all of that along with the booze. That fact was well documented in his books and speeches. Their marriage had been faithful and sexually gratifying. He had never once treated her like a piece of meat. He had never once come into the bedroom with the look these men had.

Then, the fight broke out in the kitchen. There were screams and breaking dishes and bodies pressing toward the kitchen to find out what the ruckus was. She looked for an exit. There was a press of male bodies against her, groping, grabbing and feeling her up and down. She tried to fight them off but they were determined. They had been programmed - in part by her - to animal lust. They weren't in a mood, at that specific moment, to debate the virtue of gentlemanly behavior. Two of the men chose the chaos of the moment to drag her upstairs. She was fighting back and screaming, but the screams were just another frantic voice in the cacophony of music, mayhem and intoxication that was in the house.

She recognized where she was: Hell.

The two men had her upstairs and on a bed, one heartbeat away from actually raping her when the police burst through the front door.

When the cops found her in the bedroom she had wrapped herself in a sheet and cried. In hindsight, it wasn't the near rape that made her cry - it was her own stupidity. She had invited evil to have its way with her. She thought she could reason with it, hold it in check, party with it. In her five years since separating from her husband, she never knew Ben better than at that moment. She understood his demons now. She understood what he had exorcised.

The Hambelton Clinic was minimum security. It was located out in the country, literally nowhere. She was more determined to bust out from there than anything she had set her mind to in years. Her "issues" weren't going to be resolved there. She knew where she needed to be.

It was a three-mile walk from the Hambelton campus to Lidstrom City, but at 3:00 AM it can be done without detection. When a car came down the highway, Ellen hid, sliding down into the ditch. The café in Lidstrom City opened at 5:00. She had kept one credit card taped to the inside or her shoe when she "enrolled" into the program and had surrendered all her personal belongings. While waiting for her food she called the local cab company. The driver was ecstatic at a long fare. He talked the whole way, the 45 miles into the city. She wanted him to shut up. She was not the first 'escapee' he had ferried away from Hambelton. The cabbie could have cared less if he were aiding and abetting a drunk or druggie. It was business. Before the ride began, though, he insured himself he was engaging in good business by insisting on validating her credit card in his scanner. He had been burned by drunks and druggies before.

He dropped her off at the Kowalski compound at 6:45 AM. She got out of the cab and stretched, wondering where she might get a change of clothes and a shower. The house looked empty, lifeless.

Leon Amanti had been up most of the night. The news of Arne's death had shaken them all. Their brilliant plan to commandeer Brad Pugh's rented Russian sub and rescue the Swede and his crew had been off by only a minute. Arne was dead and all of his evidence had been confiscated. Their hopes for a holy revelation had yielded nothing except a righteous corpse on the bottom of the sea.

Amanti stepped outside of the Larsen home for some air. He saw a lone female on the porch of the Kowalski mansion. He wasn't sure, but it looked like Ellen.

She was sitting on the steps wondering where on earth her husband had taken her son. This was their base of operations, after all. She heard Amanti's footsteps coming up the drive and recognized him from 100 feet away. Amanti was Ben's most loyal advisor and closest friend. He was the tactical brains of Ben's operations. She hadn't seen him in years. She had no idea what to say.

For a while, neither said a thing. They exchanged glances and Leon sat down next to her on the steps. A few silent moments passed and then he reached his hand out and placed it over hers. It sent her over the edge. She buried her face in his shoulder and sobbed.

"Leon," she said, toning down her tears. "Tell me I'm not crazy."

"Ellen, we don't want to know how or why you're here. That's not important. That'll come out in time."

They looked out at the brilliant summer day. It was early morning but already the sun was beating down and the day held promise of sweltering heat.

"Where is everyone?" she asked.

"Next door. It's a long story."

"Tell me, Leon. Tell it all to me. I've been around the world, now. I've been living in the dark and my pride just kept telling me that I could figure it all out for myself and I can't. You know why Ben never relapsed? You know why he is so forceful as a voice? It took me years to figure it out, but now I know. He wasn't running away from his demons. He was running toward the light. I know that now and I'd rather die in that light than live in the dark."

Three streams of thought began a bumper-car encounter in Leon Amanti's brain at that instant. It nearly blinded him – he couldn't effectively cope with all the electricity simultaneously firing in his skull.

First, he was profoundly aware that ever since Ellen had left, there had been a recognizable, but unspoken void in Ben's life. Amanti and Ben were kindred spirits. They had known each other long enough to know what the other thought without speaking. It was a guy thing. Secondly, Leon was genuinely impressed by what Ellen had just said. It showed a maturity, acceptance and grace he had never seen in her before. If her heartfelt expression were not just empty words, he gave Ben and Ellen a fighting chance for reconciliation.

Thirdly, and most disturbing, was that Claudia Colgate was in the house next door and there was no way to conveniently explain why she was there.

"Before we go over there we need to talk," he said.

CHAPTER FORTY THREE
Out of character

Breakfast at the Café 183 was completed in silence. Lars' buoyant mood had evaporated after stepping outside to speak with the local man, Charlie Dunwalt. By the time he returned for his meal, he was a changed man. The persecution of the Christians he had heard about on talk radio was beginning to make sense. The assault he had witnessed was not an isolated event. It was part of a larger, deliberate movement that was occurring beneath the radar of the public. It was being orchestrated at very high levels. Very high levels. There could be no other explanation.

Ethel noted her husband's silence and sensed that he had come to an emotional crossroad. It concerned her because Lars didn't do crossroads or emotions particularly well. The trip to their cabin in Canada was proving to be a bad idea, Ethel concluded. She wanted to suggest they just call off the long weekend at the cabin and just go home. If they were home she would be pruning her flowers. If they were at home, Lars would be his grumpy old self, riding his lawnmower and soaking up public radio. Instead, they were on the road and the road was a step through a looking glass Ethel was not enjoying. She wasn't sure she recognized the man she had slept with for almost 38 years. He had talked to strangers. He had sung softly. He had listened to talk radio. He had winked at her and called her 'honey.' It was disconcerting.

They walked silently to their Lincoln. When they got there Lars did another thing that was totally out of character - he went to open the door for Ethel. She stood there, not recognizing what was happening. It was a trap. Instead of allowing her in, he put his arms up on the roof, literally pinning her against the car. He looked her straight in the eye.

"That fella, Charlie, told me that eight miles up the road there's a new border station. The border guards are wearing blue helmets." He paused to let the mental picture form in her mind. "You do know what that means, don't you?"

Ethel didn't know what to believe anymore. She couldn't think. There were too many evolving situations to consider. Logic escaped her, so she did what she always did when stubborn facts got in her way. She spoke with her emotions. Her husband was the rational thinker in their house, but usually he confined his logical moments to those times she granted him. Recently he had been thinking on his own, like it was cute. She didn't see it that way. Ethel was the empath. She felt. She felt a lot of hostility at that moment - her own. She didn't appreciate her husband pinning her up against the car and violating her space. She didn't appreciate being brought up to the northern hinterlands and being forced to listen to talk radio. She didn't appreciate being awakened at 7:00 AM and told to get in the car. She didn't appreciate the Minnesota State Patrol. She didn't appreciate a lot of assumptions her husband was making. Her tea kettle started to whistle.

"And, if they are wearing blue helmets?" she asked with challenge in her voice. "If the borders have been moved and the UN has a 30-mile territory around the borders, does that change anything? Isn't it time the playing field were leveled? What makes you think what's best for America is what's best for the world? Isn't it about time we shared some of our wealth with the poor countries. Look at the big picture, Lars."

"You don't see the principle, do you?"

There was that word again. Why, all of a sudden, was principle raising its ugly head? Principle didn't butter your bread. Principle didn't pay the rent. Principle was simply pride that didn't know when to back down. She tore his arm away from the car and crawled into the cab. She barked: "Let's go! We're going to the border, or so-called border, to check this thing out. If we don't, we're just going to argue about it all the way home and - make no mistake, mister - we are going home. I have no plans to spend any time alone with you in the wilderness. No sir. I want to get back home where I can sleep in my own bed. Alone." She thought about her home for a minute, remembering that there was a small army of people renting it. It made her angrier.

"And, after you kick out all of your friends I'll give you a blanket."

Yeah, she was angry.

The cars were stacked up for a quarter mile before the border crossing. It was right where Charlie Dunwalt said it would be, eight miles north of Orr. West and east, for as far as the Larsen's could see, there were large earth-moving machines pushing, collecting and redistributing dirt in a high-tech dance of dust. It took their car eight minutes to move forward to the soldier in the powder blue helmet. The helmet had no "UN" white stenciling on it. It was just a blue helmet. The soldier was Ethiopian or Sudanese. It was hard to tell.

"When did they move the borders?" Lars asked.

The soldier looked at him blankly. He moved to the front of the car and took a digital picture of the license plate. On his video transmitter he received a picture of Lars and Ethel Larsen. He held it up and concluded that the picture on his transmitter and the occupants of the car were one and the same. He checked Lars' personal license, just to be thorough. They were allowed to pass. He handed Lars a card and motioned him to move up to the next checkpoint. Lars handed the card to Ethel. The soldier was not going to talk. Ethel looked at the card and studied it for a couple of seconds. It was a rate card. The next stop up the line was a toll booth.

"A car and boat for one day is $35 going into Canada and $55 returning. For three days it's $52.50 going in and $73 returning."

They waited in line for the privilege of paying a lot of money today for something that was free yesterday. In front of them there were angry Americans. They were animated. They were arguing with men in blue helmets and the blue helmets were stone walls. Many of the cars were turning back, going through a roundabout road built up ahead of the toll gate. The angry Americans evidently couldn't, or wouldn't, pay the toll. A fight erupted about four cars ahead of Lars and Ethel. A swarm of blue helmets descended on a Winnebago loaded with fishermen. What happened next was hard to discern from the Larsen's vantage point. A paddy wagon arrived and 50 or so blue helmets escorted six or seven Americans into it. A blue helmeted soldier got into the Winnebago and drove it up towards what should have been Canada.

Lars and Ethel told the toll booth attendant that they had changed their minds. They wanted to go back to the US. The lady was of some sort of Middle Eastern descent.

"It's a free country," she said. "You can come and go as you please. That will be $27.50."

"For what???" Lars demanded.

"To use the turnaround," she said. "It's right there on the bottom of the rate card."

Lars was about to erupt into a tirade but stopped himself short. He felt the fingernails of his wife digging into his wrist. He understood the gravity of her fingernails. Ethel spoke to him through a plastic smile and gritted teeth.

"You want to start something over $27.50? Fine. I'll take a bus home and after you get out of jail you can take a bus home because we won't have a car or a boat. Get my drift?" It wasn't advice. It was a threat. Lars got out his credit card.

"$27.50? A bargain at twice the price," he told the foreign woman. "You really ought to think about raising those prices. You know, if you want to, you can include a small tip on there for yourself. Couple bucks. Good service should be rewarded."

The attendant slid the card through the scanner and had Lars sign the receipt. She pointed them to the roundabout without saying a word. She was tired of sarcasm. She had been swimming in it since the border crossing had secretly opened for business that morning.

Once they were actually traveling back down Highway 183, Lars told his wife what he had learned from Charlie Dunwalt at the café.

"In the 30 miles buffer they're going to set up a duty-free enterprise zone. It's supposed to be a shopper's paradise. Clothing, cars, liquor, cigarettes, casinos, resorts. The idea is to suck commerce away from the States and Canada and into the UN - tax free. They're going to make their money on the rent and the tolls. Pretty ingenious, don't you think?"

Ethel said nothing. She was thinking. It was pretty clever. It was devious.

"Billy Kim," she muttered, almost in admiration. Lars sensed that she was impressed.

She looked at her husband with a smirk. It became apparent to her at that moment that everything they had seen and heard in the last few days was no accident at all. It was all part of a coordinated effort to change the very foundation of world politics. It was a new day dawning in America and Ethel was weighing in her mind if it was consistent with her own world-view. It explained a lot. It explained why the Christians had been tear-gassed at their Holy Harvest, or whatever they called it. The Christians were the most strident American patriots. They carried their faith and their patriotism on their sleeves. The gassing had been delivered to provide the Christians with a collective dose of panic. It was strategic. It was meant to disperse them, to marginalize them. It was public relations. Ethel had to reason that what they had seen at the roadside church had been duplicated on a massive scale. It just wouldn't have made any sense as an isolated incident. Then, while the Christians and the libertarians and the other fringe groups were busy making a spectacle of themselves protesting, Billy Kim and his team had put Phase One of their master plan into action.

Lars summed it up for her. "It's a coup. It's brilliant. What do you think?"

"I'm trying to keep an open mind."

Lars recognized her response. It was what she used to tell voters and reporters when she didn't want to say what she was really thinking.

CHAPTER FORTY FOUR
Stupid

Ken Quist's name had been scrolled in front of the world for 30 years. He was the most famous director nobody ever heard of. As director, his job was to call shots and compose them before telling the associate director which shot should be "hot." The associate director would then execute the order and punch a button or pull a fader bar on his console. When covering news, the director has very little input as to the content of the show - only if it involved some tricky picture composition or drop-in editing. Then, the director might have some technical reason to suggest alternatives. Mostly, he was just a technical quarterback. His job was to put together a 'shot sheet,' call the play and then hand the ball off to someone else.

As director, Ken Quist sat with his on-site producer in the conference room of the Jerusalem Hilton listening to a stern lecture, via video conference call, from the senior executives at CNN. The executive brain-trust had insisted on more fireworks - pre-recorded music, live rock bands, showgirls, marching bands, and special effects woven into the production of the temple dedication. They were also flying over a jet loaded with a lot of high-profile actors and pop stars to appear before the cameras. Quist held his tongue. He assumed they would tell him why the production had suddenly "gone Hollywood." They didn't.

Quist had been with CNN for 30 years and was assigned the temple dedication not for his technical accomplishments. He was considered competent and only modestly creative. What he did well was follow orders. That's why he lasted for 30 years at CNN. Over the decades, Quist had seen scores of other directors pass through CNN's notorious revolving door of employment - dismissed for "creative differences" when the content of what they were reporting was compromised, cut or distorted by management. Those unemployed saps had consciences. They had world-views that eventually came into conflict with CNN brass. Quist didn't burden himself with a world-view. He didn't second-guess his employers. He did his job and didn't make waves.

After the video conference was over he turned to his producer. The message from the corporate suits, even for a seasoned news director, was curious.

"What just happened there? This is supposed to be a news event. Why do they want to treat it like a Super Bowl half-time?"

The answer from his producer was a ruse, but the producer was regurgitating what he had been told.

"Ken, sponsors are lining up at $22.3 million for 30 seconds. That's unprecedented! That Kennedy thing yesterday has created a huge audience. Not just an American one - a world audience! The PR and marketing of this thing is unbelievable. We don't know the numbers because most of the people who saw Kennedy yesterday saw him on tape on another outlet. We're anticipating numbers tomorrow that will set a new gold standard. It's like the World Trade Centers attack - only, this time, we've got the exclusive. We've stumbled into Tut's tomb, Ken. We're just going to put a little window dressing on it. For posterity ."

"And profits," the director added.

Ken Quist didn't need an organizational flow chart to know what motivated sales executives. The bottom line was always revenues. He had been given his orders and, as a loyal foot soldier he knew what was expected. Still, the whole sequence of events gnawed at him. There were just too many unanswered questions. Why weren't they allowing any interviews with this JFK person/thing? What kind of technology or intelligence had saved the former president? How did anybody know that this was the real JFK? Why hadn't he aged? If Kennedy had been 'saved' he would be over 100 years old.

The director had been told not to look for answers, that they would be presented in due course. How did they know there were answers? There weren't even clear questions yet. Was there some sort of collusion between network brass and Kim and Tanner?

No, his job was just to react. His job was not to assume. "Just call the right shots," they had kept repeating. It was obvious to Quist that they were anxious about the coming coverage but they wouldn't tell him why. He wondered how the other directors, his peers who had been fired or quit on principle, would have handled this sort of treatment from the suits in executive row?

At that moment it crystallized. Ken Quist knew why he had been chosen from 30-odd other available directors to handle the high profile job of directing the temple dedication.

They thought he was stupid.

"Bringing President Kennedy back to life was no accident," proclaimed Hans Tanner as he addressed 15,000 invited guests at the temple the following day. "It's a technology that has been perfected, shall we say, from afar."

President Kennedy stood behind Tanner and nodded his assent to the comments. Overhead, the black disc hovered. On the television sets of the world Ken Quist had electronically inserted a small box in the corner of the screen that showed the black disc. Frequently, the aircraft would shift a couple hundred yards one way or the other and the camera would temporarily lose its "fix" on it. There was no explanation for the movement. But, then, there was no explanation for the disc.

In Atlanta, they were collecting polling numbers. They were extrapolated numbers. The Nielsen Company had created an empire extrapolating numbers. Their global sampling told the CNN producers that more than half of the TV sets in the world were watching their broadcast

"The wonders of the world are about to unfold before you," Hans Tanner announced. "Do not fear. The true history of man is about to be revealed."

It was Friday, 9:00 PM, Jerusalem time. The Jewish Sabbath had begun. The announcers on CNN - the only game in town, or earth - explained how the faithful Jews had gone to the synagogues for worship. They were lying or had been told to lie. The Jews were boycotting the event. Their holy inauguration had been hijacked by Hollywood and slick politicians. The temple dedication was no longer about their temple. The whole disc/Kennedy turn of events had shifted the focus from the dedication of their holy shrine to a dog and pony show which the faithful Jews were calling sorcery. They were calling it deception. They were calling it an abomination. Their words were going unreported. Had the construction of their holy site not been through the graces of the world community they would have evicted every non-Jew from the site. Had they not been suckered into being hosts for a world audience, they would have liked to cancel the whole thing. They couldn't. The forces of history were now bigger than them. They were helpless against the momentum of the event. Geography, too, had conspired against them. Over the preceding years the Israelis had relinquished more and more of Palestine until now they were, literally, an island of Jews in a sea of Muslims. If they wanted to run they couldn't. They were boxed in by their enemies. It was not an unfamiliar position for Israel.

The Jews smelled trouble. It had a familiar stench. It was the smell of rotting flesh that wafted across history and hung like a cloud over their Promised Land. Gentiles couldn't smell it. To the Jew it was the foreboding prospect of tyranny, of persecution and genocide. It was Pharoah's army pressing them up against the Red Sea, boxing them in and waiting for the right time to swoop down, kill, rape, savage and enslave them again.

Kennedy stood smiling. He remained in the background. In the shot composition Kennedy stood strategically over Hans Tanner's left shoulder on a star that had been placed on the stage for him. He had been trained to stand on it. He was standing within three steps of the secured exit. When he was introduced, again, to the assembled crowd by Billy Kim, he smiled, winningly for the cameras, raised his hands and found the star on the stage. The crowd was on their feet, but the former president, or whatever he was, simply smiled. He made smiling and waving an art. He made no motion to address the crowd. Neither Billy Kim nor Hans Tanner motioned him forward.

Kennedy was insignificant. He was a bit player. As significant as his appearance seemed, Kennedy was an appetizer.

Hans Tanner motioned to the disc in the sky. A brilliant green light flashed from the belly of the disc and scorched it's beam on the center of the stage. When the cloud dispersed, a lone Hispanic male stood in camoflague fatigues in the middle of the stage.

Hans Tanner announced the visitor. "Ladies and gentlemen, the late Che Guevara."

Ken Quist called the shot. Camera one had Guevara quickly centered and focused. The director's cell phone buzzed. There was only one source that had the number: Atlanta. The big bosses. He alerted his associate director that he had the controls momentarily and snapped the phone off his belt.

"Quist," he said.

The voice on the other end was the CEO. Quist knew it immediately. He had met him on numerous occasions, but had never had the chance to do anything more than just exchange pleasantries.

"You'll need three cameras for the next shot, stage center. Free one of your wing cameras up because I can see that you're only covering the center stage with two." There was a pause. Quist weighed what he was hearing. "Copy, Quist?"

"Copy," he said. There was a click on the line.

Without thinking he snapped into his headset: "Four! Get off your crowd shots and get positioned up for stage center. Left to right I want one, two and four. Six, give me a medium shot, stage center."

Hans Tanner lifted his hands and the bright green light shot forth from the belly of the disc again. At stage center stood three figures.

"Take one," commanded Quist. "Take two. Now, take four. Six, widen up and...take six."

"Ladies and gentlemen," announced Tanner with a regal flourish. "Through the mystery of the ages they have preserved Charles DeGaulle, Winston Churchill and Mahatma Ghandi." The three personages stood there exactly as they had been last seen in the history books, DeGaulle in a French military uniform, Churchill with a log-sized cigar, hat and suit and Ghandi in a loin cloth and bare-chested. One by one they raised their hands as they were introduced. They continued waving and smiling as they stepped back.

Another green flash emitted from the belly of the disc and three more people stood stage center amid the smoke and light.

Tanner waited for the smoke to disappate. "Ladies and gentlemen, Joan of Arc. Martin Luther. William Shakespeare." The three waved gratuitously and smiled. None of them spoke.

Billy Kim approached the podium and looked into camera two. His script scrolled down the TelePrompter as he spoke. "President Tanner and I have known about this technology and this power for a time. We have had to keep the integrity of the secret. Until now. The truth is this: From the beginning of time, we have been monitored. Throughout our history we have been protected from the influence of a higher evil by a higher intelligence. Today, we can tell the story. There is a higher intelligence. They remain...up there," he said, pointing to the disc.

In the production truck, jaws were agape. The associate director was weeping. "Do you know what this means?" he whispered through his sobs.

"Easy, Jack," Quist said. "Hold it together. We need you." Quist wasn't feeling the gravity of the moment quite as profoundly as his peers. Stupid as he was, he had figured it out.

Thirty eight singers came onto the stage. They were recording artists from all genres: Pop, country, rock, rap, soul, R&B. Everyone recognized them. They sold all the CD's. They made all the videos. They were white, black, brown, yellow and in between. They were tattooed, long-haired, bald, pierced and fluffed. As they sang, all of the historical figures swayed to the music. They sang "We Are The World." The associate director in the production truck used his fader bar to paint soft pictures of the historical figures as their smiling faces were blended in a touching palette against the faces of the world's entertainers. The entertainers themselves were visibly moved by the moment, many of them belting out their solos, fighting back sobs and tears. To a man or woman they would later admit it was probably the performance of the lives. As the song progressed, a pre-recorded piece of video was dropped into the live pictures. The clip showed children from all over the world, all of them smiling and innocent - of every hue.

The song lasted eight minutes and 32 seconds. At the final chorus the black disc lit up in brilliant hues of red, yellow and green. As a final crescendo the disc sent forth a choir of sound which was in direct harmony with the chorus of the song. Overhead, a canopy of fireworks erupted into the now-dark sky over Jerusalem and cascaded from the bomb bays of a Turkish F-15 which streaked across the southern skies. The fireworks presented a brilliant descending spiral of explosive color which consumed the entire panorama of the Jerusalem skyline. The fireworks were a breathtaking exclamation point to a breathtaking deception. There wasn't a dry eye at the dedication site.

Except for stupid Ken Quist.

"Ladies and gentlemen," Hans Tanner shouted into his microphone. He delayed a moment. It was a pregnant pause. A green light shot forward from the belly of the disc, even as it moved a few hundred meters to the south. There was a 'whoosh.' People shielded their eyes and turned away from the stage. When the light ceased a cloud of smoke lingered over the stage.

"I introduce to you the prophet Mohammed."

An audible gasp was heard across the world as the crowd at the temple dedication collectively sucked the air out of Jerusalem and into their lungs.

"Five! Get me the crowd. Five! Be alert." Muslims were on their haunches praying. Tears washed the faces of the Muslim faithful. In the course of a few seconds wailing, beating of breasts and shouts of 'Allahu Ahkbar' filled the air. What few Jews were in attendance began to quietly slip out of the area as the prophet or, whatever it was, clasped his hands in front of him and bowed to the crowd, tears in his own eyes. On the digital Maximage big screen, an extreme close-up of the prophet showed the assembled throng the picture of their historical progenitor in abject subjugation to his God. Mohammed spread his arms to the sky and the Muslim world wept with joy. The sound was numbing. The live band struck up an instrumental version of "We Are The World" as the prophet walked from one side of the stage to the other, bowing and spreading his arms to the sky. Armed soldiers in blue helmets followed him closely. The security was unnecessary. It was a love fest of righteous proportion.

Ken Quist had directed coverage at three presidential party nominations.

Once the party had selected a presidential candidate there was always four or five minutes of mayhem as the delegates sang and celebrated. The same for sports championships. Quist knew enough to let his cameramen find the best shots, to look for the pictures that needed no words. And, so it was for 14 minutes.

When the crowd was hoarse from shouting Billy Kim approached the podium and raised his hands for silence but the crowd refused. It was Mohammed, himself, who brought the crowd to silence with his raising of the hands. He held his finger to his lips and the crowd came to a spontaneous laugh as the prophet used timeless, universal sign language to quiet them. The prophet smiled at their silence.

"As you can see," began the American president, reading from his Tele-Prompter. "Death itself has been conquered. They were there when Mohammed laid the foundations of one of the great faiths. They were there at the dawn of man and planted the seeds of civilization in Babylon, in Eden. They were there when the great pyramids were engineered. They were there when Solomon's men put the last brick into this historic wall."

"What about Jesus?" came a shout from the front row.

Billy Kim tried to ignore the remark. "And, so, throughout history…"

"What about Jesus?" came the voice again. It was a snowball of a moment Another voice chimed in, and another, and another. "What about Jesus?"

Soon the entire arena was buzzing. "Jesus, Jesus, Jesus," they implored from the American president. Billy Kim turned to the European president and shrugged his shoulders. Hans Tanner tried to raise his hands and quiet the crowd. Finally, Mohammed raised his hands and put his fingers to his lips again.

The Prophet was speaking. Billy Kim took his hand-held mike and held it close to the Prophet. The language was an old Arabic/Farsi language but the name Jeshua was laced in the rapid-fire invective. The Prophet shook his head to the crowd as if to suggest it would be impossible to see Jeshua. He motioned 'no' with his hands.

Hans Tanner approached the podium. He addressed the crowd and the world. He motioned for an interpreter. A studious-looking young Arab man joined Tanner center stage to interpret the prophet's words.

"Our interpreter has worked with the prophet to chart the old Arabic language. Please," he said to the interpreter. "Tell us what the prophet is saying." Instead of using the microphone, the young man whispered into Tanner's ear. Tanner's face sobered.

"I see," said the European president. "Well, the truth needs to be known. "Tell them," he said, motioning to the crowd.

The young man stepped forward reluctantly and delivered the news. "The prophet says that Jesus, is crazy – deluded." The translator made a circular motion around his own temple and took a goofy look upon his face. "Jeshua?" he asked, motioning. The prophet nodded emphatically, mimicking the translator.

A fight broke out in the crowd. Several fights. A riot was a distinct possibility. Blue helmeted soldiers fanned out along the perimeter of the arena. Any thinking person should have deduced that Tanner did not want to incite a riot while he was in harm's way. Thinking, rational thought, however, was not the intent.

To Ken Quist it was choreography.

Panic and pandemonium reigned. The European president looked like a man who was ready to explode. He motioned for the security people to clear the stage. In the absence of order, Hans Tanner was taking it upon himself to assume control. All of the historical players - Churchill, Mohammed, Joan of Arc - all of them - were ushered through the security door at the back of the stage. The singers and musicians were led to another exit.

In a fit of pique, Tanner took to the microphone. In the control booth the audio man boosted his volume.

"You want to see your beloved Messiah? He was saved, too, you know. You want to see the man people have hung their hopes on for 2000 years?" He motioned to the sky.

In an instant there was silence. The green light blasted the stage, temporarily blinding everyone in the crowd. After the cloud dissipated Jesus Christ, the Messiah, the Son of Man, stood silently at center stage. He hung his head.

"Cut one. Five, get me wide on the crowd. Cut five." Nothing could dissuade Ken Quist from his job. He was on autopilot. Even in his doubt, he was putting out good pictures.

Jesus stood motionless, expressionless at the center of the stage while the crowd around him tried desperately to get a glimpse of what history had deemed was a man/god - the figure which had been the fulcrum on which world history had teetered for 2000 years. The crowd exploded in chaos. Hysteria and confusion reigned.

A fight erupted in front of the stage. Delerious screams, indecipherable screams, cascaded from every quadrant of the arena. Jesus stood stoically at stage center.

Overhead a hum arose from the black disc. The sound was strategically designed to begin at a set frequency and increase in pitch until it overwhelmed everything. It sounded like a thousand PA systems feeding back. The screech was enough to actually resonate in the fillings of the teeth of the people in attendance. Involuntarily there was silence as everyone covered their ears. Sound, pure sound, was a weapon. As if on cue, the sound and the pain ceased.

"This is a taste of the power," Hans Tanner said in a low, deliberate tone. "You need to hear what the man says." He turned to the Jesus figure. The Jesus figure raised his head and looked into the eyes of Hans Tanner. Tanner snuck his hand-held microphone strategically between himself and the Messiah-man.

"Forgive them," The Jesus man said.

"Ah! You speak English," Tanner observed for the benefit of the crowd.

"It is the most universal language. Of course I speak English. The Father and I divided you with language."

"I see," Tanner said, taking a step forward and backward as he formulated his next question.

"For the benefit of everyone - could you please tell us. Are you the Son of God?"

The crowd began to grumble, murmur and stir. Hans Tanner held up his hand for silence. He addressed the crowd.

"Please," implored the European president. "It's important you remain quiet so that the world can hear what this man has to say. If you can't, we can quiet you again." He turned to the Christ figure.

"Are you the Son of God?" The Jesus figure stood silent. "Tell us! Either you are or you aren't, or you're crazy! There can be no other possibilities. Are you the Son of God?"

"So say you." There were gasps in the crowd.

"Are you a man or a god?"

The Jesus figure thought about it for a moment and then spit, forcefully, into the face of Hans Tanner. The indignation of the European president flared. He wanted to strike the man but held himself in check.

"Don't you realize that I have the power of life or death over you?"

"You would have no power at all if it were not given from the Father."

Tanner walked slowly to the front of the stage. "It's been like this for 2000 years." Tanner sounded tired, defeated. "He refuses to accept that he's living a delusion. Every time we ask him to accept our authority he refuses."

From the crowd came a single voice. "Crucify him!"

The single voice was joined by others. Soon there was a growing chorus of voices demanding: "Crucify. Crucify. Crucify." Fights began to erupt in the audience.

"Stay off the fights," commanded Kenneth Quist from the control booth. It wasn't him speaking at all. It was a conditioned response. He was anticipating what the suits in Atlanta would be saying. He needed to stay on their side - for the time being.

Outside, in the arena, the screeching howl from the black disc began to build. The audience, like Pavlov's dogs, felt it coming and responded with obedient silence. Tanner walked over to the Jesus figure and spoke.

"See what you do to people? Seems we have a lot of people who would prefer to see you dead."

"I did not come to save them but to condemn them. What I do I do for the Father."

From the production booth Ken Quist had an observation he planted into the IFB's of the 20 or so cameramen, technicians, engineers and directors. "Does anyone else pick up the fact that Tanner is now speaking in the collective first person about this superior intelligence? If he's trying to be subtle it's not working. He's claiming that 'we' are the superior intelligence." The crew was silent. The director was right. The words had been self-evident, but they had missed them, having been swept up in the drama of the moment. Tanner walked to the podium.

"It is only through the miracle of an advanced technology that our friends can present this man to you today. For 2000 years we have had to listen to his claims about being the Son of God and for 2000 years we have kept him alive while he has confused us with his claims. We have no way of claiming this man's deity. And, so, I'll save you the time of trying to psychoanalyze this 'man.' He is not a god. He is a fraud!"

The crowd's screams were thwarted even before they began. The black disc emitted a piercing feedback. The dogs backed down, whimpering.

"Now you know. So, what do we do?"

"Crucify," came the cry from the crowd.

Tanner walked to the man-god with his pronouncement.

"You can tell us the truth and walk away from this stage or you can hold to your story but, if you do, today will be your final Calvary. What say you?"

The wretched man-god spit in his face again. Tanner ducked and avoided the spray.

Immediately, the crowd picked up where they had left off: "Crucify. Crucify. Crucify."

The green light bolted from the belly of the disc and three Roman soldiers in authentic centurion garb emerged from the thick smoke. They were followed by three more.

From the wings of the stage two wooden cross-beams were carried out by stage hands. One of the Roman soldiers took his spear and whacked the man-god across the back of the knees, collapsing him to the stage. Another soldier produced a spiked whip and began whipping the fallen Jesus. They swallowed him at mid-stage like wild dogs. The glint of a hammer rose above the melee and a bone-chilling scream came from the mass of bodies. Then, another hammer strike and another scream. And another. The soldiers stood back and pulled on a set of ropes attached to a block and tackle configuration. They lifted the man/god where everyone could see him.

They had crucified Christ.

CHAPTER FORTY FIVE
That pissant pothead

Lars and Helen rode silently down Highway 183 toward Walker. The radio told them that the world they left three days prior no longer existed. Their silence was the result of a mystery, a conundrum neither could put into context. After 38 years of marriage, the couple could only guess which side of the fence their mate was on.

"They're running the same feed from CNN on all the stations," Lars complained. "That's not right."

"They're the ones with the story. Since when did you become the news junkie? Why do you care who carries the story? You're getting your news."

"Something just isn't right about this. We drive out of range of one station and the next station has the same feed from the same network. Doesn't matter. AM or FM, whatever station happens to come in clearest is still CNN."

Ethel shrugged. She didn't understand why a second opinion was necessary on a news item. News was news. Besides, CNN had never once lied implicitly, or explicitly, to Lars and Ethel Larsen.

Even NPR had forsaken their usual team coverage and was airing the CNN feed. Did NPR have a choice? CNN owned the story, the rights and the coverage. While there were hundreds of reporters and allied technicians outside the temple gates, there were only CNN employees inside. Lars searched for another voice on the radio dial but finally gave up. The temple dedication and its mind-boggling "miracles" were the only story given air time. What the story meant was open to wide latitude of interpretations; interpretations neither Lars nor Helen wanted to speculate on without knowing more. What they had learned simply wasn't enough to deduce an informed opinion. Independently, they both had ideas, but neither one dared speak what was percolating in their brains. The stakes were too high. Thirty eight years of marriage was no guarantee that they knew each other well enough to guess what the other thought at that particular moment.

Outside Brainerd they had to slow down for military vehicles moving in and out of Camp Ripley. The camp was a National Guard facility strategically located in the center of the state. It had an Army air base and was 180 square miles of practice range for Army artillery and infantry training. A phalanx of camo buses stretched out in front of the camp. Guards in blue helmets directed the civilian traffic into the left lane so that a normal flow of traffic could get by.

The gas gauge told Lars that a stop would be needed. Besides, Lars' legs were getting stiff and his bladder demanded relief. At Pitkin there was a once-cozy, now run-down truck stop called Murphy's. He knew it well - it had been a regular stop for him over the years. He felt a certain familiarity as he slowed his $120,000 payload into the exit lane and onto the truck stop tarmac. Gas was especially high-priced at the stop, 20 cents more than they had paid for it just the day before. He tried not to notice because there was positively nothing he could do about it. If he complained, Ethel would have chastised him for the ill-timing of the trip in the first place. Besides, money wasn't an issue. He and Ethel were both retired and on handsome pensions, courtesy of the state taxpayers - he with his state engineer's pension and she with her three pensions for having spent eight years as a lawyer, 15 years as a law professor and another 16 years as state senator. On top of that, they both earned Social Security and had full medical coverage all the way to the grave. Money was never a point of contention with anything they did.

Still, $6.28 per gallon was a lot and it made Lars wince when he saw the price.

As he finished fueling, an Army bus pulled into one of the diesel islands and men and women in civilian clothes piled out of the bus and into the truck stop for pop and snacks and bathroom breaks. It was an odd sight - Army buses loaded with civilians.

Lars' curiosity got the better of him and he asked a middle-aged man in the parking lot what his story was.

"Goin' home," the man said with a southern drawl. It was a friendly, rich dialect and the man seemed to be receptive to a little conversation.

"Where's home?" Lars asked.

"Little Rock, sir. Gonna catch a plane in Minneapolis. That's where most of us will part company." The man looked at Lars and eyed him up and down. He had a question for the civilian, Mr. Larsen. "You figgered it out yet?"

"I think so," said Lars. "It's a coup. If you don't want to wear the blue helmet they're sending you home. Right?"

"Very good, sir," the soldier said. "I'm a captain. Seventeen years. They told me if I wanted to keep the pension I've earned and not get a dishonorable discharge, I'd better be on that bus. They gave us less than an hour."

"So, what are you going to do?" asked Lars.

"Go home and try to figger out where we lost the war. I'm not sure I can figger it out, though, because it was so subtle. Civilians everywhere in the Army now. It all happened over the last year or two. Billy Kim said he was going to reorganize the military. Well, he reorganized it, all right. There won't be a US military. He's going to turn all them blue helmets into world cops." He looked at Lars like a long-lost drinking buddy and put his arm around his shoulder.

"You own a gun?" the captain asked.

"Shotgun. Got a couple. Haven't fired 'em in years."

"Well, I'd get a couple more practical firearms if I was you. Before Kim outlaws 'em. That's gonna be his next step is my guess. Then he's gonna repeal the 22nd amendment so he can run a third time. There's a line of demarcation being drawn even as we speak and you're going to be on one side of that line or the other. Ain't gonna be a middle ground."

With a curt salute, the man turned and walked back to the bus. Before disappearing from sight, Lars couldn't help but want to know more.

"How did it happen?" It was a question the history books would ask. Lars wanted to know now. The question stopped the officer in his tracks.

"You want to know honestly?" the captain asked, stepping back toward Lars. "Here's the way I figger it: When Marshall Warren took that bullet in the ankle seven years ago, it was the beginning of the end. He'd a never been elected president if that little pissant pot-head hadn't flipped out and shot him. That opened the door for Billy Kim. Warren didn't know what he was doing. Lord Almighty, the man was an idiot. Warren's stupidity put Kim into a position where he could pull off this coup. It was a crime of opportunity. My guess is he didn't do it alone, though. He had lots of help - behind the scenes, you know. We just don't know from where. My guess is China, but we'll never know in our lifetimes. Course, who am I to say? Just a retired Army captain living on a pension, that's all. My opinion don't count for squat anymore."

The captain was about to go on a rant but stopped himself. Seventeen years of military life had conditioned him to keep his personal political opinions away from civilian ears.

He turned to leave, but stopped himself. It occurred to him at that moment that he didn't have to throttle what he thought anymore. He was a civilian! He sensed he had been striking a chord with Lars and wanted to make sure he made his point completely.

"And, don't kid yourself, mister," the captain said as if he were dressing down a subordinate. "God does have his hand in this. That whole charade in Jerusalem is sleight of hand. The Great Deceiver is at war. He's always been at war, but now, now, he's gettin' bold. Probably 'cause he knows it's harvest time. You know what I'm talking about, don't you, mister? I can read it in your face. There's lots a things you're tryin' to sort out right now and you cain't make yourself admit what you know is true."

The captain shifted his feet uneasily while reaching in his pocket. He pulled out a silver cross, showing it to Lars. "You have to excuse me, sir. It's the preacher in me."

He extended his hand to the civilian, shaking it as though they were old friends. "Captain Allan Simpson, US Army Chaplain...retired."

The captain turned and boarded the bus.

The skeptic in Lars wondered if speaking to a pastor at this particular moment in his life was coincidence. Then, there was another voice in Lars' brain that said it was Providence.

He didn't know what to believe. He had spent fifty years thinking they were one and the same.

CHAPTER FORTY SIX
Ceiling tiles

They had their laptops on the dining room table and their cell phones beside them. The television in the background monitored the crucifixion of the poor miserable man they had called Jesus up on the cross. Ben Kowalski was trying to get one of the networks, any of them, to come out and interview him. He had a theory he wanted to put forward about the man on the cross and the deception being perpetrated. He was finding no takers.

"Who's your senior editor?" he had asked a half-dozen news outlets. By the time he had to ask for the senior editor the battle, Ben knew, was lost. But, he tried.

"We're only getting one side of the story," Amanti kept complaining. He was preaching to a lonely choir. Only on the net could they find commentary offering a thoughtful analysis of what had suddenly become the Jerusalem World Fair. There was plenty of speculation from bloggers, talk radio and other alternative news sources, but CNN had stacked the deck – they owned the rights to history - and with sponsors ponying up record cash, the weren't about to relinquish the hold on their obscenely profitable reins.

The Kowalski group kept waiting for Claudia Colgate to give her take on the story, but she was holding her cards close to her impressive vest. She had said that she would answer all their questions about the fraud that was being played out in Jerusalem in due time. She kept saying 'when the time is right.' Ben thought she might just be stalling them. He was beginning to have serious doubts that she could be trusted at all. Was she a double-agent who had tricked Marshall Warren into believing that her life was in jeopardy?

The gears in Ben's head ground to a halt when Leon Amanti opened the door for Ellen. Leon made a quick, cursory glance through the window before opening the door, hoping neither Claudia Colgate nor Marshall Warren were in the room. They weren't. He had prepared Ellen for the possibility of either/or being there, but he was glad they weren't.

The room turned silent. All eyes turned to Ben. Young Jake saw his mother.

"Mom?" he said in wonder.

Ellen looked at her son and then fixed her eyes squarely on her estranged husband.

"Hiya, Cowboy. Remember me? We used to sleep together."

"That much I remember," said Ben. "How did you manage to get here?" There were reams of words rushing to his brain. There were lots of questions, but he was paralyzed by the reality of actually having his wife in the room in front of him.

"Let's leave these two alone for a while," Amanti suggested.

"No!" Ellen barked. "What I have to say I have to say is for all of you. You've been more of a family to my husband and my son than I've been. Anything I have to say is for all of you."

"If you're here to lecture us, Ellen, you'll have to stand in line," Ben added. "We don't have time for it. If you haven't noticed, there are bigger stories out there than you."

It was not a subtle shot. Ellen had expected it, just not that quickly. She took two steps toward Ben and fixed her eyes into his.

"I've had so much time to think about what to say and it all escapes me now." She paused and closed her eyes, looking skyward. "Lord, give me the words," she mouthed silently.

Opening her eyes, she took a deep breath. "So, I suppose the best thing I could do is to speak from my heart. When I'm done you can show me the door if you want. Living in your shadow isn't easy, Cowboy. You're kind of high profile and I never wanted that. I'm not refined. I'm not a socialite. All I ever wanted to be was a mom and a wife and lead the quiet life. But, I couldn't as long as you were the great Ben Kowalski. Sorry, I'm sounding sarcastic and I don't mean to be. But, you need to know how I saw things at the time. I guess I resented being told what to be. I know you didn't cheat on me with that woman. I knew it from the get-go. I used the rumor, though."

"I know you knew."

"Then why didn't you call me on it?"

"That wasn't the issue, Ellen. You and that attorney manufactured the excuse. I saw that. You wanted a ticket out. I didn't want to stand in your way."

Ellen took a deep breath. Ben was right. "Why didn't you fight for me?"

"I had other issues, dear. I couldn't run away from my issues," he said with a measured dose of sarcasm.

The implication was clear. It was inferred from Ben's tone that she, Ellen, had done the running.

It was at that point Ellen felt the urge to turn on the tears. But, she wasn't there out of sorrow or regret. The tears would not be a part of her new script. She was there to set the record straight so that she could get on with her life.

"I wanted to live my own life, Cowboy. I want to have the life that had escaped me - the life where I would make my own way - the kind of life where I could actually have my own friends and make my own money and call my own shots. I know I've hurt you. Honestly? - I meant to. I resented what you made me become. But, I was weak. I turned my back on my son and my husband and my God." She looked at the floor, searching for the next set of words.

"Are you trying to apologize?" Ben interrupted.

"Yes, but I'm not very good at it."

"Do you want to be Jake's mom again?"

"Yes."

Ben hesitated at what he was about to ask next. "Are you trying to say you want to be my wife again?"

She looked at him with measured contempt. She wasn't at that point yet. She was still pouring the foundation of her apology and Ben was trying to put shingles on the roof.

"You always interrupt, you big creep. You try to put words in my mouth. I have a mind of my own, you know. I can express myself. I wanted to tell you how profoundly ashamed I am of what I've become. How I made so many mistakes. How I've seen your demons and I know how tough they are to lose. I also know how incredibly proud I am of how you used what you've learned. You carried God's banner. I carried my own. I said I'm sorry!"

She felt more words gushing out of her now, but they were disjointed.

"And, I want you to know something, mister. I've sworn off the drugs and booze. I don't need high-paid psychologists to tell me that I'm screwed up. What I need is forgiveness and to set the record straight." She paused and turned on her heels, looking at the other men in the room. She measured what she was about to say solely because her son was among them. Jake knew the story of their separation, but she wanted to say something categorically.

"And, there's something else…I've had chances, lots of chances to cheat, but I've been faithful. You need to know that. It's very important that you understand."

"I didn't ask you that."

"I know you didn't but you need to know. You can call me a lot of things but 'unfaithful' isn't one of them."

Ben stepped forward and met Ellen face-to-face. "You didn't answer my question."

She was flustered. She couldn't remember the question.

Ben was deliberate. He asked with a straight poker face. "Do you want to be my wife again?"

The feminine pride in her was a steely shell. She tried to hide in it. She didn't move. Her eyes remained locked onto his.

"I might...consider it."

Ben looked at Amanti without expression. Both raised their eyebrows.

Leon Amanti took the occasion to interrupt. "I told her about our unwanted house guests upstairs. No surprises. She knows the story."

"Thanks, Leon." Ben was glad beyond measure that his faithful friend had sensed the land mine Claudia Colgate represented.

Ben walked over to Ellen and whispered in her ear so only she could hear: "There's a ceiling tile in our bedroom next door that appears to be coming loose. I'd appreciate it if you would look at it. It's been bothering me. A lot. You have no idea how much."

It was a school-girl giggle that came from Ellen. She grabbed Ben's hand and led him out the front door.

"We'll be over in about five minutes," Amanti said, smirking.

Ben shot a glare at his chief of staff.

When they had left and were walking across the lush Larsen lawn, hand in hand, there were four Secret Service agents, a chief of staff, an attorney and a 14-year-old son watching them through the windows. The boy wasn't sure what he had just seen.

"Leon, what does this mean?" Jake asked. "Are they back together? Where are they going? When are they going to be back?"

The men looked at Jake and wondered which one would be the one to tell the boy. Finally, Leon broke the impasse.

"Your dad ever tell you about women? He ever tell you about the covenant between a man a woman when they're married?"

The boy curled his lip. The light went on in his head.

"Gross," he said.

As they walked across the lawn Ben had a strategic, practical question to ask Ellen.

"How much money you got?"

"Oooh. You get right to the point with a girl, don't you?"

"Practical question. You may not be so anxious to do what we're about to do once you realize I'm broke." She stopped walking.

"Tell me."

"They froze all of our assets. None of us can write a check or use a credit card. It's highly unconstitutional and illegal but, hey, what's a constitution worth these days, right? We need a generator. The one we need is $8,400 and we can have our own operations back."

"You're not a cheap date, are you? Couldn't you extract money out of your guests?" She was referring to Marshall Warren and Claudia Colgate, of course.

"Marshall's broke. He invested heavily over the years in parties and booze. Not a very good return on investment there. His friends are all store-bought. Claudia Colgate won't. We asked her. Claims all of her money is out of reach. She's lying, of course, but as we've learned - that's what she does. Besides, she's still on the other team. She wants to see us fail."

"So, why do you keep her around?"

"Ellen, if she shows her face in public she's dead. Period. Besides, she's the one who has all the puzzle pieces. You don't have to like her and I don't expect you to. I don't. She's the enemy. But, it's important we know what she knows. You know what they say: Know your friends, but know your enemies better?"

"I just don't like the idea of her being that close to our son."

"That's why he has parents - plural."

She smiled at her husband, put her arm around his waist and led him to their empty, unlit house, remembering what the original mission had been: Ceiling tiles.

CHAPTER FORTY SEVEN
Class in session

It was the wee hours of the morning in Jerusalem when the medical examiner pronounced him dead. In the US it was early evening. It had been timed that way - to reach the US at prime time. The CNN announcer was somber, reserved and reverent.

"And, so it is, at 2:38 AM, Jerusalem time, the King of the Jews, the alleged Messiah, the Son of God, has been pronounced dead by the medical examiner."

Almost in unison Ben, Ellen and the other members of the Kowalski group screamed at the top of their lungs at the TV set in the Larsen's living room.

Claudia Colgate smirked. She announced her delight.

"You people don't get it, do you?"

She turned off the TV.

"It's time," she announced. "Class is now in session. We're past the point in time where anything I tell you can make a difference. Besides, I have a selfish reason. I want to see the looks on your faces." She walked over to the DVD and inserted the disc. She clicked forward to the temple dedication and the first appearance of the Kennedy figure.

"Here's Johnny!" she said. "A readily recognized figure across the globe. Those who are too young to remember him know him from history books. Note the bright green light when he is "beamed" down to the stage. The light has been measured to be just beyond the tolerable limits of the naked eye. To the modern TV camera it 'burns.' Drives the video engineers nuts because they constantly have to tweak the white scale on the cameras. For an instant the video loses clarity. The intensity of the beam is by design. Involuntarily, people have to turn away from it. It's too bright. Hurts the eyes."

"From below, there's a pneumatic tube and a lot of CO_2 injected into the tube and onto the stage in direct synchronization with the light. The actors are put into the tube and 'whooshed' up onto the stage in a split second. It's the same principle as those tubes at bank drive-thru's. Notice that all of them have to mat their hair down as soon as they arrive. That's from the air pressure."

"Who are the actors?" The question came from Ellen. The two eyed each other warily. Claudia couldn't grasp how Ellen and Ben could have reconciled, particularly after that horrible kiss-and-tell book Ellen had written about Ben but here they were. It was obvious that they had reconciled, but what wasn't obvious were the mechanics of it.

Claudia sensed no animosity from Ellen. When they had first locked eyes with each other, it was Ellen who broke the ice by saying "I'm aware of the truth about my husband." Claudia didn't want to open that chapter. Truth wasn't her ally. She knew enough not to ask, only to accept what she was seeing. Claudia chalked it up to Christian nuance, the ability to reconcile in spite of mind-numbing differences.

"As regards the actors?" Claudia said, "we'll get there. I promise."

Claudia took the remote and clicked forward to the black disc in the sky.

"The disc. Amazing, isn't it? People are willing to believe it's an alien space craft without anybody telling them. Hollywood, the universities, the tabloids and late night talk radio prepared them for it. Occultism, mysticism. Doubt. The disc is, to keep it simple, a nuclear-powered helicopter. The blades are running behind a cowling. You can't see or hear them. The cowling is black and has millions of vents in it to allow the air through. The blades are 300 feet in circumference. If the chopper got closer than 10,000 feet from the ground it would cause a dust storm which would defeat the illusion. The rotors are actually a series of 16 blades in four separate layers. They operate in a computerized timing sequence with four nuclear powered cells. They are virtually silent. The only sound is the rushing of the air, but we have a phase neutralizer that masks that sound. The phase neutralizer makes the craft run silently - it also produces the screeching sound that overwhelms the crowd. The phase neutralizer is built into the belly of the chopper. We also have very high-tech speakers installed at about a dozen or so strategic rooftop locations throughout Palestine. To mask the rushing air sound we shoot a sound pulse exactly in phase with the wind towards the chopper. It's not new science, it's just a new application of it. Now, the reason the chopper moves from time to time is because of its stealth technology. Stealth technology works great except if the stealth object being tracked isn't moving. As long as it moves from time to time it's impossible for radar to get a 'fix' on it. We couldn't risk the Americans or the Israeli's identifying it. The chopper itself is operated by only two people - a pilot and a laser operator. It's being landed and hidden at a desert complex in Syria, about 60 kilometers away.

"A nuclear chopper? Where did that technology come from?" asked Reynolds Thomas, the always-inquisitive attorney.

"Good question, counselor. Remember the '96 presidential election? Remember the flap about the Chinese fund-raiser at the Buddhist temple? Remember the allegations against Clinton that he traded military secrets for campaign cash? The allegations just kind of died, remember? Well, that was all a smoke-screen for what was really going on behind the scenes. And, Clinton had no clue. He just opened the door for our agents. The technology was being developed at Area 51. Clinton saw the Chinese money as his ticket to four more years. He made some introductions and got some security approvals. Our agents did the rest. We worked through a military contractor to get the engineering to the Chinese. Clinton never knew."

"Or chose not to know," interjected Reynolds Thomas.

"You can interpret it any way you wish, counselor. The truth will never be known," said Claudia.

"Never underestimate a man's ability to rationalize," interjected Marshall Warren. He looked at the assembled room and added: "I speak from experience."

"The actors, Claudia," Marshall Warren continued. "Are we to assume that they have all been cloned, just like your twin in Jerusalem? None of us are genetic scientists, but you need genetic material and you need a refined technology that, to date, just hasn't been developed."

"It has been developed, Mr. Warren." She paused. "Well, almost. The Chinese perfected the science of cryogenic suspension of frozen cell samples back in 1933. They weren't aware of the implications of it at the time. They had developed a process that was decades ahead of any other civilized research. Over the course of the 20th century they and their agents set about freezing samples of just about every significant political or cultural figure. Usually they bought off local medical examiners, but if they had to, they weren't beyond a little midnight grave-digging. The Kennedy cells were scraped off the back of the limo in Dallas by a Chinese operative. Churchill's sample was bought for a bottle of scotch whiskey from a mortician."

"Explain Lincoln," asked Reynolds Thomas.

"That one was odd," she explained. "One of the things that genetic engineers will tell you is that after a time the genetic information simply dies. It lives the longest though, in the pulp of the teeth. It can live in a tooth for a couple hundred years. As it happens, one of the myths about Lincoln was that the bullet that killed him knocked out two of his teeth and that those teeth were never recovered. We confirmed that the myth was true and went about finding where they might be. We put the word out that a rich eccentric, a coat tail relative of Lincoln's, was looking for them. That was back in 1961. Lo and behold, a pharmacist from Baltimore comes forward and says he has them in a bottle that had been passed down through his family. We do a little background digging and find out that the pharmacist's great-grandfather had been an Army nurse and was at the Ford Theater the night Lincoln was assassinated. We took a gamble on creating that clone, but time told us he was telling us the truth. We paid $30,000 for the teeth."

"And, what if it hadn't turned out to be Lincoln? What would you have done with the human that you had created?" asked the attorney.

"What do you think? We would have had zero use for it."

The word "it" made them all exchange glances, but no one said anything at that moment.

"So, let me get this straight," Amanti added. "The age of these clones was calculated to coincide with this weekend in Jerusalem. You wanted them to be a particular age by the temple dedication weekend. Which means that years ago someone had to target this present time to be the dedication weekend for the new temple, right"

"Yes. Give or take a year or two but, basically, you're right."

Amanti continued. "So, it all had to be planned and measured out 40, 50, 60 years ago. These clones had to be conceived, impregnated into a host, born, raised and aged to a certain point."

"And, don't forget...programmed," Ben added.

"Yes, yes and yes, "responded Claudia. "It was all done at a very secure Chinese location."

"And, after this weekend, what are you going to do with these clones?" Ellen asked.

Ben rose and walked to the window. He held his finger up in the air. He had a point to make.

"Let's think like Tanner and Kim for a moment. These clones have one purpose. They have been raised and conditioned for one function only. They can't just be assimilated into society. Enterprising reporters would be all over them if they were discovered - asking questions the clones don't have a clue about - and then the charade might be exposed." He thought for a moment.

"They'll be used as organ banks. Right?"

Claudia wasn't trying to escape the question but she was trying to formulate the answer in her brain.

"The short answer is yes. The long answer is maybe. There have been some problems in the cloning process. Seems genetics is trickier than just making a carbon copy. Most of the clones have disorders. Churchill is on his second heart and Kennedy has recurring bouts of diabetes and liver dysfunction. There are other unexplained anomalies - disorders that were not apparent in the original beings. The argument inside the cloning community is whether it is better to let them live and study them or just to farm their good organs out. But, you're right. Once their utility has been outlived they will probably be used by the Chinese as organ donors for party members. You've got to understand something, though. These are not real people. They're puppets. They've been isolated and trained for one purpose. They have been trained at a juvenile level. They know how to communicate just a few basic things outside of the lines they have been taught. Other than that, they're about as developed as nine-year-olds. Another thing you'll see in the next few days - we paid close attention to average people. There are about two dozen families, mostly Arabs, we have targeted at the temple dedication. We have taken DNA from their dear, departed, family members and have replicated them. Average people. It will provide some emotional gravity, don't you think? It's another act in the same play. Something for the masses. It's designed to put a more personal touch to our 'miracle.'"

"Brilliant. Actually quite inventive," said Reynolds Thomas, the attorney. "I applaud you. As misguided as this power play is, it's really is quite brilliant."

"Thank you, counselor. We think so. But, we never considered it misguided."

Ellen caught the irony of the comment. "Up until you were factored out of the equation, that is…"

"That did change my thinking, yes," Claudia conceded.

"Explain something," Leon Amanti asked. "Who are the ancient clones: Joan of Arc, Martin Luther, Shakespeare? They've been dead longer than 200 years. And, Jesus. Who was that poor fellow?"

"They were just a matter of type-casting. Let me show you." She clicked the disc forward in the Larsen DVD player to the appearances of the historical figures.

"Joan of Arc is actually the genetic double of a French actress by the name of Emily Trussard. Died of a cerebral hemorrhage after a fall in 1962.

She had a noble look about her, don't you think? Martin Luther was tougher. There were lots of paintings of him. We had to find a plausible double. Found him in Seattle. A night watchman for Boeing. He drowned in 1959 in a fishing accident. Shakespeare is actually the umpteenth-generation grandson of the Bard. Had a passable resemblance. Died in a car accident in Wales in 1971."

She fast forwarded to Mohammed.

"Ah, the great prophet Mohammed. Actually, his real name was Ahmed Rahmann, a carpet maker from Lyon, France. He was murdered by the father of a girl he had molested in 1964. Kind of looks like a prophet, don't you think?"

She fast-forwarded to the Jesus-man.

"And your beloved Jesus? You'll love this one. 'Jesus' was a comedy writer for the old Jack Benny radio show. A Jew named Morrie Zimmerman. Lived in southern California during the 30's and 40's. When the great depression hit he found himself divorced, alcoholic and out of work. He moved up into the hills by himself. The locals used to remark how he looked like Jesus, or at least their folk-legend image of Jesus. Wore his hair long, a beard, piercing blue eyes. Kind of looks like a man of constant sorrows, doesn't he? You should know something about his crucifixion: We had to lie to old Morrie. We told him that we were going to fake the driving of the nails. But, we did sedate him nicely. Matter of fact, the water we gave him up on the cross was laced with a very potent sedative. At the end he was given a lethal dose. He actually died from sedatives. It was all coordinated to reach the American audience during prime time."

"The abomination," Ellen said without thinking.

"What's that?" asked Claudia.

"It's what you've done. It was prophesied in the books of Daniel and Revelation."

"I wouldn't know. I've never read them."

"Figures...," both Ellen and Reynolds Thomas said in chorus.

"So, tell me something, Miss Colgate," asked Leon Amanti. "Who are you a clone of?"

"Mr. Amanti, I'd like to know as well. When I first saw my 'twin' with Billy Kim I had to do some reconciling. Obviously we were born at about the same time, but, from the same mother? Not necessarily. But, from the same DNA, for sure. But, whose DNA? My own parents adopted me. I was raised in California and brought up in what I thought was in a very conventional manner. I've learned since that my parents had a somewhat unconventional view of sex.

They thought sex ought to be encouraged in children. I was made to have sex with the neighbor boys by my mother. She coached me in all the tricks of the trade. At home I studied world history and politics and medicine when the other kids were out playing. I know now it was part of my training. My own mother and father were teaching psychologists at the UCal-Davis."

"And, they were members of the Communist Party," interjected Marshall Warren.

"Yes, you're right. I was brought up to be a good communist."

Marshall finished his thought. "When I was president, we took a close look at you."

"I figure now that I was just a secret clinical experiment for them." Her voice broke. A tear ran out of her eye and down her cheek.

"Am I crying?" she asked. "I've never done this before."

Ben stood and grabbed her shoulders with his hands. He looked in her eyes. She tried to fight and get away.

"Weak people cry," she said. "I don't cry. I'm not hurt. There's no reason for me to cry." She struggled to get away. "I have to get out of here," she said, trying to sneak by Ben. He blocked her exit.

"You have incredible intelligence," said Ben. "You must have figured out what they've done to you. Up until you escaped from that place in China you were no different than those 'it's' you referred to on TV? Do you know that?"

"I know that now. I feel sorry for the actors. And, I've never felt sorry for anybody."

"Welcome to the human race, Miss Colgate," said Ben. "Where we can feel pain and sympathy…"

"And, where we can cry tears," said Ellen, wiping tears from her own eyes. "We are also capable of forgiveness," she said, looking at her husband. "And sorrow and remorse and contentment and joy."

Claudia Colgate composed herself and said in her best clinical pediatrician diagnostic voice: "I don't have a clue what you're talking about."

Her humanity had been given a glimpse of daylight and it was too much, too fast. Her demons took over. She was the old Claudia Colgate. In control. She was in her comfort zone again with the devils she knew.

"Do you mind?" she said coldly as she blew on past them and out of the room.

CHAPTER FORTY EIGHT
Blind obedience

Ken Quist pulled the prime time shift. He slept normal hours. He kept his thoughts to himself. He knew he would be in danger for speculating about what he had seen. He had learned from his technicians about the underground pneumatic tube. He had seen the faint outlines of the plexiglass "chute" that carried the actors up onto the stage from the studio monitors in the production truck. So had his crew. His producers lectured him to keep his shots framed from below stage level. He knew, without being told, there were two reasons for the sub-stage-level shots. One was to keep the faint outlines of the plexiglass chute out of sight of the viewing audience. The other was theatrical - to suggest that what was happening was larger than life. His crane cameraman, Julius, discovered the outlines and zoomed in on them. The director knew better than to show the shot on the air.

In the booth, prickly questions began to arise in the director's brain. When his technicians talked to him about the chute it was always in confidence, alone and hushed. They could see the evidence. They sensed something sinister. Ken Quist simply told his crew that he was aware of it and would get them some answers. He also cautioned them against talking about it. An associate director and an engineer had already been called home to Atlanta to cool their heels. Secretly, Quist feared for their lives. He knew the stakes were high. Illusion was the unstated mission. Protecting the integrity of the illusion was worth more than the lives of a few video tekkies.

In his mind, Quist was trying to see into the future to a point when he could expose the fraud that was being perpetrated. Network brass was one step ahead of him. To minimize his opportunity, CNN had surrounded him constantly with producers and executive producers. They told him what a great job he was doing. They would make unending suggestions about how to cover certain shots, angles and special effects. They kept him from interviews with outside reporters. They told him, "Ken, you'll have plenty of time afterwards to give them your impressions." They were, as his father used to say, 'blowing smoke up your skirt.'

Quist found that pretending to be stupid was mentally exhausting. But, he nurtured the illusion. They had assigned him to the temple dedication because they thought he didn't have a brain of his own. Fine, he could play that game. He could be the obedient and faithful fool. But, even a fool can have his intelligence insulted. He knew the execs were looking for signs of his revelation about the fraud. He could smell their doubts. Everyone in executive row had to know that seeing the fraud wasn't a matter of 'if,' but 'when.' Everyone on the crew had slowly figured it out and most of them were smart enough to realize that talking about it would lead to a termination of one form or another. The mood had turned strictly business. The air was thick with a dread no one dared talk about.

Ken Quist knew that regardless of his ignorance or loyalty, his life depended on his blind obedience. The evidences his brain had catalogued were too volatile for public consumption. His life was small potatoes in the larger picture – a picture of deception Ken Quist wanted to frame for the whole world to see.

CHAPTER FORTY NINE
Options

"**W**hat's going on is a fraud of the first order," bellowed Brad Pugh from 35 feet beneath the waves of the Gulf of Aqaba to an audience that had grown a third in size in just a few days. His ratings had seen a dramatic spike upward immediately after the temple dedication. It was a phenomenon unreported in the major media. Nowhere in the mainstream press was his surge in popularity given oxygen. It didn't surprise Brad Pugh. As usual, he had to toot his own horn.

The submarine was clicking 20 knots beneath the waves and maintaining a submerged depth of 35 feet beneath the Gulf of Aqaba; shallow enough so the transmitting antenna could target the overhead satellite orbiting in a secret and secured pattern. The Country Music Channel owned the satellite. They held the coordinates of the orbit in secrecy in spite of legislation the Kim Administration was attempting to push through to declassify the orbit. The Country Music Channel board of directors knew declassification of their orbit would spell doom. Their satellite would be jammed or blown out of the sky. The board of directors at the Country Music Channel had made themselves unavailable for comment. They quit showing up at the office. They were running the company remotely, anticipating congressional subpoena.

In the face of pending legislation and legal action, Pugh's pirated signal was beamed to 900 domestic and 250 international stations. He was being heard all around the English-speaking world. His commentary was being interpreted, as well, in 35 non-English-speaking countries. His views had suddenly become a hot commodity. Former critics, suddenly, found his "rantings" more 'sense' than 'sedition.'

Beneath the waves of Aqaba, Captain Petrov felt vulnerable. The technology to triangulate their location was available through US channels and he wasn't sure if the US Navy and intelligence agencies were capable, or willing, to run a smoke-screen for Brad Pugh much longer. The situation was just too unstable. Now his ship was boxed into the Gulf of Aqaba. He was sure that, at the southern end of the gulf, there were ships and submarines massing to block his exit out into the Red Sea and Indian Ocean. There were options to weigh and he had many of them to consider.

"Tell your friends and neighbors," commanded Pugh. "Tell them all. The ones who hate me and have bristled at the very mention of my name - that they need to tune to this station," he intoned. "The message of hope and sanity is still being broadcast. Everyone, everywhere needs to hear it before it is silenced."

Life onboard the K-815 had taken a war-time feel. Captain Petrov warned his crew of 13 to remember the basics of ship command, operation and execution. Petrov was a commercial pleasure boat operator yesterday but today, he was ship's commander of a military vessel and probably at war.

The whole crew, including the new conscripts, Ewald and Mahrous al-Sharif, had been briefed by Captain Petrov on contingencies. They all understood that even if they managed to avoid a naval blockade at the south end of the gulf, their old naval friends may now be their new naval enemies.

"We have to assume we'll be considered pirates," said Petrov. "If we are to escape we must assume everyone is our enemy."

Petrov also explained the procedure for scuttling the craft. If he gave the order, he didn't want any confusion or stalling. If orders were balked at or countermanded, he promised he would shoot the mutineers, military or civilian.

All options were on the table. Their survival was a huge question mark and dependent on a lot of factors over which they had no control.

Brad Pugh and wife, Winnie, both understood where history and prophecy were leading. Brad had never made an issue of his faith on the air. It would have made him an even bigger target than he already was. He kept his comments confined to the political and cultural arena. In their heart of hearts, the Pugh's were devoutly Christian.

Brad wanted desperately to announce his faith, but reconsidered. His task, as he had been told in prayer, was not to provide the answers. His job was to raise the questions. In matters of faith he was a table-setter. He drew attention to man's failures. God's salvation was another department.

The end of their road was in sight. Brad felt no remorse personally. He feared for America. He had always said that the nation was only one election away from tyranny. That his prophecy was coming true gave him no satisfaction. He wished he were wrong. America, he had always said, was the last, best hope for mankind. And now, the last, best hope was teetering - seduced into a little more security in exchange for a little less freedom.

The problem, he knew, was that evil never settled for a little less anything.

CHAPTER FIFTY
Uncertainty and CO2

It was day two of the wake. The Jesus-man lay stone cold dead in the glass coffin while dancers from Ethiopia and a jazz trumpeter from Trinidad entertained the sparse audience at the temple dedication. The United Nations flag hung prominently on the stage, with a smaller Jewish flag flanking it, stage-right. There was a large digital clock on the apron of the stage that counted off the time since the man-god had been pronounced dead. It read two days, 18 hours, 36 minutes and counting. CNN ran the clock, 'wall-to-wall,' in all of their newscasts, opinion shows, round-tables and feature articles. They had the coffin and the clock in a window in the upper right hand corner of the broadcast picture.

The temple dedication/Kennedy reincarnation/alien/transporter-beam/space-thingy was secondary news for the time being. The world had taken a break from the story. The Jews had abandoned their celebration, having been upstaged by the new one-world tag-team of Tanner and Kim. Their brand new temple sat gleaming, suspended high above the Al Aqsa mosque. Only janitors occupied it. The Hebrews were waiting for the time when events would allow them to safely return to worship in their own house. The fog of uncertainty and CO2 Kim and Tanner had laid down on the temple stage made Jews everywhere skittish. They had fought long and hard for control of their temple and the sense, now, was that they had been duped.

It would be at least a couple more days before the passion play unfolded. CNN and the viewing world were waiting patiently for three days to be counted off their electronic clock. The demystification of Jesus was implied. After the three day wait the myth of a holy resurrection could be silenced. Forever. The glass coffin of the man-god sat stone cold in front of the world, cameras trained on its lifeless visage around the clock. Tanner and Kim had placed a bet they couldn't lose - that after three days a dead man would remain horizontal.

For the non-Christian world it would be a great release. No longer would other belief systems have to contend with the judgmental certainty of the Christian crowd. A world with a discredited and debunked man-god would open many new doors.

What two-thirds of the planet couldn't see was what was amassing to fill the void. Billy Kim knew. And, Hans Tanner knew. They had the best research data money could buy to tell them how to pull it all off.

The keys to the kingdom were almost within reach.

CHAPTER FIFTY ONE
Gone nuts

Helen and Lars were physically alert, awake and caffeinated. Instead of pushing their return home, non-stop, they had decided to stop and sleep for the night. The next day, they started out peacefully enough. They tried to have a civil conversation.

It lasted exactly three-quarters of a mile.

Helen drove. Lars searched the radio dial for some news about the events that had cascaded down upon them. He finally found a clear signal that was neither CNN nor NPR. 'Finally,' he thought, as he searched the dial - 'maybe now we can find out the story from some different angles.'

Helen would have none of it.

"Either we listen to NPR or we listen to nothing at all," she barked.

Lars glared at her.

"What?"

"It was good enough to listen to for the first 37 years of marriage. What changed? Besides, I don't agree with all that crap being tossed around about a conspiracy and about us becoming a socialist America on all those hate radio stations you're so fond of all the sudden."

"How do you know that's what they're saying?" he asked calmly. "You've never listened to it."

"Talk radio? Haven't you heard? That's what they talk about all the time. They're anti-government, anti-tax, conspiracy freaks. Just a bunch of white reactionaries trying to preach hate. There's talk about regulating what they say, you know. Frankly, I think it would be a good thing. Give our side a chance to be heard."

Lars counted to ten. He had heard it before. He had heard it from her for many years now. She hated talk radio. She never listened to it but she hated it without ever giving more than a cursory listen. She read what talk radio was doing from the media critics in the Star & Tribune. She heard about talk radio on NPR. They called it hate radio. She had heard about it constantly in the teacher's lounge and her party caucuses. All her friends had a visceral hate of hate radio - they were the only friends she would have. She was on her third decade of railing against all the unregulated free speech taking place on the commercial airwaves. When it came to talk radio, Ethel Larsen was totally intractable. She had staked a position about talk radio three decades earlier and she couldn't be dynamited off her intellectual perch.

He clicked the radio off. It was a battle he couldn't win.

Instead, he did something she would find even more offensive.

From the back seat he pulled out a still-sealed copy of the Bible. He broke the seal and began paging through it. He turned to the Concordance because he was looking for something specific.

"I don't believe what I'm seeing. Where did you get that?"

"Murphy's truck stop. $11.95."

She had nothing further to say. It was official. Her husband had gone nuts.

CHAPTER FIFTY TWO
One degree of dead

Two independent bits of information floated inside the bowels of the K-815. The ideas were searching for each other without any clear clues to guide them. They were like egg and sperm, each useless by themselves but with profound implications if they happened to intersect.

On the one hand, Captain Petrov, his crew and Brad and Winnie Pugh knew that the K-815 was capable of diving to depths of 3200 feet, lighting up the ocean bottom and pulling in samples.

On the other hand, Richard Ewald and Marhrous al-Sharif knew that poor Arne Karlstrom had the digital photo discs of the chariot wheel, the Mountain of God, the golden calf altar and the forensic photos of the bottom of the Red Sea in his zippered pant pocket.

The problem was that both egg and sperm had made assumptions. Captain Petrov had assumed that Arne's body was best left where it had been located by the GPS locator - exactly 2837 feet beneath the surface of the Gulf of Aqaba, resting on a ridge that digital imaging had indicated was about 600 feet wide. Mahrous and Ewald assumed that Arne's body was irretrievable. Arne's final resting place, at 2837 feet, was far deeper than any submarine was capable of diving. Ewald had served in the British Navy - not as a submariner - but still with enough knowledge about things naval to know that depths below 500 meters tended to treat submarines like walnuts on an elephant walk.

Petrov saw no reason to retrieve the body and saw no reason for mentioning his ability to do so to Ewald or Mahrous. After all, what would they do with the body? Bury it at sea? A physical examination would only confirm that he was dead. There was only one degree of dead. A murder investigation was a pipe dream. There could be no justice. Who would be willing or able to prosecute Arne's murderers? The reality in the Middle East was that Arne had died trying to perpetrate a heresy against Islam. A sympathetic jury was at least 1000 miles away.

None of the crew felt anger. They felt helplessness. Arne had died like a dog. He was meat. He had been jettisoned because he was carrying a toxic cargo - knowledge. All of them speculated how the Egyptians and/or Saudis had learned of Arne's mission, but it was moot conjecture. The deed had been done.

"It's not as if someone could just type in 'Mountain of God' or 'Red Sea Crossing' and look it up on the net, is it?" It was a hypothetical question posed by Winnie Pugh. The men all looked at each other. Was there something on the net?

In 2012, Arne had self-published a book titled 'The Exodus Files' and promoted it on the net. His strategy was twofold: To sell his book and to serve as a billboard for mainline publishers who may inquire about it. Through a search engine, Brad Pugh located the site in nothing flat. He linked the words "Red Sea" and "crossing" and "Exodus."

Bingo. There it was. The website put forth Arne's hypothesis (with pictures, drawings, charts, graphs and animation), his picture, his credentials, his scientific citations and his contact information as well as purchase instructions for his self-published hypothesis.

It was a neon sign to the Muslim world saying 'I'm an infidel. I'm a heretic. I'm over here!'

The web manager had billed Arne annually and annually Arne would write out a check to maintain and protect the site. He had sold several thousand copies of his book over time and it still paid for him to maintain it. Why not? It didn't dawn on Arne that in the 21st century a man could be targeted for publishing new scientific speculation.

Arne's naivete had been his death sentence.

A fatwah had been secretly proclaimed against him. The Egyptian naval officer who put the bullet into Arne's brain stem collected $35,000 from a Saudi benefactor. After the murder, the Egyptian captain posed with Arne's body for a few quick snapshots, as proof, before the body was disposed of. So it ended. Arne Karlstrom, a scientist and man of God had lived in a dedicated pursuit of holy evidence and died like a Syndicate snitch.

In total, there were eight discs all neatly wrapped in plastic and sealed in a waterproof pouch in the zippered pocket of a corpse which rested more than 2800 feet beneath the surface of the Gulf of Aqaba. Richard Ewald knew those discs contained two-dimensional documentation of the claims Arne had staked his hypothesis on - his life on.

Publication of the pictures wouldn't provide answers to the world, but they would raise some sobering questions - what if the Bible was, literally, telling the truth? What if it could be forensically proven that the Hebrews had been led across the Gulf of Aqaba at Nuweiba to the other side? What if the sea had been parted by a divine force? That was the central question. If the evidence existed to prove such a ludicrous claim, the implications were imponderable.

As a closet Christian, the revelations of Arne's work were just beginning to have significance for Ewald. He, Richard Ewald, had seen the evidence and wondered why God was refusing to let it see the light of day. Arne had been so close to bringing the forensic proof of an age-old claim into the sunlight. Why would God allow it to be snuffed? Maybe God wants only the faithful, Ewald rationalized.

"Blessed are those who have seen and believed, but blessed, too, are those who have not seen and yet believe," Jesus had said. The recitation of the verse in his mind made Richard Ewald shudder. That must be it.

He conceded that Arne's work had been conscripted by God to be revealed in another time, another place.

In the bow of the K-815 Brad and Winnie Pugh shared a bottle of wine over a steak and lobster meal. In the middle of the table a candle glowed. It was their 33rd anniversary.

"We've had better years," Winnie lamented as she cut into her steak.

"Oh, I don't know," Brad tried to reassure her. "The world is on the verge of a coup which will undoubtedly be a bloody massacre, we're exiles at sea, but, you know....we're together." He was trying to be cute. It didn't work.

"Brad," she said in all seriousness, "is there any way we can get out of here? Just find a place where we won't be hunted? We've got the contacts and the money. Think!"

"Honey, I have thought about it. Here's the question I have for you - assume we could find a way out - to be dropped off on a pier somewhere and disappear into the landscape. What's that landscape going to look like? It won't be the free world we knew growing up. We'll be silenced and have to live in the shadows."

"Would that be so bad, hon. Living in the shadows?"

Brad paused and put down his silverware. "That man we rescued, Ewald - he told us about the evidence of God's hand, why Dr. Karlstrom had risked his life to come here. If it tells you nothing, it should tell you that God has a plan. It's not your plan or my plan. It's His. It probably doesn't fit with our world-view but it's not our world. We need to submit to that plan, not our own."

"I know you're right, hon, but it's just not fair," countered his wife.

"Fair? Fair? - okay, imagine our lives in the US. If I wasn't dead, I'd be in prison and you wouldn't be much better off than you are now, my dear. They would freeze all of my assets and you'd be stuck living with your sister Rose and her husband Roy in that little house in Kansas City. On top of that, anything you said publicly might land you in jail or land me in the executioner's dock."

It struck a chord with Winnie. He was right. That was the likely scenario and she knew it. She also knew that she and her sister were incapable of being in the same county for more than three hours without a major fight erupting. Life in a submarine wasn't all that bad when it was weighed against Rose, Roy, Kansas City and being silenced.

"Something dire and big is happening, dear," he said with a sense of resignation as he looked out the inky bow of the ship. "We're at an endgame here, you know. Tanner and Kim are operating in tandem but they're not alone. The press seems to be working in a kind of gentleman's agreement to ignore the real story. It's not a conspiracy of governments. It's not a conspiracy of religions and it's not a conspiracy of ideologies. It's more like a conspiracy of consensus. The people are ripe to let their freedoms be taken away for a little more security. They want someone to promise them cradle-to-grave security. Anyone would want that. What people have forgotten is that that kind of power eventually gets abused. Even if Tanner and Kim were some kind of benevolent dictators, there's no guarantee that whoever succeeds them will be. History is filled with benevolent kings who were succeeded by evil dictators. The people don't see it because they're not driven to learn from history anymore. Everyone has been conditioned to live in the here and now. That whole Jerusalem fraud is the final act to some mad power play. It's filled with an evil beyond imagination. You and I are just small players in it."

"I am, dear," responded Winnie. "You, on the other hand, are keeping a flame alive."

"Maybe. But, the flame is flickering." He paused and closed his eyes. It took him 15 seconds to begin his prayer. He bowed his head and clasped his hands in front of him. "Heavenly Father,…" he began.

The submarine lurched. It took a steep dive. Brad and Winnie tumbled to the floor. Their dinner and wine cascaded down upon them. An electronic claxon sounded.

"Down bubble," shouted Captain Petrov from the helm. "15 degree, full ahead, three-quarter," he commanded the crew in Russian. Petrov had not been surprised. He had expected, and was prepared for an attack. They had been tracked by aircraft.

If war was at hand, he would expect his sonar man, Ivanov, to announce there was a fish in the water. It would mean torpedoes had been launched from sea planes. Ivanov sat silent, his headphones secure and his face rapt with deadly seriousness. The computers aboard the K-815 didn't wait for the captain's coordinates. The rudders and flaps had already been set to default toward a pre-determined location.

The floor of the Gulf of Aqaba is an inverted mountain range. If one were to stand on the shore of the gulf and look at the mountains surrounding them, they would see the mirror image of the bottom of the gulf. Like any mountain range, the sea bed of Aqaba was a contour of dips, nooks, valleys, peaks, plateaus, ridges and cliffs. At its deepest there was a ridge that plummeted to nearly 13,500 feet. Petrov had spent considerable time studying the digital and sonar images of the bottom in order to find the most defensive hole. He had purposely parked the sub above that hole while history and circumstance defined his course of action. By his calculations they were only 45 seconds away from a safe haven. The location he wanted to squirrel the sub into was 1800 feet deep and consisted of three high ridges and a plateau. The plateau was surrounded on three sides that gave them a virtual 900-foot overhang to pick off any ordnance launched at them. Only a matter of sheer luck or incredibly sophisticated torpedoes could reach them there. They would be sitting in a trough which appeared to have been designed just for them.

"Fish!" announced Ivanov in Russian. "Four of them at 1500 meters bearing 260."

The angle was good, thought Petrov. At a 48 degree approach from 260 the fish would be picked off by the mountain ridges. The K-815 settled into the silty plateau at 591 meters. Ewald and Mahrous, being tourists, were silent but saucer-eyed. It was apparent that the sub was under attack but, not having a clue about the constructs of the Russian language, they could only rely on expressions and body language.

The sub softly nestled onto the silt bottom, still and silent.

"400 meters, still bearing 260," shouted Ivanov.

Ivanov counted the explosions against the mountain range. After the first explosion, Petrov commanded they elevate the nose. Everyone hung on. The captain was positioning the ship for a quick exit if rubble started raining down on them. The concussions of the torpedoes against the mountain range rattled the sub violently after each blast.

"One hit, two hit, three hit, four missed."

The fourth torpedo had somehow slid by one of the ridges and was heading to the deep. Inside the sub they could hear a "whir" of the screws as it faded away from them and into the inky depths. Almost a minute later, the torpedo started a slow return, its onboard guidance gyros commanding it to return to the last known footprint of the sub. Almost 45 seconds later Ivanov announced it had died. Its solid propellant had been spent. It sank like a rock to the bottom. At 3830 meters it exploded against the floor. "Four hit," said a relieved Ivanov. It would be another 10 seconds before the faint concussion nudged the sub.

Petrov switched on the intercom.

"Brad...Winnie, I hope I didn't upset your meal. We had visitors. Come on up and I'll fill you in. Everything's fine now."

Brad stuck his head up the ladder, wide-eyed and announced: "We were praying."

"So was I," said Petrov. "And, I'm a communist." He laughed.

"I'm relieved you find humor in this, Captain. What happened?"

The captain gathered the civilians around him. He sat in his chair and lit a pipe. It was a pleasure he rarely afforded himself, but he felt like it now. He had just engaged in a real war-time maneuver, and he felt he had earned a smoke.

He tamped the tobacco down, lit and drew, emitting a sweet smell of rum smoke into the cabin.

"The bad news is we're at war. The good news is we didn't die," he said, collecting his thoughts. "Here is how I see the situation. If anyone disagrees, please let me know." He was getting right to the point. "We're in a gulf. It's a big gulf and we can hide, play 'chicken', as you say, against the enemy for a long time if we want, but eventually we'll have to figure a way out. The sea exit is very likely blocked. I would bet the ranch on it, as you say. We don't know by whom, but that doesn't matter. We're blocked. Eventually we're going to have to get out onto land or die in the ocean. The way I see it, there's but a few options."

"Nuweiba..." said Ewald.

"Nuweiba is a possibility. Tell me why you think so, Mr. Ewald."

"First off, it's in Egypt and we have an Egyptian, here," he said, motioning to Mahrous. "He speaks the language and can be our front man. Second, there's a road out. Problem is...it's the only road out. If they were going to look for us to escape by land, they would look there first."

"And, what do you think of the odds?" asked the captain.

"Not good," responded Ewald.

"I agree. But, you're assuming we take a van or bus out of Nuweiba, across the Sinai to Egypt." He paused. It was apparent that he was churning ideas in his brain.

"Helicopter," said Brad Pugh.

"A helicopter would have to carry 17 people, Mr. Pugh. That means it would have to be a military helicopter. Where would you find such a craft?"

"Israel?" Pugh asked.

"A possibility. We have open channels to Israeli armed forces through Mr. Kowalski. But, an Israeli helicopter over Aqaba or Sinai would be viewed as an act of aggression. There's a fairly good chance a helicopter landing on Egyptian soil would be met with a military response."

"Or," Petrov continued, "we could sneak up on Eilat, the Israeli port, scuttle the craft and go ashore there. We need to look at all the options. In the mean time, we're going to have to run deep. Take us down to 800 meters and level, Mr. Ivanov."

Richard Ewald was stunned. "800 meters?" he asked incredulously. "How deep are we, Captain, right now?" Petrov looked at the digital counter and pointed to it. "590 meters. Why?"

"Meters? I thought that was feet! Why aren't we crushed like grapes?"

"Ahhhh. I guess no one told you. You're not dealing with capitalist technology here, Mr. Ewald. This is a Russian sub. You see, communist engineers were so much more capable than capitalist engineers. When you give them a blank check and hold a gun to the heads of their children, they can invent their way out of anything." He laughed at himself. "Communism wasn't very good at feeding people, but it was very efficient at weaponry."

Ewald saw it. In that instant, the dots connected. Egg and sperm conjoined.

"Arne's body. We have to retrieve it." declared Ewald.

"I understand your grief, Mr. Ewald but just because we can retrieve the body doesn't mean we're going to." He paused to let his concern show. "Let your friend rest."

"No, Captain. You don't understand. In a zippered pocket - in his pants there are all the discs of all the still pictures. He put them there. The evidence. We can retrieve it."

CHAPTER FIFTY THREE
Wholly unacceptable

Lars flipped from one passage to the next and back again. Then, he would flip to the Concordance, find another passage and read, studiously, for a moment and begin the process over again. Ethel had given up. She had tried talking to him, but he wasn't listening. She didn't know what to do with him.

As she pulled into their driveway Ethel was fully expecting to see signs of life at their home. After all, Lars had agreed to rent the place to the Kowalski nuts after they had lost their power and needed a place to stay. When they walked into the house, they looked around for visitors. There were none in the living room, none in the kitchen and no one responded when they shouted "Hello!" The house was clean and in the same order they had left it. Ethel was relieved. On the kitchen counter she found a brief note from Ben Kowalski. It told her that they had vacated that morning, and that he would come back later to settle the bill.

"Well, at least they didn't trash the place," she said. She breathed a heavy sigh. "I'm so glad to be back home again. The past few days have been such a drain…" she said, turning around, looking for Lars.

He was in his easy chair with his Bible in his lap and the remote in his hand. He was tuning in the temple dedication, or whatever it had become.

She looked at him with a burning anger. After 37 years of marriage, what he had become in the past week was wholly unacceptable. There was a counseling session in their future, she felt. She knew it.

"Why don't you just find a church and go pray with some of your Christian friends. Give yourself to Jesus if you like."

He wasn't listening. He turned to her and said "You know what we have here?" motioning to the TV. "The abomination that causes desolation."

Even if she had been listening, she wouldn't have known what he was talking about. Ethel Larsen was a biblical illiterate. Her knowledge of things biblical were the sum of what she had seen and heard from her usual sources.

She turned and headed upstairs. "I'm going to crawl into a bath and then I'm going to crawl into bed, alone,…" she said acidly. "Then, I'm going to sleep for a day."

She wasn't kidding and he wasn't listening.

CHAPTER FIFTY FOUR
Making history and commissions

Hans Tanner walked to center stage. He was confident, self-assured and primped like a televangelist. He wore a wireless combination headphone/microphone. He knew the locations of cameras one, two and four. He understood what shots they were expected to cover. He knew, too, that camera six was a static shot of the glass coffin and that camera three was perched on scaffolding at the back of the arena to cover the wide shots. It was the only camera in the arena with an angle on the hatch in the stage. In his ear, Tanner had an IFB that was plugged into a direct line even Ken Quist didn't know about.

"I draw your attention to our friends in the sky," he announced to the 15,000 assembled at the temple and to the world viewing his movements from inside the expensive TV lenses focused on him. The green light blasted from the black disc onto the center of the stage. Three average-looking Arab types appeared. They stepped aside and then it happened again and again and again. Soon, there were 15 people, mostly of Arabic lineage standing at the apron of the old Wailing Wall. They were unremarkable. No one recognized them. Their faces appeared in a 60-foot by 90-foot digital Maximage screen at the back of the stage.

In the crowd there were pockets of hysteria. Camera three picked up the activities taking place in the crowd. The shoulder-held camera arrived quickly in the crowd. Ken Quist punched up the pictures and allowed the world to see Arab civilians in a state of panic, delight and shock.

"These people," Tanner said, motioning to the stage, "are the deceased relatives of some of those in our crowd today."

The implications were profound.

The pictures being broadcast to the world by Ken Quist and CNN couldn't lie. There was no acting in the crowd. What the world was witnessing was a genuine display of joy, shock and relief.

"Is it not apparent where the powers of resurrection are?" Tanner asked the crowd and the world.

Soon the family members of the clones were ushered onstage through tears of delight and wonder. The brothers, fathers, sisters and mothers of the replicated beings were sobbing uncontrollably as they clung onto the actors. The actors cried too. They had been trained to cry. They were actors. They blubbered uncontrollably, falling to their knees and praising Allah.

"Our friends have the technology and power to save and restore life. These are all family members of ordinary people, people whose lives have been preserved. Every one of these people have someone here today, in this crowd, to whom they are related. Imagine the implications..." Hans Tanner intoned. "Imagine the power."

Ken Quist directed the pictures from his chair in the control booth and had one question. He didn't dare utter it loudly.

How?

The question was silently echoed throughout the control booth. There were 18 people in the production truck and none of them were crying. They had connected the dots. They had seen the faint outline of the chute on the monitors. They didn't know the whole story, but the illusion that was being played out in front of them rivaled Hollywood in its special effects contrivance. The crew said nothing. The senior CNN producer in the truck noted their disbelief. It would be in his report.

The actors and their 'families' were led off-stage. What the world could not see next was the separation that appeared once off stage. The actors disappeared into a catacomb that led beneath the Al Aqsa mosque. Family members were ushered into a meeting tent. The entrance to the tent was guarded by soldiers in blue helmets. No one in. No one out.

In a matter of hours, all of the actors would be on a plane bound for China. Nicely sedated, they would be led into a replication of their familiar old compound where they would lay their head down one last time before their organs would be harvested.

At the front of the stage the corpse of the poor Jesus-man clone lay in state. The digital clock in front of it read "3 days, 23 hours, 58 minutes and counting. A throng of a thousand costumed singers and dancers had been ushered onto the stage to serve as a back-drop for the drama, or lack of drama, that was about to unfold. Hans Tanner lifted his hands into the sky and proclaimed:

"Hear, oh great God in heaven: If this is your son, over whom you hold the power of life and death, I implore you, I beg you, to raise him. Now! As you are said to have done 2000 years ago, use the powers that you alone are said to have to elevate him, to bring him to his feet. Show the world that you are the one true God! Show us that you hold the keys to the future. Show us that you, alone, hold the keys to life and death."

The world watched as the digital clocked rolled over to 4 days, 0 hours, 0 minutes and counting.

Nothing. The dead man ignored life.

"Now we know," Hans Tanner said. He motioned to the music director and the chorus and the dancers sprang into song and dance.

The song they chose for the moment was strategic - "Imagine," by John Lennon. It had all the right stuff. The lyrics matched the moment, the rhythm was controlled, it had simple and sober instrumentation and the lyrics were easy enough to teach a cast of thousands with relative ease. "Imagine no religion/it's easy if you try," the lyrics suggested. As they sung the line, the pop stars sang it with added animation. On the Maximage screen the word 'imagine' faded in and out to compliment the pictures the world and local audience were being treated to.

It lasted four minutes and 36 seconds. In his control booth, Ken Quist dropped in new footage of children from around the world and faded it into and out of the live action on the stage. The footage had been photographed by a Hollywood cinematographer. It was soft. It was human. It was touching. The filmmaker who had put together the touching montage had been hiding for 28 years on the French Riviera in order to escape a child molestation charge in the US. It was a moving tribute to the oneness of the moment. At the end of the production, the disc overhead mimicked the final chord of the song and broadcast it across the span of Israel as a single, floating, unending note that stretched into infinity. Fireworks exploded overhead as a formation of Turkish F-15's jetted from east to west in a flash, dropping a cascading trail of colorful pyrotechnics which provided a full canopy of color and sound over the temple site.

Hans Tanner levitated above the stage.

He floated about four feet above the stage without benefit of any visible means of support. The camera showed him in a reverent pose, arms held aloft as he appealed to the disc overhead. "Use me!!! Make me one with you!"

The green light shot forward onto the spot where Hans Tanner had been strategically positioned. In a heartbeat, he was gone in a blast of CO2, light and air pressure. While the crowd looked up, imagining Tanner being 'beamed up,' the reality was that he had been sucked down into the bowels of the Al Aqsa mosque. It was a good illusion. It served its purpose. The levitation was courtesy of a street magician from Los Angeles who had pioneered it. The magician had been forced at gunpoint to explain the illusion to men he didn't know. Eight days later his body washed up on a Santa Monica beach, badly decomposed and with a lethal amount of heroin in his system. Just another entertainer lost to the seduction of chemicals, the Times lamented.

In the production truck, Ken Quist received a call on his cell phone. It was the CEO in Atlanta. He wanted to see him and the crew in the conference room at the Jerusalem Hilton as soon as physically possible for a video conference. Quist knew what it was going to be - a debriefing. By executive order. It would be a company attempt to buy off what the crew had surmised. Quist had seen it coming, even through his diminished intelligence.

In the production truck, Ken Quist knew this would be the moment of his own great acting performance. While the CNN-Jerusalem executive producer was busy congratulating the crew on their superior performance in boosting the network ratings into the stratosphere, Ken Quist pulled two video discs out of the control panel and slipped them into his coat pocket. They were "out-takes," which he had been secretly recording. He joined the producer in congratulating his crew. He gave the exec a hearty slap on the back.

"We've made history," Quist commented.

The producer turned to Quist, pleasantly surprised by the director's enthusiasm.

"Yes," he said, "we've made history. And commissions," he said, winking at Quist. "As director, you won't be forgotten when the commission checks come around."

Quist smiled and shook the producer's hand again - more vigorously this time.

He had a sense that management would, indeed, remember who he was.

CHAPTER FIFTY FIVE
A dip in the deep

At 2100 feet beneath the sea, the air pressure inside the sub changed. All of their ears popped. Almost simultaneously, Captain Petrov, his crew and his guests ducked their heads and grabbed their ears. It was an involuntary reflex. The sound of their voices changed timbre when they spoke.

"Not to be alarmed, people. Our engineers trained us for this. He handed out sticks of gum. "Chew," he said. "It will help keep your ears from popping again."

At the helm Lieutenant Andrenko monitored the computer. He did little more than watch a digital screen as the sub slowly descended into the dark chasm; its rudders, diving planes and engines working in perfect synchrony to position the sub precisely in front of the GPS locator in the belt of the corpse of Arne Karlstrom.

The sub stopped its descent and began a slow, slow movement forward. It stopped again and the crew and guests felt the sensation of total stillness as the K-815 sat poised in front of Arne's body. Captain Petrov gave the order to deploy the searchlights. Inside of the bow Brad Pugh, his wife, Winnie, two crew members, along with Mahrous al-Sharif and Richard Ewald waited. The searchlight arms had finished their whirring extension outward and awaited the captain's instructions to send electricity to the filaments of the bulbs.

No one spoke.

Captain Petrov turned to the assembled members. "You're going to see a corpse. If that bothers you, please leave the bow."

No one moved.

In Russian he told Ivanov, on the bridge, to light up the bottom. The initial flash of light made everyone squint. In a few moments their eyes adjusted and they saw the body, suspended like a rag doll, floating in the gentle deep sea current, it's arms swaying slowly to and fro like an animated kite in the wind. The sub was 30 feet away from the body. A half-dollar size hole was evident in the in the middle of Arne's forehead and one eyeball was dangling in front of his face, hanging from the optic nerve. Around Arne's ankles was a chain to which a cinder block had been attached. The cinder block sat on the bottom of the shelf and the chain had wrapped around some debris on the wall of an outcropping on the bottom. Arne's body floated in the deep-sea currents like a day-old helium balloon. His arms swung as if he were motioning for them to join him for a dip in the deep.

One of the Russian submariners sat in the helmsman's chair in the bow of the sub. He slid his hand into a glove that was robotically attached to grasping claws. He activated the motors.

"This is the tricky part," said Petrov in English.

"Churmenov has been trained to retrieve objects but not humans. Once the separation and extraction is made the body will be drawn into a pressurized chamber. It may get a little grisly, so I'll warn you that the cutting tools we have are not designed for humans."

A claw extended into view. On its end was a metal fist, a cutting shears and a small circular saw. The occupants of the cabin huddled tightly. The field of vision out to the ocean bottom was very narrow.

Ewald stepped to the back of the cabin. He suddenly decided that he didn't have the stomach for what might occur next. He didn't want to look but, like watching a horror movie, found himself glancing over his shoulder to the wide angle shot of the action in front of him.

"Wait!" Ewald shouted. From his vantage point he was able to see a larger picture than those in front. The refraction of the glass nose, from his vantage point, gave him an almost 180-degree view of the scene in front of him. "Everybody! Get back here and look!"

From Ewald's vantage point they could see a wide angle of the shelf.

It was a graveyard.

Carcasses were piled on top of each other 30, 40, 50 feet deep. The flesh of the corpses had long since rotted away, having been committed to the sea worms and the tide. But the bones, the chariots, the shields, the wagons, the horse and cattle skeletons, the soldiers of Pharaoh's army had been called by gravity to this place where man had been excluded for 3500 years. The infestation of coral couldn't occur at the depth they were at. While 3500 years of silt had buried the lower levels of the morgue, the upper levels were clearly visible for what they were - the graveyard of a quarter million of Pharaoh's army.

"Captain," Ewald implored. "Please tell me you have a video camera on board."

They moved the sub foot by foot up the slope of the ridge. Ewald held his camera steady, zooming in and zooming out. Brad Pugh, the exiled voice of millions, provided commentary.

"What you are seeing is validation of a hypothesis put forth by a Swedish scientist by the name of Dr. Arne Karlstrom. Professor Karlstrom is the reason we are here. We came here to recover his body. He died, was murdered, for the truth he was trying to bring to the light of day. Today we found Dr. Karlstrom's body at the bottom of the Gulf of Aqaba with a bullet hole in his head and a brick chained to his feet. In the Russian sub K-815 where I have been broadcasting from for the past few years we have descended to 2800 feet to a place where man has, up until this moment in history, not been allowed to gaze. Skeptics will tell you that a conventional sub cannot dive to these depths. Don't listen to the skeptics. Listen to the experts. The capabilities of the Soviet K-800 class have been declassified and are available in Ford's Military magazine. Look it up before you let the press tell you not to believe what your eyes are telling you."

The graveyard of Pharaoh's army extended almost a quarter mile along the ridge. After that, the ridge dropped off and the depths swallowed up the rest of the Egyptian relics. The pictures captured on the video tape needed little explanation. They didn't lie. Anyone who had ever heard of the myth of the Red Sea crossing could deduce for themselves what the images meant.

The microphone connection was a simple quarter-inch phone jack into the camera - not broadcast standard by any stretch, but it was what they had to work with. If the pictures ever reached the airwaves they would be less than broadcast perfect. That wasn't the immediate issue.

Brad Pugh allowed the pictures to color the canvas before he spoke. "What we're showing you will be called a lie and I will be called a liar. Let me just state this for the people who distrust, for the people who discount the message because of the messenger - in 23 years as a man with a microphone I have never been witness to news. I have always been a commentator." His voice began to crack, to break up a bit. His passion began to percolate to the surface - the passion that had acted as a magnet to so many millions of people looking for explanations they simply weren't being allowed to get from most other sources.

"All of the issues we have discussed in the past were just manifestations of another reality, another dimension. This is a seminal moment. We are witness to the evidence of the ages. What was reported in the Bible is true. It ought to be the defining moment of your life. Before you are pictures that give us undeniable proof of God's imprint on human history. Moses and the Hebrews were led by the pillar of cloud and fire to cross the Red Sea. When Pharaoh's army attempted to follow them through the sea bed Moses, at God's command, brought the Red Sea down upon them. That story was recounted by Moses 3500 years ago and today we can see that those words are true. We can see the proof. That truth is going to be very, very disturbing for a lot of people. God is speaking to you in these pictures. Are you listening to God's truth or are you listening to another voice? Your heart knows and God knows what's in your heart."

Brad paused as the camera captured the skeletons of countless Egyptian soldiers, their animals, chariots and ancient armaments stacked on top of each other beneath the sea.

When they had exhausted the first video disc, Ewald stopped and frantically inserted a second disc.

"You know," he said to the crew, "Arne prayed to let God use him as an instrument to point the way. When he was murdered, I wondered why God would have betrayed him." Ewald paused and looked at all of them. "Arne got exactly what he prayed for."

Captain Petrov took the occasion to ask a question. It was a basic, simple question but one that would be recounted billions of times if the pictures ever did make it to the airwaves. The captain was stunned, unbelieving and almost in shock.

"Do you know what this means?"

Ewald gave him a curt response. "You're the godless Communist. You tell me."

CHAPTER FIFTY SIX
The devil I know

They were led like sheep. Ken Quist and the rest of the production team were ushered by unarmed soldiers in blue helmets toward the gate and onto a waiting CNN bus.

Quist didn't like it. They had been assured by network brass that they were all being led back to the hotel for a video-conference with CNN management. Why the escort? Quist didn't trust management and was looking vainly for a way to bolt. He had nothing concrete to base his feelings on other than his sense that the whole production team had been made a party to a lie. Protecting the lie, Quist assumed, was worth more than a few lives.

As they neared the bus Quist saw an armed Israeli officer on the other side of the fence. The officer was directing his gaze specifically at Quist. They made eye contact and the look from the officer convinced Quist. The officer made a simple motion with his head and eyes, motioning down the street. He was saying 'follow me' with his eyes. Quist didn't know if he could trust the officer. What he knew beyond a doubt was he couldn't trust CNN brass. He hesitated and wondered: Do I stay with the devil I know, or the devil I don't know?

He had a decision to make.

When Quist got to the bus he waited for the blue helmets to busy themselves sufficiently. For a 53-year-old man, Ken Quist broke into a pretty good sprint, dodging civilians in a determined attempt to flee his pursuers. What happened next confirmed that Quist had done the right thing. All hell broke loose. Guards everywhere scrambled to follow him. The Israeli officer appeared to come from out of nowhere. He grabbed him by the arm and led him down an alley and into a building. They went up a flight of stairs and out through the front side of the building and into another street. A jeep awaited them. Quist was pushed into the jeep by the officer and the jeep lost no time leaving. They turned a corner and there was another jeep in tandem with an armored vehicle with a soldier seated atop at a gun turret waiting to escort them.

Soon the three Army vehicles were cascading down Jerusalem's back streets.

"Why me?" Quist panted. "You weren't looking at anybody else. Why?"

"You were the director. You saw it all. We need to know what you know."

The jeep stopped almost as if on cue. The driver waited for instructions from the officer. The driver looked confused.

"Where are we going?" Quist asked of the Israeli officer. There was a pause. The officer was, Quist guessed, about 30 years old. Handsome. Noble profile. The officer's jaw muscles flexed as he contemplated what to tell the director. While he was mulling his words, the officer patted Quist down to make sure that there were no weapons on him. He found the discs in Quist's jacket pocket and pulled them out.

"I'm sure these will be instructive," he said. "The truth is, Mr. Quist, Jerusalem is about to explode. My superiors wanted me to secure you before a war breaks out. I can't tell you how much it means that you 'volunteered.'"

The officer looked at Quist and in all seriousness said "I'm not sure where we're going. We're kind of making this up as we go."

The driver turned to the captain and addressed him directly. "Captain? Orders." he said, handing the captain his headset.

The captain slipped on the headset and answered. "Simon," he said to whoever was on the other end of the radio transmission. The captain's face turned deadly serious. He waited for instructions and listened for about a half a minute before saying "yes, sir," and handed the headset back to the driver. He sat back and extended his hand to Quist.

"Mr. Quist, my name is Captain Randall Simon. Educated Princeton University. Came over to Israel to serve the homeland. They made me an officer." He pulled a cigarette out of his pocket and offered one to Quist. When Quist refused the smoke he offered one to the driver who gladly accepted it.

"I told my wife I was going to cut down," he said as he lit his smoke.

"Our original mission was to get you and bring you back for interrogation. That mission is already changing," he said. "I'm not sure what to do with you now. We're at war."

The director's face went blank. Quist had painted himself in a corner. To be a hunted animal in a war-torn country was not what he had signed on for when he had accepted the original CNN assignment. He didn't know much about geopolitics but he did know that the Israeli army didn't have many friends.

"War?" he asked. "With whom?"

The captain took a long drag off of his smoke and looked at the corporal's face in the rear-view mirror, smiling.

"Everyone."

"What do you mean, everyone?" Quist asked.

"The US is our only international friend, but behind the scenes there is every indication that President Kim is working against us. Israel is probably not the best army to be aligned with right now, but, here you are! We're quite outnumbered and surrounded. But we do have God on our side. That ought to reassure you."

Quist bristled. "Forget God. What about me?"

"Mr. Quist, I have orders to take you to a small seaside port on the Gulf of Aqaba called Eilat. We're trying to get you together with Brad Pugh."

"Brad Pugh?" Quist asked incredulously. "I thought he was dead."

"You should know better than to believe what you hear on your own network. Pugh has been in contact with some of Israel's friends and they want any intelligence we have brought to Eilat, and you, Mr. Quist, are that intelligence. They want to know what you know and they want you to tell the world what you know."

Quist became suddenly animated. He didn't like what was happening, no, not one bit.

"What? To be a spokesman for the Jews? You want me to defend the Jews to the world. Why can't you do it? You know as much as I do," he yelled. "My life won't amount to a hill of beans."

Captain Simon held the two discs up in front of Quist.

"Knowing the truth is an awesome responsibility. Defending the truth can be deadly. Not defending it can be worse. You Americans seem to have forgotten that."

CHAPTER FIFTY SEVEN
Another media dance

Ben had changed his mind. He had given up trying to get a reporter from the mainstream press to get his opinions. The mission had changed. True to Murphy's Law, as soon as he decided the networks were worthless, they began calling and asking if they could come out and talk to him. They showed up alone and, at other times, stacked one on top of the other. Leon Amanti chased them away with a certain measure of fervor. He would have liked to plant a boot in their hind-quarters, but resisted.

Ben knew what they were up to. They wanted 'the opposition' to say something critical of what had happened over the past 24 hours in Jerusalem. The networks wanted to demonstrate their balance. Ben knew better. He had been reading the scuttlebutt on the net. There was a move in congress to fulfill what Marshall Warren had prophesied. Now that Christ was dead, Kim's congress wanted to kill Christ's church.

What the networks wanted was to show the face of enraged Christians. They would balance their coverage, of course, with their own calm and reasoned clarifications. To make certain their point of view was solid, they wanted to juxtapose Christian anger against what they contended was the undeniable proof that Christ was a myth, a legend, a fairy tale.

It was another media dance Ben was all too familiar with. He concluded it was time to be quiet. Now was not the time to speak. The battle had been lost. He didn't want to lose the war. Ben had lots of opinions worth airing, but network TV was not the medium to air them. Not now. He knew the media. He knew they couldn't be trusted to deliver what he had to say in context. They would cut and chop and juxtapose his words to suit their own conclusions. Talking to them now would just give them ammunition.

All Christian organizations were back-pedaling. In just 24 short hours they had been put in the position of having to fight for their financial lives. The IRS was auditing them. The full force and scope of the IRS had been given new powers overnight, in emergency session. Billy Kim and his congress acted quickly. Since Christ was dead, it was argued successfully, Christianity was a de facto cult. Cults, congress declared correctly, are not and have never been, protected by the US tax code. There wasn't a pastor, reverend, minister or priest in the country who wasn't consumed trying to find shelter for the financial assets of their church. The same thing was happening to any Christian group claiming to be a ministry, a non-profit organization with Christian ties, or a Wednesday evening bingo bazaar. One congressman from San Fransisco, a career agnostic, had even gone so far as to say "they might as well be worshipping Elmer Fudd. And, for that they get tax protection? C'mon, this is a new day."

It summed things up for a lot of people. It was a new day. Whether or not the charade in Jerusalem was believable wasn't the point. It was credible enough for those who wanted to believe it.

Christ was dead, it was asserted with little congressional opposition. And Tanner was missing in action. No one at the Kowalski compound was surprised when, on the third day after being 'beamed up' to the mother ship, Tanner miraculously reappeared. In the morning skies over Cairo the black disc appeared, hovering and humming. It moved slowly, slowly west out and over the pyramids of Giza. Cameras from a dozen news organizations locked onto it as the green light and CO_2 beamed onto the apex of the pyramid of Khafre, 455 feet above the desert floor. Video cameras captured Tanner atop the pyramid on his knees with arms held aloft. A helicopter was dispatched to pluck him off the top. When he was brought to earth he had a brief statement before being whisked away in a jeep. He appeared weak and glassy-eyed. He said, "I have tasted the fruit of knowledge and it is delicious beyond belief."

The quote was a headline on the front pages of every major metropolitan daily on the planet.

In a subsequent news conference Brian Vandervoort, chief of staff for Hans Tanner, said the EU president was drained, but exhilarated by his alien experience. Vandervoort said that his boss was busy preparing a written statement - a vision for mankind. Cynics, skeptics and the faithful knew what it would be: A manifesto - a mission statement for the next millennium - a statement which, no doubt, would hold little tolerance the Christian or Jewish traditions.

The illusion was complete. The new order had supplanted education. It had taken them two generations to convince students that the world they knew and the history their parents had learned was littered with half-truths - that every righteous or evil act was the result of a conspiracy of oppression.

Secondly, they had killed Jesus Christ.

Finally, a new god was emerging from the void.

Game, set, match.

CHAPTER FIFTY EIGHT
Hot

The television uplink had been established. Video, being on the FM band, had to be targeted directly in a line-of-site at the satellite and the satellite had to be in precise synchronization with the signal. It was supposed to be a covert operation and Ben Kowalski was betting, hoping, praying that the Kim Administration was as incompetent at acting on intelligence as he believed they were. The Kim team had demonstrated their disdain, over seven years, for military intelligence or intelligence gathering. Their focus had always been on what Kim called "social and economic equity." Kim and his team simply didn't trust the military or the intelligence necessary to make the military effective. Billy Kim's gifts were in the cultural arena. Billy Kim was a master at public relations. When it came to the practical matter of insuring the common defense or protecting the property rights of the citizens, he was indifferent. His administration reflected the indifference he felt toward constitutional or military matters. Kim was, in the classical sense, a socialist. He never used the term to describe himself, even though Brad Pugh had made a career out of calling him one. No, Billy Kim called himself a progressive. Those in the know knew there was no difference, but there just weren't that many in the know. Most of America had learned what they knew about the frailties of their freedoms through the public school system. They had only a basic, cursory understanding about democracy, the workings of a representative republic or the moral foundations necessary to maintain a civil society. Instead, they had learned about the lofty and impossible virtues of being progressive, forward-thinking, and equitable. Morality was defined by the criminal code. Ethics were fluid constructs, situational and highly debatable. Truth, if one could define it without offending someone, was just another point of view. Good intentions, in the Kim paradigm, were as laudable as good results. The result, after 50 years of cultural assault on tradition and norms was an American public that had been intellectually arrested at a juvenile level. Video games, movies, music and tabloids had become their natural brain food. Feelings, emotions mattered. Facts got in the way of a good, self-righteous smugness. Matters of intellect required a labor Americans no longer felt required to perform. They could hire foreigners or, worse - academics - to think for them. The American landscape had lived on a slippery slope for decades. The slow, inexorable slide downhill was not seen as an historical event - because history itself had been framed as a series of ancient accidents.

Into the cultural swamp of moral symmetry, situational ethics and ambivalence, Billy Kim had stepped into a national void and fueled the American slide toward a 21st-century Sodom and Gomorrah. He was their pied piper.

Kowalski knew the juvenile profile of the American masses were no mistake. He also knew there were too many juveniles, now, to have an adult debate. Kowalski had seen America's decline long before it happened. It wasn't a vision. He wasn't a sage or prophet. He had no crystal ball. He was more like a cultural meteorologist. He studied the social clouds, the cultural winds, the political humidity, the poll barometers and the increasing density. He had learned how to predict a storm when there were bluebird skies. Generally, his predictions were right on the money, and generally they were ominous, which was precisely why Ben wasn't broadly sought for his timely opinions. People, as a rule, didn't want to hear bad news, but it was all Ben could peddle. In time, the American public was coerced into accepting the New York Times' editorial page assessment of the once most trusted man in America: "Ben Kowalski is a washed-up political hack whose commentary is a vain attempt to prop up a fundamentalist Christian dogma the American people have outgrown and are far better off without."

The Times' opinion of Ben was far easier to digest than actual thought and served as a guidepost for journalists seeking a handy bucket in which to store Ben's legacy.

The editorial took root in the journalistic intelligentsia. In time, the reporters didn't quote Kowalski and the networks never called for his commentary or insights unless it suited their foregone conclusions. Instead, they quoted themselves. Kowalski was insignificant. The Times said so. Ben had become like an overprotective parent constantly warning his children about the cliff they were playing too close to. His words had become meaningless, even in their accuracy.

Within his grasp, though, Ben now had pictures that verified, provided concrete evidence, of a truth higher than that residing in media boardrooms, or the halls of Congress, or academia. Kowalski harbored no illusions about the impact of the pictures. To those who would accept them for what they were, the pictures were a key to a treasure chest of possibilities even the mainstream media could not whitewash.

Why God had allowed them to be revealed at this moment in time wasn't a question Ben could answer. It was only his to ask.

What Ben knew with reasonable certainty was that the broadcast of the pictures would mark him and his team as refugees in this New Order. The truth revealed in the pictures would be suppressed with extreme prejudice and the messengers would be sought out and discredited with equal vigor. That much was certain. Left unchallenged, the damage contained in the Red Sea pictures could take Tanner and Kim a generation to cleanse from history.

Ben knew the pictures were an atomic weapon. He also knew, for the sake of setting the record straight, the bomb had to be detonated.

The staff and families of the Holy Harvest had spent the day calling every ministry, church and pastor in their database. The instructions were simple: Put out emails to everyone in your church to tune into the Country Music Channel that evening and record the broadcast. They couldn't give specifics. They didn't want the Kim Administration to get wind of why Christians were being mobilized. Were the feds to become aware of the content of the broadcast, Billy Kim might be tempted to exercise an executive order and shut down the studios. The Holy Harvest people just said 'watch.' They didn't say why. They were hoping enough would accept the message on faith and faith alone.

Ben and his cadre of board members were praying – hard - that the K-815 had enough time and resources to complete their secret mission.

Without discussing the larger consequences, Ben, Ellen and Jake Kowalski went, as a family, to complete their new mission at hand. Once their task was done they were heading to an Indian reservation in northern Minnesota. Millions of Christians would soon be heading to Indian reservations. They would be adopted and protected there. It was the one and only executive covenant Ben had secretly negotiated in his brief tenure as president. The Christians would be bringing their assets and their expertise to the Indian reservations in return for protection within the sovereign boundaries of the Native American nations. The escape plan had been anticipated by Ben. He had seen the day coming. He never told anyone about the ominous American future he saw evolving in his visions because no one would have believed him. As president, though, he had taken measures by signing an Executive Order stripping congress of some of the authority they had in Indian internal matters. He had constructed an escape plan.

He was covering his Christian rear flank.

The Kowalski's drove to a pay phone at a convenience store about a half mile from their home. They couldn't trust their privacy to a cell phone. At the store, Ben fed Ellen's still-valid credit card into the scanner and completed his call to the chairman of the Country Music Channel. When the chairman picked up the phone they both knew, without elaborating, that they were two pirates walking short planks. Neither blinked. Ben told him that the K-815 would be uplinking pictures from a pre-set coordinate. He gave the chairman the times and coordinates. The chairman took all the information down and repeated it back to Ben. They exchanged no pleasantries. When all had been said Ben concluded by saying, "may God be with you."

The chairman responded almost cheerfully. "I'll see you on the other side, my friend."

On the K-815 they had no means to digitize the pictures. The broadcast would have to be "hot," in real time. The uplink went from the transmitter on-board the K-815, up to the Country Music satellite orbiting in a secret pattern 240 miles above the Gulf of Aqaba. The time window would be narrow. The entire broadcast was 27 minutes. The tape included the pictures of Pharaoh's vanquished army at the bottom of the gulf along with Brad Pugh's commentary and a roughly edited Q & A session with Kenneth Quist.

Quist explained the temple ruse credibly and explained in detail the depth and manner in which CNN had executed the deceit. To back up his assertions, Richard Ewald had edited in out-takes from the stolen discs provided by Quist showing the distinct lines of the plexiglass chute on the temple stage.

Quist was a reluctant participant at first. He had been delivered to the sub by an Israeli naval ship in the middle of the night. Ewald showed Quist the video of Pharaoh's vanquished army as a measure of gaining the director's trust. Quist, a fallen-away Methodist, knew what the pictures meant without elaboration. His eyes welled when the first frame of the video showed the ancient graveyard. He wept.

He wept not only because of the evidence it showed, but because it validated the sense of shame he had felt during the temple dedication. The director knew he had been used as a tool to perpetrate a fraud. Suddenly, he was relieved that he had been kidnapped to Eilat. He realized he had a chance to atone for the lie he had helped disguise.

The Aqaba broadcast interrupted the regular programming on the Country Music Channel. In the middle of CMC's highest-rated late-night video countdown the screen went blank and then reappeared with the full face of Brad Pugh.

"Ladies and gentlemen, if you have the capability of recording this transmission, do so now. I urge you to put in a disc and record what you are about to see. We are counting on you to spread these pictures to every corner of the world. I'll explain why as we go along, but please, please, put in a disc to record what you are about to see. We're only going to get to show it once."

The next pictures the audience saw were of the graveyard at the bottom of the ocean.

It took the Syrian Air Force, under the leadership of UN and NATO military officers, six minutes and 15 seconds to triangulate the signal being shot to the satellite from the antenna of the K-815. It took another eight minutes for them to scramble to the airspace outside of Eilat. When the Saudi, Syrian and Egyptian planes came within range of the K-815 they were intercepted by the full force and fury of the Israeli Air Force. If it was a dogfight, it wasn't fair. The Israeli pilots were better trained, better motivated, better armed and with better technology. In the course of a few minutes nine Saudi, Jordanian and Egyptian fighter jets had been shot down.

The war was engaged - and since the Israelis had shot down UN-directed aircraft, the implications were reported as the first volley in a "global" confrontation - the kind of confrontation Tanner and Kim salivated over: Israel against the world!

Captain Petrov's crew and guests watched the dogfight from a pier in Eilat. Petrov had ordered they be ferried to Eilat. Captain Petrov stayed with the ship until the end. It was the final clause in every captain's contract. He would be the last man out. He had one final act to perform.

Egyptian, Syrian and Saudi naval vessels had spotted the Israelis shuttling Brad Pugh, Petrov's crew and his guests towards the Israeli port. The Arab vessels were waiting for the right opportunity to shoot them out of the water, but their fingers froze on their triggers. The sight of Israeli helicopter gunships overhead served as a suicidal reminder of the price of such aggression. The order had actually been given by one Saudi officer, but the men balked. The officer never repeated the order, realizing that if he barked the command again he might be the only casualty.

Against an azure-blue Middle Eastern summer sky, Petrov sat alone atop his sub watching the aerial gymnastics. As a military man, it invigorated him. He lit his pipe and stuck out his chest as he watched the battle overhead. He was still the captain of a formidable ship and was proud to be where he was. He didn't fear going down with the ship. What he feared was having the ship go down before the transmission was complete. He had seen the evidence and could never deny its larger meaning. He knew, without the benefit of a press release or an editorial summary, his sub could be a flashpoint in an operation of stunning proportion. Since the demise of the Soviet Union, Captain Petrov had little passion for being a sub commander. It was only a business. Still, he had an almost romantic understanding of the passion required to carry out a military mission. Going to war was not a normal human response. People wanted to run away from armed conflict. It took training, preparedness and commitment to act aggressively in the face of attack. Captain Petrov had regained his battle passion. His enemy, now, was anyone who would thwart the pictures being broadcast from his sub. He knew what the pictures meant. They represented a truth he had come to understand only in the past 24 hours.

In the middle of a still and serene Gulf of Aqaba, about six miles south of Eilat, Captain Petrov waited for the video disc to finish its uplink to the satellite. In his hand he held a transmitter that was programmed to scuttle the boat, blow the ballast and flood all the chambers. Capture of his vessel was not allowed. He would commit it to the deep. It was what he had been trained to do and it made sense. If he were to abandon the ship, the technology aboard could fall into the wrong hands.

Petrov glanced at his watch. The video was 27 minutes long and it had been transmitting from his ship for almost 26 minutes. He was still alive. He owed a debt of thanks to the Israeli Air Force. He waited for the time to wind down and he clicked on his radio.

"Is the transmission complete?" he asked in English.

Brad Pugh, on solid ground for the first time in over a year and a half, in Eilat, was waiting for the question. "Affirmative, Captain. Come join the party. The land is solid. It hasn't moved once since we landed. Feels great."

"Have a cold beer waiting for me. Out."

"Out, Captain," Brad said.

The captain began to lower himself into the inflatable raft. Once in the raft he started the engine and began to move far enough from the ship to scuttle the craft without being swamped by the wake.

An Israeli helicopter appeared on the horizon, swinging in a wide arc around the sub, making certain any enemy ships were kept at a distance - and to serve as Petrov's personal escort to Eilat.

Petrov turned the engine off and lifted the destruct key necklace over his head and stuck the key in the transmitter. He began to enter the code.

From beneath, Petrov felt the whine of the torpedoes cutting through the water. He didn't need to be told what the sound was. He recognized the drone of the screws: Russian. Ironic, he thought. He smiled. He raised his arms skyward. He closed his eyes and remembered the images of Pharaoh's army at the bottom of the gulf. The picture was burned into his eyeballs. He wanted that snapshot to be the picture he took with him. He felt grateful and privileged to have learned about Jesus from his American shipmates. He knew in this instant that the man on the cross had risen because Petrov, himself, had seen the evidence of the Father's word being constant and true.

He didn't feel cheated.

The concussion of the blasts shot his body 300 feet into the air, toward Heaven.

Scuttling the ship would be redundant.

CHAPTER FIFTY NINE
The cobwebs of comfort

He sat at the chair in his study with his finger poised over the "enter" button. One keystroke. That's how far away Lars was from the potential of torching his marriage and his life as he had come to know it. One keystroke and he would complete a plan that might totally undermine everything his wife was plotting to accomplish. One keystroke and he would run the risk of being branded by the New Brotherhood, whose blessing Ethel coveted.

He rationalized that there was a better than even chance Ethel would never find out about his nefarious plans. But, he knew, there was a chance she would. He withdrew his hand without punching the key and sat back in his chair, reflecting.

It was quiet in the house now. Ethel Larsen, thankfully, was asleep. That was why it was quiet. She had gone to St. Paul that day, trying to resurrect her political career. Her party cronies had called for a war council. She had spent the day in a hotel ballroom with an army of legislators, former legislators, lawyers, teachers and party reptiles. They were trying to decide how to carve up the carcass of America. They would never refer to their actions as such, but that's how Lars saw it. Billy Kim, Hans Tanner and the New Order had redefined the pecking order and the politicians in Ethel's camp were abundantly aware of it.

What concerned Lars beyond the politics was that he had a 27-year-old son/lieutenant in the infantry in Palestine. He was right in the center of whatever was coming next. Lars wanted him home. He didn't want his son to die for refusing to wear a blue helmet. Or, worse yet, consenting to wear one.

When they had returned home from their aborted Canadian mini-vacation Ethel had slept for 20 straight hours. She was mentally, physically and emotionally spent. Lars was happy to let her sleep. In that time, he studiously surfed the net for answers to what had happened over the prior week. The chat rooms were overloaded with conspiracy and end-of-the-world talk. He didn't know enough about prophecy to comment intelligently. He just watched and read. Were all these people nuts, he wondered? There sure were a lot of them. They seemed to be of a like mindset, as well.

From NPR the size and scope of the Christian world had always been made to seem minimal - the Christians were always irrational automatons who lived on the social tundra, apart from humanity's actual gravitational pull. On the net, though, Lars was seeing a Christian community that appeared to be the center of an ant farm. It was in a chat room that Lars was alerted to the video transmission of the Red Sea occurrence. It seemed too ludicrous to be true.

He keyed the story from the link. What he saw jolted him. Lars had spent his adulthood running away from faith. The pictures on his computer screen represented a rebuke of everything he had become. His first reflex was to dismiss them as being doctored pictures. Lars had spent 28 years as a civil engineer for the state. He was logical. He was an engineer by trade. He had been trained in numbers and graphs and equations. He wasn't spiritually prepared for the sight, the possibility, of the pictures he saw from the bottom of the Gulf of Aqaba. They spoke to a larger school of engineering. It was shocking, but like the chorus of "How Great Thou Art," it gave him a peaceful center of gravity. The weight of the evidence he saw broadcast from the bow of the Russian sub put his and Ethel's issues into a new and understandable framework.

He spent the next six hours surfing the net and discovering who Brad Pugh really was. He needed to separate the myth from the reality. He had only heard of him as a verbal gunslinger. Why would he command an audience so large if he wasn't saying something that smacked of reason? Was he credible? Lars spent a solid hour reading biographical summaries and sketches of a man he had voiced an open contempt for for over 20 years - without ever asking why.

Switching gears, he checked out Ford's Military Magazine online and confirmed the existence of the Soviet K-800 class. The K-800 class could, according to Ford's, dive that deep. For an engineer, it was quite impressive. It was an amazing feat of marine engineering for which Lars could find no citations or analysis from his usual trusted sources.

He wanted to talk to someone of like mind about the recent squall of events and checked himself into one of the ubiquitous chat rooms which had sprung up overnight. Instead of engineering, however, he found himself in a running theological discussion of the Red Sea miracles and their larger implications. He clicked away from the bear trap trying to ensnare him. He found his way into one of the ancillary chat rooms and struck up a conversation with another guy much like him. He was a 59-year-old skeptic, a chemical engineer from Ohio. The man had, in just the past day, given his life to Christ and wanted Lars to do the same. Lars said he would think about it and signed off. The man from Ohio didn't know Ethel, Lars thought. She wouldn't stand for anything like that.

Lars opened his $11.95 Bible and turned to the Gospels. He read and he catnapped. When he awoke, something uncontrollable gripped him. The Gospels were singing to him. In the span of a week, his 67 years on earth had been given a living, breathing superstructure which transcended the boundaries and fences he had spent 50 years constructing in order to keep God out. If what he was feeling was real, he had to know how he could have been so blinded.

To look forward he looked, temporarily, backwards.

He had been sent to college by wealthy parents. He had married a county attorney. She hated being an attorney and became a law professor. She eventually hated that and won election as a state senator. She hated that, too, but loved the power and the attention. As Ethel's prominence rose, Lars' life became secondary, incidental. Ethel was his primary identity. He was Lars Larsen, husband of State Senator Ethel Larsen, the majority leader of the Minnesota Senate. Politically, she had become the most powerful woman in the state. He ignored her notoriety. He wasn't a political animal. He mowed lawn. He went to movies. He listened to NPR. He watched CNN. He was an engineer. He was objective. He was analytical. He couldn't be shaken from his rational, reasoned point of view.

He was, in a word, comfortable. He wanted for nothing and viewed his comfort with guilt - believing everyone was worthy of his comfort and since he couldn't provide it, he concluded it was government's function to assuage his guilt. His wife and his radio station had told him so.

Now he had seen helicopters gas church-goers. He had heard about persecution of people from the radio. He had found comfort in old hymns. He had seen his own country relinquishing its sovereignty. He had witnessed his neighbor forced out of his own home by the government. He had seen his own country's military forces compromised in what was undoubtedly a coup.

The pictures from the Russian sub were pushing him towards a place he could no longer keep at arm's length.

Seeing the pictures of Pharaoh's army in an eternal repose defined in a moment what Lars had been searching for his whole adult life - resolve. In the middle of the transmission he found himself wiping tears from both eyes. To no one at all he silently muttered. "Do you know what this means?" His tears turned to audible sobs and he throttled himself, not wanting to wake his sleeping wife.

He was seeing through new eyes. His past made him grimace in shame. The Red Sea pictures made him realize he was dealing with a design. He was an engineer. He knew design. He knew the constructs of mechanical and civil engineering. They were principles that allowed buildings and bridges to stand and machines to work. Lars was struck with the revelation that the same principles applied to men, only in a spiritual realm. At his core there *was* a spirit. It was the engine of his humanity. The realization gave him new eyes - he had the right to discriminate because he had been given the tools to discern right from wrong. Truth was not an opposing point of view. It was a tool toward understanding. Relative truth was the stuff that made lies digestible. Why had those concepts escaped him for 50 years? They weren't difficult concepts. They were incredibly easy. Truth! Finding truth didn't require invention. It required Grace. Grace. Lars understood, now, what the word meant.

He had heard Grace talked about in the sermons of Pastor Jacob McNearny at the Second Baptist Church in Calumet, Illinois, a half century earlier. The pastor painted the picture of an undeserved salvation called Grace. The young Lars Larsen had barely heard the sermon then. But he heard it now. Lars knew there was no turning back from his revelation. The Designer was extending that Grace to him personally.

How had he managed to ignore the signs for half a century? For the first time he was able to put his lifetime into a context which would satisfy himself – and history.

Lars and Ethel had lived in the suburbs from their first married moment. They never knew urban blight, the struggle of poverty or the recurring cycle of ignorance. They read about it - and NPR preached it to them unceasingly for four decades. Over time, NPR had leveraged their taxpayer-subsidized signal into the hearts of the Larsen's. NPR, academia and Ethel's political involvement had slowly extinguished the flame of faith Lars once had.

Instead of being a responsible, successful engineer with a sense of gratitude and charity, Lars had spent his adult life as a cynical, dour, cranky, rich, white suburban vessel of guilt. His wife fed his guilt and wore it, herself, like a badge of honor. Ethel was high-profile and influential in the white guilt community. Whenever someone in the black community was wronged, or perceived to have been wronged, the reporters headed to the rich, white suburban home of Lars and Ethel Larsen to get a recitation of the injustices Ethel Larsen believed were deserving of a government program. She always made certain she was interviewed inside, where the cameras couldn't reveal the opulence with which she had surrounded herself. She wielded her mantle of despair, concern and guilt like a giant Caucasian wrecking ball. She was always "devastated." For the local media outlets it was worth the trip to the suburbs to find out just how devastated one white woman could be. By being the official Minnesota face of white guilt and blame she defined Lars' identity. Lars conceded to his role - he was white and he was guilty and he was willing to shoulder the blame - if he could do it privately. It was easier than trying to correct the record and admit to his indifference to almost everything requiring a judgment. In fact, Lars discovered he didn't have to become socially aware as long as his wife was. Basically, he just had to go to work for 28 years until he could collect a full pension from the state. If people wanted to identify him as the husband of a guilty, devastated state senator from the suburbs, that was fine with him.

As a county attorney, college professor and state senator, Ethel had three pensions waiting for her at the end of the road. The Larsen's were public servants who earned more money in retirement than when they worked. Money wasn't an issue for them in the autumn of their lives. In fact, they were so comfortable that Lars didn't have to think. She took care of that, too. Pretty much, he had been allowed the luxury of unplugging half his brain for about a quarter century.

Up until the last week.

The pictures of the graveyard at the bottom of the Red Sea were a reawakening of what a long-ignored part of his brain Lars had mothballed decades before. The skeletons Lars witnessed beneath the sea were also the skeletons of Lars' faith. The pictures shook him out of his white guilt and suburban, gated-community security. Out of his comfort zone, a nagging set of questions arose which neither his wife nor his radio station could answer. For the first time in decades he jump-started his brain, pumped the gas on his cerebrum and fired up some dusty synapses. At first it hurt, but he found the facts his brain digested were both disturbing and challenging. What he determined, all by himself, without the aid or urging of his wife - was that God was showing His hand. Why? The engineer in Lars needed to know the Designer of the puzzle he was now seeing with surprising clarity. For the first time in almost 30 years he felt a sensation that had been covered in the cobwebs of his comfort: A child-like fascination.

The aborted Canadian vacation, Lars was beginning to believe, had been set up by something outside the physical realm. Was this God's last, desperate attempt to fan the dying ember of his faith by pointing out the sin of his own willful ignorance? In that moment Lars knew: He had to let go of Ethel. She was the firewall preventing him from discovering a truth he could no longer simply ignore.

When they had returned from their Canadian debacle, Ethel had gone on a sleeping binge. When she finally crawled out after a day of suspended animation, neither one spoke much. There was still an animosity hanging in the air - a coldness Lars had earned by openly reading the Bible and listening to AM radio in her presence.

She wasn't the kind of person who could let those acts go unpunished.

While she had been asleep she had received an e-mail to contact one of her old political cronies. When she returned the call, her voice became absolutely, positively buoyant. The party was meeting to carve up turf and they were asking her to show up with her knives sharpened. She had been shopped around, in some circles - it was said - as attorney general.

"Attorney general," she beamed to Lars. "It's the job I was groomed for." She could barely contain herself as she showered and fit herself into a smart gray and black pant-suit. It was feminine without compromising the testosterone side of her. Lars told her it looked great. The truth was he would have told her bib overalls and a T-shirt looked great if it would have gotten her out of the house any quicker. When the car cleared the driveway Lars knew what he had to do.

He had to gain some perspective.

The walk to Kowalski's house was about 100 yards. The conversation Lars had with himself along the way was confusing, even for him. There were just too many things happening too fast. But, at the bottom of the page he knew what the score was. He just didn't understand how it all added up.

Lars knocked on the door and waited like a teenager coming to pick up someone's daughter for a date. When the door opened Ellen Kowalski answered. It caught Lars flat-footed. What was she doing here? Hadn't she written that spiteful book about her husband? Hadn't they been estranged for five or so years? It was a new social dynamic he was totally unprepared for.

"Um, um, Ellen…it's a surprise to see you here. I came to talk to your husband, I mean, to Ben. That is, if he's still your husband. I'm sorry, I'm just…"

Ellen saw the awkwardness of the moment and grabbed him by the arm, leading him into the vestibule.

"Ben," she yelled into the house. "It's, um, Mr. Larsen. Our neighbor. I'm sorry, I've forgotten your first name," she said.

"Lars," he said.

"Of course, how could I forget. We're in Minnesota. Of course it's Lars." She tried to make light of the moment. "Just so you know - we've reconciled. I'm no longer promoting the book. It's a pack of lies anyway. They waved a lot of cash at me and I was weak. I took it."

"My wife will be interested to hear that. She thinks it's a definitive study of your husband as a hypocrite." He wasn't sure he should have said that to her, but it was out of his mouth before he could think.

"Well, I'd be happy to tell her face-to-face if you think it would help."

"Nah. That's not going to happen. Trust me."

She could tell from the way he spit out the line that it was true. Ethel Larsen, Ellen remembered, had opinions. She was not someone who could be persuaded off a point of view once her mind had been made up. She was exactly the kind of person who bought 'The False Prophet' and swallowed it whole. Ellen didn't want to dwell too much on the inner workings of Ethel Larsen, but was compelled to ask one question.

"So, if your wife thinks it's a study of a hypocrite, what do you think?" She was buying time. Ben was still not there.

"I didn't read it. That kind of stuff never appealed to me. It's all opinion and kiss and tell stuff. It's usually very self-serving and amounts to nothing."

"Bravo, Lars. The publishing world hates people like you."

Ben entered the room and exchanged greetings with his neighbor. "What can I do for you, Lars?" he asked.

"Can we talk in front of her?" he asked with a tilt of the head towards Ellen.

"Would you rather not?"

"Yeah, honestly, I would. It's kinda personal."

"Let me do something wifely," Ellen said, excusing herself. "Maybe I'll make a casserole."

"Maybe you could beat the kid," Ben added. "Needs a whuppin'. It's been days."

It cracked Lars up.

"The picture of you beating your kid is what my wife would like to believe."

"I take it she read Ellen's book?" Ben asked.

"Sheesh. Couldn't put it down. Strutted like a rooster for a week. Tried to get me to read it. Didn't have to, though. She told me everything in it. Boring stuff. You know you're basically a boring guy, Kowalski?"

"Yeah, I do." They both sat down on the wicker couch and looked at the brilliant summer day that had unfolded in front of them. There was a tension in Lars that Ben couldn't put his finger on. He waited for his neighbor to volley the first serve.

"I'm going to leave Ethel," he finally said.

Instead of uttering the predictable 'Oh No!' Ben waited. It was a powerful volley and one he couldn't easily return.

"Why are you telling me? I'm not what you would call a close friend."

"I don't have any close friends," said Lars. "I figure that I should tell you because in a way it's you who broke up our marriage."

Ben took in a cleansing breath. The political, cultural and economic world had blamed Ben and his Christian causes for everything from AIDS to intolerance. Breaking up Lars' marriage was a new charge.

"Explain, Lars."

Lars looked off into the distance and pulled the glasses off his face. He wiped the lenses with the tail of his shirt as he spoke.

"Last week we went up to our property in Canada, but we never quite got there because along the way we listened to the radio. Not just NPR like we usually do, but I found some time to listen to the other radio stations. Even listened to Brad Pugh for a while. I found out that a lot of what they were saying was not really outrageous. Fact is, made some good, common sense. Except, of course, that Ethel doesn't much care for common sense, but don't get me going on that. I kept thinking back to what you told me about the Holy Harvest. Then, when we were on our way up to Canada there was a Holy Harvest site outside of Baxter. So, I decided to stop and see what all the talk was about - I think I told you this when you called. They tear-gassed them church-goers, Ben. Our own government attacking people who were gathered peaceably! I look for news of what happened but it's unreported. Well, as the week goes on, we learn a whole lot more about things that shouldn't be happening. There's a UN buffer zone that's been constructed around the Canadian border. Our military is being forced to wear the blue helmet, you know. No one's talking about it. Well, all of this gets me to thinking about the One World Order and some of the warnings I remember from my youth when I was a good Baptist. We cut the weekend short because we're just learning too much to make it comfortable. On the way back I buy a Bible and do some digging into Daniel and

Revelations and the Gospels. Come to learn that all of this has been foretold. I think you know that."

He stopped. It was as much talking as he had done in one sitting in several years. An internal stop sign signaled his brain that he was ranting. He looked at Ben, continuing almost sheepishly.

"I watched that Red Sea crossing story from Brad Pugh on that submarine. Saw it on the net last night. You seen it?"

Ben nodded. He had volumes of text he could tell him about the inner workings behind the story, but decided now was not the time.

"They're already calling the story a fraud," interjected Ben.

"You ain't surprised, are you?"

"No. I'd be surprised if they didn't. Truth is a moving target for them."

Ben looked at him seriously. He wanted to get to the nub of his neighbor's issue. "I sense that you're coming to grips with something. What?"

"The truth," he said. "It's different today than it was a week ago."

"Think so? You don't think the truth is constant?"

"Truth is. I ain't."

Kowalski laughed. It was a deep belly-laugh. "Welcome to the human race, Lars."

Lars wasn't sure how to take the laugh. He was glad he could bring some levity to the moment, but he was thinking that his plight demanded more sobriety. Lars stared at the horizon.

"I told you, didn't I? - I been readin' the Bible?" he said as if he were admitting to a capital crime.

"Yeah, Lars, you did." Ben's intuition kicked in. He knew now why Lars had come over. It wasn't just to share marriage matters. Lars was wrestling with a question Ben thought he was incapable of asking.

Lars inhaled and asked, "are we at the End of the Age?"

Ben sighed. He rubbed his chin. "I don't know. No one knows. Even Jesus said only the Father knows that time. But Jesus said, too, that we should be aware of the signs. The abomination..."

"That would be Tanner at the temple, the crucifixion of that poor Christ fellow."

"Jesus said that the gospel would be spread to the four corners of the earth."

"We've done that. Ain't hardly a soul on the planet who doesn't at least know *of* the gospel."

"He said that there would be wars, famines, earthquakes."

"He also talked about the tribulation of the saints. What does that mean?"

"Lars, let's not get ahead of ourselves. There's a lot of things…"

Lars interrupted him. "And, what about the Rapture? Tell me about that."

Ben didn't want to sound rude, but he wanted to set the record straight.

"You never saw that word in the Bible. The Rapture is an invention. It's reading between the lines. It's interpreting Scripture into something that may or may not have been intended."

"You mean it ain't gonna happen?"

"I didn't say that. I said it's an interpretation. If God wanted us to know exactly how history plays out, he would never have created men with free will. He would have created robots - clones."

"Now I'm really confused," confessed Lars. He stood to leave. "I thought you had the answers."

"I'm not God. All we can do is follow his road map. Part of our faith demands that we trust in Him. Does that make sense?"

"Well, what I've learned over the past week is that my faith has been put in the wrong place. I let myself be blinded. I was lazy. I let my wife do the thinkin' for me. She's part of the lie I been livin.'"

"Is there any chance you two could reconcile? Does she know how you feel? Has she rejected faith altogether?"

"She's got faith. In her party. In lawyers. In academics. In philosophy. In lots of stuff, but not God. She thinks Christianity is everything that's wrong with the world. And, honestly…all she sees now is that the party is talking about her becoming the next attorney general. Her god is herself. She's like most of 'em. They see themselves as the center of the universe."

Ben had heard enough. Particularly about Ethel becoming the next AG of the state. If he were a CIA agent, his next sentence would be ill-advised by his superiors but Ben's intuition told him that Lars could be trusted. There was no science to what Ben was concluding at that moment - it was just that old prescient feeling.

"Let me ask you, Lars. What do you think is going to happen on the world stage in the next week?"

"I suspect Hans Tanner is going to come out of his exile and declare that he is filled with some kind of alien wisdom. They'll warn of some kind of environmental disaster, maybe. That would serve a lot of their purposes. And I expect most people will buy it because the papers will regurgitate it. People don't know how to think for themselves anymore."

"What do you think is going to happen to the residents of my house?"

Lars hadn't thought about it. It was a consideration off his personal radar. "Tell me," he said.

"Well, they've already frozen our assets. Got a secret for you: Marshall Warren is living in our house. He's a drunk. He's headed for detox but my guess is he'll relapse. Claudia Colgate - the real one - lives inside, too. She's putting on weight like a sumo wrestler - got an orange butch haircut and put on some biker leathers. Tells us she's headed for Mexico."

Lars looked at him as if to say 'yeah, right.' Fifty one percent of his brain told him that his chain was being yanked.

Ben winked at Lars. He wanted him to think he was kidding. He gazed at the horizon and spoke dispassionately. He had something to say and he didn't want Lars to think he was selling.

"They quit paying our Secret Service agents about a week ago. They're gone. We're just average citizens now. Pretty soon the government is going to find a way to tax us out of existence or close us down. The truth at the center of the whole charade is really quite easy to understand if you place it in its context. All this talk, this movement to be inclusive and multicultural and tolerant towards one another is a seduction. It's Satan's strategy for men to justify tyranny - to legitimize it. The seduction is that we can all be equal in every measure - income, status, height, weight, influence. That way none of us can complain that life isn't fair. History ought to tell us that the surest way to tyranny is to agree to let government make life equal. That's the seduction. And that's what's coming, my friend. It's called the Tribulation and it is coming. Now? Who knows. The target of this culture war has never been Christians, though you could argue that they are sometimes the worst possible ambassadors for the faith. The target has always been Christ. You'll see it soon. Now that they claim Christ is dead, they're going to go after his followers. We'll be displaced. Everything that's contained in this house will be foreclosed on and boarded up. I have no idea where we'll end up. Same for Christians everywhere. We're going to be shut out of the system. That's a part of the Tribulation. It's been foretold, if you want to know."

"Unless the Rapture happens first..."

"Don't assume. That's dangerous, my friend. Let me ask you a question: What do you think we do in our house?"

"What do you mean?"

"There's always been a lot of traffic here. You know that. Why do you think all those people - all those Christians - visited here? Let me tell you: In our basement are four servers with a lot of private data about a lot of things Tanner and Kim want. We've already established a covert financial network for thousands of churches and millions of parishioners. The Administration would love to find out where that money is going. We have to move the data soon because I'm a high-profile target and our operation is going to be one of the first casualties of the coming purge against us."

Lars looked at him askance. "Why are you telling me this?"

"Because, brother, we need you to make a sacrifice for us. We need you to stay married to Ethel. It will require some acting, but she's politically well-connected. Knowing what's going on in her world could be a real asset to us."

There was a palpable pause. Lars heard the words Kowalski had said but couldn't come to grips with a motive. He was trying to weigh their gravity. Then it dawned on him: In that moment Lars felt relief. He didn't have to be a passive observer. There was a way to serve against the imminent siege.

"Do I have to sleep with her?"

"Do you now?"

"Only after she's snoring."

CHAPTER SIXTY
Actor

In the lion's lair Ethel reclined in her easy chair. Lars looked at his watch. It was 9:55 PM. His wife never lasted past 10:30. After five minutes in the recliner she was sawing logs, head tilted back with her adenoids declaring to the world that she was no longer young or discreet. Lars shook her feet and helped her out of the chair.

"Was I asleep?" she asked.

"The whole neighborhood could hear you, dear. You need to go to bed."

"I do. It's been a long day, hon, but…" she stopped halfway out of her chair and remembered something.

"Oh, I forgot to tell you: Kowalski's name came up at the war council today. They want to know what we know. I can't do anything officially until after I'm elected but, you know, they want to start putting together a file on him. So, don't be surprised if someone from the FTC or IRS comes around asking questions about him. I told them we'd cooperate. I don't know exactly what they have in mind, but they're tightening the noose. Once Tanner and Kim deliver their State of the West address next week there's going to be a lot of changes. Good changes. You and I won't ever have to worry about a thing. We'll be taken care of."

"We don't have to worry about anything now," Lars responded.

"Well, maybe, but just think about all the good we can do for the poor and the children," she said as she moved to the top of the stairs. "We can use what we've earned to level the playing field for a lot of people."

She began to walk back down the staircase again. She wanted to talk! Lars tried not to show his disappointment. He wanted her up the staircase - in bed - asleep. She wasn't going to cooperate. He maintained a curious look. He wanted his face to say 'my, this is interesting dear. Can you please tell me some more?' He was play-acting, but realized in that moment that he had been play-acting for decades. A few more minutes wouldn't kill him.

"Did I tell you, Lars, that there's something in this for you?" She was trying to be seductive. It wasn't working. "What I mean, Lars, is that we expect some new roles for government officials. That means new compensation. You'll be getting your own per diem. And, they figure you'll be getting some other perks like golf club memberships, time-share condos, opera tickets..."

"I hate opera," said Lars.

"Oh, come on. Tell me you wouldn't like to wine and dine at the finest places, be taxied around town, have memberships to the best clubs."

"Wow!" Lars said. He was trying to sound sincere.

"Stick with me, honey. I'll take care of you. There's going to be some short-term pain in the economy, but we won't feel it. We'll be insulated from it. No one will be able to touch our house, our money, our per-diem or our pensions. We'll be a lot richer tomorrow than we are today, that's for sure."

"Yeah, because a lot of other people will be a lot poorer."

"You've got to quit being such a cynic. We're about to inherit a lot of influence. Influence we can use to make the world a much better place. Only now we can set the terms."

Hon," he said, looking into her eyes - "it doesn't matter - as long as we're together." It was the best acting he had ever done.

"Come to bed, Lars. It's been so long."

His acting was a little too good.

"Nah," he said. "I'm going to try to e-mail Joey over in Palestine. We need to see if he's wearing the blue helmet yet."

"Let's pray he is."

"Pray?" he said, "I thought prayer was for hypocrites."

"All right, let's just say I hope he wears the blue helmet. We raised him right, dear. He will."

She turned and walked back up the staircase. "Don't take too long, hon. I don't know how much longer I can stay awake."

Lars stood in his study looking out the window. The instant replay in his brain was his way of stalling, he knew. His jump back from his daydream to the present didn't lessen the gravity of the moment. He was about to become a traitor to his wife. He was about to become an undercover agent for a faith he had only re-discovered in the last few days. If he were discovered he would be jailed or killed. He wasn't sure how the New Order would handle him if he were caught. It didn't matter. His mission was resolute. He was a new creation. The calendar said he was 67 years old but he felt like he was 17 and without a curfew.

He pulled the chair up to the computer and made sure Kowalski's port device was inserted into the 'J' drive. He double-checked the e-mail address. He had no clue where the data was headed, but Kowalski had told him the transmission had to originate from someplace outside of the Kowalski compound, someplace beyond the suspicion of the New Order. Lars had a relative comfort that it would never be traced to his house. After all, who would think to look inside the Ethel Larsen household for treachery against the New Order. Lars, because of his wife, was beyond suspicion. He poised his hand over the 'enter' key again.

He stroked the key and listened to the drive engage. The genie was out of the bottle. It hummed and whirred for 20 seconds and quit. The encrypted data on the disc would allow the phantom at the other end of the transmission to access the Kowalski servers and unload all the data. Kowalski had told him their four servers would be trashed once the download was confirmed.

When the data was unloaded and a confirmation received, Lars flicked his back porch light on and off two times. The signal sent the Kowalski compound into a scramble.

Their exit strategy was a model of preparation and efficiency. Within an hour the Kowalski compound was dark and lifeless, all of them headed to unknown venues. Lars regretted losing Ben's friendship. Ironic, Lars thought. Ben was the closest thing he had to a true friend in the last 30 years. It had lasted only a few minutes.

Ben knocked softly on the window glass. He didn't want to wake Ethel. Lars knew it would be the last time he would ever see him. When Ben appeared at the door, Lars handed him the disc and Ben handed him their house key. They looked at each other for a moment before Ben spoke. There were volumes of words waiting to be said but no time.

"We're trusting you, you know. You could easily betray us."

Lars knew exactly what he was talking about. Lars wanted to say something reassuring to Ben but realized time was short and words were insufficient. Lars had memorized the e-mail address of a chat-room where he would be able to go late at night and pass along what Ethel was made privy to by the New Order. He took the scrap of paper with the chat room address on it and tore it up; placing the scraps in Ben's hand, reciting the address to Ben as he did.

"I know where to reach you. It's here," he said, pointing to his temple. "No one knows what I know and no one ever will because I am the firewall protecting you from them."

"And what happens if you're found out?" Ben asked.

Lars thought about it for a moment. "They can't kill me Ben." He picked up his Bible. "I'm going to live forever."

The answer caught Ben by surprise. The faith of Lars Larsen was not emerging, it had blossomed. In his brief answer, Lars told Ben volumes. Ben waited for a moment, looking straight into Lars' eyes, trying to divine any sense of doubt. He extended his hand. Without breaking the stare, Lars shook his friend's hand one last time.

Lars watched, motionless, and waited until Kowalski's car had left the cul-de-sac. He turned off the outside light and locked the door.

He sat in his recliner and aimed the reading light. He opened his $11.95 Bible, put on his reading glasses and turned to the book of Revelation. He wondered in which verse of St. John's incredible vision he might be inspired to discover the past few days.

EPILOGUE

The Israeli armed forces were programmed to survive. In the community of international intelligence and counterintelligence they had no peers. Their survival skills were honed not out of desire, but out of necessity. Their ingenuity in security matters stemmed from the inescapable fact that, for nearly four millennia, most of their neighbors wanted them dead.

While the Saudi, Syrian and Egyptian Air Forces had been sacrificing their best pilots over the Gulf of Aqaba, trying vainly to destroy the K-815, Israel had taken a calculated preemptive measure. Flying in from the Red Sea in the south, Israeli bombers attacked the Saudi air complex located in the northwest corner of the country at Tibuk. Aerial reconnaissance had told Israeli intelligence that significant numbers of F-15 and F-16 fighter jets had been flown in under cover of dark and stored in hangers there.

While Saudi officers huddled in Tibuk, monitoring their own aerial defeat in the Gulf of Aqaba, Israeli B-2 stealth bombers approached from the south, over Saudi air space, flying right over Jabel El Lawz, the Mountain of God. They unloaded enough ordnance to quickly paralyze the airfield and destroy the jets being staged to attack Israel. They were followed up in their campaign by a flight of eight A-10 Warthogs which blanketed the airfield with electronic cannon fire that provided a symmetrical strike of 40 caliber armor-piercing cannon shells every 4.4 square meters up and down the length and breadth of the airfield. After the A-10 cannon carpet was laid down only those officers monitoring their Aqaba defeat from secure underground bunkers were left to attend to the dead. Communications were non-existent. A counter-strike, were it possible, would have had to be initiated with rocks, fists and name-calling. There was nothing mechanical, electrical or animal above ground that projected any semblance of life.

It was Phase One of the larger Israeli mission.

At the same time, a ground force of Israeli commandos had little trouble securing the site at the base of Jabel El Lawz. The Saudi guards were captured in their sleep. The security fence restricting the mountain to trespassers was disassembled by a survey team from the Israeli Council of Antiquities. Israeli archeologists then set up crime scene tape perimeters around the mountain, around the "Golden Calf Altar" and all other curious anomalies. It was at this point that a curious "graveyard" was discovered 2000 meters to the east of the mountain. Thousands of upright and fallen monoliths, headstones, had marked the site of a mass burial. In the book of Exodus, thousands of the Hebrews had been slain by their Hebrew brothers when Moses ordered their extermination in response to the abomination of golden calf worship practiced while he had been up on the mountain. Could this be their final resting place? It would take a survey crew, stratigraphers and archeologists long months of careful excavation to determine the era of burial, but the initial evidence suggested Late Bronze Age, or the general time of the Exodus. It dovetailed perfectly with Scripture. Besides, why would a graveyard of thousands exist on real estate where no one had ever lived permanently? Still, the evidence would have to be systematically evaluated. In due time, the Israeli government would allow an international team of archeologists to excavate and authenticate the findings at the Jabel El Lawz site.

Mount Sinai had been secured in order to establish an archeological analysis. That was Phase Two.

Phase Three of the plan was to establish a military perimeter in the northwest corner of Saudi Arabia and annex Israel to their mountain. This would be a little more problematic than a simple military occupation as there were pockets of indigenous Saudis and Bedouins who lived in small enclaves throughout the region. The Israelis knew the only way to secure the area would be to evict every native. It could reasonably be presumed the Israeli occupation would not be embraced by the locals. They would have to be physically escorted off the premises. After capture, the Saudis would be marched to the edge of the annexed Israeli property, given a stipend for relocation expenses and told not to bother returning.

Next, the Israeli Corps of Engineers and security forces efficiently erected double lengths of razor-wire fences across the extreme northwest corner of Saudi Arabia. By the time the new boundaries were redrawn, Israel would stake a claim to over 400 square miles of former Saudi real estate.

Ben Kowalski learned the Israeli sequence of events from his Internet mole in Eilat several weeks after the fact. Ben had to rely on his Israeli contacts for hard news. Most communications from Israel were so heavily edited by the media that fact and fiction had become indistinguishable.

Kowalski had moved his headquarters and his people to the Red Lake Indian Reservation in northern Minnesota where a base of operations had already been built for them, courtesy of the Red Lake Indian Tribe. The complex had been secretly constructed and financed through a generous contribution from the federal government. Ben Kowalski had authored the Executive Order during his brief tenure as president; establishing almost three dozen Indian Reservations for "infrastructure upgrades." The plans were to establish regional operating posts, bases of operations for those who were willing to forsake citizenship in the New Order for a small area of free, protected, sovereign territory. The new American patriots emigrating to the reservations brought their resources, their brainpower, their skills and their unrelenting thirst for liberty and freedom to a new land, a new fragmented America.

All the while, Arne Karlstrom's still photos and the Red Sea video saturated the Internet. In spite of the obvious conclusions, the evidences were being largely discredited by the unrelenting media machine Tanner and Kim had set in motion.

What would remain unreported in virtually all major media outlets were the spontaneous and unannounced pilgrimages by the new Hebrews as they ferried down the Gulf of Aqaba and trekked across the wilderness - to their mountain.

They were returning, as had been prophesied, to their mountain, to renew their covenant with God.

Jerry Lindberg has been a man in need of a miracle. Alone, he has stood as a beacon of clarity in the world for over a decade, waiting patiently for humanity to come around to his way of thinking. As a prolific editorialist, blogger and commentator, he has plied his craft in the shadows, content with the warm glow of his own wit - patiently awaiting his miracle.

Prior to 1993, Mr. Lindberg's history is fuzzy. He graduated from college with a double major in communications and chemical consumption. This qualified him to work as a disc jockey and, later, as a singer in a rock and roll band — where he exploited song, dance and drink to a critical mass. While it can often be said that an author spends a lifetime perfecting his craft, the same cannot be said of Mr. Lindberg. For two decades he began writing stories only to have Happy Hour interrupt his creative process. Having survived many years as a "misappropriated" believer, he finally read The Book in earnest and, in it, found a Truth stronger than beer. It was at this point Mr. Lindberg discovered he could record a sentence with some level of coherence. This was the missing part of a writing equation he had been grasping to solve. Eventually, this epiphany led him to construct a paragraph.

"The Fingerprint of God" was originally a screenplay of mystery and political treachery Mr. Lindberg wrote in 1996. He was operating under the delusion Hollywood was hungry for an uplifting tale of spiritual awakening. He failed on two levels: First, putting "God" in a Hollywood title is a deal-breaker. Second, his story had too few corpses, exploding body parts or mystical references to the Deity consisting of A) light, B) fog, C) ether, or D) happy thoughts. The mysterty of how to uplift without the benefit of special effects rattled in Lindberg's brain for five years (taking time out for meals and naps, of course), until he read "The Exodus Case," by Dr. Lennart Moller. The hypotheses put forward by Dr. Moller were a mother lode of new science and forensic understanding which gave Lindberg's story, literally, a chariot.

This was his miracle.

Mr. Lindberg currently masquerades as a taxpaying, responsible, home-owning parent and husband. He resides somewhere in the Midwest and owns a mini-van. To the untrained eye he and his family appear to be normal human beings.